The Care and
Management of Lies

THE CARE AND MANAGEMENT OF LIES

A NOVEL OF THE GREAT WAR

JACQUELINE WINSPEAR

HARPER ● PERENNIAL

NEW YORK ● LONDON ● TORONTO ● SYDNEY ● NEW DELHI ● AUCKLAND

HARPER PERENNIAL

A hardcover of this book was published in 2014 by HarperCollins Publishers.

P.S.™ is a trademark of HarperCollins Publishers.

HarperCollins books may be purchased for educational, business, or sales promotional use. For information, please e-mail the Special Markets Department at SPsales@ harpercollins.com.

FIRST HARPER PERENNIAL EDITION PUBLISHED 2015.

Designed by Fritz Metsch

Library of Congress Cataloging-in-Publication Data has been applied for.

ISBN 978-0-06-222051-6 (pbk.)

15 16 17 18 19   OV/RRD   10 9 8 7 6 5 4 3 2 1

To Amy
With love and gratitude, always

*Every intelligent person in the world knew that
disaster was impending, and knew no way to avoid it.*

—H. G. WELLS

*The home front is always underrated by generals in
the field. And yet that is where the Great War was
won and lost.*

—BRITISH PRIME MINISTER DAVID LLOYD GEORGE,
WAR MEMOIRS

*What is certain, is that war will not leave us as it
found us.*

—*WOMAN AT HOME,*
February 1915

THE CARE AND
MANAGEMENT OF LIES

CHAPTER 1

JUNE 1914
LONDON

*A tactful woman is one who will never hurt
another's feelings. She will always respect the
little foibles of her friends and refrain from
holding them up to ridicule.*

—*THE WOMAN'S BOOK*
by Florence B. Jack, first published in 1911

The country was in the early weeks of a summer that would become memorable for its warmth and, despite worries farther afield, there was a sense of being cocooned in Englishness. If ever the natural world conspired to create the perfect summer, then this was the beginning of a charmed season. People—country people—would reflect on this time and remember cricket on the village green, with ladies seated, drinking tea, while men and boys ambled back and forth between the stumps, the ricochet of leather on willow accompanying a run here, a sprint there, followed by light applause from members of the audience not already lulled into an afternoon doze on the pavilion veranda. A gentle sound, as if small glass beads had been run across fine writing paper, would on occasion fill the air when a light breeze caught leaves so fresh they might have unfurled especially for these days. In London, the heat became oppressive as it wafted down into the subterranean tunnels of the Underground. On the street, horses grew impatient with their sweat, stamping their feet when required to stand. Cabbies, too, were becoming ill-tempered—well, perhaps no more ill-tempered than usual. Women might have perspired, but only to the extent that embarrassment could be dealt with by an extra handkerchief well placed and a parasol set just so. It might have been possible to forget, for a moment, that the country had been beset with strikes, and that the government was at the time preoccupied with "The Irish Question." A stench from the Thames, her tributaries and canals, would be intolerable within a month, and for the poor there was at least no fog, no pea-soup smog, and no biting winter to endure, though hardship and disease still cast a pall over their lives. The city's poor lived a different life, remember.

Kezia Marchant had been staying for a few days with her most beloved and dearest friend, Dorothy Brissenden, at Queen Charlotte's Chambers, the women's boarding house close to Russell Square where Dorothy had lodged for some five years. Both women were twenty-seven years of age, and in late afternoon were comfortably seated by a sunlit window in the confined quarters that Dorothy—Dorrit, to her family and those who had known her since childhood—had lately referred to as her "gaff." This was a new locution for Dorrit, once so correct and unassuming—or so it might seem, at first blush—even for a farm-born country girl. Having spent the earlier part of the morning window-shopping for items they could not afford and would consider it profligate to indulge in anyway, they'd had tea and were lazily leafing through a pile of women's monthly books a fellow boarder had given Dorrit. Though a picture of idleness, each woman offering a comment here or an observation there as she licked a finger to turn the page, they were endeavoring to reestablish the companionship enjoyed in earlier years. Kezia was distracted by considerations of marriage—she would be wed to Dorrit's younger brother, Tom, in just four days, and since her engagement eighteen months ago this past May, her thoughts had been peppered by a commentary that became ever more resonant as time passed. "In a month, I will be a married woman." Or, "By the time I wear my winter coat again, I will be wed." Or, "When I walk into this shop next time, I will be Mrs. Tom Brissenden." This propensity to reflect upon her anticipated status would continue until the day of her wedding.

Though the two women appeared to be animated by their connection and intermittent conversation, the more intuitive onlooker might have detected something amiss, which further consideration would reveal to be the bonds of friendship loosened by choices each had made, as if one were a boat and the other the harbor. It is the nature of the vessel to set sail, and of the harbor to remain solid, waiting until the boat returns laden with tales of travel and experience, of rough seas and calm. If this thought had crossed her mind, Kezia Marchant—at this point Marchant for just four more days, mind—would have recognized that she was the harbor. She was a well-read, academically adept woman, and of late she had felt—but not consciously acknowledged—an irritation blended with sadness at this turn of events. The once mild yet solid Dorrit had changed.

They had been friends since girlhood, from their first day at the prestigious—and in this instance prestigious also meant expensive—Camden School for Girls in Tunbridge Wells, where both were recipients of a scholarship to fund an otherwise unaffordable education, plus their keep as boarders. Kezia's father, a vicar in a small town at the London edge of Kent, had always been a staunch supporter of his daughter's education and took delight in her intellectual gifts. Such was their love that she had seen herself as the adored Margaret to his Sir Thomas More. But Reverend Marchant—whose family lived in an ivy-clad

Georgian rectory with a housekeeper, scullery maid, and cook, as would befit a man of the cloth in safe tenure—had not the funds to finance his daughter's attendance at Camden, so was overjoyed when news of the scholarship was received.

Jack Brissenden farmed land deeper into Kent, outside the town of Brooksmarsh and not a mile from the village of Turndene. His father and grandfather before him had worked the same land until their hands were raw, until they were bent and spent and the earth was ingrained in the folds of their skin. He was not short of a bob or two, but could see no point in spending good money to further his daughter's learning. A scholarship amounted to free coin, however, and was therefore not to be turned down. Jack knew that his son Tom—Dorrit's brother and, more recently, Kezia's fiancé—would in time take over the farm. So as far as Jack was concerned, investment in the broadening of Tom's mind, of *his* view of the world—especially that of commerce, of buying and selling for market—was not such a bad thing at all if the family were to continue this run of prosperity, which was the cause of some envy among others of his ilk. Thus, unlike that of many local young farmers in the making, Tom Brissenden's education had extended beyond apprenticeship to his father. He had been sent to the Royal Agricultural College in Cirencester, so that from beyond the borders of his Kentish home, he might open his mind to fresh ideas about working a holding of not inconsiderable acreage. He would gain, as Jack suggested when he announced Tom's departure, "a new perspective" on a farmer's life. He pronounced it " 'spective." Tom would return to the business of running the farm, which, it was predicted, he would manage a good deal more efficiently than even his father, in time. This had been the forward-thinking Jack's intention, though the patriarch could not have known just how forward-thinking his plans were, or that by his forty-fifth birthday he would be dead, his life shortened by a heart attack. Jack had been predeceased by his wife, Mary, who had passed away just one year earlier, having ignored a lump on her breast until such a time as saving her life was well beyond the skill of any doctor, even if Jack had been disposed to withdraw sufficient funds from the bank to take her to a good hospital.

Kezia and Dorrit had been inseparable from the day they were allocated neighboring beds in Camden's austere Austen House dormitory. Austen House was one of four "houses" to which girls were assigned for all sporting endeavors, for academic competition, and to instill a sense of camaraderie among pupils. Dorrit had expressed more of an allegiance to the novels of Elizabeth Gaskell and had rather hoped to be assigned to Gaskell House, though Kezia had idolized Jane since first reading *Persuasion*. It was later, during a visit to the farm at Dorrit's invitation, that Kezia met Tom, to whom she would soon be wed. In fact, if she had glanced at the clock while Dorrit was speaking, she would have known that at that very moment in four days she would have already walked down the aisle of her father's church, where the vicar from a neighboring parish had officiated so that her father could give her away.

Upon matriculation from Camden—"old girls" referred to themselves as "Cammies"—both Kezia and Dorrit had commenced further studies in London, at a teacher-training college in Chelsea, again with scholarship assistance in pursuit of their chosen calling, the education of children. And from there they parted ways; with Kezia accepting the offer of a position as English mistress for the upper school at her beloved Camden, while Dorrit remained steadfast in her refusal to leave the city. Dorrit's choice was made in defiance of her father, who thought the village school more than good enough for a young woman in wait for a husband, who—if Jack had pressed his preference— would one day be a son of farming Kent. She was employed at a private academy close to Regent's Park, where her daily charges were the younger sons and daughters of the better-off. She assuaged her guilt—Dorrit had acknowledged within herself a sharp leaning towards the establishment of a more equitable society—by taking food parcels to the East End poor. She suspected that those in receipt of her largesse thought she was a bit stuck-up. Dorrit, in turn, could not understand a word the East Enders said, outside a grateful, "Fanks, miss."

The nub of Kezia's doubt regarding Dorrit had for some time been the latter's immersion in the world of suffrage. Not that Kezia disapproved of the vote for women, but she had noticed Dorrit becoming more forceful, and suspected her friend was being sucked into something quite dangerous. It was one thing to march; one thing, even, to clamor for the attention of politicians, and to wear a green banner across her chest while pressing pamphlets into the hands of passers-by, all to further the cause of ending the disenfranchisement of women. But Kezia considered it another thing altogether when Dorrit's language became increasingly belligerent; the word *fight* spiced with the venom of a viper. Whenever Kezia visited Dorrit in recent months, she departed with the sense that something was being hidden from her, as if soiled laundry had been shoved under the bed to make room on a chair for an unexpected guest. As a further surprise, Kezia's very best friend had announced on Friday evening that she would be known as Dorrit no longer. With her father dead and buried, she explained, there was no longer any reason for her to endure her family's obsession with Charles Dickens, a trait inherited from her grandfather, who had named every field on Marshals Farm in honor of the author's work—Marshals itself being an abbreviation of Marshalsea, the debtors' prison where Dickens's own father had languished. The family had suspected that the chosen name was by way of a warning—unless they worked hard and took care with money, a similar fate might await them. Jack's mother had put her foot down upon becoming mistress of the house, and insisted upon the alteration that changed the farm's name, stating that it was enough to be stuck in the kitchen all day; she would not have the shadow of a prison thrust upon her home. Had Jack Brissenden prevailed at the time of his son's naming, Kezia would be engaged to a young man named Pip.

Dorrit had informed Kezia that she was in future to be known as Dorothea—abbreviated to "Thea" for friends—and she would be grateful if Kezia would pay tribute to their friendship and address her as such. In fact, if she heard the name Dorrit from any quarter, she would ignore it. Though it might seem that her social leanings would have caused Dorrit to cherish her given name, in truth she was glad at last to be rid of it.

Kezia felt as if she were in mourning, as if she had lost something very precious. How she had admired Dorrit—Thea—even from those early days at Camden. Though Thea was a quiet girl then, it had seemed to Kezia she could do anything, drawing upon a solid strength from the land that raised her. The Dorrit she loved as if she were a sister could ride a horse like the wind, and knew how to light a fire without a match. Dorrit would not draw back from the task of cleaning a pheasant or pulling the neck of a chicken, and would march across muddy fields as if the ground beneath her feet would never give to her step, for she owned it. Now she had become this woman of the town, a strident Amazon who peppered conversation with the word *fight* more times than she may have realized.

If Kezia continued to feel a little sorry for herself, blaming the fissure on Dorrit—how could you suddenly begin calling someone by another name, she thought, unless that is, it were the surname you were changing?—then Thea, as she would now forever be known, or ignore all attempts to gain her attention, also felt pushed aside. When was it, exactly, that Tom and Kezia looked at each other and saw themselves as joined, without her in the middle to reflect one to the other? At what point had she become unnecessary, ceasing to be Tom's first confidant, and Kezia's dearly adored sister—of the heart, if not in name? When had Tom grown up enough for Kezia even to have noticed him? Had he always loved her, since she first came to the farm, sitting down at the kitchen table as if she were a visitor from another world? And she was. Jack Brissenden had never held with the church—especially a town church. He considered churches, with their spires and towers, with their buttresses and chancels, naves and narthexes, as useful only for the official naming of children, for the joining of two people in matrimony, and, of course, for the burying of the dead. Thea wondered how he might have felt about that now, having been committed to the cold earth not six months past.

Thea often felt an acute sense of unfairness when she considered the features that marked Tom and herself as brother and sister, an unequal division of the shared traits in appearance and demeanor that seemed to bless him while rendering her less attractive—in her estimation, at least. Their mother's fair hair was light and sun-kissed on Tom, even in winter. Yet on Thea, that same tone became straw-like by late spring, and dull and mousey in the dim light of shorter days. Dark eyebrows, long lashes, and hazel eyes gave Tom's face definition. Thea considered those lashes to be wasted on Tom—why had she not been blessed with such bounty? And how she hated those same brown eyebrows on her own face, so much so that as a girl at Camden, she had filched a pair of tweezers from the school infirmary to rectify the situation. Her error had been in allowing

Kezia and another friend to pluck away the offending hairs. It was some time before her eyebrows grew back enough to allow another try at shaping them.

Tom was a good height for a man, but Thea was three inches shorter than Kezia, who was in turn just one inch shorter than her husband-to-be, though of the two women, Thea was the physically stronger and more adept. Even in childhood, as Tom's accomplishments were lauded by their mother and father, Thea pushed herself to match him, and surpass him if she could. The scholarship to Camden was a blessing, though it was a sword with two edges. One neatly cut away the moorings tying Thea to her family, allowing her to leave the farm and begin to establish a sense of herself. The other side of the blade separated her from Tom. For all her moments of resentment when she considered evidence suggesting that Tom was the more favored child, it was obvious as he grew that she would have fought battles to protect him, and might even have given her life for him, because Thea loved her brother beyond measure. And in return, Tom had nothing but adoration for his older sister, and had understood how his parents' preference had wounded her. He would wink at Thea across the table when his father admonished her for not being as good as Tom with the sheep, or the horses, or he would come to her later and ask for her help with some task on the farm, or inquire if she would like to walk down to Micawber Wood. It was as if he were putting a precious piece of china back on a high shelf after it had been knocked down, handling it with care in case the crack might become a break. Tom had missed Thea with a terrible ache when she went away to school, even though there was little discord in the farmhouse during her absence, and he liked the calm.

Thea's irritation with the forthcoming union between her best friend—was Kezia still her best friend?—and her brother had rendered her less than generous in her wishes for them. She could not see Kezia as a farmer's wife, and neither could her late mother, who had maintained from the first indication of a courtship that she would not share her kitchen with another woman, even if that woman was dear Kezia, who had first visited the farm when she was but thirteen years of age. Of course, such potential discord never came to pass. However, it was under the influence of this prejudice that Thea had bought her friend a gift in advance of the wedding. It was a book chosen—if truth be told—for the title alone. Thea leafed through only two or three pages at most before paying for the heavy tome, knowing she could pass it off as a worthy offering from the bridesmaid to the bride.

The seemingly benign offering represented a dig not lost on Kezia, who accepted with grace, kissing her friend on the cheek. "Dear Thea, how thoughtful of you." The book was laid bare of its wrapping. "Oh. How . . . nice. *The Woman's Book*." She leafed through the first four pages. "Well, this has everything, doesn't it? 'Contains Everything a Woman Ought to Know.' " Kezia looked up from the book and smiled at Thea, unshed tears pricking her eyes. "Now you can be assured I'll be the perfect wife for your darling brother."

"I thought it might be something you could use—it has all you might need to learn about being a woman in the home. There's a section on cookery, though I think you'll find my mother's old copy of Mrs. Beeton somewhere in the kitchen, just in case. She was a fair plain cook, so I doubt she ever needed it."

"Then there will be nothing missing in my reference library of housewifery." Kezia closed the book and patted the cover.

"And there will doubtless be times when this will be a lifesaver," she said, setting the book to one side, her smile forced.

She knew the gift was Thea's comment on her life to come, as if any depth of intellectual inquiry on her part would henceforth extend no further than a list of ingredients for the next meal or the best way to black a stove. The book had hurt her pride, though she knew very well that Thea—she had a mind to call her Dorrit again, to get under her skin—was more than aware of her Achilles' heel. Kezia had never had reason to cook, or clean, or tend house. Even while lodging in Tunbridge Wells after she'd taken up her position at Camden, every meal had been prepared for her, and at school she took her meals in the staff dining room. After she was married—*in three days, nineteen hours, and fifteen minutes*—and became mistress of Marshals Farm, the feeding of men and boys would be up to her. She would be stoker of the farm's engine.

Thea thought Kezia saw the land through rose-colored glasses, never having paid attention to the running of the farm. For a farmer's wife there was only toil from well before the first light of dawn, until the wick was turned down at night—even with help from Ada Beeney, the girl who came in from the village to light the fires, scrub the floors, and fetch and carry, it was a hard life. Kezia was an intelligent, educated woman; Thea knew that, and cherished the well of conversation that had been a hallmark of their friendship. But Kezia was also a dreamer. Once that ethereal quality had enchanted Thea—she had never met anyone like Kezia. Now her friend's naïveté festered under her skin. It was as if Kezia saw her future on the farm in a bubble, a life in which she would spend her days with daisies in her hair, wandering across sun-drenched fields bringing bottles of fresh lemonade and warm scones to her strong farmer husband, her one true love, who would sweep her into his arms with joy and gratitude.

"By the way," said Thea, flicking newspaper pages as if to underline the fact that she had better things to think about than white lace, and no need for books on keeping proper house and being a woman, "did you read about this business going on with Austria and—where was it?—yes, Serbia. It's all to do with the archduke and his wife being assassinated in Sarajevo. Anyway, I do hope any trouble blows over before August. I don't want my walking tour of the Alps ruined—Edith, Avril, and I have been planning it for such a long time." She turned another page, having recited the names of her new friends to accentuate her separation from Kezia. Indeed, Thea had no real interest in what happened in the Balkans, or anywhere else on the other side of the English Channel, but the news gave her an opportunity to test Kezia. "Of course, what happens on the world's stage won't worry you, will it? After all, by the time I'm picking edelweiss, you'll be dealing with that noisy coterie of women from the village who come to wash and mend pokes ready for the hops. There'll be a multitude of piece-workers swarming the farm to put up with. And it'll be down to you to keep the farm books—that's after making breakfast for the men at half past five in the morning. Fortunately for you, they bring their own dinner, the men, which is just as well, because Tom's like my father, ready to eat a horse when he comes in for his tea at six o'clock. You'll need the best part of the afternoon to prepare a meal fit for a king." She sighed. "I sometimes wonder whether you've ever grasped just how much hard work it all is. Three meals a day to be cooked, on top of everything else on your plate. Anyway, it's a pity you'll have your hands full—you might have liked to come to Austria. That is, if Tom would allow it. They say the Alps are beautiful beyond measure."

Kezia, who was herself not above needling, picked up the book again, resting it on her lap. "Oh, I've seen the Alps, *Thea*—don't you remember? I went with my dear father and mother when I was fifteen. For the *whole summer*. You might recall that you were invited to join us, but your father put his foot down—I think it was because my father's a man of the cloth and we were the guests of an Austrian parson, an old family friend." She smiled. "Anyway, Tom and I will be so thrilled to see you again when you come home—and when you come to stay, we'll have your old room ready and waiting." She paused and patted the book's cover. "Do you realize that in four days you'll be raising a glass to Tom and me? To our future, to the happiness we bring to the farm again, and the home we build together. The two of us making the house a home again."

Thea turned away at the word *again*.

Kezia lay back on the narrow bed in her room, watching fronds of lilac blossom scratch against the window, framed in dawn light. A cotton robe was loose around her body, naked and still warm from her bath. She ran her fingers through her hair, free of pins and splayed across the pillow, and looked at the white dress upon its hanger, hooked on the picture rail. It was a fine piece of stitchery, with lace laid across soft lawn and petticoats underneath, cut to accentuate her slenderness. A high neckline embellished with pearls would draw attention to her prominent cheekbones, though she hoped a tiny scar at the side of her left eye, reminder of a childhood accident, was not too visible. In time her mother would come to wake her, though she must know that her daughter had hardly slept. Soon Thea, dear Thea, her best friend, would knock on the door, ready to be her maid of honor on this day, when she would be wed to Tom

Brissenden. In six hours, I will be wed, thought Kezia. And in the silence of her room, her childhood room in her parents' house, she loosened the robe and allowed her fingers to trace a line across her breasts, then downwards, traversing her belly to her thighs. Before this time tomorrow, before twenty-four hours had passed, Tom's hands would grasp her, and his body would press against hers, and at last it would be done. She would belong forever after to Tom, beloved Tom whom she had known for years, even before it seemed they had seen each other at last. Until that moment, Tom had always been Thea's younger brother— young Tom, capable Tom, sensible Tom. Tom who worked the farm, who brought home from college fresh ways of drawing income from the land, and who had toiled to win the respect of workers who were his father's men. Tom who had a laugh like sunshine, and who had kissed her for the first time when he was twenty-three and she two years older, would be her husband, her spouse, her helpmeet and lover. Kezia rolled over on the bed and closed her eyes. This was the body she would give to Tom— the man who was still a boy when she'd first come to Marshals Farm. But Tom, now tall and capable, with hands callused and worn and shoulders broad from working the land, was her Tom, dear Tom whom she would love for the rest of her days.

Tom and his best man, Edward—Edward was a farmer in Sussex; they had met at the agricultural college—were staying at a local inn. He would have preferred to be married from the farm, but he could not argue with custom—and it was custom that the marriage took place in the bride's parish. He had tried, once, to press his point, arguing that Kezzie—he had called her Kezzie, it seemed, since they first met—had lived most of her life in Kent, attending school and working at Camden after college in London. And though he knew she too would have chosen the village church, he did not wish to cross either her mother or her father, for to do so would be tantamount to arguing with God, and though he was not a churchgoing man, he wouldn't take a chance on anything untoward coming to pass on the big day. Now, while Kezia was awake, imagining the hours ahead, Tom slept. There were few days for him to call his own, but today he would rest his head until at least half past nine. Edward would wake him. In time, with Tom dressed in the suit he had bought for his father's funeral, the two men would walk to the church to await his bride. Tom was not nervous; he had no qualms regarding his choice of the woman he would lie next to every night for the rest of his life. *Old head on young shoulders*, they said about him. When all was said and done, even Thea—grudgingly—agreed they were a good enough match. Despite Kezia having few skills to prepare her for keeping a house and being a farmer's wife, the foundation of their union would be Tom's solid nature and Kezia's ability to lighten their days.

It might seem to some that Tom was one who kept his thoughts to himself, who would never be caught supporting this opinion, or that argument. He was solid even as a boy, someone who knew what he had to get on with, so proceeded to get on with it. The men who worked for his father had come to respect his straightforward manner, and—increasingly—the finality of his decisions. No one, not even Edward, not even his mother, who swore she could read both her children blind, had intuited the depth of his enchantment with Kezia Marchant.

At first it had been a crush, a boyish beating of the heart first experienced when his sister brought her friend home to the farm and introduced her to the family. His babyish name for Thea was Dorry, for that was all he could pronounce when he first began to form words, so the name had been kept, albeit with a Dickensian twist. Of late Tom had felt rather put out when asked to call his sister Thea. It seemed as if the childhood bond was lost, as if someone had snipped the fine yarn that had joined them from the moment he reached for her hand to steady his attempt at walking, saying, "Dorry, Dorry." But Tom was not a complainer, so he called her Thea and referred to her as such ever after.

He had looked forward to Kezia's visits to the farm, anticipating her noticing him, drawing him into the conversation.

"Hello, Tom. Dorrit tells me that you've your own flock now—you'll have to show me."

The boy had flushed; the mother noticed, and the father raised an eyebrow as he cast a glance towards the girl who would one day become his daughter-in-law, though he would not live to see the day. When the engagement was first announced, he accepted it with a smile, slapping his son on the back, though without obvious enthusiasm.

If Tom had been asked to explain, to describe to another, why he had chosen Kezia for his wife, he might—predictably— have shrugged his shoulders and said that he had better things to do than talk about private matters. But in his heart and soul, he knew very well why he wanted Kezia by his side. The childhood crush, a time when a single look from Kezia, just a comment of interest or observation, would flood his body with warmth, had developed into something more over the years. He admired Kezia; he took account of the way she held herself, of her confidence. Her dress was neither ostentatious nor plain, but always drew attention from passers-by—a second look by a woman, the raising of a gentleman's hat. Her features might have seemed sharp on another woman—eyes that moved quickly from person to person in a conversation with family and friends—and she had dexterous hands, large hands, really, for a female; yet in her movements she was deliberate and thoughtful.

Whether walking on the farm or meandering around the shops in London, Kezia would stop to peruse anything that caught her eye, and would not be rushed. Thea had found this trait annoying at times, cursing Kezia as their bus pulled out in the distance or as they arrived late at the cinema, forfeiting the first fifteen minutes of the picture on account of something Kezia just had to see. Later, though, Thea found she missed those little things about Kezia that had once been the source of some frustration. Kezia had a throaty laugh that, when she came to know the family, seemed to have no governor. Jack Brissenden would laugh with her, and Tom would notice the sparkle in Thea's eyes as she tried not to giggle, at which point he could not help but laugh. Only his mother executed control—her cheeks twitched, but her stare was less than warm. Tom knew then that his mother was jealous of Kezia, for it irked her that all her family was in love with this girl who seemed to know little of the country, and nothing of the farm.

What Tom knew, now, was that he wanted Kezia by his side. His work was hard, and despite his apparent success in managing without his father's guidance, he often felt as if wolves paced the perimeter of his land. Not only had he been fortunate in his inheritance, but his father's foresight had bolstered his chances of running a good farm in what were proving to be troubling times. Jack had realized that Tom would need more tools to serve the land than he had ever had in his day, if the land were to serve him in turn, and his son after him, God willing. He might have the theory of agricultural college under his belt, along with a deep innate understanding of the soil, but the days were long, and a farm could take its pound of flesh in return for a good harvest. Tom wanted to come home to a warm, fragrant kitchen, a fire in the hearth at night, and a woman with whom he could share his joys, his worries, his laughter—and he so wanted laughter. In truth, his parents had thought Kezia unsuitable, and would have preferred to see him paying court to a daughter of the countryside, to a girl who understood what it was to put her apron on in the morning and take it off at night only when her spouse had made his way up the creaking farmhouse stairs to the room above. She would bank up the fire, swab the red tile floor just one more time. Not before she had settled the wicks in flickering lamps would she take to the staircase and then to their bed. In marrying a Brissenden, Tom's mother had set aside a desire to continue her education, and devoted her heart to the farm, had given her spirit to the business of her husband, her complexion to worry, and her hands to hard work. Though her formal learning had ended early, she had been a steady reader in her day, and now she harbored envy that Kezia, with her light touch in the world, the way she skimmed across the surface of concern, might find the softer way of being a farmer's wife that had eluded her.

Edward nudged Tom as the organ bellows wheezed, drew breath, and exhaled fresh energy into the ancient church. The "Wedding March" filled the rafters with joy. Tom felt a line of perspiration run down his neck and along his spine, and fingered the starched collar that would leave a red horizontal stripe on his skin. He felt a warm blush reach his cheeks and ears, and thought the entire congregation must see this sign of his delight, fear, anticipation, and—yes—excitement. Edward nudged him again. And again.

"Look, you bloody fool. Look and remember. She's right

beautiful." He pronounced the word "boodiful" in his rounded rural Sussex brogue.

So Tom turned his head, and at once a shaft of light seemed to render all others invisible as Kezia walked towards him, one hand on her father's arm, the other clutching a bouquet of white garden blooms—her mother had begun to cultivate a bed of white flowers next to the house on the day Tom had called to ask for Kezia's hand. No veil could keep the bride's wide smile from captivating her groom, and no crown of orange blossom could shadow the coppery nut-brown hair drawn back in a braided bun. Kezia had been the wife of his heart for years, long before the minister asked who giveth this woman and her father lifted her hand towards his; long before he set a ring of gold upon her finger, and long before the bells pealed and they walked past a blur of faces as man and wife. And she would be his wife for as long as they both might live. God willing.

Chapter 2

A good housewife will not rest content with the fact that the meals in her house are well-cooked. She will also see to it that they are well-served, knowing that dainty table equipment and skillful service does much to enhance the enjoyment of the fare provided.

—*THE WOMAN'S BOOK*

Tom looked up from his plate and began to laugh.

"What's the matter with it?" asked his wife of two and a half weeks, herself smiling, unable to resist her husband's apparent amusement.

"Kezzie, love, what have you done with this cauliflower?"

"What do you mean?" asked Kezia Brissenden, rubbing her hands on a pinafore still bearing the crisp creases of newness amid a garland of stains. "What's wrong with the cauliflower?"

She leaned across to look at the food she had set before him. There was a meat pie; admittedly, she'd had some trouble with the pastry, and it seemed pockmarked. The mashed potato was quite well divested of the lumps she'd fought against earlier, and the cauliflower appeared well cooked. Tom liked his vegetables well cooked, color drained from the green to the extent that it appeared bleached, with creamy white florets almost indistinguishable from the mash.

"I just wondered why there was string in it."

"Oh, dear, you've got the string. I didn't see it when I dished up. Here, allow me . . ." Kezia leaned towards him, pulled at the string he'd lifted with his fork, and removed it with a flourish.

Gravy splattered the tablecloth. She giggled as she carried the
length of twine towards the sink to wash in cold water and hang
to dry on a pipe running from the copper at the side of the stove,
which supplied hot water to the tap. "Waste not want not. Your
mother would be proud of me!"

"I daresay she would, but why did you cook the cauli with
string in the first place?"

"To keep the bits in, silly. All those little flowery bits might
drop off, if you don't tie them up."

And with that Tom shook his head, tried not to laugh, and
slipped his fork into the pie. They were in the first flush of marriage, and this was another source of fascination for the young
husband, that this wife of his had no attachment to her prowess
as a cook. She didn't seem to care that pastry might be under-
done, meat overdone, that bread was too doughy in the crumb,
too hard on the crust, or that the men looked at their eggs and
bacon and then at each other every morning. She seemed like a
sprite assigned to a factory job, flitting from stove to table, then
out to the kitchen garden, cutting rosemary to garnish an egg on
toast—and not one of the farmworkers had ever seen garnish,
nor would the word be part of their vocabulary.

Other women, Tom knew, set stock by their accomplishments
in the kitchen, as if their identity, their essential wifeliness, were
attached to the range, the mixing bowls, knives, crockery, and
cutlery. His mother had entered her rich eggy sponges in the
annual show, though at home cake baking was generally left
until Saturday so that Sunday tea might have something special about it. She'd had a limited repertoire, his mother, though
the food she set upon the table was good and hearty, each day
assigned a menu that never changed. You knew it was Monday
when pie topped with mash was dished up, the meat minced
and left over from the Sunday joint. Tuesday toad-in-the-hole,

Wednesday hotpot. And so on. No fish on Friday, though, unless one of the men had brought trout from a summer's eve spent with rod and line. Experimentation was not his mother's forte; setting up a good table for hungry men who showed appreciation with the doffing of a cap or a nod in her direction as they set off for their day's work was good enough for her. She did not ask for more.

But Kezia had taken to heart a nugget of advice discovered in a hardly used recipe book found in her late mother-in-law's larder:

Never omit that trifling touch of decoration which makes the simplest dish seem appetizing, and the homeliest table attractive. Even a jar of woodland or hedgerow blooms makes all the difference—a meal at once appears, something more than merely eating to satisfy the wants of the body. It becomes a pleasant affair, beneficial and a tonic to the soul.

So she set the table with best silver brought from the parlor for men who tied their trousers in place with rope. On her first day as the farmer's wife, she'd put out fresh linen towels on the kitchen draining board as the men walked in through the back door, and soon it became a habit for them to form a line at the sink as they waited to wash their hands. At first they looked at Tom in dismay, wondering what life must be like with this woman who didn't appear to know her place, who pulled up a chair to the table, her mug of tea held with both hands, asking them questions about their wives, their children, and what they thought of this or that, when the only thinking that engaged their minds was whether cows were to be moved from Barnaby to Pickwick, and whether their wives might get a bit of work, pin money earned darning pokes up in the oast house, still bearing the spicy must of last year's hop-picking season. But soon there grew among these men something akin to envy. Though not a soul could articulate such feelings, it was clear that the farmhouse had been bathed in new light, as if it had been given a stark coat of white paint—and they wouldn't put that past Mrs. Kezia Brissenden, Miss Marchant, as was. They could see that Tom had a freshness to him too, as he left with his workers to go out into the fields each morning. And it wasn't that Kezia didn't respect her role, or Tom, or the farm she had married as much as the man. She took it as it was, loved it for what it would forever be, just as she loved her husband. Kezia was Kezia, and nothing, it seemed, would change who she was, or who she might be in her world. Tom knew all this, could see and feel her establishing her place. She was not simply filling the role of another woman before her. It entertained him, this Kezia-ness that was enveloping Marshals Farm, named for a dark prison in Dickens' day. And it never bothered him; he knew that at the center of Kezia's rural life, they stood together, hand in hand, and all else would grow from there.

It was when they had been married precisely twenty-four days that Kezia realized that she had become somewhat disengaged from life beyond Marshals Farm, and decided to venture out beyond her immediate wifely domain of the house, the kitchen garden, or the village shop. She had been thinking about her mother. Mrs. Marchant had supported her husband in the many ways expected of a parson's wife. She was active in the parish, with coffee mornings, flower arranging, visits to the sick and bereaved, and committee work. But she took her "days out" without apology or explanation, and Kezia could never remember a time when she had questioned where her mother might have gone at those times, or when she would return. Was it weekly that this happened? Or every fortnight? She wasn't sure, but she supposed her mother had taken the train to London, or to the coast. A visit to an exhibition, or to Whitstable, where she might enjoy a plate of oysters, a cup of tea, and a walk along the seafront. On the morning of Kezia's wedding, Mrs. Marchant came to her daughter's room—not, to Kezia's surprise, to give a lesson on married life, on what might be expected in the kitchen or the bedroom, but to slip into her hand the grand sum of ten pounds.

"Keep a nest egg, Kezia, your private money. Keep it safe and add to it, if you can, but never let it go. A woman needs money of her own, as much as she requires time beyond the home. Start as you mean to go on, Kezia, dear. Claim what you require at the beginning with no explanation, and beyond that day you will never have to account for yourself, as long as the house is a good house, the food is on the table, and your husband sleeps well at night."

Then she kissed her daughter, placed her hand on her cheek, and left.

Kezia had a nest egg of her own, held safe in the bank—money earned while working at Camden, together with a small bequest from a maiden great-aunt. But she took her mother's advice, and kept a tin in the bottom drawer of her dressing table, into which the ten pounds was duly placed.

On this, the first day that Kezia claimed for herself, she dressed in a sturdy walking skirt, her stout leather boots, and an old cream linen blouse that had seen better days—all good enough for what she planned. She packed a sandwich, placing it in a knapsack along with an earthenware bottle of lemonade. She took a book and a bound journal—she had kept such a daily record of her life since childhood. Kezia left Ada to the kitchen and the cleaning, and upon the table set a fresh pork pie and a loaf of crusty bread—probably too crusty, again—along with a wedge of cheese, two tomatoes, and an apple. She added a jug of lemonade covered with a doily, and set off. Tom might expect a cooked dinner at noon, with a pot of strong tea, but Kezia knew there was enough food to see him through the rest of the day. She would be home in time to prepare a hearty tea and have it ready when he walked through the door at six. It was coming on harvest time, and he would go out again later. There was always more work to be done on a summer's night.

Kezia had no idea where she was going, only that she would set off towards what she believed to be the perimeter of the farm beyond Micawber Wood, and then along the edge, which she expected to be marked with a fence. She planned to explore the forested acres flanking Twist, the largest of the hop gardens, where the spicy hops with their dense, green, and pungent fairy-wing petals lay heavy on the bine. She thought she would even ramble to the edge of the Hawkendene estate. She knew little of the property abutting Marshals Farm, only that there was a wealthy man and his wife, their son—older than Tom, or Kezia—and a host of lackeys to do their every bidding. The family opened their gardens once a year, in late August. Trestle tables would be set up with linen tablecloths rippling aimlessly in a light breeze, like sails on a ship becalmed. There would be triangled sandwiches and small fancies with pastel icing. The tea would have a fragrance to it, and at least one of the villagers would be heard to comment—in a low voice, of course—that the lukewarm beverage was only fit to dab behind the ears, and wouldn't set you up for anything, of a morning. When Kezia went into the village, it seemed that everyone was talking about the party, even with a month to go before the anticipated day. Thea had written to her—since the wedding, they were both endeavoring to nurture the friendship, for weren't they now joined as family?—and told her that she should not go. She maintained that this inequity, this fawning on the rich by the poor, should have died with the old queen. Kezia thought she had a point, but at the same time found herself getting caught up in the excitement. She wondered, though, as she jumped over a stile as if she were a schoolgirl, if her enthusiasm was due to the fact that the people who set such store by the party were referring to her as "Mrs. Brissenden" for the first time. After almost a month she was getting used to her new name, and in the village shop now ceased to look round when greeted, in case the ghostly specter of her late mother-in-law had appeared behind her.

Hawkendene Lake was still, the summer sun reflecting surrounding trees into the water as if copied there with oils. Kezia chose her spot, a place at the foot of a giant oak where thick roots reared up from the earth, providing a place for her to sit and rest her head. She pulled a square embroidered cloth from the knapsack, setting out her repast. She closed her eyes and sighed. This was it, a perfect place. Across the lake, just visible, the house in which the Hawkes family lived appeared to lounge amid perfect lawns and pruned hedges. It was, she thought, somewhat intimidating. Spires rose up from rooftops, poking their way skyward as if in competition with the pines. It was a tableau to be painted, one day, this image now scored into memory; the house, the woodland, the lake with water lilies in bloom. The light buzzing of worker bees toiling in the fields behind her seemed to settle her soul. Bliss, she thought. For two hours, perhaps more, she would read her book and pen whatever thoughts came to her. Soon, though, despite her best efforts to resist the heat of the day, the gentle swoop of birds across the lake, and the meadow fragrance, her eyelids grew heavy and she slept.

"Did you know you're trespassing?"

At first the voice seemed to come from far away, and, she thought later, had even entered her dream, though she could not remember any detail of that slip into another world. But then, when she realized she was no longer alone, Kezia's eyes opened in a snap. She shook her head and leapt to her feet, only to find herself looking down at a man who had, it seemed, been sitting alongside her for some time.

"And who are you, sir?" She felt as if she had fallen down a hole marked "Slumber" and was struggling to grapple her way out.

The man laughed, leaning back on one elbow. He was dressed in twill trousers, his white shirt open at the neck and a kerchief tied at his throat. He wore a brown weskit and leather shoes that appeared to have been polished to a shine before he set off across fields of hardened ochre Kentish clay soil, picking up dust along the way.

"It's all right, I'm not going to take you to the constabulary. I just wondered if you realized you had encroached beyond your land."

"How do you know what or where my land is?" Kezia leaned forward, her hands on her hips as if to establish an impression of importance.

Splaying his fingers on the ground to steady himself, the stranger stood up and faced her. He rubbed his earth-soiled hand on his trousers and held it out towards her.

"Edmund Hawkes. You're in my favorite spot—since I was a boy, actually—but I won't scold you for it."

"How long were you there?"

"And you are?"

"I beg your pardon, sir." Kezia took the proffered hand. "Kezia Mar . . . I mean, Kezia Brissenden." She felt her cheeks redden. "Mrs. Tom Brissenden. From Marshals Farm."

"Yes, I know that much—Tom's new wife. I guessed who you were, but I didn't know your name. Congratulations, Mrs. Brissenden."

"Thank you. I apologize for the encroachment. Now I must be on my way. I will be sure not to come here again."

Kezia turned and knelt to pack away her book, her journal, the spent bottle, and the white linen cloth in which she'd wrapped a sandwich. Hawkes knelt next to her.

"It's all right, I can do it," she said.

They stood, facing each other.

"Look, don't worry—if you want to visit the lake, please, be my guest. You're not hurting anyone," said Hawkes. "It gives me pleasure, knowing that someone else enjoys my spot."

"That's very kind of you, Mr. Hawkes. But I think in future I will find plenty of interesting places within the boundary of Marshals Farm. Now I have to be on my way."

They shook hands once again, and Kezia set off at as fast a clip as she could manage across the field towards the stile. She turned, once, to look back. Edmund Hawkes had not moved, and was staring in her direction.

Two days later Kezia had all but forgotten the meeting. She was in the kitchen, leaning across the table, wiping it dry following another swabbing. The top was a thick, solid piece of wood akin to the block upon which the butcher would swing his cleaver to chop through flesh and sinew into bone. It was more part of the kitchen than Kezia, or her mother-in-law before her; it had been in its place for generations. Now it had been scrubbed twice this morning, ready for Kezia to knead a lump of pastry dough into topping for a meat pie. The mix was too dry, but she had yet to get the feel of different types of dough in her hands. Meat pie had become her stalwart friend, a dish she could execute without too much ado. *Execute* might have been an appropriate verb to describe her skill, though her dexterity in the kitchen had improved. She had studied the recipe, and was confident in her ability to prepare the dish for her husband's tea.

She was using leftover meat taken from a joint of beef, which she cut into cubes, pressing them into the meat grinder as she turned the handle. The grinder was screwed onto the table for this part of the job, and Kezia could never quite turn the nut tight enough on the screw—the grinder wobbled a good deal, so crumbs of meat dropped onto the floor. She fried onion and celery, along with grated carrot—her mother-in-law would never have grated the carrot, but would have instead cut root vegetables into small cubes. She added thyme and savory to the mix, along with the meat, onto which she poured some gravy.

The one ingredient not specified that Kezia added to each meal, and in copious amounts impossible to be weighed on the kitchen scale, was a love for her husband growing beyond affection, beyond the familiarity that led her to accept his proposal. It must be mentioned that there were those—both in the village and farther afield among others familiar with the Marchant family—who wondered if, and therefore, why, Kezia Marchant had married below her station. There was speculation that she might have envisaged spinsterhood looming and rushed into marriage at the first opportunity—though the long engagement would suggest not; indeed, the young couple had been putting money by for their future. Others thought Kezia had "settled" or that the Brissendens were attempting to better themselves. The truth was perhaps more simple. Each recognized the honesty in the other and felt—with an acknowledgement that had no need for spoken confirmation—that their trust was well placed. Their love was thus seeded in the rich soil of mutual understanding.

While kneading, rolling, and lifting the pastry to line the pie dish, Kezia could think only of Tom, imagining him in the distance, a moving speck against the plane tree on the hill, walking down towards the farmhouse and along the road, his jacket thrown over a shoulder and held by a single finger. Tom's hands were working hands, broadened by shovel and pick, by steadying the harness and driving a saw to coppice a few acres of woodland. Soon the kitchen would be filled with the fragrant heat of pie blended with the aroma of vegetables overcooked. With the meal almost ready, Kezia kept an eye on the window, a vigil for her spouse. When she saw him, off came her pinafore, consigned to the hook on the back of the kitchen door. She pushed back a stray hair and quickly checked her appearance in the mirror on the back wall, to ensure no flour had rubbed off on her face.

"Hello, Tom." Kezia went straight to him, always, when he entered the house, and this day was no different. She took his jacket and pressed her lips to his. Tom could not help but smile, pulling her into his arms. He had never in his life known his mother to greet his father in such a manner, and wondered if she ever had.

"I smell a meat pie," said Tom.

"Ah, but a different meat pie today," replied Kezia, putting on her pinafore once more.

Tom washed his hands at the sink, scrubbed his nails with the brush, and picked up the clean linen towel Kezia had placed on the draining board. His father never washed his hands; never had water, soap, and a linen towel touch his skin between work and a meal.

"What did you do this time?"

"I've added a little something to the gravy, and some herbs to the vegetables—but don't worry, I've massacred the greens for you."

Tom laughed and sat down, waiting for Kezia to set plates upon the table. The tea had been made and left to brew, so Tom reached for the pot, removed the knitted cozy—a wedding present from one of the villagers—and poured for them both. He had noticed that Kezia was thinner. Not awkwardly so, but in contrast to his own weight. One of the women working in the blackcurrant fields commented upon it, saying, "Ah, love, you're a married man now. It's contentment in your belly, that's what it is." And he'd blushed, then measured the woman's picked fruit and moved on to the next row to check the trays.

"You need a bit more food, Kezzie," said Tom, pointing his fork towards her plate.

"It's enough for me, Tom. Plenty. What do you think of it?" Kezia waited for his appraisal of the dish before lifting her own cutlery.

He had never heard his mother ask for an opinion upon her cooking. She put food on the table and expected it to be eaten. She would nod when his father patted his belly and said it was a good table she'd set for them, or she might add, "It's entitled to be, it took me all morning." But Kezia liked to talk about each dish, what he liked, what he thought would have been better. So Tom became used to this discussion as he ate his dinner, a meal that Kezia's family would have called luncheon. His tea was their supper. His mother's supper was a thick cheese sandwich after mopping the floor at ten o'clock at night, whereas Mrs. Marchant's was likely a cup of cocoa with a slice of toast, and possibly the only meal she prepared herself each day. It was funny, thought Tom—this naming of each meal, and how it changed from here to there, whether the here and there was a division by geography or by the station of the person sitting down to eat. But one thing Tom knew—he liked to recognize the food on his plate.

"What's this bit?" he asked, cutting into his pie again.

"Oh, a few sprigs of rosemary laid under the crust. Gives it a more piquant flavor."

"Piquant, eh? Well, it's very nice, but it gets a bit stuck in my teeth."

Kezia frowned. "Hmmm, I should probably have cut the leaves off the sprig. Never mind, I'll do it next time."

Tom commented on the gravy, the potatoes—fried, not mashed—and in general was well pleased with his meal. He added that he thought it would be fit for one of those restaurants—not that he would ever set foot in one, after all, you don't know what you're eating when it comes from a kitchen you can't see into.

Kezia, resting her arms on the table, looked poised to counter this opinion, but instead shared news gleaned from the village that morning. "It's getting very tense, you know, this talk of war. I'm rather nervous about it. I mean, what will we do, if it comes to it? Mrs. Coombes said her husband went up to London last week and came back with all sorts of stories about what people are saying up there. He said it was like another planet down here, when all we think about is the hop picking, or the barley."

Tom reached across, took her by the arm, and pulled her to him, seating her on his lap. He wiped his mouth with a napkin; now they had table napkins, boiled white so that they might continue to match the wedding-gift linen cloth that covered the old table. Mrs. Marchant's housekeeper told Kezia about boiling for whiteness, and adding a blue bag to the water.

"I don't pay much mind to it all, Kezzie. I've too much to do all day with the farm. Don't worry, love, it won't come to us."

"Tom, you have four men on this farm, two apprentices, and pieceworkers besides. What if they all go to war? What if you have to go to war?"

"I'd like to see Bert try to go to war—he's my right-hand man, and he's too long in the tooth; they'd send him packing. Danny wouldn't get into the army, on account of his leg, and Bill Hicks and Mattie Wright, we were nippers together—they've worked here all their lives, and their fathers too. As for the young lads— they're still so wet behind the ears, it's all they can do to lift a shovel, never mind a rifle. War's a young man's game."

"But you're young, Tom."

"Come on, Kezzie, I'd better get back to work—if I linger too long, we'll be up those stairs, won't we?" He kissed her on the mouth. "Don't worry about me, I'm a farmer born and bred, and if there's anything that'll be needed if it comes to war, it's what I've got—food to put on the table."

As Kezia began to clear the plates, Ada came into the kitchen, a pail in her hand. Kezia blushed.

"Anyway, this'll never get the cows moved, will it? See you later, love." Tom walked towards the back door, rolling up his sleeves. "Did you put something in the gravy, by the way?"

"A little sherry, actually."

"Sherry? Mother only kept that for Easter and Christmas." Tom winked at his wife. "Nice in gravy, I must say."

Kezia had become more worried about this business of war. She'd bought a newspaper in the village and read every word reported on the subject. No one she met seemed to be paying much attention. Perhaps Mr. Coombes was right; perhaps they were cocooned in their round of work on the land, in the home or a wealthy someone else's home. The Brissendens were considered somewhere in the middle of the village social order, better off than most, with Tom becoming more of a gentleman farmer than his father before him. In fact, most people didn't quite know where to place Tom, especially following his marriage to Kezia. But they liked him—he was one of their own—and they couldn't help but take to Kezia, whom many considered very ladylike, though not perhaps lady enough to have someone else to do her shopping. She drew attention when she rode the mare into the village on days when she wanted only a few bits and pieces, putting them in her knapsack before riding back to the farm. It was clear she was something of a novice in the saddle, though she was trying to learn. Sometimes she brought the gig, but it was generally considered that if the mare, Mrs. Joe, hadn't known her job, Kezia Brissenden would have been in a good deal of trouble.

By the end of July, and wed all of twenty-seven days, it seemed to Kezia as if the roots of her marriage were beginning to break through into the earth, ready to grow deeper with each year. For Tom, she knew, it was as he expected. You sow a seed and it either flourishes or it withers, and it never crossed his mind that his marriage to Kezia would ever be anything other than a good one. He saw his future clearly. The farm would be strong, and there would be no setback that he could not counter with hard work. He had never looked at the land through rose-tinted glasses, and he knew how it could break a man, how it could wound body and soul. He had a responsibility that came with providing a living for men who worked on the farm and their families—men he had known his entire life. That the farm was his at all had been down to sheer luck—and he knew better than tempt fate. In time there would be children, and their children after. Tom trusted—though he had never thought about it consciously—that he would die on this land and be buried in the churchyard, and that his son and his son after him would work the fields that generations of Brissenden men had farmed.

But there was something beginning to scratch at the smooth veneer of Kezia's new married life. It was not a constant annoyance, like the branch that scrapes against the windowpane night after night, but more like a small fragment of grit in the shoe, something that is felt now and again. Though Tom would have argued otherwise, had she confided in him, Kezia wondered if she was on the cusp of losing an element of herself. She had claimed two half-days alone, walking, reading, and writing in her journal, but she considered Thea's life—and, indeed, her own before marriage—and wondered if in time she would feel that she was missing something, and whether she had bartered her character for contentment. Indeed it was in the village hall, which also served as a library of sorts, and where Kezia had stopped to read a women's monthly or two—she was still undecided upon the question of placing a subscription with the newsagent in Brooksmarsh—that she came upon a comment that caused her to sit down and read further. Women's books in the village library were always out of date; however, from a copy of *Woman At Home*, dated January 1913, she copied down a paragraph on the back of her shopping list:

> *The modern girl prefers to live independently, and earns two hundred pounds a year, rather than marry a man with an income scarcely more than her own.*

The writer asked if it was surprising, then, that the latest statistics on the matter revealed that 1912 reported the lowest marriage rate ever? Kezia wondered if she was a statistic, perhaps a dying breed—the married woman.

She had given up a reasonable income to be married, but more so had given up a job she loved. Would her new life sustain her? And of greater importance, would she have enough about her to hold the love of her husband? A line in another book taken from the same pile declared, "The twentieth century is discovering the woman." Kezia was appalled. Weren't these questions she asked of herself simply indicative of her self-interest, and at a time when her husband was working his fingers to the bone to build a life for them? She cast the book back onto the pile, but not before making a note that Hoe's Sauce provided an excellent flavoring for soups, stews, and other dishes.

These thoughts continued to trouble her. The grit became a stone in short order. Over Sunday tea, Kezia suggested to Tom that it might be a good idea for her to go up to London to see dear Thea, from whom they had received only one letter since the wedding—athough Kezia had sent her two long communiqués, the second with a note from Tom added at the end. Kezia informed her husband that she would go up to Charing Cross the following day—even though it was a bank holiday. She had checked, and there were some nineteen trains timetabled on the up line from Tonbridge, and she had the times noted down. She told him she had prepared plenty of food for him, which Ada had only to heat in the oven, and there was a goodly supply of extras in the larder to tide him over for a couple of days. She planned to be back on Wednesday afternoon. She was sure Ada could manage the men's breakfast for two mornings.

Tom offered no counter to the plans. Given that he too was worried about Thea—"dotty Dorrit," as he referred to her, with affection, on many an occasion—he was glad that Kezia was looking out for his family. It warmed him.

Edmund Hawkes watched Tom Brissenden bring the gig to a halt outside the Brooksmarsh branch-line station. The farmer stepped down from the cart, then walked around to attend his wife. With his hands about her waist, he swung her down onto the cobblestones, whereupon he took off his cap and held her to him, kissing her as if he might never see her again. Hawkes turned away as the couple came towards the ticket office, Tom carrying a small leather case. A third-class fare for one was purchased. Tom led Kezia out onto the platform and, after looking back at the clock, kissed his wife once more to mark his departure. He set the case down beside her and left the station. Hawkes could not ascertain their conversation, though he realized that he was frowning as he watched them, scrutinizing their expressions as they bid farewell. There was only one other passenger waiting, an old woman reading a book, a pince-nez held up to her eyes. She paid no attention to Tom and Kezia; indeed, Hawkes thought she might be deaf. Apart from the ticket master, he was the only person who'd seen them at the station, and they had not even noticed him. Edmund Hawkes felt an unfamiliar emotion over this event that had lasted perhaps five minutes. He was envious of Tom Brissenden.

CHAPTER 3

Women, like men, have the desire to expand their realm of intelligence, to take part in the affairs of the world, which bear upon their lives, and the restraint and force of mere tradition, prejudice, or caste, have become intolerable to them.

—*THE WOMAN'S BOOK*

Edmund Hawkes was liked in the village; indeed, he was known and well thought of across the county. Not to the extent that he was feted, though his batting average for the local cricket team was talked about every year. He was simply liked. He had an easy way about him. He smiled readily, but not overly. He was gracious to shopkeepers and to the landlord of the Queen's Head, where he occasionally stopped for a pint of ale, his Labrador dog, Millie, resting her head on his knee, and his hunter, Bella, tethered outside. He was considered a kind man. More than anything, it was generally agreed that he was a sensible Hawkes, not one of those foolish members of the family, like his father and great-grandfather before him. The Hawkes family were not lords of the manor, not aristocracy, though they were well-heeled gentry with business interests overseas and at home. Four large farms belonging to the estate brought in a good income. It had once been five, but due to weakness on the part of his great-grandfather, the most productive of those farms now belonged to the Brissenden family, who had gone from tenants to owners in the time it took to throw a double top in a game of darts.

Hawkes did not grieve for land that had never been his, though he could not escape what appeared to some to be a pre-ordained element of character. It seemed that, throughout the history of the family, an heir of good sense followed an heir who could best be described as a dilettante. It was as if each generation bred a son at odds with his father. His great-grandfather had been a gambler, a man who would sit in the pub—any hostelry would do—and within a short time draw someone into placing a bet, even if that wager were money risked upon which of two raindrops would descend the windowpane first. There was no limit to what stake he might put on the table. His son, Edmund's grandfather, had subsequently run a very tight estate, with every penny in or out of the accounts marked in a ledger at the end of each day. The restriction was like a noose around the neck of Edmund's father, who grew to manhood with a liking for drink and a leaning towards profligacy. And so it began again. Edmund grew up knowing how to keep his father at arm's length—and fortunately, his father had little interest in the activities of his son. A good estate manager kept Hawkendene Manor from complete destitution, and it was this man—Albert Hodges—who took Edmund under his wing, and taught him how to care for the land he had inherited. With his father rendered incapable by senility, Edmund could look back and know that it might have been worse for him. He'd spent most of his childhood in Sussex, at prep school, and then on to Bishopswell Hall, a senior school for boys where he had worked hard enough to secure a place at Oxford. He had studied politics and economics at university, but would rather have read novels all day and written poetry. Now, though, his work was the maintenance of the Hawkes fortunes, ensuring a good foundation should another generation fall foul of the whisky bottle or a passion for cards. If Edmund had a weakness, it was, as the village postmistress put it, *He can be a dreamer, that one* . . . Knowing this element of himself, he feared his son—a son yet to be born to a women yet to be met—might be a fierce man of purpose who forever moved at a brisk clip, in response to a father who preferred to stroll, and ideally to sit by the lake and work with verse rather than stocks and shares or trusts and investments. So Hawkes tried to balance desire and responsibility, and was generally considered to be a good man.

"Kezzie, what are you doing here?" Thea came downstairs to greet her sister-in-law, having been summoned by the warden.

"Did you not receive my postcard? It should have arrived this morning, second post at the latest. I actually sent it before I told Tom I was coming, dear love that he is." She set down her leather case. "I've come to see you—to stay, if that's all right. Just for a couple of nights."

"What—is my brother driving you to leave the farm already?" said Thea, responding to Kezia's open arms, holding her close. She smelled the freshness of a Kentish morning in Kezia's hair, and realized she had missed her friend very much. "And you're forgetting—there was no post today, not on a bank holiday."

Kezia stood back but held on to Thea's hands. "Oh, dear. I did forget. We hadn't heard from you, so I decided to come. Tom agreed with my decision. I came up on the train. We thought you might have been upset when your friends backed out of the excursion you'd planned. Don't you think they were a bit hasty, in calling a halt to it all?"

"Hasty? Well, I might have risked it, but . . . Kezia, don't you keep up with what's happening?" Thea bent down to take

Kezia's leather case, but Kezia shook her head and reached for the handle.

"I can manage. And what do you mean, don't I keep up? Of course I do, but you know how the farm can be." She held her case in two hands. "And you should see Charing Cross— it's packed with Belgians, and people trying to organize them, running round with ledgers, taking names, and doing their best to help out. I think everyone's just overwhelmed by it all. And when I changed trains at Tonbridge, there were notices warning of delays due to troops being moved to the coast."

Thea led the way back up the staircase towards her room. She responded as if she had not heard Kezia. "Didn't you take account of what it's like on the streets as you came from the station? Everyone's waiting for news. And you would think it was the Jubilee, what with people drinking and dancing." She took Kezia's case and put it in her wardrobe. "If you didn't notice, you must have walked here with your eyes closed."

"Of course I noticed, but it seemed so strange to me, that people would celebrate the idea of going to war." Kezia faltered, and she felt her eyes water. "You don't think it will actually happen, do you?"

Thea nodded. "I don't think there's any going back now. And that puts *us* in a difficult position. Mrs. Pankhurst is coming out in support of the government by ceasing our battle to finally get voting rights for women. Frankly, I'm not sure where that leaves us. And as far as war is concerned, I'm for the pacifists, you know."

"The pacifists? You mean, you wouldn't support your country if it happens, if we go to war?"

"Oh, Kezia, you are a strange one, surely you are!" Thea folded her arms and stood by the window, looking down at the street. "I have friends who are German. Emily is walking out with a German boy, and he's even met her parents and they like him very much. Now they're frantic." She sighed. "It's all coming down like a pack of cards. And you know who it will hurt most at the end of the day? You, Tom, and me, people like us—and all those people walking along the street." She pointed towards the window. "Everyone out there."

Kezia hated to see Thea so impassioned, so taken; it was as if she were in pain. She had seen it so many times over the years—Thea, always standing for something, whether it was small children who came to school without food in their bellies, or London's women of the night, many just girls, and most of them with little choice in how they could earn their keep. Kezia wanted to bring Thea out of herself, to stop her fretting about things she couldn't change in the world. She wanted them to sit down together and share their confidences, as they had years ago. She had imagined Thea being so thrilled to see her, she'd want to go out window-shopping, or take an evening walk through the park. Kezia had brought cash from the tin in the bottom dressing-table drawer; her mother would doubtless agree that now would be a good time to dip into the fund, to give them both a good supper. She had hoped to see something of her best friend of old once more; she missed Dorrit.

"Come on, Thea, let's go out to a dining room, somewhere we won't be expected to have a chaperone. We'll have something lovely to eat. It will be my treat."

"Delving into your nest egg, Kezzie? Or is the harvest looking to be better than expected?" Thea's response cut like a blade.

"This is my money," said Kezia, who had instinctively laid her hand upon her heart as if to protect herself. "Now, I would like to dine, and I would like you to join me. Is that better for you?"

"I'll get my coat."

Soon they were back on the street, where Thea linked her arm through Kezia's.

"I'm sorry, Kezzie. I don't mean to snap."

"I know. We'll leave it at that, shall we? Now then, let's go to that little Italian restaurant, the one where we went to celebrate when you got your job at the school. They were always so nice to us there."

"Perfect," said Thea. "Yes, perfect."

As they made their way to the bus stop, they had to push past people going in and out of the pubs and talking on the street. Kezia thought it was like swimming against the tide. A newspaper vendor waved a fan of papers above his head and called out across the throng.

"England ready for war. Forces assembling. England ready for war . . ."

Kezia sipped from her glass, having been encouraged to order a dark cream sherry by Thea, who chose the larger pour, a schooner.

"I don't think I've been here since the last time," said Thea. "Not that I have much to spend on going out to eat. And it's not as if you're entirely sure you know what you're eating, in a restaurant."

"Oh, you're just like your brother, no imagination. If it doesn't look like anything he's ever eaten before, he pokes it around as if it were something found on the road. I have to disguise almost everything I cook as a pie." Kezia laughed, half choking on the unaccustomed sherry. She pointed to the glass. "I only ever use this for cooking."

The two women sat back in their chairs, at last settled in each other's company. Kezia twisted the sherry glass, as if afraid that someone might see her and judge her worth. She thought this fear might be a residue from her church upbringing, a leftover from always having to watch what she said and did, knowing it would reflect upon her father and—ultimately—God.

"Thea, I can't remember if you ever told me how your family came to own the farm. I mean, it was leased, originally, wasn't it? From the Hawkendene estate?"

"That was years ago now—years ago. In my great-grandfather's time." She tipped back her glass and emptied it. "Gosh, I do believe I could do with another—but better not. Tomorrow will be a busy one, mark my words." She looked at her hands, then at Kezia. "Have you seen it, the estate?"

"I have, yes. I went for a walk not long ago. Packed a lunch and set off across the fields, then followed the path at the back of Micawber Wood, through the forest there."

"That's not really a path, you know. Not any path you'd see on a map. It's the old poachers' way—leads through the woods, across another path, and right up to the lake."

"That's right."

"You're lucky their gamekeeper never caught you and hauled you in. He'd love to bag a Brissenden, and that's a fact."

"No, fortunately I never met him. I met Edmund Hawkes, though. He's the son, isn't he?"

"You met Hawkes? Well, I never. I haven't seen him in a long time."

"He was very nice, actually, considering he found me trespassing."

"Oh, I bet he was all smiles and accommodating noise, was Edmund Hawkes."

"Yes, to a point. He said I could go there any time I wanted."

Thea looked at Kezia, as if searching for something in her countenance.

"What?" asked Kezia.

"Nothing. Did you tell Tom you'd seen him?"

"I can't remember—I came home and was busy with his tea, so . . . um, I'm not sure. I probably did tell him, now I come to think about it."

Kezia could feel Thea watching her, and hoped her friend would not credit any sign of her discomfort with significance.

"I'll tell you what happened, and why those Hawkeses have never really forgiven us Brissendens."

"Mr. Hawkes seemed as if it didn't matter."

"If he's still like he was when he was a boy, he has that way about him, as if nothing matters enough to spur him to do something big. He probably said, 'Oh, well, never mind,' or something like that."

"He had that air."

"I will say this about him—and his great-grandfather, God bless his stupidity—they are gentlemen and keep to their word."

"So, what happened?"

"Don't tell Tom I told you, will you?"

"Whyever not?"

"He just doesn't like to talk about it. He cherishes the farm, probably more than Dad, even, but he hates the thought that it was earned by means other than hard work. Mind you, if it had been down to hard work, rather than a bit of good fortune at the right time, then the land would have been ours in the Bronze Age. If toil got you a roof over your head and food in your belly, London wouldn't have half the problems it has today. That's why you see all those boys in a long line to enlist, and we're not even at war yet—the king's shilling will go a long way, and so will having food set on a plate in front of you if you become an army man."

"But what about the farm?"

"Oh, yes, that. Well, here's what happened, according to what's been said—and I reckon it's as close to the truth as makes no difference. We don't talk about it in my family, you see—the farm's just ours, and we get on with it. And Tom has always kept well away from Edmund Hawkes. Not that he's got anything against him, but Hawkes came round once, to ask if Tom would like to join a shoot. I suppose Tom was about nineteen, and Hawkes would have been a bit older, perhaps twenty-five. Tom flat out refused, and that was the end of it." Thea leaned across the table. "Anyway, Edmund Hawkes' great-grandfather was a man who liked his drink, and he always liked a wager. He played the tables in London, and took himself off to France when he fancied, to the casinos over there. His father before him had been a canny fellow, and the estate was wealthy enough, but this Hawkes seemed bound to flutter away every penny—whether on cards, the horses, or if the sun would shine on Christmas Day. Bet on anything, that was him."

"He sounds dreadful." Kezia rested on her elbows to edge closer to Thea.

"He was, by all accounts. In any case, he was home from London one Friday, having come down on the coach. They had their own carriages and a whole stable of horses, but he'd come on the coach—we think—because he'd already lost a good deal on speculation and wanted to sneak home. He went into the pub to drown his sorrows and saw my great-grandfather playing darts, all on his own. It was the only drink he would have all week, on a Friday evening. My granddad said it was as if his father just wanted to be on his own, but in a comfortable place in the warm where he could enjoy his pint of ale. But old man Hawkes could never let the chance of a wager pass, so he pressed great-granddad Brissenden to a game with money. He refused—he wasn't a gambling man, and he didn't put up his hard-earned money on a bet. But Hawkes went on and on, apparently—and though it was only thought to be joshing, he said that my great-granddad was afraid he'd lose. According to my grandmother, Tom's very much like the old man—a slow burn. And you don't want to get near him when his patience is done. Finally, he said, 'Put up the farm and you can have your game.'"

"But he could have lost everything," whispered Kezia.

"No, not really. Hawkes would have known that if the Brissendens left the farm, they would be hard pushed to put a better tenant in there. And if old Hawkes had any sense, he would have walked out, laughing, and they would have both forgotten it. But he had a crowd, and he could not resist the wager. So he put up the farm on the best of three games of darts."

"But what if he'd been a good shot with a dart?"

"Great-granddad knew that Hawkes was tired after a day in London, that he'd been drinking the local ale—and it would have been after wine in his City haunts. And he knew himself, that he had a good eye for the board, and if he wanted to hit a double top, he could."

"So what happened?"

Thea drew back, laughing. "Oh, you are a silly—he won, of course, otherwise we wouldn't have the farm! Hawkes had to keep to his word, because there were witnesses and the bet had been written up with both men's signatures. It was over and done with quite quickly, the transfer." She sighed. "I think the worry of it all took a toll on my great-grandfather though, but he worked hard to make the farm a good, solid going concern to leave to his son, my grandfather. And he renamed the farm and the fields—I think just before my father was born—to be a lesson. According to my father, his own grandfather was always saying that the way he won the farm for the family should be a lesson never to gamble on anything and never to be a debtor. He admired Dickens, and thought him some sort of morality messenger." She shook her head. "If it had been up to me, it would be Brissenden Farm by now, and that would be it. But seeing as it's no longer my home, well, it's not up to me, is it?"

"Oh, Dorr—" said Kezia.

"See—that's one reason why. I'm who I am here. There on the farm, to everyone in the village, I'm nothing but little Dorrit."

"Sorry, Thea. It was just a slip."

They slept as girlhood friends that night, in Thea's bed. It was as if they were at Camden again, at a time when both felt homesick for a place that, in truth, they'd been happy to leave—for Thea it was the farm, and for Kezia, her role as daughter of the parsonage. It had been fear of the future that brought them together in sisterhood, a sense that neither quite belonged because they were scholarship girls. They'd had to prove themselves again and again to feel deserving of an education that came with strings attached. Now another kind of fear had taken root in their hearts, a fear that began to grow with talk of war, as if it were disease spreading through the body.

"Who knows what tomorrow will bring, Dorry?" said Kezia, in the darkness of Thea's room.

Thea did not rush to correct Kezia this time, perhaps feeling comfort in a name she'd so easily discarded.

"Can you hear that, Kezia? There's still people on the streets. It sounds like they're letting off firecrackers."

"I can hear them. I wish they'd all go home."

"I do too. I've to work tomorrow—we may have ended the

term, but we have a number of children coming back during the summer for private lessons, mainly in French and English literature, and of course arithmetic. So many have trouble with their addition and subtraction." Thea sighed and turned in the bed, pushing Kezia even farther towards the edge.

They spoke no more, and eventually Thea's breathing changed and Kezia knew she was asleep. The bed was uncomfortable enough for one; for two it was impossible. They were girls no longer, after all. Kezia lifted the covers and stretched out her legs. She crept over to the armchair, pulled a cardigan around her shoulders, and looked out of the window to the nothing of a dark night. She wondered if this was the difference between London and the country, that on the streets people kept each other up waiting for something to happen, whereas in the country it seemed that everyone went to bed knowing exactly what the next day would bring because the land dictated their work, and unless that work were done, the land would not reward them. Kezia would stay one more night with Thea. Tomorrow she would go to the shops, to the markets too, where she would buy spices and herbs she knew could not be found in the village store, or even in Tunbridge Wells. She'd buy some good coffee, the sort her father had introduced her to on her twelfth birthday. She'd winced at first as the strong black liquid touched her tongue, but soon acquired a taste for coffee midmorning and after supper—and since her marriage she had made it in the small cafetière her father had bought her as a special wedding gift. Yes, there was much to do today; when she returned, she would cook her lovely Tom a meal fit for an emperor.

Sleep claimed Kezia at last, and when she opened her eyes and yawned into the morning light, Thea was already pouring tea.

"There you go, Kezia. I'll be home at about half past three today. Will you be all right on your own?"

"Do I seem such a country bumpkin already?" Kezia sipped her tea. "As soon as you're gone, I will get myself ready and go out with my shopping list. I'll go to Hatchards first to browse the books, and then to a good grocery shop to buy some bits and pieces for the kitchen. I might even go for a new blouse to wear to Hawkendene Manor for the party. I want to do Tom proud."

"You do him proud anyway," said Thea. "Even if that sort of thing should have gone down with the ark—the squire and his missus lording it over the rest of us, and especially the Hawkes family and their shenanigans." She sipped her tea. "Watch out on the streets, they'll be packed today."

Kezia had loved living in London when she and Thea first came up to attend college. She remembered being fascinated, excited, as if she had arrived in a different country. And London felt and sounded like another country. All around her on the streets, people were marked by their different modes of dress and the languages of foreign lands. She could hear Russian, German, French, Spanish—was that Maltese? And there were Italians and Americans, walking along side by side. Gypsy women from Bohemia stood on corners offering posies of lucky white heather for sale. Kezia remembered she could hardly stop staring at them, their colors and flounces, the hooped earrings and vibrant scarves covering rich black hair. Now she ventured out on the bus, all the while wishing she had remained at Thea's lodgings; reading, knitting, anything to soothe her mind while she waited for her friend to return. It seemed that so many more people were out with no purpose except to wait, lingering outside pubs and restaurants, as if with food and drink came the comfort of togetherness: a force waiting for news. It was, thought Kezia, as if everyone felt more solid surrounded by other people; they even seemed to move in a mass, like a giant snake slithering here, then there, across the road and down the street. Newspaper vendors called out the headlines, and for one moment, before she at last reached Hatchards, Kezia thought she might faint, so clammy was the air. She did not want to consider war. She did not want to think of people she knew joining an army. And more than anything, right now, she wanted to be at the farm. There, she could count on things not to change. There was not this frenzy of emotion in the countryside villages. There was just the day ahead, with no talk of enlistments, no talk of Germans invading British soil.

The errands she had imagined would take just a couple of hours seemed to take so much longer. Arriving back at Queen Charlotte's Chambers, she hoped she would have time for a rest before Thea arrived home. But Thea was already there, waiting.

"What are you doing here?"

"The school closed at lunchtime. Some mothers started coming for their children or sending their servants, so it was decided to get them all home. Most live quite close, and it's a small area we serve, so we walked children back to their nannies in those big houses." Thea grasped the back of a chair and leaned forward as if she were about to fall.

"Thea—Thea." Kezia dropped her bags and went to her friend, holding her by the shoulders. "Come, sit down. You must be all in. Let me get you some tea. I can nip down the road to the bakery for some buns."

Thea shook her head. "No. You can't." She scraped back the chair and looked up at Kezia. "I dropped in on my way home—I thought I would buy some of Mrs. Backer's lovely strudel for us. But the shop is boarded up. I saw Mr. Backer nailing in the last plank of wood. He told me that some lads had come along earlier and smashed the windows with bricks. It wasn't a spur-of-the-moment attack either—it had been planned. So they're going to her sister in Wiltshire, away from London. And all because of their German name." Thea took Kezia's handkerchief and wiped her eyes. "I'm so angry. That's why I'm crying. I am so fiercely angry that people can be so stupid—Mrs. Backer is English, and her husband was born here. His parents have lived here since they were just married. They set up that bakery and they all worked so hard. Now look—suddenly they're being treated like the devil, and we're not even at war yet. Part of me wishes they'd had the sense to call themselves 'Baker's Bakery' years ago—but then, why should they? For goodness' sake, half the king's family are bloody German!"

"Thea!"

"Oh, please don't be a prude, Kez. Not now, not here with me. I've used stronger language than that, you know."

"But it might not happen, the war."

"You and your head in the sand, Kezia." She sat back in her chair and rubbed her face. "Come on, I'm not sitting here waiting—let's go out and see if we can get news anywhere."

Outside, the two women made their way along the street, passing the boarded-up bakery and another shop where the butcher was in the process of mending a window, while his son waited with wooden planks to secure the premises before they left. Thea stopped.

"Mr. Van Althuis—what's happening? Surely you're not going too."

The man put down his tools and wiped his hands on a cloth tucked into his belt. He pushed back his cap and answered in a broad London accent. "It's the bleeding fugs, ain't it? Whadda they know about the difference between German and Dutch? Van, Von, it's all the same to them. Nah, we're off."

"But where will you go?"

"I've got a bit put by, and my son's been bringing home his keep, so we won't starve. We've got relatives in Rotterdam, so we thought we might go there."

"Have you ever been there? Can you speak Dutch?"

"Granddad spoke the language, and I can understand a bit—but nah, it's all Greek to me. I'm London born and bred. My wife says we should lay low for a bit, then open the shop under another name. Might work. Might give it a try. Althuis means 'old house' so I thought 'House & Son, The Butchers.' Give people time, they might forget they ever knew us as Van Althuis—in point of fact, most of 'em call us Van Old House anyway! I reckon we might get out of London and think about it—mind you, if you're a Londoner, the only place you belong is London, innit? Everywhere else you might as well be another outsider."

Thea's complexion reddened. Kezia said nothing as she stood by her side. She had discovered, lately, that it was sometimes better to say nothing around Thea.

"I think this is just disgraceful. Putting bricks through the windows of innocent shopkeepers," said Thea.

Kezia thought her comment was a bit rich, seeing as Thea's suffragette friends had lobbed many a brick through the windows of innocent shopkeepers. She wondered if Thea had narrowly escaped arrest for such a crime. It would not surprise her. Nothing surprised her about Thea anymore.

Thea held out her hand towards the man, then his son. "I wish you both well. And give my best regards to Mrs. Van Althuis. You know where I live—in Queen Charlotte's Chambers, the ladies' boarding house—so let me know if there's anything I can do. My brother has a farm in Kent—this is his wife." Thea nodded towards Kezia. "I daresay you could stay in one of the cottages. In any case, I am sure they would help—wouldn't you, Kezzie?"

Kezia felt herself flush, and stammered a reply. "I could talk to Tom about it . . . yes, I could do that."

Mr. Van Althuis smiled at Kezia. It was a half smile, and as he looked at her, Kezia thought that if there were two photographs, one of each side of his face, you would see different men—one sad and angry, and the other pleased and relieved. The duality unsettled her.

"Much obliged, but to be honest, the wife don't like the country much. All that earth, and them trees and animals. She likes it here, so for all my talk about going to Rotterdam, we'll find a way to stay. Truth be told, I couldn't see us even getting out as far as Tilbury Docks. Never mind, it'll all come out in the wash. Always does." He turned to go back to his work. His son had looked on, silent, throughout the whole exchange. "But I know one thing," he added, turning back to Thea. "We'd better get on with the job and put a stop to that bleedin' kaiser before we've got them Germans marching all over London, and that's the truth. My boy's going down to enlist as soon as he can, aren't you, son?"

The young man's blushes were a match for Kezia's earlier flush of embarrassment. His Adam's apple moved up and down as he swallowed, as if words were caught in his throat. Kezia saw the fluff of adolescent hair on his chin and around his jaw, and a cut where he had tried to shave. She felt a catch in her throat, seeing this youth trying to assume the beard of manhood.

"You don't have to go, you know, Tim," said Thea. "You can wait. It's voluntary enlistment, and there's plenty of others lining up to sign their lives away."

"It'll all be over in a few months, Miss Brissenden, just you watch," said the boy's father. "But Tim should show willing, after all, we have to look after our country, don't we?"

Thea sighed, then wished the man and his son well. Kezia smiled at them both as they continued on their way.

"Look at that. Just look at that for a fine example of this war talk. That man and his family work their fingers to the bone, all hours, going across London delivering meat, with Mrs. Van Althuis on her feet all day, putting food on tick for those who haven't got two ha'pennies to rub together. They get their windows broken by stupid idiots under the influence of a crowd and whatever they've read in the newspapers. Those papers have a lot to answer for, mark my words." Thea picked up speed as she walked, her temper rising as she all but spat out her opinion. "And there they are, encouraging their only son to enlist. Sending him to his death."

"Thea—surely it will not happen. Surely this is all bluster. I mean, it's not like this in Kent, not in the villages." Kezia felt as if she were running to keep up the pace set by her friend.

"Not yet it isn't. But it will be." Thea marched ahead and, waving back to Kezia, picked up her skirt and ran towards the omnibus stop, calling to her to hurry. Kezia went after her, and they both leapt on the vehicle's running board, then upstairs. The conductor rang a bell, and the horses moved off again.

"Where are we going?" asked Kezia.

"Buckingham Palace," replied Thea. "People have to gather somewhere to wait for news, so that's where they'll go."

"But news won't come from there. It's not as if the king is going to stand on the balcony and shout the news if war is declared."

Thea turned to look at Kezia, her voice peppered with exasperation. "But Kezzie, the people will gather behind a figurehead, won't they? The king stands for Britain, far more than the Prime Minister."

"I don't know where you get all this from, really I don't.

We'd do better to go to Downing Street, or even St. Paul's—the church always knows what's going on."

"No. Buckingham Palace. Asquith will have to go to the king first, if there's to be an announcement. Then we'll know. Yes, then we'll know."

CHAPTER 4

It has been said that the essence of all good breeding is tact. A tactful woman is essentially a woman who knows how to adapt herself to varying circumstances, who has that keen perception which enables her to see and do what is best upon occasions when discrimination between the wrong and right methods of action is necessary.

—*THE WOMAN'S BOOK*

Kezia lay awake, uncomfortable, tossing and turning in the armchair. Despite her exhaustion, sleep did not come easily. She felt tormented, as if her thoughts were conspiring with the coiled springs of upholstery. She felt prodded and poked in body, mind, and soul. The crowds at Buckingham Palace had overwhelmed her; she had put her arm through Thea's as her friend shouldered her way into the mass. She saw a man with his wife and sons, a length of string joining them lest they became separated among the surrounding bodies pressing together. This was not many people, this was one, a massive being buoyed on by the promise of a fight. The boys' capped heads reached their mother's narrow shoulders, with the youngest—perhaps an inch shorter than his brother—tiptoeing to see over the heads of men. There was yelling and shouting, a sound that from a distance was like the wheeze of a kettle left on the stove at night. But as they'd drawn closer, the crescendo seemed to reach down into the ground, only to ricochet up through Kezia's body. She'd felt assaulted; if this were civilization, what had happened to civility? And now, as the grainy light of morning fingered the curtains, the noise was growing again, with newspaper vendors calling out once more, baying like wolves in the night. It was later, when she bought two newspapers at Charing Cross Station, that she wondered if she'd been caught up in a play, a school pantomime. The front pages of both papers said little of the still-new declaration of war. There were small columns of advertisements and square private announcements to temper the grand pronouncements of patriotism; that the nation would be filled with fresh courage in the face of a fight.

But for now she waited, wondering when Thea might wake, so that they could have tea together before she departed for Kent and the farm. If she could, she would have left earlier, would have crept around the room gathering her things. She would have penned a quick note, words chosen with care to pour oil on the troubled waters of their friendship. Perhaps she had not understood Thea. Perhaps she could have been more accommodating, more . . . what? While they were moving through the crowds, Thea had searched among the faces, on occasion jumping up to gain a better view. It was in front of the palace gates that she had found what she was looking for—a gathering of pacifists shouting their message. Thea stepped forward, nodded to her friends—Kezia could tell at once that they were all known to each other—and took a banner from a woman struggling to grasp a megaphone at the same time. Having relinquished the additional burden, she began to shout her message.

Peace is the only worthy fight!
Be a soldier of peace, now!
March into the battle for peace!

Kezia had never seen Thea so filled with passion, her eyes alive in the madness of the moment, calling out her message, raising her fist as if to fight. Kezia wanted to pull her back, wanted to feel the muscle of her arm through her jacket, wanted to drag her away, out of the crowd. She wanted peace and quiet. She wanted to be back in her father's study with only the grandfather clock's *tick-tock, tick-tock* punctuating their conversation. She wanted to hear his smooth voice, never raised to counter a point; softened, even, when he felt she was wrong. She wanted to hear the farm, the cows coming in for the milking, a deep lowing as they moved at a deliberate pace, full udders swinging from side to side. Kezia wanted to know the dinner was in the oven, and that Tom would be home soon. She was tired of London, done with this madness. War had not even begun, and she felt the weight of worry bearing down upon her.

"Thea. Thea! Thea, let's go home. Let's go home now! You could be killed here," she'd pleaded.

Thea shook her head and continued calling for peace, for men to lay down their arms, for government to navigate the ship of political crisis back from the brink.

Mounted police had broken through the crowd then, fanning out as if to tear through the fabric of the mob, scattering people back away from the gates. They did not raise their truncheons, did not strike a soul, just pushed the horses forward slowly, giving people a chance to move, to be a person again, to be individual and not part of this behemoth waiting for news of war.

The pacifists were scattered too, and it was then that Kezia saw her chance, taking Thea's arm, the arm she had focused upon, the limb she would pull until her friend was with her again, and they were away from this place. They'd exchanged hardly a word on the way back to the boarding house. Thea's eyes seemed aflame, and though Kezia was afraid to speak, she could not stop herself.

"Everyone's gone mad, Thea. I feel as if I've escaped a lunatic asylum."

Thea stopped walking and looked at Kezia under the strained lamplight. "You think you've seen madness tonight. That was only the beginning, Kezia. There will be more lunacy to come unless there's a refusal to fight."

"But the army won't refuse to fight," replied Kezia, now walking with a quick step to catch up with Thea, who had already turned away.

"No, they won't, which means they'll need more men. Then see where you are, Kezia. When Tom's called to war, let's see what you think of the pacifists then."

"Oh, but it won't come to that," said Kezia. She could feel the childish smile on her face, formed not in joy but in response to fear.

"Won't it? Well, we'll just have to wait and see. Won't we?"

They had gone to bed without another word, and now Kezia was ready to leave. London held nothing for her. She doubted she would ever again feel the familiar excitement as the train pulled in, steam filling the air when the loco reached the buffers at Charing Cross. She could not imagine the anticipation of window-shopping, of going into Liberty's and fingering fine cloth she could not afford. And there was no fulfillment in her friendship with Thea. It had vanished, like sodden autumn leaves washed down a drain. She would not wait a moment longer. She would make ready to leave, and if Thea did not rise from her deep sleep in the meantime, Kezia would write a note and depart. She would say that she had to get back to the farm, that it had all been very exciting, and that she wanted Thea to visit them soon. She would remind her that her room had not been disturbed, and that a sojourn in the country would do her the world of good. Kezia wrote all of these things, with a pen dipped in ink and the message scratched back and forth on cheap vellum found in Thea's desk. She set the envelope against an unwashed cup on the bedside table, and without a sound gathered her clothing into her bag and left the room, turning the handle slowly so there was no creaking to signal her departure. It was a false message she'd penned, and Kezia tried to brush away the feeling that Thea would think her light, that she would see right through the words, written as if from one polite matron to another.

Thea opened her eyes as the door closed, raising her head from the pillow to listen as Kezia's steps receded down the stairs, where she opened the front door, closed it, and walked away, down the street and into the distance. She sighed, relieved that her sister-in-law had left, relieved that she would not have to feel the sharp prickle of annoyance, the intense jabbing of envy, even. She knew when Kezia had left the chair where she'd spent the night. She had heard her brushing her hair, splashing water on her face. With her eyes closed she'd followed the sounds of Kezia dressing, finally lacing up shoes as she was ready to leave. Thea had not opened her eyes, not changed her breathing. She had just listened, knowing that, while part of her wanted to embrace Kezia, wanted to cling to her because everything might change—because she herself was changing and couldn't stop now she'd begun—another part just wanted Kezia to leave, to go back to the farm and be whatever she planned to be if she really wanted to waste her mind. More than anything, Thea felt—as did Kezia, descending into the depths of the Underground, sitting on the train as it rattled from side to side, then making her way up onto the street and into Charing Cross Station—that perhaps they were, in fact, in a similar state of mind. They were both afraid.

For Tom Brissenden there had been little in the way of a hiatus in his responsibilities over the bank holiday. The farm had been quiet, with the men enjoying an extra day off. Tom didn't think that joining the village charabanc outing down to Hastings for the day represented much of a rest, but quite a crowd had gone—the children with buckets and spades, the men ready to roll up trouser legs and dip into the sea as far as their calves, and the women laden with baskets filled with sandwiches, pork pies, sausage rolls, and lemon barley water. Of the farm's workers, only Bert Grace remained at home, allowing himself an extra hour in bed before leaving his tied cottage to walk across the fields to Marshals Farm with his dog, Whisky, at his side. The dog's name revealed everything a person needed to know about Bert's favorite tipple, in which he indulged just once a week on Saturday night at the Queen's Head. Bert had been working on the farm since boyhood. His wife, Mary, had died in childbirth, and on that night he swore he would never marry again, for she was the love of his life. Now, bent forward, his trousers tied in place with a length of baling twine and his jacket oily with the years and bearing the smell of many a harvest, Bert could not imagine a better day than one spent on the farm.

Bert admired Tom, had known him since he was born, and he'd known his father before him since boyhood. He had seen Tom grow beyond his father's shadow and knew he would only have pulled free from the elder Brissenden upon his father's passing, which came sooner than anyone would have thought.

Bert was well versed in matters of life and death, on the inevitable cycle from first breath to last, from seed to threshing machine. He might have been surprised when Tom took Kezia for his wife, but he was not disheartened. The girl tried hard and was a worker, and he suspected she knew very well that her attempts to provide a hearty breakfast for the men were met at times with surprise and, indeed, the occasional look of incredulity. But he also knew the locals had a soft spot for Kezia. You could see her innocence, thought Bert. You could see there was still dew on her petals. Sometimes he thought that, if he were young again, he might like to catch her eye himself.

Tom and Bert worked for only as long as the farm needed on that Monday. The younger man was always respectful of his foreman and never drew back from asking his advice. Bert thought that said a lot for the lad—it took a man to admit when he wanted direction. Later they would go to the Queen's Head together, where Tom would lift his glass of ale to touch the whisky tot that Bert held with gnarled forefinger and thumb. They spoke of what all this business of war might mean for the farm, and agreed it would be good—an army marches on its stomach, after all, and if there's one thing the farm provided, it was a good-quality crop and the finest livestock. It never occurred to either of them, to young man or old, that the other men who came to the farm each day, who sniffed Kezia's poached eggs with a leaf of mint on top, and who then marched out to fields thick with barley and wheat, putting their backs into nurturing the land, might themselves march away to war.

Kezia arrived at Charing Cross in something of a daze and easily distracted. She felt like a butterfly caught on the wind, jostled by people waiting for announcements running towards their platforms. Already the regular army was on the move, with soldiers lining up to entrain for the coast, whereupon they would be ferried across the Channel. A swirl of khaki moved towards the same platform as Kezia, and when she pressed forward, holding out her ticket, a guard informed her that the Dover train would be delayed. Troop trains took precedence. Kezia sighed, and hoped she would not miss her connection. The branch line ran alongside the eastern perimeter of the farm, its sooty steam punching up through the trees flanking Scrooge Field. If only she could ask the driver to stop, she would leap out, run across the fields and into Tom's arms. Kezia looked down as her eyes became wet with tears. How would she ever bear it if he had to go? But no, he wouldn't. The farm was where he belonged. Who would look after the farm, if there was no Tom to direct everyone each day to do their work? What would happen if there was no Tom to sit at the head of the table with his men, to wipe his plate clean of golden egg yolk with a slice of fried bread, and then to pick up his mug filled with piping hot tea and say, "All right, Danny, I need the horses up on Pickwick this morning—and make sure you get that plough in the corners, all right? Check Mabel's right front hoof before you put her in the traces, and if that shoe's loose again, bring her over to Bert—Bert, do what you can with it, and if it won't hold, Dan will have to walk her down to the smithy. And if it comes to that, you can ride her home, Dan, give your feet a rest—that's if she's in a mood to let you on her back. And if she's gone for a few hours, we might as well let Ted have a bit of time to himself— Bert, if the old girl's off work today, probably best to put him in the pasture for a good roll; he'll think it's holiday time." And so it would go on, Tom giving orders, directing the men before they all went about their work for the day. And he trusted each one to do his bidding, and to know what the land needed and when.

Bert would add his advice, and soon chairs would be pushed back and off they would go. Another day, another round, another opportunity for Kezia to be a good wife.

"I say—Mrs. Brissenden? Are you all right?"

Kezia felt lightheaded, and at once the heat of the station engulfed her. Sweat drizzled down her spine, and she thought that if she moved to pick up her bag, the stains under her arms would embarrass her beyond measure.

"Oh, Mr. Hawkes, this is a surprise." Kezia reached into the pocket of her linen jacket for a handkerchief, which she pressed against her brow. "It's so busy here today, and it's very close, isn't it?"

"May I escort you to the train? I take it you're on your way home." Hawkes leaned down to pick up her bag, and offered his arm. "It's this way, on platform three—they've just changed it again."

"I don't think I have ever seen so many soldiers—even when I was a child and my father took me to see the changing of the guard. I could never imagine seeing something like this."

"Well, you'd better get used to it. This is only the beginning."

Kezia stopped, steeling her face to dam her tears. "Surely it's all a storm in a teacup, Mr. Hawkes."

Edmund Hawkes looked at her, and she felt as if she were being judged. Was he disgusted at her naïveté? Annoyed at a childish assumption? He bore just a flash of attitude.

"I think it will be quite a tempest, Mrs. Brissenden." He nodded towards the platform. "Ah, there's our train." And at once he was the gentleman again.

Hawkes opened the door of a third-class carriage for Kezia and, having seen her situated, raised his hat and continued along the platform to a first-class compartment.

Kezia would have liked to talk to him on the journey. She

would have liked to talk about literature, to find common
ground so that she might know him better—she noticed that he,
too, had been to Hatchards. She wanted to converse with him
to distract herself, to take her mind off the moment when she'd
lifted the lid of Thea's desk before leaving Queen Charlotte's
Chambers. It was an old desk, brought home from the school
where she worked when new furniture had been purchased,
so it always seemed as if she were a pupil, leaning against the
angled lid to write in her composition book. Kezia had lifted the
lid and seen a letter to Thea, written on the finest linen stock.
There was no return address on the envelope, but the letter had
been left open, visible to anyone who took the liberty of looking,
though of course the only person she ever imagined delving into
the depths of the ink-stained desk was herself. Or had she anticipated Kezia seeing the letter?

Dearest Thea,

*To my sister in our cause, how lovely it was to walk
together and then continue our long conversation while
lingering over tea. I have found a new, beloved kindred
spirit, and I cherish our friendship, which I am sure
will last as long as we both walk this earth. We will go
forward together and rejoice in our victory.*

With affection,
Avril

Once the train reached Brooksmarsh station, Kezia lingered
with the door ajar for as long as she could before stepping down
onto the platform. She didn't want Tom to see her walking out of
the station with Edmund Hawkes, for she felt sure the landowner

would be a gentleman and insist upon helping her with her case and parcels. She waited until Hawkes had exited the station, though she was anxious to be in the safe embrace of her husband. But Tom was not there to meet her; he had sent Danny Hatcher in the gig. Danny was Bert's nephew, a quiet young man, twenty years of age. He had been lame since birth, with his grandmother setting blame upon the head of the midwife, who—she said—held him up with such a strong hand on the day he was born that she disjointed his ankle. No one knew if this was true, and doctors could not account for the lack of muscle between knee and heel—though Danny's widowed mother had only ever taken him to the hospital once, when he was a small boy. It seemed that Danny was lame, and that was all there was to it. He was given no quarter at school, and at work he always made an effort to pull his weight along with the other men. Bert had brought him to the farm when the boy was twelve, saying it was about time he learned to be a man. While Tom tried not to favor Danny by giving him the lighter jobs—he knew better than to belittle the lad in front of the men—he was mindful that Danny's leg sometimes ached, so he would assign a "special" task, one to which the boy was best suited. Mrs. Joe, the little mare who was more pony than horse, seemed all affection with Danny, which might have had something to do with the apple he'd bring, or the mints he kept in his pocket.

"Danny, how are you?" said Kezia as the boy took her bag and stowed it behind the seat, then held out his hand to steady her as she stepped up into the cart.

"Very well, Mrs. Brissenden. What was it like up there, in London?"

"Overwhelming, what with war being declared. I bet there's been talk in the village about it."

Danny shrugged, tapped Mrs. Joe on the rump, and they

moved off. "There was a bit, I suppose. Some of the lads in the village have been jawing about having to join up, but I reckon we just get on with it, eh? Mattie and Bill have both said they think they ought to go—after all, we're right in a striking line of the Channel here, so if the Germans come over, we'll be among the first to cop it. They reckon it's best to get over there to France and do something about putting a tin lid on the kaiser's plans before his army get that far. And Mr. Brissenden says we might have to change the crops, and that there'll likely be men down from the ministry soon, telling farmers what they want more of. He said that as long as there's a war, farming becomes part of the ammunition."

"Did he? I never really thought about it like that," said Kezia, looking out at the fields, golden in the sun. The air held a loamy fragrance, a blend of the heat from barley almost ready for the harvest, and hops waiting to be picked. She slipped off her linen jacket. "So, what of village news? How was the expedition to the seaside?"

"The first thing is that the Hawkses' harvest party has been canceled, on account of the war. And as for the seaside, well, the charabanc broke down on the way back from Hastings, but Tub Watkins from the garage sorted it out. He reckons he'll be getting more passing business now, what with people going to and from the coast, you know, army and what have you."

Kezia felt a wave of fatigue. "Oh, that's a shame about the party. But did everyone have fun at the seaside?"

"From what I saw, everyone caught the sun a bit, and Mrs. Finch was fair burned across her nose—mind you, my mum always says she'll get her nose burned off one of these days, if she don't keep it out of people's business."

Kezia laughed, knowing the shopkeeper's wife to be a great

source of village gossip. She had learned the importance of not adding to the woman's arsenal of information.

They talked of local news until they drew closer to Marshals Farm and the oast house, with its witch's-hat cowls signaling that home was just minutes away. Whenever she left the farm to go into the village, Kezia had felt a rush of joy when she finally caught sight of those white cowls on her homeward journey. She imagined them sometimes as courtly women in voluminous skirts, beckoning her back to her house, to her kitchen, and to her husband. It was where she belonged now.

"Mr. Brissenden said to tell you that there's a chicken hanging in the larder, and that he fancies a bit of chicken tonight," said Ada, turning from making up the fire as Kezia came into the kitchen.

"Yes, that does sound lovely." Kezia was putting on her pinafore, having set her leather case in the bedroom.

She had recently read in a monthly that it was important for a lady to take the time to talk to her servants, so that they might form a loyalty to their mistress and be more inclined towards accommodating behavior if required to work on their day off. Though Ada was her only staff, and they had so far rubbed along nicely, she felt it important to heed the advice, and be sure to acknowledge her employee.

"Did you go down to Hastings, Ada?"

Ada shook her head. "No. I didn't. Mum took the other children, but I had to stay with Granddad, because he can't be left on his own."

"Oh, my, that is a shame." Kezia pinned a loose hair in place and took a recipe book down from the shelf above the stove.

"Could your granddad not have gone too, with a little help? There were plenty of big strong men on that charabanc."

Ada sighed, and Kezia wondered if she were annoyed at the questioning, or perhaps it was because Kezia didn't know something that most of the village knew already.

"It's on account of his waterworks."

"Oh, I see," said Kezia. "Yes, of course." She turned and went through to the larder, returning with the chicken. Kezia enjoyed roast chicken as much as the next person, and loved the way the farm chickens waddled up to meet her when she came out with the scraps pail in the morning, but she was well aware that the journey from farmyard to plate—from farmyard to roasting pan, even—was somewhat sketchy in her imagination. She realized she had never cooked chicken for Tom. They had eaten beef and mutton, already cut for her to cook. And they had eaten pork, but again, she had not been the one to actually take the life of the pig. She had cleaned a fish once. She'd gone fishing with Tom and come home with two fine trout. Tom had washed the fish, placed them on the kitchen table, and demonstrated gutting. Holding the trout upside down, so it seemed as if it was looking back up at her, Tom had cut down behind the gills to just half an inch below the top of the head.

"Then you just pull," he said. "And the guts will come out with the head. Or if you like, you can slice him open here, and clean out the rest under the tap—see?"

And yes, she did see, and though she felt a salty phlegm rise in her throat, she had taken up a trout and followed Tom's instruction.

"Good girl." He'd smiled, and kissed her on the mouth. "You'll get the hang of it."

She flicked through the pages of her mother-in-law's recipe

book until she found what she was looking for. "To Draw Poultry." Now she had to get the hang of this.

Kezia opened the kitchen table drawer and took out a boning knife—she hadn't realized there was such a thing, but fortunately there was an illustration of the knife in the book. Then she pulled the bird towards her and lifted the knife.

> . . . *pass the knife under the skin, cut off the neck at its junction with the body, taking care not to cut through the under skin of the neck with this motion.*

Kezia lifted the knife and touched the point to the chicken skin.

"Mrs. Brissenden . . ."

Kezia looked up, as if startled.

"Yes, Ada?"

"Mrs. Brissenden, do you want me to do that?"

"No, I should get on with it, though I will confess, this is the first time I've drawn and trussed a chicken." Kezia lifted the knife again.

"Mrs. Brissenden . . ."

"What is it, Ada?" Kezia, her nerves on edge at the thought of a task that in truth turned her stomach, realized as soon as she'd uttered the words that her tone was sharp.

"I just thought I'd say that it's easier to take all the entrails out after you've plucked it."

"Oh. Yes, of course it is." Kezia stepped back. The room was warm now, with the range burning to heat the ovens and the sun outside beating on the clay path. Everything seemed yellow and hot.

"Let me, Mrs. Brissenden." Ada put down the towel she was

holding and came to the table. With a deft movement she lifted the chicken, moved it to the draining board, and placed a bowl in the sink. As she did so, blood ran in a trickle from the bird's beak onto her hand. She turned on the tap, washed away the blood, and turned off the tap. Kezia watched these movements as if in slow motion, then fled out of the back door towards the privy.

At the sound of her retching, which seemed to echo all the way to the kitchen table, Ada smiled. Before noon the following day, most of the village was apprised of the fact that Marshals Farm was to be blessed with a honeymoon baby. But it was not new life that had caused Kezia to hold her stomach and retch into the dark hole of the earth closet—and when would they get a proper lavatory at the farm? Surely it could be done, she thought. The source of her nausea was something else—a dread that had escalated at Charing Cross Station when she'd been caught among the mass of soldiers setting off towards their platform. It was a second's terror, as if she were being dragged into the sea by a wave, and the feeling had not released its grip until she came back to the farm, where everything seemed to be as it was before she left.

Her new neighbors in the village—people she was coming to know, people she passed the time of day with—were taking the news of war in their stride. Or were they? wondered Kezia, as she wiped her mouth and used her apron to draw beads of sweat from her brow. Were they simply waiting for London to come to them, which is what those from the towns believed countryfolk did anyway? Would the war end before it reached Kent? She cast the question aside. She was not in London, not caught in the melee . . . and then she remembered preparing her notes for last year's matriculating class, and the book she'd chosen for the oral examination, *Far from the Madding Crowd*. Oh, she loved Hardy, loved the measure of his language, the heft of his stories. And now a favorite image from the book came to her, and though it had been only a matter of weeks, it seemed so long ago that she was a teacher, when her favorite lines from so many books could be recollected with ease.

And at home by the fire, whenever you look up there I shall be—and whenever I look up, there will be you.

And she saw Tom as Gabriel Oak, saw his solid form by the fireplace, as they would be this evening and in years to come. *There you will be.*

CHAPTER 5

The purpose of Edmund Hawkes' journey to London had not been simply to sit in a leather chair at his club, reading the *Times* and jawing with City grandees about the state of affairs in Europe, or the effect war might have on the mighty Bank of England. Despite his father's best efforts, Edmund had steered the fortunes of the family estate in a positive direction. His banker was always happy to see him— indeed, doubly happy that he did not have to deal with the current Hawkes senior. Hawkes' credit was not in question, and he was not indebted to his tailor, his shoemaker, or indeed to his club. A valet attended his room, and while he was in the capital, his every need would be met. There was no reason to think that anything in his life would change—but the one thing he was about to do would change everything.

His first task, after settling into his rooms and taking lunch with one of his advisors, was to take steps to enlist in the army. He would not wait to be conscripted; because for Edmund Hawkes there was the question of honor. He had followed the news, spoken to men older and wiser—his father not being one of them—and decided that a landowner in his position must set an example. He had been an army cadet at school, and upon going up to Oxford he'd thought it wouldn't do any harm at all to join the Officer Training Corps. Since then he had been an officer in the Territorials—there was only the obligatory commitment of twelve or so days each year in the army—so it was up to him to honor his status in the county, and ultimately, to honor his name by presenting himself for service before he was called. He did not want this war to be one that a Hawkes avoided, but instead one where his willingness to step up and be counted reflected well on his name, his village, on his beloved Kent, and on his country. It was time, thought Edmund, that a Hawkes was prepared to stand for something of greater import than the next round of drinks or another wager.

It had taken him aback, the different responses to news of war in Londoners and county folk. The crowds both fascinated and appalled him, and it occurred to him that it would all change once war was under way, that when people had to get on with it—whatever "it" might be—they would not be on the streets but instead would be going about their business, whether the business was that of fighting, or of keeping the country running for a few months until it all ended, like a storm blowing itself out with gusts of its own energy. While many young men seemed to be spoiling for a fight—men wearing their summer straw hats and light suits, men who laughed together as if it was all a bit of fun, as if going to war would be another distraction, a sort of prolonged day at the seaside— Hawkes thought that most people, when war was declared, would take solace in the ordinary things in life, whatever they might be. Of course, what Edmund Hawkes did not know— and, to be fair to him, could not have known—was that so many of those young men, especially flat-capped working-class lads from the poorer areas, were after the king's shilling, a steady job, three square meals a day, and a warm place to bed down. They had seen their share of death at home. Most had watched siblings die in infancy, and perhaps lost a mother in childbirth. Grandparents passed away at home, and in many cases a father had lost his life at work. If they saw that, and it held no fear for them, then the threat of war was nothing more than words. The Hun was just Backer the Baker with a gun in his hand. So off to enlist they went, cheering and back-slapping along the way, pals all.

After making his inquiries, Hawkes had set off to present himself for service, with the good wishes of men at the club, men in their pin-striped suits bearing the shine of age, men who said "Good chap" and slapped him on the back before reclining in leather chairs and reaching for a glass of port or brandy. Edmund Hawkes stepped into a waiting taxicab and, once settled, reached for the notebook always kept in his jacket pocket and wrote, "Mirror image—leaving the quiet ease of the club into the noisy street—like leaving life in Kent, like departing from peace into war. What will it be like? Will I see men killed? How best can I serve, and make a good account of myself?" Later he would add to those notes, and in time, he knew, he would begin to compose verse, his scattered thoughts taking on form and rhythm, catching the beat of the heart like an army marching. But, he wondered, whose heart, if he kept the poems to himself?

In the depths of a guarded building in Whitehall, Edmund was interviewed, weighed, and measured. His eyes were tested, his teeth inspected, and another doctor fingered his manhood.

"Just checking the crown jewels, sir. We know you're fit, but just want to make sure. Now then, cough! Good—we don't want hidden ruptures or any other funny business getting in the way of an officer's work."

And so it went on. When he emerged into the bright sunshine again, it was with a travel warrant for Aldershot. His next stop would be Hyam and Co. on Oxford Street, an outfitter that claimed a tailored uniform could be ready in a matter of hours. He would report for duty the following Monday.

Edmund Hawkes returned to his club and ordered a whisky and soda, which was brought to him as he sat by a tall bay window overlooking the street. The red velvet curtains seemed heavy for a summer's day, but they obscured the sun. Hawkes was glad to be in the shadow, for the brightness felt a little too much at such a time. He closed his eyes and tried to transport himself to the seat of earth under the oak tree by the lake. He imagined Millie by his side and Bella, unsaddled, unbridled, munching on sweet grass while she waited. She'd lift her head, watch her master for the merest second, then, head down, would begin pulling grass once more, her ears bobbing from side to side as she teethed each tuft from the ground. And though Hawkes had paid attention to the tide of events since June, and had made plans for himself and the estate accordingly, he realized now, as the first sip of whisky burned his throat, that he had been fooling himself. Hawkes was given to introspection—he was, after all, a poet in his secret self, a man of words and thoughts that came from places he could never identify, as if his heart were rooted to something beyond the earth upon which he walked. But now, taking another sip, and another, he realized that in controlling the estate's fortunes in recent years, then in formulating his plan to enlist, and last week, as war seemed even more imminent, in visiting the family solicitors, he was trying to direct events. And in enlisting before any pressure to do so came from another quarter—and of course it would—he was kidding himself that he could control what might come to pass in his life.

Thea was aware that her temper was changing, and sometimes it felt as if a new person were inhabiting her physical body.

Though sometimes labeled a "quiet one" while at Camden, she had never been what might be called shy, never a precious flower of a girl—but she had never imagined feeling the welter of anger that often assailed her now. She suspected London might have something to do with it. There she was, teaching children of the well-heeled, earning a sufficient wage to live in comfortable, clean lodgings for women of good reputation. The mothers of her charges arrived at school in chauffeur-driven motor cars, or a carriage and pair, and could be heard talking to each other about how much better it was to have children at school, where they could mix, rather than having a governess at home. And Thea had thought, *Mix?* And the children in their uniforms would come into the class and do as they were told, when they were told, though there was always the one. Wasn't there always the one, wherever you were a teacher? Yet if she had been a teacher in the East End, or south of the river, there would be more than the one—there could be three or four or eight or nine little thorns in the side, and every one bearing the welt of a clip around the ear for some infraction committed before they'd left what passed for home, and with no shoes on their feet, while thinking themselves lucky if they'd had bread and a scrape of lard inside them before setting off for the parish school down the road. Bread and scrape for breakfast, bread and scrape for dinner and then again for tea. She'd been to those houses—volunteering her time to help the poor by delivering discarded clothing, shoes, warm blankets, and the like from wealthier homes—and most of the time there were no plates, knives, forks, and spoons, because anything that came to the table was mostly eaten with the fingers. On Sundays a big pot of broth would be put out, with any scraps floating on the top that could be picked up off the street after the costers passed on their way home. She'd see the children running to claim the odd leaf of cabbage, or a floret of cauliflower as it fell to the ground when the horse and cart clattered over the cobblestones. For a few pennies the butcher might have a pig's knuckle or a rabbit head—oh, how the brains were treated as a rare delicacy, white and curled, as if the mind of the animal had caused ripples of thought to run across the membrane. If the father was in work—and even if he hadn't a job to go to—he'd have the best of whatever came to the house. These were the poorest of the poor, and Thea did everything within her limited power to help them. Was it any surprise, really, that so many lads wanted to go to war, when every day was a battle anyway?

But there was another Thea, the Thea who knew that, even though she worked for people she despised for their place in the social strata, and where they lived, and their ignorance about those who had nothing, she loved the children. Children brought her joy, whoever they were. It wasn't the fault of these young ones, her pupils who went to their own beds at night after a warm bath and with a cup of hot milk served by the nurserymaid. It was their good fortune that they had been born to plenty. They were innocent, and—she knew this—so were their parents. They'd simply never had cause or perhaps the opportunity to learn. This Thea, the Thea who understood human nature because she understood children, saw her chance in the latest letter she'd received from Avril. Then she made ready for school, smiling into the mirror when she put on her hat before leaving the house, as if to remind herself that her face could be arranged in such a way.

About a fortnight following her return from London, Kezia set off for the village shop. Driving the gig was now well within her capability, and she depended less upon Mrs. Joe to make decisions regarding where to stop and which way to go. She considered it fortunate that the horse appeared to have a fine mind, and Kezia always came with a good provision of carrots to reward the animal for her kind nature. Now, as she waited her turn to be served, Kezia could not help but notice two things. The first was that talk of war had increased, though there seemed to be no escalation in venom towards the Hun, despite stories appearing in the newspaper—the local edition came in on a Friday. For the most part, dailies did not sell in the village, and one only saw a *Times* or a *Daily Mail* or the *Evening Standard* if a copy had been found on the train and then made the rounds of interested parties. Staff at the four large estates in the area would bring copies home, which went into circulation in due course. Thus, the village was in general a well-informed community, but not completely up-to-date. Perhaps it was an appreciation that their news of world events, of parliamentary debate and stories of poor little Belgium, was delayed that tempered the villagers' response; however, it occurred to Kezia that while London boiled with opinion and rhetoric, inspiring young men to march to war, in this rural area there was a slow simmer—and, as she had discovered, a slow simmer could generate just as much heat underneath the pot.

It seemed that the sight of Edmund Hawkes in the uniform of an officer had been the source of some gossip. During her visits to the village, and especially to the shop, or to the library run by the vicar's wife and a coterie of women whose husbands worked in London—*He works up in Town*, they would say, or *He's in the City*—Kezia came to understand that the village's confidence in the Hawkes family had never been that high, but that Edmund Hawkes was looked upon with an interest bordering upon fascination. It was noted that he traveled to London several times each month, that he had a serious demeanor and was always dressed in an appropriate manner for such an excursion. At the same time, he was spoken of as a man who would rather while away his days scribbling in his notebook—yet his management of the estate, his guardianship of the land, suggested otherwise. It was said that he had an arrangement with the landlord of the Queen's Head and several other hostelries within a ten-mile radius that if his father were to venture in, there should be a limit to the number of times his glass could be refilled. It occurred to Kezia that Edmund Hawkes might like to perpetuate a certain idea of himself, and in so doing had the upper hand, as if he held a cloak of invisibility over his true character. It also came to mind that if she had time to think about the likes of Edmund Hawkes, her brain was becoming stale.

Then there was the second thing that Kezia noticed as she awaited her turn to step up to the counter and read out her list of groceries, listening as other women asked for a pound of this, or half of that, taking account of the fact that she never saw the poorer women in the shop, or if she did, they bought only bread and dripping, or perhaps a quarter pound of the cheapest cheddar. Kezia noticed that each woman—and some remained to chat even after purchasing their goods—seemed to cast her eyes in the direction of her waist and then turn to nod to another woman, or frown and begin a natter. Such was this interest that Kezia thought the clasp on her belt had come loose, or the cloth puckered, bringing up her skirt. An unusual quiet seemed to fall when she read out her list—flour, butter, currants and raisins, some spice for stew, a bottle of gravy browning—and though she could not be sure, it was as if she had disappointed the company gathered behind her.

As Kezia drove back to the farm, she hoped Tom would not mention that she had already gone into the village every day so far this week. His mother went but once a week at most, doing all her shopping in one fell swoop and returning with her baskets laden. And as for her mother, Kezia was well aware that merchants called upon the parsonage, and that the cook placed the weekly order, to be delivered on a Friday. Kezia admitted to herself that it was company she sought. It wasn't that her days weren't full enough—there was the laundry, which took the better part of a day, and more if it was raining; there was cleaning and polishing, and the blacking of the stove, which kept her and Ada busy until the girl left at half past three to care for her siblings after school. Kezia found that she looked forward to the girl's company. She discovered that Ada had been required to leave the village school earlier than most to look after her mother, who had been sickly after the birth of her eighth child. Only four had survived past the age of five, a fact that the girl took in her stride, as if such wounds were only to be expected. Most of the children in the village had lost at least one sibling—an infant stillborn, a little one taken by fever, an older child suffering an accident. Ada therefore could not read at a level that Kezia—who was discovering that relinquishing her role as a teacher was harder than she had anticipated—thought appropriate. Each day after Tom left to return to the fields following dinner—which Kezia still considered to be "lunch"—she would sit down with Ada at the table and tutor the girl in her numbers and letters. If she delved a little more into her heart, Kezia might admit she was trying to create an avid reader, another Cammie with whom to talk of novels and poetry. She used the books to hand, and began in the kitchen, so Ada might develop two skills at the same time.

"Now, this is what I plan to cook for Mr. Brissenden this evening, and I must start now. So, Ada, would you read to me from here." Kezia had taken down her mother-in-law's recipe book from the shelf above the stove, its yellowed pages dry and cracking as she pressed the spine, and set the open book before Ada, who leaned forward, placed her finger by the first word, and began.

"Cuh . . . cuh . . . a-a-a . . . b-b-b—cabbage. Cabbage w-w-w, i-i-i, th-th—with a wh-y-t." She sighed. "Cabbage with a white sss-sauce. Cabbage with a white sauce." Ada looked up at Kezia. "You go and put a sauce on the cabbage? I bet Mr. Brissenden never had that before."

"No, I bet he hasn't, and I've never cooked it. So we can get into trouble together, can't we, Ada? Now then, carry on."

And so they stumbled through. And by the time Ada's work was done and she had returned home to the end cottage in the village, she knew that cabbage could be cooked with a sauce of water, salt, butter, the tiniest pinch of soda, and some flour. She also knew that Kezia hummed while she cooked, and that she strained lumps out of sauces with the sieve, and still managed to make the sauce lumpy again when she returned it to the stove. She knew that Kezia threw away all the goodness of the cabbage with the water—which Ada would have made a gravy with, if she'd had the browning and a bit of corn flour—and that this dish alone would have been a whole meal for her family. But Kezia had also bought fish, which she put on to bake a good hour before Ada thought she should have—fresh fish never took that long, and she knew the shop only ever had fish when it had come up straight from the boats at Hastings, or when they sold it round the back because it had been caught at the Hawkes' lake without the gamekeeper knowing. But she also knew something else, an impression garnered while she watched her employer prepare food or stand at the stove, contemplating the sauce as it came to the boil—contemplating, mind, not stirring, which is what she should have been doing. Ada noticed that when Kezia cooked, it was as if she were blessing the food. Her brow knitted when things did not go smoothly, but she smiled again when a problem was solved. She lifted pots and pans with a gentle flourish, as if carrying something very precious. And though Ada could never have articulated her observations, there was something about the way Kezia moved in the kitchen that made her feel warm, as if she were caught in a glow.

Tom had been working long hours throughout the past week, as hop pickers began arriving from London. The annual hop-picking season was a holiday for the East Enders, a few weeks away from the Smoke, a time to get a bit of sun and fresh air, and all without losing money—even, with a bit of luck, earning more than they expected. Gypsies—who as a rule camped on Wimbledon Common, or who went from town to town, searching for work—turned up at the same time, looking to make enough to see them through the winter, and on the side the women would sell their posies of white heather, going door to door and persuading with their guttural, throaty tongue, "Gorn, luv, bring a bit o' luck, that will." They sold paper carnations, and clothes pegs made by the men, and as long as they kept to themselves, everyone rubbed along out in the hop gardens.

Amid the melee of the incoming tribes, there were always villagers too, taking stock of the outsiders and wondering how much they could get away with and blame it on these people who sounded nothing like them, and not even like one another. Tom loved the harvest season, whether it was soft fruits, hops, apples, or barley. The fragrance of ripeness filled the air, the spice aroma from hop pollen, the tang of blackcurrant, and the sweet waft coming from the orchards. This would be the last year of blackcurrants, though; men from the ministry had already come calling, and with the fruit picked and gone to jam makers and bottlers, the field was to be ploughed in ready for turnips and potatoes, hearty vegetables to keep an army marching. His father had always taken a chance on the fruits anyway, because money was in livestock. Wheat came in cheaper from Canada and America, and it seemed that output from farms across the Empire and refrigeration in ships had eased the need for British farmers to grow so much. Tom knew men who'd been letting land lie fallow, with trees coming back to re-form the forests of old, woodland that had been cut down when ancient Britons learned to furrow and plant. Young men had left the counties for urban employment, exchanging fresh air for smoke, for the factory and another master. But now, when the hops were ready to be picked, the city came to the country, and the farmer was happy to have it be so.

On this day, as Tom walked across the hop gardens, making sure everyone was settling in to the work, greeting people he hadn't seen since last year, it was getting on for dinnertime, so the hoppers were already setting up kettles for tea, bringing out bread and dripping sandwiches or, if they were feeling flush, a bit of cheese. Tom pushed back his cap and felt the growl in his stomach—it had been a long time since breakfast, so he was ready to walk back to the house for whatever delicacy his wife had prepared. Since he'd married, Tom looked forward to meals for more than sustenance to get him through the next part of the day. Kezia fascinated him with her imagination. Time and again he wondered if life on Marshals Farm would be enough for her, but she smiled with ease, and was becoming softer against the land, as if all those sharp edges of the town were wearing away.

Yet he was a man with a hint of worry amid his contentment, as if he were like a sailor on calm seas who saw dark clouds in the distance. He'd lost Bill, Mattie, and one of the apprentices to the army already, and when the pickers began arriving, walking along from the station with prams, pushchairs, and handcarts filled with pots, pans, bed linens, and boots, he could see that it was mainly women, children, and the old who'd come. If there were young men among their number, they were the lame, the thin, the sort who looked as if they'd been sickly as children and never quite recovered. And already Tom was beginning to feel something akin to guilt, as if he should be with his men who'd left the farm, alongside those who'd enlisted from the village. These were men he'd known since he was no taller than his own thigh.

"When you coming, guv'nor?" Mattie had called out, on the day the whole village had lined the street to watch their young men marching away to war. He was all smiles and teasing. "We're all in this one together—let's show 'em what us Kentish lads are made of. Come on, join up with us." And then they were gone, marching through the village with regulars sent to bolster recruitment, like a band of Pied Pipers taking away the children. So Tom was thankful for the workers who came this year, grateful for the Londoners and gypsies, and even for the fact that Danny would never be able to enlist, and Bert was too old. When all the harvest was in, winter would come, and surely the three of them could manage the farm as the days became shorter.

CHAPTER 6

Many women find it difficult to begin their letters—others find equal difficulty concluding them. One sensible rule to observe in beginning a letter is to avoid starting off with the pronoun "I."

—THE WOMAN'S BOOK

Dear Tom and Kezia . . .

Thea held her pen above the paper and made a series of dots around the *i* in Kezia's name, so it resembled a child's sketch of a fountain gushing upwards. Frustrated, she scribbled across both names, then crumpled the barely started letter and started again with a new sheet.

Dear Kezia and Tom,

I wanted . . .

But what did she want? What did she want to say to her brother and sister-in-law, or to her sister-in-law and brother? She felt uncomfortable writing to them together, as a single unit. In fact, when had she last written to Tom, or he to her? When her parents were alive, it was far more simple; letters were sent to Mother, who would of course read each out at the dinner table, as if it were a story—she imagined—or pass it to her husband first, who would read a bit here and there before handing it to Tom. She could see her brother in her mind's eye, placing the letter to the side of his plate and reading it while eating dinner. Mother would scold him—*Be careful with that gravy on the tablecloth*—but not really; it couldn't be called a scold, because any reprimand from their mother directed at Tom was always mild, never forceful, as if she were going through the motions of dismay. Tom could do no wrong in his mother's estimation. *You're her blue-eyed boy*, Thea would tease.

Even Kezia belonged to him now. She put down the pen, sliding it onto the groove next to the inkwell. She twisted the paper into a tight knot and threw it into the wastepaper basket. She didn't want to write to Tom too. She wanted to write to Kezia. Kezia alone. It was not that there was a secret to tell, or anything untoward to communicate, but she could not write to Tom and Kezia together, even though the letter would likely be read out at the kitchen table. And having given the matter due consideration, she realized that all she wanted to do, really, was let them know how things were, because she knew the village, she knew the farm, and she believed the war had probably barely touched them. And that made her angry. It made her angry that they could sit there and not know what was happening, that they were oblivious to it all.

Dear Kezia . . .

One more sheet for the wastepaper basket.

My dear Kezia,

By now you will be in the thick of the hop-picking, and I am sure that, even though you've known the farm since we were girls, it has come as a bit of a surprise to you. I don't think you ever came at hop-picking time, did

*you? When the hoppers arrived from London, you were
always in Europe with your family, or on the Norfolk
Broads, or in the Lake District, so you never saw the
farm at the busiest time of year.*

*I wonder what news you hear of war. I imagine
nothing's changed much for you, though I can tell you,
London has changed. You never know what you're going
to hear next—the papers are full of it, and on the street
people are very excited about the boys going over to fight
for Belgium. One of the women boarders here works at
the London Hospital as a typist, and she says they've
been bringing in wounded late at night so no one can
see them. She heard from an orderly that some of the
men are in a terrible state, and they arrive with their
clothes reeking of dirt and rats. You would read nothing
in the newspapers about it. They want to keep that to
themselves.*

*Germans are leaving London now. Elsie's best boy
has gone, and she is heartbroken—and so is he! I think
most of the waiters here have gone, so heaven knows
what the restaurants will do, not that I would notice,
as I haven't the money to pay for fancy suppers. And
you would have thought the larders of London were
absolutely bare, as there was nothing to be had in the
shops for a time, though I think people have calmed
down a bit and realized there is still food to eat.*

Kezia was at the kitchen sink, rubbing a thick green bar of
laundry soap back and forth across the neck of one of Tom's
shirts, when she saw the postman walking up to the house along
the farm road. The collies, Sloppy and Squeers, rushed at him,
but he waved them away and they grew bored and trotted off,

noses down, to find shade in the lee of the oast. She shook the suds from her hands and looked again. Mr. Barham had stopped to talk to Ada, who was pushing sheets through the wringer; with a deft hand she was keeping both the sopping side and the damp side out of the dirt. If the day was fine, it was always best to wring the laundry outside before pegging it on the line to dry.

"Mr. Barham, good morning to you!" said Kezia, wiping her hands on her apron, then lifting her left hand to shield her eyes from the sun. "You have some post for us?"

"Two for you, Mrs. Brissenden," said the postman, who took the opportunity to cast a glance towards Kezia's waistline.

"Oh, lovely—there's one from my father, and another from Thea—" She looked up. "Dorrit—she's known as Thea now, remember?" She smiled, glanced at the postman, again shielding her eyes. "Are you in a rush, Mr. Barham? Would you like a cup of tea, or some fresh lemon barley water?"

"Not today, Mrs. Brissenden. Got to be on my way now." He looked down at the ground. "Not a good job to have today, this."

"Is something wrong, Mr. Barham? Are you sure you wouldn't like a cup of tea?" Kezia turned to Ada. "Ada, go and put the kettle on, would you? Just let that sheet back into the basket."

Kezia waited until the girl had gone inside the house, then turned back to the postman. She was a vicar's daughter, and intuited when trouble's shadow was moving in to cross the sun. Her father had encouraged his parishioners to tell him about problems causing sadness or worry; as he explained, "Bad news can't settle inside, Kezia. My job is to bring it out and see what the Lord will do with it, and how He might want me to serve."

She placed a hand on Barham's arm. "I can see there's something troubling you—please tell me what I can do to help."

The man shook his head, and reached into his delivery bag.

He took out a telegram. "I've to deliver this today—to Ada's aunt. She was widowed last year, and now this—her eldest, Jimmy, has gone. Killed over there. I don't need to see what's inside, I know already. He was with the regulars, so he took his chances when he joined up—you'd be simple to think you'd never have to go to war, being in the army. Happened at a place called Mons. Our boys were driven back by the Hun, you see— and they copped it. I've been walking around with this envelope, knowing what's inside."

Kezia's eyes filled with tears, which she wiped away with the corner of her apron. "Jimmy was one of ours, Mr. Barham—I remember it was almost two years past, when he joined the army. Not that I knew him well, but I remember Tom remarking upon it, that he was joining up because there wasn't enough of the world to see around here. Oh, Jimmy's poor mother—how will she bear up? I must pay a visit."

"Best to leave it for now, Mrs. Brissenden. I wouldn't be surprised if young Ada doesn't come to work tomorrow, just so you know." He pushed back his cap and scratched his head where perspiration had gathered. "I knew it would come to this. They all go off, you see, these young 'uns, and they don't know what it's like. They think it's going to be a big adventure, like going off to the seaside for the day—I daresay that's what Jimmy thought. And they say the Hun is a terror to fight." He looked across at the oast, at the giant pokes filled with dried hops pressed down, ready for the brewery, now loaded on the cart to be taken to the station. "You're lucky to still have your horses—you watch if the men from the army don't come round and want them. You can't say no to them, not if they want your horses."

Kezia nodded. "They were both lame when they came, and they're getting on in years—Tom told the men about it, about how old they are and that he's thinking he'll have to go to market soon for more, if there's any to be had. So they left them with us. And they didn't take Mrs. Joe—they said they needed horses with some size to them, not a pony."

"The Shires were too old, eh? I reckon I remember when Jack Brissenden brought the pair of them home—never would have thought them too old."

Kezia nodded, and began to turn away. "Well, they're not good enough for the army anyway, the man said so. And what with the food we're sending off from here, the horses are doing their bit for the war."

"And that's a fact, Mrs. Brissenden."

Kezia looked along the road where it vanished among the trees and led to the fields of Marshals Farm. She drew her attention back to the postman. "I wish I could do more for them, the mothers who've seen their boys go—they must be worried sick."

"Oh, and there's more still of an age who'll march away, you mark my words."

With the heat of the day upon her, Kezia felt a sudden light-headedness.

"Are you sure you won't come in for a cup of tea?" she asked.

Barham shook his head. "Best be off." He touched his cap and, as he turned to walk away, the two collies came alongside, ready to accompany him until he reached the main road.

Kezia stood for a while, then slid the letters into her pocket and returned to the kitchen, where she settled her hands down into the now-lukewarm water. She felt along the collar of Tom's best shirt, then lifted it from the suds so that she could press it against her face, and across her cheeks, as if to wash away her tears.

"Mrs. Brissenden?"

Kezia turned, releasing the sopping garment back into the sink. "Oh, yes, Ada, is everything all right?"

"I made the pot of tea—would you like a cup?"

"Um, not yet. Put the cozy on and let it brew, and I'll have a cup in a minute."

Ada nodded, and reached for the tea cozy hanging up above the stove. "I'll finish the wringing and then put those sheets on the line—they'll dry in next to no time, I shouldn't wonder, with this heat and the blow they'll get."

"Yes, of course. And then you should go home, Ada. I can do the rest. I'm sure your mother would like to see you walk in the door a bit earlier today."

Ada looked up at the clock on the mantelpiece. "But it's not even dinnertime yet."

"I know, but we've got a lot done between us, and you've not had a moment off your feet all morning. Go on, Ada, you go home when the washing's on the line. I'm going to set to and prepare something special for Mr. Brissenden's dinner—something he hasn't had before. Oh, and don't worry, Ada, nothing will be docked from your wages. It'll all be the same as usual."

Kezia waved as Ada left the garden and went on her way down the farm road towards the village. It was a tight little place, that much she knew already, so when Ada walked into her home, it would be as if her own brother had died. All the children in the village had grown up together, in and out of one another's houses. They courted within the villages, and for the most part they married local, so when someone went, it was always as if family had been lost.

Lambs' kidneys. Kezia did not care for kidneys, but Tom had brought home four fresh lambs' kidneys from Maidstone market just the day before. They should be cooked or they would spoil soon enough. Kezia had placed them in the coolest part of the larder, while considering what she might do with them. In truth, she did not even want to touch them, did not want to finger the smooth flesh, blood oozing out onto the plate. It had pooled almost to the edge of the china, and already she could see a mark forming as the blood began to dry and congeal, working its way back to the kidneys as if it were an outgoing tide. Lifting the plate, maneuvering it with care, she attempted to get it to the sink without spilling a drop. Since Mr. Barham had called with the post, she had been thinking of Jimmy Hart. Poor dead Jimmy Hart, killed by a German gun. She tried not to hate Germans. She tried to imagine German boys being killed by British guns, by French cannonade. And she thought of Thea, and wondered what she would say, now that the war had come to the village.

ONION AND KIDNEY SAVORIES

Take one large onion and a paring knife. Take out the middle of the onion as if coring an apple. Wash the kidney, dry with clean muslin cloth. Skin the kidney. The oven should be hot. Place the onion in a baking dish and insert the kidney. Bake, basting with cooking butter. When cooked, serve with thick brown gravy.

How, thought Kezia, would she know when the kidney was cooked? Would she touch the meat with a knife, checking that no blood oozed from inside? Did kidney change color when cooked? And how thick, pray, was thick gravy? She had four kidneys, not one, so four onions were required. Tom would walk down the lane from the oast house in just over one hour, so she had better get on with it. In the kitchen garden, Kezia pulled four onions, and then some parsley. Her mother-in-law had only ever grown parsley, and rosemary seemed to grow by itself. Kezia wanted to experiment with other herbs, and had ordered seeds from a catalog—oregano, basil, thyme, sage. In the meantime, she'd purchased a small envelope of dried mixed herbs when last she went into Tunbridge Wells on the train. The village shop did not have dried mixed herbs, and the only spice available was a mixed spice cube for casseroles and stews. The recipe did not mention herbs, but this was to be a special dinner, a medley of flavors to set before Tom.

Kezia wept over the onions, felt queasy handling the kidneys, and at last began to enjoy herself with the parsley and dried herbs. She blended them together into a mash with cooking butter, and pressed a lump down on top of the kidney, as if it were a fragrant hat. How might it turn out? She had no idea, but there was something staid about the recipe, something middling, something run-of-the-mill. And everything she did for Tom, she wanted to be different. Even if it meant taking a risk.

As she moved about the kitchen, as she banked up the fire and opened the dampers to make the oven hot, so hot that when she opened the door she felt as if her eyelashes would scald together, Kezia thought about Thea. Or, if she were to distinguish her thoughts with more accuracy, she considered how Thea was changing. It was as if Thea were becoming more defined, so that when Kezia saw her friend in her mind's eye, she saw her still, as in a photograph, only someone had taken a black pen and traced around her frame, outlining her, making her stand out. And then, limb by limb, button by button, and now the shoes, the ears, the hat, each part of Thea was becoming bolder and sharper. There was no part of Thea that might disappear. Kezia straightened her spine, a kidney held in one hand. While Thea was acquiring more definition, she felt as if she, Kezia, were fading at the edges, drawing back into herself, like the blood on the plate. It was as if, when she looked at her body, she would see herself vanishing—disappearing. Had she ever been defined? The collies started barking again, and Kezia looked at the clock on the mantelpiece above the stove. Now she finished the dish, adding even more herbs, more pepper— more edge—to the recipe. This would be *her* onion savory, not anyone else's. Her onion savory, served with mashed potato, to which she would add just a little cheese, and perhaps some fresh cream, too. And the gravy would not be thick, would not be sludge, lumpen on the plate; no, it would slip across the potato, slide into the onion, and it would be a dish fit for a king. Her king.

"So, what's this?" Tom brought a sliver of something clear, something he could not identify, out of the onion. "It looks like onion, but it isn't."

"I found a fennel bulb in the garden, so I chopped it and added it to the butter."

"Tastes like licorice." He held out his fork to Kezia. "Taste."

And though she had her own fennel, her own kidney-filled onion, drenched in herb butter of her own concoction, Kezia leaned forward to receive the offering, taking Tom's wrist to steady his hand.

"I quite like it," she said, dabbing the corners of her mouth with a clean table napkin. When she'd first put out the wedding-present linens, Tom left his at the side of his plate, instead using his handkerchief, pulled from a dust-filled pocket, to wipe his mouth.

"It's different, Kezzie, I'll give you that. It's different."

"Do you like it?" she asked.

Tom smiled, picked up her hand, and brought it to his lips, kissing her palm as he smiled. It was a smile of suggestion, a smile only for Kezia. "I like it very much—though I think I'd like to taste a bit less of the pepper next time." He took his hand from hers and pinched her cheek, and at that moment she felt two things. She felt a rush of love rise up from her center, though at the same time, a little more of her definition vanished into the fog, and she realized that they were becoming one instead of two. And though part of her was filled with pleasure at this newness, still another part felt bereft.

"I have some bad news, Tom." Kezia could not have said why she chose that moment to tell Tom about Jimmy Hart, though when she looked back, she wondered if there could have been a better time, or a worse time. Tom's cheeks seemed to draw in when Kezia told him the news, as the weight of knowing settled upon him, that a childhood friend had been killed in a war that barely seemed real in his cocooned sameness of morning, noon, and night on the farm. In the middle of a season that followed another season and came before yet another, a life had been stopped, a body would never grow infirm, a face never age. All of this came to Tom. He took a handkerchief from his pocket and wiped his mouth.

"I'll have to tell the men," he said. Not the lads. Not the boys. Not any term of light affection. He had to tell the men. Now they were men who would stand tall, who would take the news with straight backs; backs that would be set to the land again with pick and shovel, with their shoulders into the plough. Now they would work all the harder to absorb the loss of one of their own.

"I'm sorry, Tom. I didn't know when to tell you."

"Not your fault, Kezzie. You're not a bloody Hun, are you? And you're not a general, or a Kitchener, or anyone who has anything to do with all this, and Jimmy left to go into the army nigh on two years ago, before we went to war." He stood up, scraping his chair, the screech against earthenware tiles like a score underneath his words. Outside the back door the collies had heard his boots move, and scampered up from the dirt, ready to follow.

"I'm going to tell the men," he repeated. Tom kissed Kezia on the cheek, and turned to leave. "Don't give me that fennel again, love. That taste—it'll only remind me of losing Jimmy."

Kezia sat for a long time, though it was probably not as long as she thought, but it was enough lingering when there was washing to be brought in from the line, when there was ironing to be done, a fire to be banked again, and a tea to be prepared and set before her spouse. She went to the washing line and gathered in the sun-bleached sheets, pulling them to her so that she might bury her face in the folds, drowning her senses in the fragrance of something scrubbed and blown through with a fresh wild breeze.

Hop-picking days were long. No sooner had Tom finished his tea each day than he stood up from the table, kissed Kezia on the cheek, and left to go up to the oast house once more. He had barely spoken a word over their early-evening meal, one that Kezia had planned especially. She thought something simple would be best, so she cooked a bacon and egg pie, chipped potatoes, and peas. Food to comfort him, food with no herbs added, no garnish of dandelion leaf, no fancy chutney to frame the chips. It was into the pudding she'd poured her imagination, for she wanted Tom to feel the comfort of sweetness. Scalded cream, raw cream, sifted sugar, sherry, and brandy, whipped together with lemon and grated nutmeg, then poured into wine glasses. Syllabub cured all ills, according to her mother—though Kezia thought Tom might consider it extravagant. She watched as he ate the syllabub, holding the slippery taste at the back of his throat before swallowing. He scraped the glass clean, took one last teaspoonful—the cutlery delicate, almost like a sparrow's leg in his rough, bruised hands—and then came to his feet.

"I'll see you later, Kezzie. Lovely tea. Lovely."

And then he was gone, the kitchen door closed behind him, putting his cap on his head as he walked along the farm road, the collies slinking in his wake.

Kezia sighed. She knew, already, what was on his mind. And if she were to admit it, she had known since she came back from London. She would wait him out though, and not encourage him. Kezia sat at the table for some time. She knew her mother-in-law would have been up already, washing the crockery, scrubbing the stove, sweeping the floor before bringing out the mop and bucket. She would be checking to see if the tablecloth could be used the next day, and she would bustle.

It was as she lingered, pouring salt onto her palm, then using the lines on her hand to funnel it back into the pot, that she remembered the letters. She flung the grains of salt remaining over her shoulder—for luck, because salt should never be cast aside without proper disposal—and went to the mantelpiece, where she claimed the letters brought by Mr. Barham.

Tom did not return to the house until after ten that night, and when he'd sipped the last of his cocoa, he set the earthenware mug on the kitchen table. "I'm going up, love." He reached across and took Kezia's hand. "Been a long day."

She nodded, and he stood to make his way to the staircase.

"I'm going to finish work on the books, Tom. I've got to be ready for the wages on Saturday morning."

They exchanged smiles, and all the unspoken words between them seemed to surge forward and then retreat.

Later, when Kezia had added and subtracted, multiplied and divided, when she had checked the books and reckoned up the amount of money she would need to take from the bank this week, she closed her ledgers, put them away in a drawer in the parlor desk, and made ready to join her husband in their bed. She undressed in the dark, slipping on her cotton nightdress and taking down her hair, brushing it one hundred times like her mother had taught her, and as she had been taught in turn by her mother before her. Then she wrapped a silk scarf around the brush and drew it across her hair; if there were moonlight, it would shine back at her reflection in the windowpanes. Kezia crept across to the bed, not wanting to wake Tom, but when she slipped between the cool white sheets, he drew close to her. He did not lay his hand upon her thigh, did not lift her nightdress to touch her skin. Instead he rested his head on her breast, as if he were a child seeking solace.

"Kezzie," he whispered into the dusky night, as if interlopers were eavesdropping.

"Tom."

"Kezzie, I've come to a decision."

She swallowed, the movement in her throat almost constricting her breath. "Yes, I know you have."

"I'm going over there. To fight."

She kissed the top of his head and drew him even closer. "Oh, Tom."

"I won't go yet," said Tom. "I'll take us through the last of the hopping, and get everything in. It'll be a few weeks yet, and then by the time spring comes, I daresay I'll be home again."

"Shhhhh. Come morning, we'll talk about it. Not now."

"Do you understand, Kezzie?"

"About Jimmy?"

"And the other lads. They're all going from the village—lads I've known since I was a boy. It won't be right if I don't go."

She nodded, and Tom felt her hair move against the pillow.

"I love you," he said.

Kezia moved her head again. She rested her chin against her husband's hair, and closed her eyes.

CHAPTER 7

*Words of Command. Commands will be
pronounced distinctly and sufficiently loud
to be heard by all concerned, but no louder.*

—*INFANTRY TRAINING*,
1914

While Kezia lay in her bed, asleep and yet not asleep, feeling as if she had just escaped a sinking ship and was lingering, spent, sodden, and kept afloat by her life jacket in a sea that at once lulled and threatened her, Thea was wide awake in her room at Queen Charlotte's Chambers. According to the letter she'd received that afternoon—a letter with no address at the top of the page or on the back of the envelope, no postmark, for it was delivered by hand, and no date to mark its creation—if she still felt the pull of opposition to the war, then a meeting of like-minded individuals would convene at seven o'clock this evening at an address just off Marylebone Road.

Thea wasn't sure what she'd expected when she set off at six o'clock—perhaps a darkened parlor filled with desperate souls trying to stop a boulder of some magnitude from rolling down a steep hill. She imagined the meeting to be something akin to a rendezvous between Guy Fawkes and his collaborators, men in dark coats, with wide-brimmed hats pulled down over their faces, and all with the pockmarked complexions of those afflicted by terror. She found the address with ease, and followed instructions indicating that she should employ several means of transport to reach the destination, including her own two feet, to ensure she was not followed. This rather scared Thea, though at the same time she was filled with a sense of purpose, an impassioned belief that she was flying in the face of authority to stop a monster. And whenever she imagined that authority, it had her father's face.

A woman answered her knock at the door—a woman who might have been pegged for a rector's wife had she not seemed so perplexed, looking both ways along the street before taking Thea by the shoulder and leading her into the hall with some force, as if an offer of shelter from a storm had become an order. Perhaps this *was* shelter in a storm, thought Thea, though the way the woman glanced this way and that to ensure no one had followed the latest visitor reminded Thea of Mrs. Bracken in the village, a busybody who would come out onto her front doorstep when she collected her milk, peering down the street to ascertain who else might be there to exchange gossip. But this was no convening of idle talkers. Thea was required to show her letter before she was ushered in among the company.

"Good of you to come. Welcome."

A tall, thin man stood up as she entered and came towards her, hand outstretched. He guided her towards a chair. Thea thought he reminded her of how she had once imagined Casaubon in *Middlemarch*. A sudden longing for Kezia's company enveloped her. Together they would have whispered and giggled, and then tried to match everyone in the room to characters in the book. And then she remembered—though how could it not have entered her mind as soon as she'd given the man an identity?—that George Eliot's Dorothea had married Mr. Casaubon. Thea took her seat. It seemed she was among the last to arrive. Men and women had all found places on the available chairs, though there were apologies here and there, an "I do beg your pardon" as a foot was nudged by another foot, and a mouthed "Excuse me" when knee knocked against knee. The youngest woman present appeared to be about twenty-two and was accompanied by a man some ten years older, whom Thea assumed to be her husband. The oldest was a woman who might have been a thinner Queen Victoria, dressed in black from head to toe, and wearing a bonnet from another age.

"Thank you all for coming this evening." Casaubon stood up, and introduced himself. "My name is Ian Thurber."

Ah, not a Casaubon, thought Thea. No, this one had the name of a factory clerk, or perhaps a teacher, like herself. Mr. Thurber, the geography teacher. Or the physics teacher. Or perhaps Thurber wasn't his name at all.

"As some of you know, I am secretary of the United Pacifist Society, though there are a few here who know me from my occupation. I would like to affirm, before anything else, the gravity of what we are about to discuss, and the importance of keeping these meetings in confidence. There is no need to introduce yourselves; in fact, it would be better if you remained anonymous to those present who do not already know who you are. As a further precaution, there are two different exits from this building, and we will leave at intervals, spacing our departures so as not to look like it's closing time at the White Hart."

Thurber smiled as low, tension-easing laughter rippled through the room.

"If you have reason to discuss any aspect of our work here—and it is crucially important work—then you must do so via the person who is your immediate link in the line of communication. I would urge you to keep such conversations to a minimum and in a location where you will not be overheard, or will not cause you to be observed as unnatural in your manner."

Thea looked around. There was Avril, just arrived, leaning against the door. She was late—Avril was always late. She gave an almost-nod towards Thea, then smiled as a man stood up, extending his hand towards his seat. He took her place by the door.

"These meetings will be rare. The climate of response to the war is too fraught with danger, and those of you"—Thea felt as if he were looking at her directly—"who have been members of the suffragist societies will already be known to the authorities." He paused. "Be assured of that."

Thea felt herself redden. She had suspected as much. Though she had never been caught, she had known what it was like to have a close shave. It was last year that it had happened, in early spring. She was walking with Mary Williams on a fine afternoon—she must have had a day off work, but now could not remember the reason for the holiday—when, without warning, her friend had taken a brick from her shopping bag and thrown it through the window of a gentlemen's outfitters. Thea had no recollection of the name of the shop, but for a split second, having seen the woman's arm arch and the way she bowled the brick, she had the incongruous thought that Mary must be the sister of a brother, because surely she had played cricket as a girl. It was a random notion, and one she knew, now, was born of shock. And then Mary had yelled, "Run! Run for God's sake, woman." And the police whistles came closer, and soon Mary was gone, and Thea ran and ran into the crowds on Oxford Street, whereupon she began to walk, her head down, with the cool air diffusing perspiration across her cheeks and above her lip. Without looking back, she made her way into Selfridge & Co., trying to breathe at a more measured rate so her heart might stop beating as if it would break through her ribs. She stopped behind a pillar and placed her hand on her chest, and when she had finally gained control over her breath, she went on her way, exiting the store on a side street. She walked all the way back to Queen Charlotte's along streets she didn't know, but all the time setting one foot in front of the other in the direction of a place that was, at that very moment, as good as home. Once there, she penned a letter to the school's headmistress and paid a boy to deliver it at once. Claiming a fever that she did not wish to pass on to the children, she informed Mrs. Gibson that she would be at school on Monday, fit and well. Thea left London as soon as she could, but did not return to the village. Instead she went to Kezia in Tunbridge Wells. *What a lovely surprise.* Kezia had taken her down to the Pantiles for tea the following day, and they had listened to the band playing.

Mary, though, had been apprehended, charged, sentenced, and dispatched to Holloway prison for three months. Once incarcerated she refused to eat, and after a few days of this perceived insolence, something akin to gruel had been poured into her stomach through a rubber tube rammed down her gullet. When Thea saw Mary again, she had just been released. She was rail-thin, the bones on her wrists blue and so fragile, and though her hair was beginning to grow back, her body's malnourishment had caused it to fall out in small, soft clumps. Mary would never again feel long hair against the length of her spine. She took her own life, throwing herself into the Thames from Westminster Bridge under the gaze of the Houses of Parliament. Thea wondered if any man inside was looking, or would have been concerned had he witnessed Mary's desperate drowning. But something had come to pass, though not down to Mary ending her life—the so-called Cat and Mouse Act was now law. Women who went on hunger strike were released upon the point of death, only to be arrested again when—if—they recovered.

Now, as Ian Thurber spoke, his words breaking in and out of her memories, Thea felt a sickness rising within her. Mary had died about two weeks before Kezia and Tom were married.

"It's important you understand the danger involved in the risk each and every one of you are taking—but know this; you are putting your cards on the table and you are gambling your livelihoods, your family life, indeed your own personal well-being, in the name of peace in Europe, and in the name of the men—both Allied and those from Germany—who are at this moment being butchered on the battlefields of Flanders."

Thurber then motioned an older woman to the front of the room. Her name was not given. If this meeting was so fraught with danger, Thea wondered, why did Ian Thurber even bother to give himself a name, even if it was a fiction? Or perhaps he was not so big a catch if he were apprehended. She felt the bile rise in her throat again, and tried to press from her mind the memory of the day Mary threw the brick. It was after leaving Selfridge & Co., on one of those side streets, with barely a soul about, that she had stopped and, leaning against a cast-iron railing outside a house, vomited onto the flagstones. A woman came running up from the dark downstairs of the four-storey house, wiping her hands on an apron, the cap keeping her hair at bay marking her as the household's cook. *Oi, what do you think you're at—all over the bleedin' path? You can clear that up—your sort always think you can roll out of the pub, chuck it all up, and then make up the money lying on your back some-where.* And then Thea had spoken in her good Town voice, her I-am-one-of-your-betters voice, and told the woman she had been shopping and began to feel unwell, so had thought a walk would be best, but now . . . She let the words linger. The cook had taken her downstairs, pulled out a chair for her, and when she was settled, had gone up to the street again with a pail filled with water and bleach, which she threw across the flagstones. She went back twice more before she was satisfied that the contents of Thea's stomach had been sluiced well away. Then she returned and grated ginger into a cup that she filled with hot water from a stove-blackened kettle. *There, that'll sort you out.* And it had. For the moment. Thea had had trouble keeping food down since Mary died.

"The plan to raise small groups—four, five, or six together— will enable us to deploy you across parts of London at the same time. We can distribute our literature, make our point, and then disperse into the crowd. We will convene in popular locations where there are many people gathered. Arrive as individuals, depart as individuals. Go home, and await instructions for your next demonstration. Do not retain pamphlets; simply leave them if not distributed among the populace." The unnamed woman paused. "Expect confrontation." She paused again. "But know that the illustration on the pamphlet—which you will not see until the day of your participation—accurately depicts what is happening to men at the front, and to the local populations where war has arrived on the doorstep. We are a pacifist society, so we go forward in peace. We will not rise to the bait of argument, and we will turn the other cheek if attacked—though again, departure and dispersal should be employed."

A hand went up, and a man spoke. "May I ask a question?"

Thea began to look at the man, then turned away—she did not want to know who he was in case she saw him in the street.

"Aren't we putting ourselves at risk, being in such small groups? We could be set upon by a larger gang in support of war."

"We must not be afraid of our remit," said the woman.

Thea felt the man shrink into his chair.

By the time the meeting was disbanded, and Thea had waited by the rear exit for directions back onto the Marylebone Road, she had learned that she would soon receive her instructions. The letter must be memorized and destroyed, as must any other correspondence from the society, and she would be expected to be present at the demonstration. Was she fearful, as she ran to catch a tram, and then a bus, and then walk to Queen Charlotte's Chambers? Yes, it must be said that Thea felt it in the pit of her stomach, a duality of emotion—a conviction that she was doing something that was right and true, and a sense of terror that someone might press a thick rubber tube into her mouth, that she would feel it snake to her stomach, and then the warm mush slopping into her gut. She pressed her hand to her mouth and hoped she would get home in time to avoid embarrassing herself on the street once more.

Edmund Hawkes was wondering if he was nothing more than a glorified scout leader. He'd been here not yet a fortnight, in France, and all he wanted to do was go home. Have this terror end, and all go home. Did they do this to every junior officer? he wondered. Sling them into the deep end to see if they would sink or swim? Well, the Honorable Edmund Hawkes—not feeling very Honorable right now—knew the answer, and he didn't feel as if his head were above water. It was baptism by fire—fire, fire, and more fire.

There was a cough behind him, a phlegmy attention-demanding clearing of the throat. Hawkes looked up. His sergeant stood to attention. Edmund sighed—the man did not intimidate him, but rather saddened him. He liked his sergeant, who, he knew, had more experience of soldiering in his little finger than the average newly minted officer had in his whole body. He understood that his sergeant's most difficult job was in making sure his officer knew what he was about.

"Well, Sergeant Ellis. Are the men ready?"

"Five minutes, sir. The bombardment ends, we count—"

"Very good, Sergeant Ellis, very good. Issue the rum, and give me a minute."

"Sir!" The sergeant saluted, turned back, out into the trench.

Here we go. Hawkes looked around the dugout, his eyes resting on a photograph of himself with his mare and his dog—dear Bella, dead already within a day of landing in France, when a makeshift stable sustained a direct hit from an enemy shell. He should have left her at home, should have left her to canter across fields, to linger by the lake, blowing into the water and then drinking her fill. He closed his eyes and tried to remember how her gallop felt, how she powered herself, carrying him across the fields, over a gate, and another, then slowing to a canter, then trot, and down to the lake. Would he soon be dead too? Would his early luck hold? And if it did, how many letters would he begin to write, telling a wife, a mother, that the man had not suffered, that he had died instantly in the service of his country? *Died instantly?* Hawkes remembered studying classics at school, and it seemed Aeschylus had it down: "In war, truth is the first casualty." But what else can you say when a man has been blown into a million pieces, a million pieces and his blood seeping down into a foreign field? *He died instantly.* Of course he bloody well died instantly—no one can live without a head, a heart, or a brain. Would he, too, die instantly within the next five minutes, or ten?

The Honorable Edmund Hawkes pulled at the cuffs of his uniform jacket, checked his Webley revolver, replaced it in the holster, and moved out into the trench. Men were lined up, each with a sixty-pound pack on his back and a Lee Enfield rifle. *How the bloody hell are they supposed to run with that?* Hawkes pushed his thoughts to the back of his mind and put his hand on the shoulder of a man whose whole body was shaking. *Man? No, boy, more like.* A Kentish boy with blue eyes and cherry-red lips, a boy who had never known a woman's love and might never yet.

"It's all right, Saunders. Chin up. Your mother's proud of you, you're a good soldier."

He caught the eye of one infantryman after another, not flinching, not drawing back. Two days ago he had become the most senior officer in his unit—promotion by war's attrition. His inadequacy pulled at his gut, but he walked all the taller for it—it was what the men expected. He cleared his throat.

"You fight for the honor of our land across the Channel, for the honor of every town and village, for every man, woman, and child in the British Isles—remember that! Remember that, and go forward, and may God go with you, and with us all."

He nodded at his sergeant, who gave the command to fix bayonets. He stepped towards the ladder—*ladder into bloody hell*—and put his foot on the first rung. He took his pistol, readying it to fire.

"Are you ready?"

"Yes, sir!"

"Bearers up!" he called, summoning the stretcher bearers to attention.

Edmund Hawkes could not hear himself speak. His teeth rattled as the cannonade escalated, with shells flying over the trench and towards the enemy. He looked at his watch, counting down the seconds now. *Tick-tock, tick-tock*. Then silence. A split second, *one, two, three* . . .

Hawkes glanced at his sergeant, remembering their first charge together. Ellis had thrown a football over the top when he gave the order to charge, so the men had kicked the ball one to the other while running towards the German guns. *Play up! play up! and play the game.* Now he caught sight of the shaking boy; his men were looking towards him, waiting, waiting, one second after another, time expanding and contracting about him, his ears ringing, no sounds, not even his voice, *not even his voice*, as he raised his arm, his arm with the hand that grasped the pistol, and his sergeant lifted his whistle, and then one after another, though it was slow and fast all at once, Edmund Hawkes, the Honorable Edmund Hawkes, ran up the rungs, and within another second could hear someone shouting. . . .

Charge!

And the voice came from within him, tearing into his throat, bursting into his ears, as he ran into the fog, into the smoke, and into the shells and guns.

"For king and country!"

And though he could barely see, Hawkes ran, and alongside him his men ran, holding out their rifles, running as if running were all they had to do. He fell, picked himself up, and ran. Now more men were in front of him. It was a horse race, a Grand National of war, a Derby of running soldiers. He saw the boy fall, the boy who'd been shaking. He'd found his legs and was galloping hard, screaming into the smoke, screaming at the Hun to get the effing hell out of his England. And then he'd gone down.

Hawkes came to his knees alongside the boy, looked down at the blood-black hole in his stomach, then at the boy's face. And in that moment he thought he saw everything there was to know about that face, and it was as if time were standing still again and the noise receding, scared away by the running bellowing men, who opened their mouths but no sounds came out anymore.

"I'm dead, aren't I, sir? I'm a dead man."

Hawkes reached for the boy's hand.

Dead man. Dead boy. It was all the same, really.

"You'll be all right, son. You've done yourself proud, done your mother proud."

Hawkes knew this already; he knew mothers were important. The dying and wounded always asked for their mothers, their lips working like babies seeking the milk of sustenance.

"Tell her then, sir."

"I'll tell her you're one of the best. I'll see her myself."

A sweet sickly stench came from the boy's center, yards of bloody rope seeping from his body. Then at once the hand became lifeless, and it was done. All around him, men were dead and dying, calling with their last ounce of life, the sounds of shelling and gunfire giving way to something that reminded Edmund Hawkes of the mournful baying of dogs.

"Retreat, sir. Go back. Call the men back."

Hawkes turned to Ellis, who had his head down as he staggered towards him, his right arm hanging, held in place by his left hand.

"Sir! Retreat! Now!"

The sounds came back, whooshing into his head almost as if he had been struck by a shell, and again he heard the voice, the voice that came from his mouth yelling to the men to pull back. And bearing the weight of his wounded sergeant, the Honorable Edmund Hawkes—Captain Hawkes, now—staggered home to the trench, because in that moment the trench was home. But he knew, even as he fell down into the earth, as he pulled his almost-unconscious sergeant to him, that he would return to the battlefield. He would go out with the stretcher bearers into the night to bring back wounded, even if it meant prizing their torn bodies from barbed wire. But he knew, too, that he had not surmounted fear, that he might never overcome the terror inside. He knew it lived with him, would eat with him and would go to bed with him at night and come to him in his dreams. Yet he was not afraid of death, of that final moment of life. He was afraid of the dying that came before the end.

The letter came on a Friday at five o'clock in the evening, instructing Thea to be at Hyde Park the following afternoon. It cautioned her to destroy the communiqué once read. She was to wear plain clothing, and no jewelry or other identifying accoutrements. She should not stand out from the crowd. There must be nothing to distinguish her from any other woman in the park that day. Thea followed the instructions to the letter, and on Saturday afternoon made her way from Queen Charlotte's Chambers by foot and by bus to Hyde Park, at the Lancaster Gate entrance. When she arrived, not one face was familiar, though she had known the others she was to meet as soon as she saw them clustered. There were two men and two women, and another man joined them just after Thea, a man she might have passed in the street and never noticed. He walked up to the group and nodded. The taller man passed a clutch of pamphlets to her. He was wearing a bowler hat and a suit of plain dark grey worsted—she noticed the trousers had a shine where a hot iron had been taken to them without a pressing cloth in between. She looked at the pamphlet; her stomach turned as she saw the drawing, an almost photographic depiction of a British soldier dying, tangled in barbed wire.

"Right, my friend here and I will hold the banner and call out our message. You, you, and you"—he looked at the women, nodding his head toward each one in turn—"you will distribute pamphlets, call out to people to join us. We are representing everything that is peaceful—do not be drawn into argument or dispute, simply state your message. Do not hold a gaze with anyone, because you must not be remembered. We are here to uphold peace in our country, peace for the people of Britain, and peace in Europe." He paused. "Are you ready?" He cast his eyes across the group. "Shall we?"

The man waited for each person to nod their agreement, and then set off. Holding the banner high, the two men marched along the broad walk, with the women and the young man who had been late marching behind. Thea held out her pamphlets, and at first she smiled, then remembered that no one should recollect her face, so she kept her hat low, and saw only hands as she pressed a leaflet into them—hands with gloves; small, childish hands; hands with long fingers and ink-stained hands. Then she pushed a pamphlet into a thick, work-worn hand, a hand that might have been her father's or Tom's, and she felt the stab of nausea touch her again.

"What do I bleedin' want this for? You wicked piece of nothing—my boy's over there, fighting, and all you can do is go on about peace. Tell the bleedin' kaiser about peace, girl."

Thea turned, and as she did, the young man of their group came closer.

"But sir, surely your son should be here, in England. He should be with his family, perhaps helping you in your work—surely he should not be on a foreign battlefield."

Thea felt the group cluster and heard the banner flapping in the breeze. A small crowd had begun to form, and soon people were calling, telling them to go home, go back to where they came from.

"We come to you in peace, with a message of support for our soldiery, and a desire to bring them back from the brink of death—the people of France and Belgium have suffered even more from bombs and shelling since war was declared."

The man's voice was drowned out. A woman shouted, "What

about the poor Belgian babies, what about the Germans, knif-ing them right through!"

And still the crowd grew. A woman pulled the pamphlets from Thea's hand and twisted them into a ball, which she threw over her shoulder.

Then, in the distance came the police whistles. The sound of authority catching up with her again.

"Disperse!" said the first man to speak when they'd met. "Go now!"

Thea did not wait for a second instruction. She felt a hand take the arm of her coat.

"See what this one does when they nab her for sedition! See what she does, the little trollop! So much for defense of the realm!"

Thea pulled her arm away and ran. She ran towards the gate. The park was busy on such a sunny day, so she slowed as she mingled with sweethearts arm in arm, with families and children, and then she walked as quickly as she could to the Underground. Her breath was echoing in her ears, and behind her she heard footsteps gaining on her. She turned a corner and stepped to one side. Three boys on the brink of manhood ran past, teasing each other and pushing as they galloped on.

Tube, bus, and walk. Walk with a brisk step, head down. Walk to the front door, take out the key, in the lock . . .

Thea closed the door behind her and walked upstairs to her room. Everything was as she left it. Neat. Tidy. Fresh flowers in a vase on the table. She closed the curtains and turned on the gaslight, then took off her plain coat, hat, and gloves and sat down in the armchair. She pulled the pillow to her stom-ach, curving her body around its softness, and rocking back and forth, her eyes closed.

Rap-rap-rap at the door.

"Miss Brissenden?"

Thea started, her eyes open wide.

"Miss Brissenden, are you there?"

She came to her feet and, still clutching the pillow, opened the door. It was the warden. A woman in her fifties, she was of Thea's height and always dressed in a black skirt with a white blouse and wide belt. It was the belt that changed with the season or the occasion—today the belt was deep red, and matched the combs in her hair and the rouge on her cheeks.

"Oh, Mrs. Montague, good afternoon," said Thea.

"I thought you mustn't have seen this parcel waiting for you—and there's some post, too. I'd left it on the downstairs table—you walked right past without noticing."

Thea nodded. "I was in a bit of a hurry."

"Well, here you are then." The woman smiled. "Nice day?"

"Yes, thank you. I—I went to the park—Green Park. It was quite beautiful today, but I do have a headache now."

"Right you are, then. I'd best be off—I've a friend coming round for a bit of supper tonight."

"Oh, lovely," said Thea. "Well. Have a good evening, Mrs. Montague."

Thea smiled and closed the door.

She brought the box into the room and set it upon the table. With scissors she cut the brown paper, and a second layer of paper underneath. It was a cake tin, with a letter on top.

Dearest Thea,

I know how much you love walnut cake, so I baked one to my very own recipe. You will find there are lots of walnuts to pick out—do you remember at Camden, when we would buy a little round walnut cake and cut

it into small pieces so we each had the same number of
walnuts? I wanted to make sure this was the best walnut
cake you could possibly taste, ever. You will find I have
put in a goodly amount of brandy, so it keeps nicely in
the tin. I have mixed in everything you love in a walnut
cake, dear Thea. I do hope you enjoy it.

"Oh, Kezzie."

Thea sat on the chair, holding the tin in her lap. In all her years away from the farm, even when she was at school, then college, she had never been sent a cake. Her mother would not have thought it necessary. Food was something you put on the table, or took in a basket to a sick friend, or to a husband, out in the fields at harvest time. Thea lifted the lid, drew the tin towards her face, and breathed in the sweet, spicy fragrance of rich walnut cake. It was as if she could distinguish each and every ingredient—best butter, eggs from the farm, flour from Dallings Mill, cinnamon, sugar, golden syrup, candied cherries, and walnuts. Whole walnuts, not chopped walnuts. And there was another ingredient that Thea knew was there, but had no distinguishing fragrance, though it was fresh and sweet and she knew it had been bound in with each sweep of Kezia's wooden spoon. It was as if Kezia had poured her heart into the cake, so that when Thea took a bite, which she did, later, with a cup of tea, she felt the old warmth of friendship return. She could taste companionship itself, and she longed for her beloved Kezzie to be there, in the room with her, crumbling the cake and counting out walnuts.

CHAPTER 8

Religion and politics are topics of conversation which
should always be avoided. They are subjects upon which
difference of opinion is very rife, and may often lead to
heated arguments which are as tiresome and unpleasant
as they are ill-bred.

—*THE WOMAN'S BOOK*

Dear Sis . . .

Tom could not bring himself to write "Thea," though he often
felt that he had lost Dorrit anyway. It no longer mattered that
she had changed her name, because the girl he had once run
across the fields with, had followed to the top of the big climbing tree, limb by limb, and who had been his close confidante,
felt lost to him. Calling her "Sis" brought her back, reminding
him—and her, he hoped—that they were once as thick with
each other as siblings could be, like twins, until he had chosen
Kezia, and she had chosen him back.

He had decided to tell Thea himself. Kezia had offered to write
the letter, and had then left the idea hanging, so that he might
choose to set pen to paper. That's what he loved about Kezia—
she made him do what was right, but left it up to him to know
what right was. He didn't think she even knew she had this quality, and sometimes suspected that being the daughter of a man
of the cloth had imbued her with a certain knowing that eluded
him, and others. Perhaps being brought up with righteousness
was a gift, after all. And it was usually when he caught himself

with fanciful thoughts that Kezia altered his viewpoint, and there was always something special on those days—the discovery of a posy of dog roses next to his plate, as if to garnish the table while he ate. But it was clear that Kezia believed it should be Tom who wrote to Thea to announce and explain his intentions.

"But don't ask her to come back to the farm, Tom. I can manage—with Bert and Danny and anyone else I can get, I can manage. Thea won't want to come home, Tom, so don't expect it of her."

Tom took Kezia's words to heart, and set to writing again.

Dear Sis,

This is your brother writing to you.

Tom always began a letter in this way, as if Thea would not be able to tell the solid hand, with the stream of lettering divided in places where he had pressed hard with the nib, which had separated so two lines of ink ran apart, then together, then apart. He had not written a letter to Thea for some time, usually choosing a postcard to reply to her, with quickly scratched news from the farm, and always an invitation. *Come back soon, Sis.*

Dear Sis,

This is your brother writing to you. I will come to the point, because neither of us likes dithering, and we've always been straight as arrows with each other, even when we didn't like what the other was saying.

He could imagine Thea in his mind's eye, reading that sentence, and thinking of the letter he'd sent—when was it? Two years ago? *There's no need beating around the bush. I want you to know that I have fallen in love with Kezia, and intend to make her my wife.*

He looked down at his page, and continued.

> *. . . even when we didn't like what the other was saying. I don't think you'll like this, Sis, but I have decided to put myself up for the army. I've seen men of my age and with not so much about them, going off to enlist to fight for our country, and I reckon I should do my bit with them. According to the papers, the war won't last that long, so I would say that by the time I'm trained up, then it'll be close to finished and I'll be home again. Bert knows what needs to be done here, and Danny is as good as any of the men, though he would never get into the army on account of his leg. Kezia has been a dream girl, a real farmer's wife. I went out to the field to check on Danny yesterday and found her out there with Ted and Mabel, and Dan showing her how to drive them on with the plough. Her line was fair straight as well, though I reckon the horses felt it, because I saw Mabel look around just to see who had a hold of her.*

Tom dipped the pen again. He had hated the pen since schooldays, hated dipping it into the black ink, hated the knob of skin on his middle finger, where it touched the nib and an ink-stained ridge would remain for a day or two afterwards. He didn't mind the earth in his nails and ingrained in his hands, but ink stains across his fingers reminded him of school, then college.

> *There's no need for you to come home. Don't you think that we would want to change your London life for a*

*minute, because Kezia has told me how much you set
by living there and being a teacher, so we don't want
you to do that, though I would say that we would love
to see you if you come for a Saturday and Sunday.
Kezzie would collect you from the station in the gig.
And I daresay she'll come up to London to see you soon
anyway. She likes to do things like that, on her own.*

*I will sign off now. I plan to enlist as soon as all the
harvesting is finished. The hop pickers have nearly all
gone home, so once I've left, Bert needs only to concern
himself with getting everything done through the winter
so we're ready for spring. I reckon him and Dan can
do most of it, and there are young lads in the village
looking for a bit of man's work. A few of them, not yet
four and ten, tried to enlist and were sent home with a
clip round the ear for their trouble. So now they think
they're men Bert can put them to work when he needs
them. The farm will be in good hands, so don't worry—
Kezia has taken up the books and made a much better
job of it all.*

*Your loving brother,
Tom*

Tom looked up from his letter writing, setting the pen in its
cradle. Kezia had moved the desk to a place by the window,
so she could look out over the garden while she was doing the
farm accounts and preparing the wage packets. He could see
Kezia now in what she called "my kitchen garden," and realized
he hadn't lingered to watch her for a while. He saw her every
day, indeed, still flush with new marriage, he felt his heart move
whenever she came into a room, or when he sat at the table to
talk while she cooked at the stove, pushing hair from her eyes

as she put her finger on a line of instructions in her recipe book. Now he watched as she moved around the garden, and wondered about her. She was different. He could never before have put his finger on the why of it, just that each day she did or said something that he had never heard his mother or Thea or one of the women in the village say or do. Two days earlier she had gone through his father's old clothes and come out with a pair of corduroy trousers that had been small on the old man by the time he'd expanded to a fair size around the girth. She'd used a hot knitting needle to add holes to a leather belt, and worn those trousers into the garden, tucked into a pair of gum boots that must have been several sizes too big for her, but she maintained that gum boots kept everything out that shouldn't be in. He would buy her a better pair before he left, a pair that would fit so she didn't trip and trudge.

Now she moved along the runner-bean row, her basket on her hip, leaning forward to clip each bean from the vine with her forefinger and thumb. She'd planted herbs in the garden, first nurturing seedlings in the greenhouse—a greenhouse hardly used until she'd taken it into her head to clean it out and set up trays with rows of eggshells. Into each half-shell—she got through a lot of eggs, trying to perfect her cake baking—she had placed some soil and a seed, so as each green shoot struggled to break through the earth, it seemed as if a chick might one day appear instead of a plant. It occurred to Tom that he should have told her it was the wrong season for starting the growing of herbs, but he kept quiet. In any case, he thought that the time and attention she lavished upon her young would cause them to flourish in a desert. Then his concerns caught up with him, and he sighed a long-winded breath of worry. He wondered how she would manage. She seemed confident enough. Kezia had not wept, had not pleaded with him to stay. She had simply told him that he must do what he thought best, and she would do what had to be done for the farm while he was gone. She said she would be at the gate every day waiting for his letters, and would be there still when he came home.

The clock struck the hour, and Tom sighed again, such was the weight upon his heart. It was strange, he thought as he watched Kezia from the quiet of the parlor, with only passing time for company. It was said that marriage settled both man and woman. He considered what it meant to be settled, because there was something in Kezia, something he'd felt since their marriage, and even more since his decision to join the regiment. She seemed like a young branch that had passed the time when it could be bent this way or that, a limb becoming stronger with maturity. He watched as she picked up her basket and walked to the gate, stopping to talk to Bert, who was leading Ted and Mabel out to the paddock. She lingered to give them treats from her pocket, then rubbed each horse with a firm hand swept down the neck. Tom felt tears in his eyes as she laughed with Bert and walked towards the house, closer to the window, so he took up the letter, folded it, and inserted it into the envelope, which he addressed to Miss T. Brissenden. And at once he felt the wash of fear again, and he realized that it was not so much a worry that Kezia could not do without him as the realization that she and the farm might do quite well together.

FROM KEZIA BRISSENDEN'S
EXPERIMENTAL RECIPE BOOK

Pork, diced; Onion, chopped; Thyme, chopped. Salt and
    Pepper (check oversalting)
For Pudding—Baked Apples
Four large apples, Butter, Dried fruit, Cob nuts

At some point in each day there came a moment when Kezia itched to be among different people, when she missed the days before she gave up the classroom and her life in Tunbridge Wells. But at the same time, she found there was something in the rhythm of the farm and what she now considered to be her work that warmed her heart, giving her a sense of the rightness of her place. It was as if the farm had lungs and she were caught in its breath, swept inward, at one with its life force. She tried not to think about Tom going to war, because every time she read a newspaper or heard people talking about what was happening in Belgium or France, she felt as if war itself were alive too, breathing in and out, breathing fire towards her. She wanted to write to her father about her feelings, and about the dreams that came; dreams that she was running from a fire, with the flames coming ever closer. But something had changed—she didn't want to have him quote a reading from the Bible, or the work of a scholar who might explain her nighttime fears. Instead she sought solace in the kitchen, which cocooned her, brought her into its rhythm. Outside it was another warm day, but the dampers were open and the fire was blazing to heat the oven and the hot plate above, and she was preparing another meal to present to Tom, who would surely tell her it was the best meat that had ever passed his lips, with the most succulent vegetables—minted and peppered, but no salt, not today—and the baked apples would be the sweetest yet.

Kezia was about to throw the potato peelings onto a newspaper to take out to the compost heap when a snippet of print caught her eye. She read the news whenever she could, but always found something she'd missed when about to use the paper for something else—perhaps to step across a just-mopped floor, or to line a tray for the greenhouse. There it was again—the casualty list. The never-ending rows of names, of boys and men lost to battle. She drew her eyes away, then to another snippet that had eluded her attention at an earlier reading.

SUFFRAGETTES ARRESTED IN PACIFIST MARCH

It wasn't the headline that caught her eye, but the sudden feeling that she'd seen something familiar, something that resonated in her memory. There was an element of the story she recognized. Her eyes scanned the column of text, which told of women who had been taken into custody, then into Holloway Prison, on account of a disturbance in Regent's Park. The charge of sedition was suggested, and though Kezia held her breath, looking for Thea's name, she could not find it. But a woman named Avril had been one of those arrested, and Kezia remembered that Thea had a friend named Avril—a new, close friend, a friend she would have gone to Austria with, had it not been for the war. Avril was the friend who had usurped her in Thea's affections. She wondered whether Thea might be in trouble too.

Kezia felt dread wash across her skin as if it were a wave shimmying up a sandy beach, and wondered how she might find out more without annoying Thea, who seemed so prickly of late. Letters had gone unanswered; now, when Kezia thought of Thea, she saw in her mind's eye a person alone in her room, the curtains half closed as if she were intent upon shutting out all society. And she felt in her heart a yearning to go to her friend, to pull those curtains wide open, allowing sunshine and warmth to flood in. Perhaps Thea had wandered close to an abyss and needed to be helped back with a hand held out. But would she accept the proffered hand? Kezia shivered, folded the peelings into the newspaper, and put them by the back door. She returned to her cooking, and was struck by the idea that perhaps she would change things around, just to see what happened. Why would she cook baked apple for pudding when apple went very well with pork anyway? Why not combine the two and see how it might turn out? Immersing herself in the creation of a new dish, she felt relief as she moved away from thoughts of Thea and the dark chasm she saw in her mind's eye when she worried about her.

Kezia cut the pork into small pieces, frying them to a golden brown, then she added the meat to a bowl containing the filling of honeyed sultanas and chopped cob nuts she'd originally prepared for the apples. She mixed the sugary-savory blend then filled each of the cored apples, finishing the recipe by setting the tops on the apples. She covered the dish and placed it in the oven, closing the dampers a little to control the heat. There. Meat and sweet together, opposites blended, like her and Tom. She imagined him coming back, holding his head still, his nose raised a little as he tried to distinguish elements of the aroma. He would tell her how much he liked this new recipe. He would come up behind her and snuggle his nose into her neck. Then, later, she would tell him, *I must write to Thea. I miss her so.*

Thea sat in her room. Each day she returned to her job, and if it was Saturday or Sunday she remained in the room, sitting, waiting. Avril had been arrested. She knew that. The letter had been delivered the night before, the envelope plain, sealed and crossed with ink on the back so any disturbance could be identified.

Miss Dorothea Brissenden.
By Hand.

And then inside, on a small card, the informal message:

Thea, I do believe you should give up teaching. Trying to teach people does not suit women such as us, and I have discovered that it has had a very poor effect on me and what might come to pass. Leave it to others. I do not think I will be able to see you in the near future, so do not write or call. Best not.

Avril

At first Thea's head seemed to swim with confusion. Leave teaching? Then the truth dawned. This was a warning. They were coming for her. Her name had been discovered, and it was only a matter of time before Thea herself would be caught in the net. *Give up teaching.* Yes, give up teaching that peace is a better way than war, than bloodshed, than fighting.

She felt herself begin to shake, felt the welter of emotions she had to counter every time she joined a group to mount a demonstration—always different people, always the same out-come. The shouting, the swearing, the names and calling, then the running, the footsteps behind her, and then safety, some-where, anywhere—behind a wall, another building, always saved by her own inconsequential looks. Then the retching. Now the terror returned. It had begun to rise again when she read her brother's letter.

I plan to enlist as soon as all the harvesting is finished. The hop pickers have nearly all gone home now, so once I've left, Bert needs only to concern himself with getting everything done through the winter so we're ready for spring.

Thea struggled to her feet and stood before the mirror. She pulled out the pins in her hair, brushed it, and pinned it again, tidy. She put on her hat and jacket, and before leaving her lodgings, she drank a glass of cool water. Then she walked. She walked and walked. If she walked, if she was out and window-shopping on a Saturday morning, no one would think anything untoward. No one would look at her and say, *There she is, the suffragette!* They would not point and say, *Aha! The pacifist!* No one would accuse her of sedition, or of being a traitor. No, she would walk. Walk and not look. Walk and be seen to be a good woman, a nice woman, a woman who had no reason to be afraid.

And so Thea walked. She set one foot in front of the other without seeing, without looking at hoardings, without noticing shops closed, boarded, without noticing those around her, and without feeling as if people were simply going about their business when everything inside her was in turmoil.

"I say—Dorothy Brissenden! Dorrit!"

The voice seemed to boom along the pavement, bouncing off the shop window as Thea slowed to glance at her reflection, just to make sure she looked as ordinary as she was trying to feel. She turned back in the direction of the voice.

"I thought I would never catch up with you. Where are you going at that clip, anyway? Off to the races?"

At first Thea could not place the woman, though there was something in the voice, in the manner. *Camden.*

"Is that Hilary Dalton?" asked Thea.

"Yes, it's me, old Hilly. Must have changed a bit—I suppose we all have. After all, it's been almost ten years since we became old girls, isn't it?" Hilary Dalton leaned forward, concern etched into her wide cowlike eyes. "I say, you don't look well, Dorrit. Let's get a cup of tea inside you, and you can tell me everything."

Thea pulled her arm back so Hilary could not link through hers—she could not be sure, but it seemed that Hilary was the type to walk along the street arm in arm. At the same time she smiled, so as not to seem churlish. Hilary Dalton had been like Thea and Kezia—not quite like other pupils at Camden, though she was not a scholarship girl. She was taller than most, big-boned and athletic at school. She loved mathematics and physics and wanted to be an engineer, following in her father's footsteps—and she claimed she would, whether the world and her mother liked it or not. So she was an outsider, and on occasion joined Kezia and Thea at school, rubbing along with them when loneliness claimed her. Now she seemed so much more confident, her clothes of fine cut and quality, her movements assured. Yet there was still no frippery about her, though a few rough edges had been smoothed in the intervening years.

Hilary chose a tea shop nearby, insisting it be her treat. Over tea, she chatted about her life after Camden. "It was finishing school that did it—Mother insisted that if I was set on going into the family engineering firm, then I must go to Switzerland, so no choice. Then I went to university, and now I'm an engineer, though the men hate it." She paused. "Anyway, I told my father—last week, in fact—that it's about time I did something for this war. So I just went along and joined up."

Thea looked up. The tea had warmed her stomach, and she cut into the teacake, thinking she might keep it down. "Joined up with what?"

"A medical unit. They needed drivers. It's private, sponsored by a woman named Mary Rathbone—well heeled, sided with the suffragettes, though not to the extent that it embarrassed her husband. She decided there should be more women doing something for the war—blah, blah, blah—and I knew some-one already in to be my sponsor, which helped, and now I'm in too—start training on Monday. And there's a stipend, which helps, though we are considered part of the voluntary aid de-tachments. I shall be in France by Christmas, I would imagine."

"In France?"

"That's where the war is, or hadn't you noticed?"

Thea nodded. "I'm sorry, Hilary, I just wondered, that's all—you're the first woman I know personally to have enlisted for war work." She paused to sip her tea again. "Perhaps—"

Hilary tapped the table with her forefinger. "You know, Dorrit, I—"

"Please—don't call me that. It's Thea now. I am Thea, not a stupid name given to me by my Dickens-adoring father. Thea. Thea. Thea."

Hilary raised an eyebrow and sat back. "I thought you said 'Fear, Fear, Fear' for a minute!"

Despite herself, Thea smiled. "I'm sorry. I just got a bit tired of it, that's all."

"And I don't blame you. But you know, if you want to do a decent thing, you could join up with me. I could sponsor you—I'm on passing good terms with our fearless leader, you know. And I think they would snap you up. Any girl who has the stom-ach for a wild horse or the strength to drive a plough would be welcomed with open arms—and I know for a fact that you can do both, despite present appearances." Hilary pulled a note-book and pencil from her bag. "Look, buck yourself up and take some Beecham's, because you're clearly suffering from some-thing. Then on Monday, meet me at this address—could you be there by half past four? I will do the honors, introduce you to she-who-must-be-impressed when it comes to recruiting fresh blood—Daphne Richards. I'll tell her I can vouch for you, that we were at school together, etc., etc., then I'll leave you to it. How about it? I know I sound like a sergeant major already, but I really think we women need to step forward, and not just leave war to the men."

Thea hesitated, then took the small sheet of paper. Was this her salvation? She knew that Avril would be pressed to talk, would be deprived of food or fed too much, would be questioned until she gave up names, and Thea's was likely the only other name she knew. Thea was convinced that she was now on borrowed time, and she was scared. And she hated herself for her fear. Perhaps that's what she had said, after all—*Fear, Fear, Fear. My name is Fear.*

"Well, all right, Hilary. I can go along, can't I? They might not want me, but I can see someone. I'd feel better anyway, because my brother, Tom, is enlisting."

Hilary smiled and sat back in her chair. "He married Kezia Marchant, didn't he?"

"Yes, that's right," said Thea.

"Can't say that I could see her a farmer's wife. Interesting girl, wasn't she? Sort of passive until you realized that really she was quite a force in her way, and could be a bit stubborn too. But you two were thick with each other, weren't you? You must be very happy to have her in the family fold."

Thea nodded. "Yes, I suppose I am." She realized then that Kezia was family and, for the first time since receiving Tom's letter, wondered what the woman who had been her dearest friend might think when both she and Tom left for France. And as Hilary Dalton raised her hand to the waitress to call for more tea and cakes, Thea caught herself. *When.* She had thought *when.*

As she walked home, back to her room, which she had come

to think of as her lair, she thought she might not go on Monday after all. She had felt more than a little strong-armed by Hilary, who had always been a pushy character. She suspected Tom might have found himself in a similar position, pressed to enlist, except it would have been his own sense of duty that pushed him, not the pressure of another. She wondered why Kezia had not stopped him, had not put her foot down and demanded he stay.

Arriving at Queen Charlotte's Chambers, Thea was at once pounced upon by Mrs. Montague, who must have been lying in wait for her, twitching the curtains in her flat and watching the street to monitor her return. No sooner was Thea's key in the lock than she was on the threshold; Thea stumbled as the door opened with the warden's pull.

"There's been two men here looking for you, Miss Brissenden."

Thea felt the flush evaporate from her cheeks; she was now both hot and cold at the same time. "Looking for me? Do you know who they were?"

"Didn't say, but it looked like trouble, and if there's one thing I won't have here, it's trouble among my women."

"Oh, Mrs. Montague, I assure you, I have neither courted, caused, or been the source of any trouble—you know that very well. I go to my work, I continue my work in the evenings at my desk. I keep myself to myself, and I pay my rent on time."

"That's as may be, but they looked like trouble all the same. I'll have to ask you to be careful—I wouldn't want to see them again. Men aren't wanted here."

"I know that very well, Mrs. Montague, and I assure you, I do not know any men. I wonder if something untoward hasn't happened to my brother or sister-in-law. Did they say they would come back, or did they leave a message—a note?"

The woman shook her head. "No. They just said they would

return early next week, in case you were away until Monday. They know you're a schoolteacher—that much is evident."

Thea smiled and made to move on. "Well, it doesn't seem to be bad news, so I will just have to wait and see. Thank you, Mrs. Montague."

She was well aware that she had left the warden standing, her mouth shaped in a perfectly round O, such was her surprise at not having the last word in the matter. Thea unlocked the door to her room, let herself in, and turned the key behind her. She leaned her back against the door, and as the full weight of realization seeped into her body, her legs went out from under her and she slid to the ground. *They're coming for me. I'll be charged under the Defense of the Realm Act. I'll end up in Holloway.* She staggered over to the sink for fear that her stomach could not contain her anxiety on top of tea and cake.

She would see Hilary Dalton on Monday. She would put her best foot forward and persuade the "fearless leader" that she would stand tall before any foe, and could turn her hand to any task in support of the men of her country. She would do this because she knew she could not face a judge and jury. She would do it because she could endure the terror of a gun and the shell, but she could not see Kezia or Tom again if she were accused of being a traitor. And then she wept. She wept because she felt alone. She wept because she was powerless against the monsters of war and want. She felt trapped by her own passion. She wept because she was burning with a deep, searing pain, as if she had pierced her own heart with the knife of betrayal and was bleeding her failure to hold true. What irony—that the only way she could make amends with herself was to go to war.

CHAPTER 9

The housewife requires the qualities of a field-marshal. Instruction in selecting subordinates, tact in managing them, organizing of daily work, financial ability in handling the household budget, the taste that imparts charm to the home—these are not common facilities.

—THE WOMAN'S BOOK

As Ada was scouring egg from the knives, Kezia stood at the back door and looked down at the collies, both shaking in anticipation, their ears like folded envelopes. "He's gone, sweet boys," said Kezia. "He's gone to be in the army, but he'll be back. Don't you worry."

She knelt down and ruffled the scruff of each dog, then came to her feet again. "Let's go and find Bert, shall we?"

The sky was silvered with clouds hardly distinguishable from one another. It was late October, yet November's nip was already in the air as Kezia marched along the farm road, past the pigpens, past the oast house and then the orchards on the left and the new fields of turnips on the right, just beyond the old barn. There was no sign of Bert and Danny, or the four lads taken on to help settle the farm for the winter. There were fences to be mended, fields to turn, and cattle to be moved. Spent bines from hop picking were now piled along the empty rows of the hop gardens, left to brown and bracken, ready to be burned later when they'd dried, filling the air with that scent once again, but now filtered through smoke and flame that lent splashes of red to a day devoid of hue.

Kezia stopped at the top of the hill, where the road slipped down towards Dickens' two cities, and stood for a while. It seemed at once that the landscape had ceased to breathe against the cold, its color dull, as if she were looking through a window-pane with grey muslin drawn across. She inhaled deeply, trying to bring Tom back to her, now, in this place. And she realized that she must fight her fear of being alone, of having taken on more than she ever imagined she could accomplish as both mistress and master of the farm.

One of the collies barked, its head forward, nose to the wind. Bert and Danny were bringing sawn wood up to the farm, each driving a cart, Bert with Mabel's reins in his hands and Danny behind, working the more amenable Ted. Kezia waved. When Bert was alongside, he rested the leather on his knee.

"Mornin', Mrs. Brissenden." He touched his cap. "I've got them lads out in the hop gardens, cleaning up so we can let them sit till spring."

"I'll walk down and see them—I was making my way over there anyway, then up towards the railway line and back to the house." She paused, looking at her feet and at the mud sticking to her boots. She used the foot of one to dislodge mud from the other, holding on to the side of the cart to steady herself. "Look, Bert, I know you and Danny have brought your dinner, but I thought you might like something hot today. Would you like to come into the kitchen? I've got some soup on the stove."

Bert pushed back his cap. Mabel stamped her foot, ready to be off.

"Well, I don't know, Mrs. Brissenden. I mean, it's not like breakfast, is it? We've been at work since then, and we're both a bit ripe, if you know what I mean. And besides, we're used to taking dinner in the oast house. Just the two of us."

Kezia smiled. She did not want to press the point, and she wondered how the men felt, now Tom was gone. Did they pity her? Did they think she was lonely? More to the point, did they wonder if she could cope when the rudder was in swing against a tide freshened by storm?

"I don't mind, Bert. If you like, I can bring soup to the oast house—nice with your sandwiches."

Bert nodded. "Right you are. We'll be there at the usual dinnertime."

"Good. That's good, Bert. I'll bring the soup."

Kezia smiled and went on her way, bidding Danny good morning as she passed him. Ted seemed content enough to stand, showing none of Mabel's impatience.

When she had circumnavigated the farm and arrived back at the farmhouse, Kezia felt her spirits rise. There was no soup on the stove, and none had been prepared yesterday, so she set to work. She would imagine her soup was for Tom, and it would be a good soup, the best soup, a soup that had her imprint on it. Bert and Danny would talk about the soup, and it would become known that she, Kezia Brissenden—Mrs. Tom Brissenden—was a good farmer's wife.

Kezia chopped the vegetables, simmered the broth, plundered the larder for peas she'd dried in summer and beans that had been soaking since the day before. She went to her kitchen garden and searched among the tied-back and cut-down sprigs for thyme and rosemary, savory and parsley. And as she cut into each, she held them between finger and thumb to breathe in the aroma. She added curcumin bought in London, and some tiny peppery seeds found in a jar in the larder, seeds she could not identify because the label had fallen off ages ago. She thought the bittersweet flavor that settled upon her tongue when she bit into a single seed would add something to Tom's soup. And it wasn't until Ada came in from the front of the house, where she had scrubbed the doorstep—not that anyone ever came to the front door—and asked, "Was someone here, Mrs. Brissenden?" that Kezia realized she had been talking to Tom, telling him all about his soup as she moved vegetables to the pot, as she peppered and salted the broth, and as the beans and peas and lentils merged with carrot, onion, swede, parsnip, and celery root. And just because she liked the idea, she added a chopped pear brought from the cold shed next to the kitchen garden. This would be the very best soup Tom had ever tasted, and she would write to him as soon as it was on the simmer, as soon as she was ready to pour it into a small saucepan and take it to Bert and Danny. She would serve them soup in her china bowls, and give them white linen napkins to wipe across their chins when they ate so fast the liquid dribbled into their stubble.

Dearest Tom,

Marshals Farm misses you. The men miss you, Sloppy and Squeers miss you, and I miss you most of all. But we are all looking after the farm, so you must not concern yourself. We know you have enough to worry about without wondering if this or that has been done. It's all well in hand. We've still got Ted and Mabel, thanks be to the Lord. The men from the army came again last week, but they were both looking a bit tired (the horses, not the men), and Mabel was ready to knock a fly's eye out if anyone but Bert came near her. I think she misses you too. I told them I was a woman trying to run the

farm on my own, with only two men left and one of them
lame, and I told them we had already been under orders
to plough up a meadow and take down an orchard for
more growing, and asked how they thought we would
feed their army without our horses. I mentioned that
my father had enlisted as an army chaplain—not that
he's gone any farther than a London barracks, as far as I
know—and I would like to think the word of God settled
in their ears and kept Ted and Mabel with us. I don't
know what we would do without the horses.

Kezia read the letter, and shook her head. No, she could not
tell Tom of her concerns. It was unfair to tell him he was missed,
and she could not possibly worry him about the horses, about
the orchard to come down—she realized it had not been mentioned before, and would keep him awake at night. She decided
it would be best to write the letter in pencil as a draft, then edit
it before copying out her final version on writing paper. It took
her two hours.

Tom was hungry. His hunger gnawed at his backbone. Nev-
ertheless, he wondered if he could eat what was put in front of
him. He had never been among savages, but he thought jungle
tribes must be like men in a mess hall. Hundreds of men, hundreds of khaki ants, and big men, cooks—men cooks, mind—
men serving up food, not with spoons but with their bare, soiled
hands, hands that became cleaner as dirt adhered to the meat,
potatoes, and bit of bread they shoved onto the next plate. *Move*
along, move along, no slacking. A sergeant stood in attendance
to make sure the new recruits ate, to make sure they didn't
linger a moment where a moment could not be spared.

The line shuffled along, elbows into ribs, knee into the back of another knee, man moving man. Tom hated it, could hardly stand the lack of space around him. Dinner was supposed to be private, personal, just him and Kezia, together. And no one else. Her hands were clean, the tablecloths laundered and crisp. Flowers were on the table, and all for him. Now this. He felt as if something were being taken from him, that he was no longer Tom Brissenden but a private among many privates. Funny, that—now he was Private Thomas Brissenden, yet everything was far from private, or personal, or individual. It was one lumbering beast of man animal. An army.

"Come on, move along, lads. Get on, move your arses and get that food down yer! On the double!"

Some of the men laughed; others paled—in particular the younger lads, many not even with a bit of fluff around their chops—and looked sick. Food had always been cooked by a mother or a wife. And even if the lad had been in a family of six children and one pot of broth, and the army food looked better than at home, home and mother were still a long way past. Weeks, even.

"Scum, that's what it is. Look what they're feeding us." The speaker sat down next to Tom. It was a hut mate, Cecil Croft, who now pushed his food around on his plate. Croft had been a teacher before enlisting, a university man.

"I'd get on with it, mate, if I were you. That sergeant over there sees you playing with your food, you'll be on a charge," said Tom. He nodded towards his neighbor's tin plate. It held stew, potatoes, and a hefty slice of bread.

"It's not as if we're not getting the calories, is it?" said Croft. "It's what they do with the food to make them add up that makes me suspicious. I mean, it all looks the same. And brown bread."

"They say it's better for you."

"Try telling the other men that—look at them, ready to throw it back. There'll be a mutiny before we get to the boats, at this rate. White bread is cleaner, you know."

Tom shrugged and poked at his food.

"Not good enough for you, son?" The sergeant loomed over Tom.

"Just getting the gravy onto the meat," said Tom.

The sergeant leaned forward, the waxed end of his moustache tickling against Tom's ear like an errant fly on a summer's day. "Stand to attention, Private Gravy, now!"

Tom set down his knife and fork and scraped back his chair.

"Do it again, and this time do it faster, Private."

Tom sat down, his behind barely touching the chair before he stood up once more. The noisy clattering of knives and forks had diminished, though few had stopped eating.

"Just getting the gravy onto the meat, what?"

"Just getting the gravy onto the meat, *sir*!" said Tom, his eyes to the front.

"Just getting the gravy onto the meat. Looked to me like you were playing with your food, Private."

"No, sir."

"No, sir. No, sir. Well, you've no time to get your gravy now, or your spuds, or your meat." He turned his attention to the other men gathered, who were looking back and forth as if watching a tennis match. "Atten-shun!"

Men scrambled to their feet, standing with straight backs, facing forward.

"Private Brissenden here was poking round his gravy looking for a bit of meat. Was anyone else having trouble finding their meat?"

There was a low mumble.

"Did anyone else have trouble finding their meat?"

"No, sir!" the soldiers answered in unison.

"Well, now you'll all have a chance to show Private Brissenden how to find his bit of meat, because it's down to him that I want you all on the parade ground. Now!"

There was a stamping of feet to attention, and a turning around as one when the men marched from the mess hall. Tom remained at attention, only marching when the cohort at his table began to move.

"Not you, Private Gravy. The cook wants his floor scrubbed. The cook wants no filth in his kitchen, nothing to taint the rations." The sergeant looked at Tom, who continued to look ahead. He pressed his face close to Tom's and shouted a command. "About turn!"

Tom turned in the direction of the kitchen.

"Quick march!"

It was later, in the hut, that Cecil Croft came alongside Tom's bed. "It's all part of the game, Tom. Like surnames only, like the mass of men eating like pigs—men who have never had a good meal sitting next to men who've had better than you or I—it's all done to make us into an army."

Tom nodded. He went on polishing his boots, cleaning his webbing.

"Putting the mass of men against one is all part of the play. I've seen it before, at school," added Cecil.

"I never went to a school like that." Tom didn't look up.

Cecil put his hand on Tom's shoulder. "I did, Tom. I don't think I ever heard my Christian name between the ages of six and sixteen. Croft this and Croft that—even my father called me Croft or Boy."

"Then how come you're different now?" Tom turned round, for the first time facing Cecil Croft.

"Because I wasn't like any of them, Tom. That's why I won't

call you Brissenden and you won't call me Croft, because we'll do our level best for our country, and we'll play their game, but that's all they'll have of us." And Cecil Croft looked at Tom for one more second before turning around and stepping along the line of beds to his own, where he slumped down and began writing in a notebook.

Tom finished the polishing, finished the spitting and the blacking and buffing, and in turn lay back on his bed. He pulled an envelope from under his pillow and took out a letter from Kezia.

My Dear Tom,

Let me tell you about the tea I cooked for you today. I am sure you will love it, but please let me know if there's anything you think I could do to flavor it more to your taste.

Bert brought a rabbit to the door yesterday. Thank goodness Ada skinned and quartered it for me. I thought a hot pot would be a good idea, so I fried up the rabbit parts and put in a whole onion, chopped. But here's what I thought to add—some sultanas. They come out big and juicy when they're cooked and add a sweetness to the rabbit, so it's like a little bit of summer in France added to winter in England. When this war is done, you can tell me all about France, can't you? I daresay you'll be home by spring in any case.

Now, back to your tea! Next I put in some chopped parsnip and carrot, and let the whole thing heat up together with a good knob of best butter. Can you smell it? The kitchen is still full of it, and the dogs are pawing at the back door. I poured everything into the big brown dish with a little sherry (I won't have a glass at

*Christmas unless you're here too), and made a stock, and
then before I put the lid on, I did two things—I added
some rosemary from the kitchen garden, and then I rolled
out some bread dough into a long sausage-shaped rope,
and sealed the lid with it. That way, when the casserole
cooked through, the dough became a lovely bread to dip
into the gravy. I dished up some for Bert and Danny
and took it to the oast house for them, and they said that
if the army had this, well, the Germans would be sent
running by our boys and you would be out at the front,
leading them. Though I say so myself, it cooked up a treat.
Close your eyes, dearest Tom, and tell me what you think
of the casserole. It was made for you, only for you, really.*

Tom read the letter twice and felt a soporific wave wash
over him. What was it Kezia's father had called it, once, when
they'd gone for a Sunday visit and sat down to dinner—what
the Marchants called "luncheon"—and when everyone felt tired
after the roast chicken and roast potatoes and vegetables and
gravy? Postprandial torpor. *Torpor.* He'd meant to look up the
word, but forgot. Now he felt tired, weary, but in truth he knew
it was for want of a meal he felt like eating. Perhaps that would
change soon. Perhaps if he just imagined the army's pungent
meat and mashed potatoes to be like something Kezia would
cook, it would go down a bit easier.

Tom took a small sheaf of paper and some envelopes from
the chest next to his bed.

Dearest Kezia,

*The casserole was lip-smacking. My mother never called
anything a casserole, so I wonder if that's French, or*

*something foreign like that. The rabbit was cooked right
and tender, and it made my mouth water, the way the
flesh fell off the bone. The gravy—*

He stalled at *gravy*. Private Gravy, now a washer of floors
and a recipient of name-calling.

*The gravy was different from anything I've ever tasted
or that you've cooked before. I think you should
have gone a bit easy with the rosemary though, love,
because you know a little goes a long way as far as I'm
concerned. And perhaps a few less sultanas, though
I liked the flavor. Did you sneak in a bit of honey? I
could have sworn I tasted honey in there—mind you,
parsnips can bring that sort of sweetness, can't they?
The bread was good and yeasty, and the way the gravy
dripped off it, I thought I would hardly lift it to my
mouth before it ran down my chin. I bet Bert couldn't
wait to get that down him, but I reckon Danny poked
at it a bit before he had a taste. Now then, don't you go
giving the dogs anything from the table that you could
eat yourself. I don't want them getting fat and you
getting thin.*

*You didn't say much about the farm, but I was glad to
hear that Ted and Mabel are still working for us. I can't
see them apart, and not everyone can get a firm hand on
Mabel—even I haven't got Bert's way with her. If they
took her, they'd have to take Bert as well, and I can't see
him in Kitchener's Army.*

*Sid Rawlings, who comes from a farm the other side
of Frittenden, said he heard from his missus that the
Ministry are going to order woods and orchards to be*

ploughed in. Have you heard anything about it? Has anyone been around?

It's going all right here. The other lads in my hut are a good lot. They're feeding us well, so you'll be happy to know I'm full to bursting—and with your cooking, how could I want for anything? I'm looking forward to the next dinner you set before me, I feel like a king sitting down at his royal table.

Have you heard from Dorrit?

Thea arrived at the station on the early train. There was a small fireplace in the carriage, between two facing rows of seats, and in this emptiness, with only the almost-spent coals for company, Thea felt in two minds regarding her decision to come to the farm before she was posted to France. It was Kezia's letter that persuaded her.

The door opened, and a guard, feeling his balance as the train moved from side to side, came into the carriage, bearing a coal scuttle.

"Make up the fire for you, miss? It might be a sunny morning, but it's still November, and they say it'll be a hard winter, 'specially after that summer we had."

Thea moved her legs to one side, allowing the guard to poke at the embers and add more nuggets of coal. She wondered why he had not enlisted—not that she would ask, for she had seen men harassed on the street; men who were lame, or who had been wounded already, or whose disability was not visible to the women who questioned their loyalty. It was always women who asked. Brazen and volatile, they demanded to know why that young man had not stepped forward to be counted among those who would lay down a life for their country. Thea closed her eyes. She had seen how her country had treated the poorest souls, and how they had been the first to press their sons into the army.

"Sorry about that," said the guard, noticing Thea's closed eyes as he drew back. "The fumes don't half knock you back when the flame hits that coal. Goes right into your chest, it does." He waited for the fire to take again, his legs braced as the train slowed coming into Sevenoaks. "That's why I'm here and not over there, you know." He thumped his chest with a closed fist and coughed for good measure. "I went up to the board, but the doc took one listen to my chest and shook his head. Said it was a wonder I could breathe at all. I told him about the pleurisy when I was a nipper, and he said my lungs were scarred, he could hear it, and he couldn't pass me fit. Not that doing all this shoveling of coal makes me any fitter—but it's a job, and it was my father's job before me."

"Perhaps there's something else you could do for your country."

"I reckon I'll get over there eventually. The way our boys are coming back half dead." He looked at Thea and leaned towards her. He reminded her of a woman, a gossip about to tell a secret she was bound to keep. "I've seen them, you know. At night. They bring them in on trains when there's no one to see them—men with no faces, with no legs, and all the blood on their uniforms—they don't even have time to change them, all that French mud still on them. But I'm not supposed to know, see."

Thea nodded, feeling the locomotive pull as the driver applied the brakes. She closed her eyes and was thankful. She had nothing to say to the guard. She had heard the story already.

"I didn't want to say anything, but I've not seen many women in uniform. Not like that anyway. What're you doing, then?" asked the guard.

"I'm with a medical unit."

The guard laughed. "Oh, rolling bandages and making cups of tea for the doctors, eh?"

Thea shook her head, felt her temper blacken. "Not quite, young man—" She could hear the sharpness of her words, the knife nicking his skin. "I am a driver and a mechanic. I leave for France soon, probably in the next few weeks. I'll be bringing our wounded from the battlefield, to safety." She smiled. "And just in case, I've learned how to take apart a motor engine and put it all back together again, which will come in useful when the war's over, I shouldn't wonder."

Passengers pushed past, hurrying through the carriage to step off onto the platform, though few joined the train. The guard touched his cap and turned away, caught in the press of bodies making their way towards the doors. Thea looked at her hands, clasped together on her lap. She had soured herself again; she had turned the knife and felt empty for it, and she felt tears prick the corners of her eyes. It wouldn't have taken much to just agree with the man. After all, how was he to know?

Kezia was waiting in the gig outside the station. She was wearing a familiar tweed jacket, one treasured as best several years ago, and a muffler was drawn around her neck against a sharp wind that made the clear November sky shimmer like cut glass. For a second Thea thought Kezia and the mare resembled trains waiting at the station, their breath visible in rhythmic blasts as it condensed in the chill air.

"Thea!" Kezia waved and leaned to kiss Thea on the cheek as she clambered into the gig, throwing her kit-bag into the well behind the driver's seat.

"You look the part, Thea—just look at you in your uniform! I hope you're hungry, because we've been busy, Ada and me, making sure you'll want for nothing before you go off."

"Oh, you shouldn't have—I've a modest appetite these days," said Thea.

"Not when you sample some of my cherry and leek soup, you won't."

"What?"

"It's a treat, I promise you."

They talked of the farm as Mrs. Joe stepped out, her gait light with forelegs high and footfall firm. It was when they arrived and Ada came to the back door, wiping her hands on a cloth, that Thea held her surprise in check, for as Kezia drew back the blanket that had protected them from the cold and stood up to jump down from the gig, it was Tom's woolen trousers she was wearing, tucked into sturdy working boots.

"Where's Danny, to unhitch the gig?" asked Thea.

Kezia laughed. "Can't spare him to look out for me, Thea— Danny's in the old orchard with Ted. We're doing the Ministry's bidding now, you know—well, to a point—and it's a shame the Ministry doesn't pay as well as the market. Now then, you go in and Ada will get you a nice cup of tea. I've to go down to Pickwick to have a word with Bert. Or do you want to come with me?"

Thea shook her head and turned to Ada, who nodded at Kezia in a conspiratorial manner, and Thea wondered what had been said, and perhaps Ada had been told that Thea hadn't been herself, what with all the suffrage business, and now this volunteering. Together they watched Kezia step up into the gig once more and set off in the direction of the hill, which in turn would lead down to Micawber Wood and Pickwick field. Thea wondered who this Kezia was, and felt the loss of something she had grasped in her hand, as if it were fine sand sifting through a tight fist. She had thought she was leaving Kezia behind, that her friend was ceasing to be important, somehow, here on the farm. But instead, it was as if something of Tom had settled inside her friend and sister. The farm was becoming hers.

Ada held the door open into the kitchen. "Come in and sit by the fire, Miss Thea. Mrs. Brissenden made a lovely cake, you know, though we're short on a few things now, but she did it all the same. It's got pears and lavender in it—lavender, who would have thought it? But I tell you, she has a knack with things you wouldn't wonder to put in a bowl together."

Ada chatted on, and Thea let her ramble about the farm, about the wind and how the fire wouldn't draw some mornings, or there was a downdraft and the kitchen would be filled with smoke. And she said there would be plenty of water in the copper, so if Miss Thea liked, she would draw off some into the tin bath and leave her in peace in the kitchen, because it couldn't be comfortable for a woman, being in a uniform like that, all itchy. And Thea listened, nodding, agreeing, and then she said she'd go up to her room because she needed the familiarity, though it wasn't familiar, because someone—Kezia, she knew—had filled a vase with small branches of autumn leaves, with cascades of November berries and chrysanthemums taken from her garden—no one had ever grown chrysanths there before, but Kezia had written to tell her that it was important to grow certain flowers amid the vegetables in the kitchen garden, as they kept pests at bay. When had Kezia learned this? When had she become mistress of the farm, as opposed to the farmer's wife?

Thea took off her leather belt and unbuttoned her woolen jacket, removing one item of uniform after another. She pulled at her leather boots and stood in front of the long beveled mirror—when had there been a mirror in her bedroom? Her mother had always said a mirror was a woman's distraction, that a wife with a mirror would pay more attention to her face than the mind of her husband, and it was the mind of the man of the house that counted. Now she looked at herself in her regulation undergarments and her regulation hat. She felt comfortable in the uniform. She remembered her uniform at Camden, how it protected her, how she felt safe in the blue serge skirt, with its regulation—always that word, *regulation*—six gore, two inches above the ankle. Two inches, no less, no more. There was the high-collared white blouse, worn with a blue ribbon at the neck, to be secured with a navy blue pin embossed with the name of the school. It was as if the word was placed under the chin to make girls hold their heads high because they were pupils of Camden. But she believed that wearing the uniform had allowed her character to form—there was no competition in dress, no obvious distinction between the scholarship girls and those of wealthy parentage. It was down to who you were to make something of yourself. And of course Kezia had worn the very same uniform, though the skirt seemed to have more swing on the taller girl when she strode out along the corridor. Thea wondered if anyone else noticed that Kezia could cover a fair amount of ground in a short time—if she chose to do so, and not linger.

She glanced out of the window, then, and watched as Kezia walked out of the barn, along the farm road towards the house. Her sleeves—Tom's sleeves—were rolled up, and she carried her tweed jacket on a finger over her shoulder, as if the wind no longer mattered. She was striding now, the collies at heel. It occurred to Thea that in her campaign for suffrage, when she had been asking for an enfranchisement she believed in, she sometimes felt as if the request had become a deep black bellow of a yell. She had worn her green sash of hope against a white blouse, and she had run from the authorities to the point where she could not keep her food down. Now Kezia was marching towards the house, marching back to the kitchen. It was as if she were queen, and this her domain. She had assumed her position, not asked for permission.

Thea removed her underclothes and pulled on her old dressing gown, freshly laundered and laid across the bed ready for her. Stepping out onto the landing, she could hear Kezia laughing with Ada downstairs. It was a comfortable laughter, a laughter of inclusion, of belonging, and she could not wait to be in the kitchen, enveloped by Kezia's warmth and Ada's caring. As she lowered her head to avoid the beam above the door to the kitchen, Thea thought it would be sensible to consider the future, to talk about it with Kezia, because the future was bound to be different. She smiled, making up her mind to say something over dinner later—over whatever Kezia was dishing up for them. But as she walked into the kitchen and saw Kezia look up while filling the tin bath for her, she checked herself, realizing that she felt as she had with the young guard on the train. Some rogue element in her character compelled her to show off her strength, to avoid feeling less than worthy—though afterwards she felt the worse for it. A childhood memory surfaced—the day she stepped on a bright May beetle she'd seen crawling across the kitchen floor. The act was quite deliberate. She'd felt a deep regret at her action. But to open the window, to use her hand to steer it towards freedom, would have meant giving in to the softer part of herself.

CHAPTER 10

It was after supper, after the plates had been washed and the fire banked for the night, after the collies had settled on a blanket in front of the stove—a privilege never allowed by Tom, who would have said mollycoddling would soften a working dog's heart—and after two bricks heated in coals had been wrapped in towels, one placed between the sheets of each bed, that Kezia and Thea made their way upstairs, carrying oil lamps to light the way. On the landing Kezia turned towards Thea and kissed her on the cheek.

Thea felt herself lean into the kiss as if she were a child, and though she drew back from articulating the feeling in her heart—she would not even say the words to herself, silently, in her mind—she felt a mothering warmth as Kezia's lips brushed against her skin, and as her hand rested on her shoulder. Thea looked down, drawing herself back from the inner realization that perhaps Kezia had always mothered in her way. As her dearest and perhaps only friend, Kezia might have intuited that the former Mrs. Brissenden felt little affection for her children, but could be swollen with pride when it came to Tom's accomplishments. Yes, she put food on the table, clothed her offspring, and set them off on life's road, but she was a farmer's wife, and it was her husband, her son, and the farm that took the milk of her love.

"It's a cold night, Thea—bring your brick and come into my bed. I've put an extra blanket on, so it'll be just like Camden. We can pretend we're still girls, can't we?" Kezia smiled, resting her hand on the door handle.

Thea hesitated, but was persuaded by the chill air. "All right. I don't want to remember those cold dormitories, though."

"Or the anthracite stove at the end of the room—threw out no heat, but filled the air with fumes."

Thea laughed. "I'll just get into my nightclothes."

Kezia could not have bundled herself more thoroughly. She wore a flannel nightdress with Tom's thick woolen dressing gown wrapped around her, and heavy socks pulled up above her ankles. Thea clambered in beside her, similarly mummified.

"Grief! Who would have thought it could be this cold—and the day was so bright."

"There was no cloud to keep the land swaddled, that's why we're all feeling it."

"Spoken like a true farmer's wife." Thea elbowed Kezia, who elbowed back.

They giggled, heads together. And in this proximity, it was as if they were retracing their way along time's byway, down the years and back to Camden; back to a time before they went on to college, even before matriculation—to a moment before their paths diverged.

The giggles had subsided, and they were quieted in the room, sheltered by gentle lamplight. The walls felt closer, the nighttime quiet, comforting.

"Thea."

"Yes?"

"What made you volunteer? You've never liked anyone telling you what to do, have you? And you love your London life—you worked hard for your little slice of independence, Thea. You even changed your name. And now you're set to go to France. I just don't understand."

Thea's body tensed.

"I'm going, Kezia, and I can't change my mind now, you know."

Kezia sat up, staring into Thea's eyes. "I'm not interested in trying to change your mind. You've made your choice. I just want to know why." She folded her arms into the copious sleeves of Tom's dressing gown.

Thea was silent, then spoke, parsing her reply with care. "It just seemed to come up while I was thinking about looking for another position. I met an old friend—you remember her, Hilary Dalton—she'd joined a medical unit as a driver, and she took me along."

"Oh, so you were swept away."

Thea shook her head but moved closer to Kezia, who leaned back against the pillow. "Not really, Kez. I wasn't so much swept away as I caught the tide. I wanted to be in something. I wanted to belong, and . . ."

"Belong to what?" Kezia pressed.

"Well, I belonged to other things, societies and so on, because I wanted to do something worthwhile—it doesn't really matter what they were. But when war came, none of that made me feel as if I'd been doing something really, well, important for our boys. I wanted to play a part."

Thea was aware of Kezia, nodding her understanding. She remembered a certain look, from the very early days of their friendship. Kezia would often take her time with a question, ruminating over it in her mind, chewing on it like a cow with a clump of grass, grinding it down from side to side to get the goodness—only with Kezia, it was as if she were looking for something in the middle of the problem. The truth, perhaps. Thea had attributed it to having a vicar for a father, for surely life in the parsonage meant that you thought about everything more than anyone else, because God had his eye on you all the time.

Thea turned onto her side and looked at Kezia, at her long hair braided for bed, at the collar of Tom's dressing gown pulled up around her neck, and at the shallow wisps of her visible breath, turning into little puffs, like sheep's wool caught on a hawthorn hedge.

"Do you think everything will be all right, Kezzie?" said Thea.

"Yes, I do. It'll be over soon, just like they say it will. Look at you—you'll go out there and be back in five minutes. And Tom will come home, I'm making sure of that."

"What do you mean?"

Kezia's eyes met Thea's. "I'm tempting him with my cooking—he'll come back for that, just you see."

And then, in their burst of laughter, Thea felt joined to Kezia in the way that childhood friends are connected. As girls they had wanted to be mistaken for twins, because the error would simply add another layer of glue to their sisterhood.

Kezia reached out towards the lamp and turned down the wick, then burrowed under the covers once more.

"Thea."

"Yes?"

"When do you leave for France?"

"Up to London on Thursday, then more training, and as soon as that's done, I'll be on a boat from Folkestone, I would imagine. It might even be before Christmas, or soon afterwards."

Kezia drew breath to speak, then paused.

"What?" said Thea.

"Well, when you said you belonged to other things, you weren't talking about social clubs, were you?" Kezia waited for a response. Thea said nothing, so she continued. "I mean, was it something dangerous? Were you in some sort of trouble, Thea? Is that why you volunteered—to go away?"

"Of course I'm not in any trouble. What gave you that idea?" Thea felt the tone of her voice rise.

"It was nothing, really. I mean—well, I'd read about an Avril someone or other being arrested at a pacifists' rally, and I remembered, at Buckingham Palace . . . and I know you've a friend—a good friend, I think—called Avril."

Thea laughed. It was a forced laugh, and she knew Kezia would recognize it for what it was, a prelude to the bending of truth. "Avril? I haven't seen her for ages. Not since she decided she didn't want to go on an Alpine walking tour. I have no idea what she's doing, actually. No idea at all."

"I suppose there are quite a few Avrils."

"It's not an uncommon name."

The women were silent for several more minutes, until Kezia spoke again.

"Thea, are you scared?"

"I'll be safe—don't you worry."

"I'm not worried. Of course you'll be safe. But are you scared, Thea?"

"No more than you are, when you have to unhitch Mabel."

Kezia chuckled. "As God's my witness, there never was a more contrary mare, truly there wasn't."

More laughter, then they reached towards each other to embrace.

"Night, Thea."

"Good night."

And in the darkness, each felt the other shiver, and as they continued to hold hands, they understood that it wasn't the cold air, or the cooling bricks, for now they were warm beneath the bedclothes.

Edmund Hawkes sat at his desk in a tent, one tent in an encampment of tents. He was safe, for now, unless shelling reached this place, a farm chosen for its seclusion behind the lines. Seclusion was, of course, a relative concept, for the trees—those still standing—were bare of all foliage, and there were orders to go up the line again in forty-eight hours. Another push. Push and shove, thought Hawkes. Push here, shoved back, push forwards, shoved sideways—shove them, and we're pushed. And in the middle of all that pushing and shoving, men—his men— would lie dead. Men that lay buried, now, in hasty graves; bodies wrapped in ground sheets and set in the cold, wet earth. Only the words of a soldier's prayer to see them on their way, so far from home and love.

"Sir!"

Hawkes looked up. A month ago he might have felt inept, inadequate, and ill prepared when facing a sergeant with years in uniform, but now all care had left him.

"Sergeant Knowles. Good. At ease, Knowles."

"Sir!" Knowles eyed Edmund Hawkes and saw a man beyond intimidation.

"Right. How are your raw recruits to the game?" Edmund Hawkes looked directly at Knowles.

Knowles appeared to bristle when he heard the word *game*. Hawkes understood that Knowles was an army man through and through, and that he had only so much time to knock his lads into shape, to knead them into a fighting corps, a body willing and able to take a man's life, and to die. Recruits should have had a year of training, but for some it had been whittled down to not much more than a month. It was no game to Knowles. And Hawkes knew that Knowles considered him just one more new officer, raw and disillusioned—another enlisted man to be trained up enough to save his own life.

"All present and correct, and ready for the Hun, sir."

"Well, that is good news." Hawkes ran a finger down the list. "I know some of these men—come from the same village. I—"

"Sir?"

"This chap—Brissenden. How's he shaping up?"

"Not one of the best, sir."

"I'm surprised. He's a farmer, a good worker. He didn't have to enlist, he's got a farm to run."

"Sir." Knowles made no other comment.

"What's the problem?"

"Couple of incidents, sir. Troublemaker, I would say. Didn't like the food, sir."

"I don't think any of us like the food, Knowles."

"Didn't keep it to himself, sir. Gets the men going, comments about the ration."

"Well, we'll see how he gets on here. Not that we'll all be here for long. Anything else?" Hawkes looked up when there was no immediate response. "Sergeant Knowles? Anything else?"

"Private Brissenden. Personal letters—very odd, sir. Not good for morale, I would say."

Hawkes felt a wave of fatigue flood his body. He wanted nothing more than a hot bath, a soft bed, and a good meal. "Describe how the letters are 'odd,' if you wouldn't mind."

"Well, he reads them out—the men ask him to. But it makes them dissatisfied, to my mind. And that sort of thing can cause trouble."

"Keep an eye on it, then." Hawkes sighed. "Frankly, I can't see how a personal letter can change matters here, but I will bow to your better judgment. Now then, I will inspect the men in precisely one hour. Tent inspection."

The sergeant saluted. "Sir!"

Knowles smiled as he emerged from his officer's tent. He didn't like Edmund Hawkes, but he had sown the seed. There was always one, ever since he'd joined up himself, over twenty years ago. He'd seen his sergeant find the one, and he knew it was the way to keep the men together. Separate the one, and make him the enemy inside—made all the difference when they went after the enemy outside. Private Gravy was his one—not a complainer, but not a man to let anyone trample over him either. The perfect one. Push him too far, and he would push back. Make sure the men bear the brunt of it. Yes, he knew how to run a bloody army—and he knew how to get the Captain Edmund Hawkeses of this war where he wanted them. Bloody toff wouldn't last long anyway—it was a wonder he was still here now, the way they were going down like flies. Still wet behind the ears, most of them, though this one was older, looked wiser. As if that would help the poor bastard.

Tom sat on his camp bed and checked his khaki tunic—buttons gleaming—then his webbing and boots, to which plenty of spit and polish had been applied. He had pulled a soft cloth on a string through the barrel of his Lee Enfield rifle so many times

that not one speck of dust lingered to delay the passage of ammunition. Every part of his weapon would shine where it was
supposed to shine in the low winter sun. He checked his AB64
pay book, tucked into his breast pocket, and made sure that the
First Field Dressing was in its place. Now all he needed was a
helmet. Now what any of them needed was a helmet. Helmets
were in short supply—like proper uniforms, which had only
been distributed before they set sail for France. Tom counted
everything in his pack, and checked again. He knew Knowles
would be after him, so he had to be ready. There would be nothing, *nothing*, in Tom's kit or about his person that the sergeant
could identify as wrong, out of place, or not up to snuff. He
knew full well that he was the sergeant's choice for singling out,
for humiliation. He would give him no excuse.

A bugle announced inspection. Cecil Croft was the neighbor to his right, so they gave each other's bed and uniform the
once-over, just to make sure. Then they stood by the ends of
their beds. Knowles and the officer would come in, walk up and
down, and when the inspection was finished, the men would
be quick-marched to the parade ground. Such as it was. A
field flattened and rolled by the sappers. A field that would be
pounded to such a degree that mud would form only after the
most plentiful rain.

Knowles entered the tent and stopped at each bed. He lingered when he came to Tom. He dropped a ha'penny on the
blanket to check the coin's bounce, a sign that the covers were
drawn tight across what passed for a mattress. He took Tom's
rifle and peered down the barrel, and with a flourish he used a
magnifying glass—a glass not used with any other soldier—to
study the buttons on his tunic. His boots were scrutinized, and
he asked Tom to open his pockets. Pay book, field dressing. All
present and correct.

"Private Gravy." Knowles' mouth was so close to Tom's face that he swore he could smell yesterday evening's coffee and this morning's tea rolled into the sergeant's night breath.

"Yes, sir!"

"A good show, Private Gravy. Keep it up. Keep it up every single day. Every single day, Private Gravy."

"Sir!"

"Good morning." Given the attention focused on Sergeant Knowles and Private Tom Brissenden, the voice at first sounded disembodied, before the men realized their commanding officer was present. The greeting came from the tent opening, where Captain Edmund Hawkes stood with another soldier at his side—his batman, Pullings.

The soldiers' feet thumped to attention on the rough boards beneath them.

"At ease, men." Edmund Hawkes looked down the row of men, each standing at the end of his camp bed. His eyes stopped moving when he came to Tom Brissenden, and then he turned to his sergeant and nodded.

"Brissenden," said Hawkes, as he approached Tom.

"Sir!" said Tom, standing to attention, his salute firm.

Hawkes smiled. "At ease, Private." He paused. "You've left a good deal of work on the farm, Brissenden—winter coming and then the spring sowing. And I've no doubt there's been men down from the ministry to tell you to plough in the orchards."

Tom glanced directly at Hawkes, but was brought up short by Knowles.

"Eyes front!"

"That's all right, Sergeant Knowles," said Hawkes.

"I've a couple of good workers, sir, and the boys in the village will like to earn a penny or two for piecework—the older lads have enlisted though. We're not ploughing in the orchards—the russets have always done well for us." Tom's voice was modulated.

"Very well," said Hawkes. "Good man for enlisting to serve your country. You had no need." Hawkes turned, his eyes once more taking in each man standing. "None of you had need to enlist, but you came forward to the call of your country. Now your country asks you to march on to defeat the enemy—and each and every one of you will set forth on that march with a full heart, knowing the gratitude of the British people is at your back." He looked at Knowles and nodded.

"Attennnn-shun!" ordered Knowles.

The men snapped their backs even straighter and thumped their heels together. Hawkes nodded, and left the tent, Knowles following in his wake.

The men stood to attention for another second or two, then looked at each other.

"Aren't we supposed to wait for the at-ease?" said one soldier.

"He probably forgot," said another.

"He didn't bleedin' forget anything. Attennnn-shun!" The tent flap was open again, and Knowles stepped in. The men stood at the end of their beds. "Well, that was all very nice, to be congratulated for turning up to fight for your country. There's plenty dead and gone that did the same a lot sooner than you lot, and you're going up after them. If you want to come back, you'd better toe the line." He stepped towards Tom, a sneer on his face. "Even you, Private Gravy." He turned to the men. "Otherwise, the man at your back will be me, and you don't want that. I promise, you don't want that." Knowles paused. "Right then, my little nancy boys, after a turn on the parade ground, you'll be cooking your own breakfast this morning, giving them *you-ten-sils* in your kit a bit of a go, so you don't starve up the line when the cookhouse goes up because a shell has just hit it, and the only meat coming your way is a bit of the horse that just pulled your dinner along the road in the first place." Knowles continued to give instructions, but Tom was only half listening. Kezia had told him she'd managed to persuade the army men who'd come to take the horses that their plough horses weren't up to the job. Apparently Mabel had gone for one of them, then turned and kicked out, while Ted snapped away and took off at the first sign of her temper, so the men shook their heads and went to another farm. He smiled, imagining the scene.

"Oh, so now Private Gravy is finding something funny. Tell us what you were thinking about that was funny, while your compatriots"— he pronounced the word like a child in school, getting his mouth around each syllable, *come-pate-rye-ots*— "get shelled into little pieces."

"Nothing, sir."

"Nothing, sir. Nothing, *sir*! Well, for the trouble of your finding all this very funny"—he turned to the men—"all this serious business of soldiering, funny"—he looked back at Tom—"you, Private Gravy, will be on latrine duty today—because I for one have had enough of your S-H-one-T." He paused, smirking. "Now then, at the double."

Dear Kezia,

I hope all is well on the farm. I was very glad to hear that you still have Mabel and Ted, though I am surprised the army walked away from them. Perhaps Mabel really did put them off, because believe me, you don't want trouble out here. Mind, she is a sturdy girl, and we need her on the farm. I saw Hawkes today. Captain, he is. He asked about the orchards, whether the farm still had the apples, because the ministry had been giving instructions to plough them in for other crops to be planted. You never said, so I told him we still had our russets.

Your last dinner was very nice indeed, and I felt a bit of a pig after eating so much. But my love, how could I refuse your cooking? That roast lamb fair made my mouth water. I've had a bit of mint sauce with lamb, but never had it cooked into the lamb, and with blackcurrants. You did a good amount of bottling in the summer. Makes all the difference to winter, having a bit of the taste of the harvest in the food. I don't know anyone who would have roasted lamb with mint and blackcurrants though. And that mashed potato. I've never had it that way before either, squeezed through an icing bag into little hills on the tray, then put into the oven to crisp up the top. Looked like browned model mountains on the plate. You do overdo the sherry in the gravy, you know—we won't have enough for Christmas at the rate you're going.

We did a bit of cooking ourselves today. The recipe would make you laugh—straight from this little book we've each been given, on billeting and cooking. Before I enlisted, I never thought you could get a book on how to go off to war, but the army gave us all one. We had to set up a camp according to the book, and then cook ourselves a dinner. It was not one speck on your dinner.

Sitting at the kitchen table on a frozen December afternoon, Kezia folded the letter and placed it in the envelope. She was grateful Bert and Danny had brought their own dinners, because food was becoming scarce, even for a farmer's wife.

They were down to just eggs for the morning's breakfast, and you had to stand in a queue at the butcher's for a bit of bacon. They said all the food was going to the army, and there wasn't enough coming in by ship anymore, from across the Empire or America, on account of the U-boats, though it was predicted it wouldn't last long, unless Germany built more of the underwater vessels.

She dipped one slice of bread into a bowl of broth made from the last chicken she'd cooked, to which she'd added an onion. The meat off that chicken had lasted her a good five days before she'd rendered down the bones to make the broth. As she took each sip of the warm onion-infused broth, she wondered what she would write to Tom about next. It would be another story about a dish she'd cooked for him. She closed her eyes and let the broth linger on her tongue. No, it wouldn't be turkey—but pheasant. Pheasant that had been hung for a good while to let it ripen. Pheasant with . . . pheasant with . . . oranges. Yes, she would lay small cartwheels of cut orange, complete with the skin, across the chest of the pheasant—she would make up a story about getting one somewhere, even if it were only a Seville orange, sold for marmalade. And she would fill the bird's cavity with herbs. What herbs? Sage and thyme and then some of those tiny onions you couldn't get anymore, only in her recipe—her special recipe for Tom—she would definitely use the little pearl onions, so that when you cut into the flesh, roasted to perfection, the smell would waft across the kitchen and set his juices going. Roasted potatoes, his favorite, would be set in a large dish on the table, and perhaps some winter greens, just shy of soft, especially for her Tom. She took another sip of the broth and felt her stomach growl. Yes, this was the meal she would describe.

Dear Tom,

*Did you enjoy the dinner I cooked for you today? It
was a treat, when Bert came to the door with a brace of
pheasant. I know you don't like anything too funny, but
what did you think of the oranges laid across the bird's
chest? And what about those lovely little onions, the
way they fell out onto the plate . . .*

Edmund Hawkes looked at the pile of letters, in unsealed envelopes, ready to go out to wives, sweethearts, mothers, fathers,
brothers, all the people loved by his men, and who loved them
back. He had come to hate this particular job, the censoring of
military post. He dreaded the humanness of the messages sent
home from men who might be on borrowed time. And he could
hardly bear the fact that tomorrow he would march up the line
with his men, and—God willing—march back again a week later
or two weeks later—perhaps more, or even less; perhaps four or
five days later. Nothing was set in stone; reinforcements were
always delayed these days. And when he marched back into the
encampment, the line behind him would be about a third as long
as it was when he set out. He sat back in his chair, in his room
in the large country house abandoned by its owners and requisitioned by the army. The men had tents—cold, damp tents—and
for a while there was no room for him in the house, so he was also
under canvas, which he thought was no bad thing, for it gave him
an opportunity to show he could bear the same circumstances as
his men. But a more senior officer had gone up the line, so for the
time being he was inside, enjoying warmth and comfort. A treat
before death? He pulled his notebook towards the edge of the
desk, took up his pen, and wrote "A Treat Before Death."

Then he didn't know what to write. Fine poet he made. What
would he want to say? That a treat before death for most of his
men was a visit to the *estaminet*, a goodly measure of beer, a
girl on their lap, and then a girl on the bed—never *in* the bed,
never the time. And was it two minutes with the girl on the bed,
or three? Different treats for the men and the officers, who fre-
quented a different establishment. Three minutes with the girl on
the bed, then out the door, still fumbling with the buttons, passing another man going in for his three minutes. It was a treat. *A
full warm belly, a drink, a girl.* And where was love, in all of this?
Hawkes pinched the finger and thumb of his right hand into the
corners of his eyes, then brought his attention back to the letters.
Knowles had set aside two, especially, for him to read. He flapped
the envelope destined for England, written on thick paper, penned
in a hand more dexterous than he would have imagined.

> *... Your last dinner was very nice indeed, and I
> felt a bit of a pig after eating so much. But my love,
> how could I refuse your cooking? That roast lamb fair
> made my mouth water. I've had a bit of mint sauce with
> lamb, but never had it cooked into the lamb, and with
> blackcurrants. You did a good amount of bottling in the
> summer. Makes all the difference to winter, having the
> flavor of harvest in the food.*

Hawkes read the letter, folded it into the envelope, and secured it, ready for its journey across the Channel and to Marshals Farm. Then he took the second letter, this time from Tom
Brissenden's wife.

> *I don't think I've ever told you that I've never liked
> marrow. Cook would always remove the seeds and then*

cut the marrow into large pieces, and boil it until it was soft—too soft for my liking. I hated the way it seemed to slither on my tongue, almost as if I'd put a jellyfish into my mouth. I saw a jellyfish once—a whole cluster of them had washed up on the beach at Broadstairs while we were on holiday there. Funny, wobbly things they were, with a sting if you trod on one. But we have quite a few marrow in the kitchen garden, and as I always suspected the vegetable had more to offer, I have been experimenting—and I must say, I think it's turned out very well indeed. Now, imagine this for your dinner.
I cut the marrow across in one-and-a-half-inch rings, and removed the seeds but did not peel it. I placed the rings in a casserole dish. Then I boiled some rice—and before you cringe, I have discovered there's more to rice than a sugared pudding with a spoonful of jam on top. When the rice was cooked, I fried some onions and tomatoes (bottled in the summer), with a spoonful of mixed herbs and added the rice to the frying pan. This was the stuffing for the marrow—to fit nicely into those round holes. And here comes the interesting part—I made a lovely cheese sauce with sharp English cheddar and poured it over the stuffed marrow. I thought it needed a bit of crunch to it, so I crushed some cream crackers, and sprinkled them on the top with a little more grated cheese and put the dish in the oven. I must say, I was a bit worried about how it might turn out, but when the top was a rich golden brown, I knew it would be just right. I knew you would love it—the marrow was soft enough but not soggy, and with the rice and cheese, it was a meal in itself. Can you taste the cheddar sauce? Isn't it a delight? Soft on the tongue,

*yet different with the rice and tomato, and the crunch
on top. Tell me what you think, Tom? Did you ever taste
marrow like it?*

He rubbed his eyes again, pushed his chair back, and walked
to the fireplace. Pullings had kept a roaring blaze in the grate,
with logs procured from a pile at the back of the farm. And as
he looked out of frost-dusted windows, across the encampment
of men—men standing alongside braziers, or setting off into
town for one last evening out with their pals and a chance with
a woman—his mouth watered. Tom Brissenden was eating the
same food as any other man in the encampment. But with these
letters, he was tasting love, and Edmund Hawkes wanted so
much to taste love. It would be a rare treat.

CHAPTER 11

*A cake to be baked to perfection should rise
evenly and be smooth on the top, and by the
time it has been in the oven half its time a
light brown crust should be formed.*

—*THE WOMAN'S BOOK*

Despite the cold, Thea was not hungry. Though perhaps she was. Her mouth did not feel the pull of food, and though her stomach growled, she felt as if she might retch as soon as she swallowed. But she knew she must eat, because her strength depended upon fuel, and she needed every ounce of power her body could pump out. And she was not even in France yet, but instead on a cold, windy, and wet Salisbury plain, in charge of a recalcitrant vehicle with an intemperate starting handle. She had cleaned every part of the engine, slathered oil where oil was needed, and removed scum from those places where scum soiled points and plugs. To no avail. Her back hurt, her fingers were frozen, and it crossed her mind that she would rather be responsible for encouraging a sweet mood in Mabel than a ticker of life from her ambulance. She leaned into the starting handle again, and cranked. And cranked. And cranked. The engine coughed. She cranked, it coughed again, and again, and finally took the juice, so she clambered into the driver's seat and applied the throttle. Not too much choke. God, the last thing she needed was a flooded engine. She sat there for a full two minutes, her breath in short gasps lest any movement change the engine's mind—she knew it had a mind, because it had been set against her all morning.

"Very good, Brissenden. That old girl's a nasty one—bears a grudge. Now then, onward across that hill, where you will find wounded. You know what to do. On you go."

The woman issuing instructions seemed to have been constructed for her chosen milieu. She was broad of shoulder, sturdy of hip, and had a stride like a major general. It seemed to Thea that her fellow volunteers were of this ilk, yet she knew it was the uniform and the determination that made them seem so, for in civvies they assumed a quite different demeanor, their femininity displayed in silk and fine fabrics. She tussled the ambulance into gear and maneuvered the steering wheel, so the nose moved into the direction of the "wounded."

"Brissenden!" The woman held up her hand. Thea applied the brake. "Brissenden, you forgot something!" She reached forward, rendering herself invisible to Thea, who peered over the steering wheel. When the woman stood up again, it was to wave the starting handle. She stepped around to the driver's side and handed the handle to Thea. "For God's sake don't lose this thing, whatever you do."

The wounded—stuffed scarecrow-like straw bodies with red paint—were strewn across the field and made deliberately heavy with sandbag innards. Thea leaped from the ambulance and treated each one as if it were a much-loved man taken down by the Hun. She filled her ambulance and went on her way, the engine shrieking and moaning over every bump, every ridge that caused a slide into mud. She turned this way and that, imagining she had the leathers in her hands and two draft horses afore the plough, and returned to the encampment.

"Well done, Brissenden. All present and correct. Now let's see how you do with real soldiers."

There was the hospital training, the driving, riding on

horseback across the plain, and the never-ending task of taking apart the engines and putting them together again. Whether it was a spanner in her hand, a wrench, or the bloody dressings from an amputation with the stench of gangrene not beaten, Thea knew this was a heaven lived before the hell—and she expected the hell, for it seemed that whatever she did in recent years, she ended in a corner of a darker place. She still lived with the sickness of imminent discovery—not of her involvement in the quest for women's suffrage, but that her courage had failed her and she had run so many times from authority. The truth was that, here in this sodden field, she was running again.

Thea had been informed that she would be on a ship for France towards the end of January, or sooner if the request came for immediate reinforcements. It seemed that, far from being over by Christmas—and the London shops were full of the festive season—the war would linger into 1915. There were those who said it would even stretch into the following year, that it would become a war of attrition. She wondered how she would bear up in France, for at times her strength failed her, and her lack of appetite was obvious in her physical ability. It was at those times that she willed her bones to move, to bear weight, to push and pull and tug and lift. It was as if she were drawing strength from sheer determination—and she was a Brissenden, which meant determination was in her blood.

Edmund Hawkes and his fellow officers led the column of men closer to the cannonade. He missed his beloved mare, missed the fact that she knew his every intention almost as soon as the thought had crossed his mind. Following her death, he had been given Wellington, a former hunter, a brave gelding intent only upon going forward, on jumping the next obstacle. Wellie seemed to question why they were breaking away and trotting back along the column, rather than remaining at the head of the field. When moving out to the front, it was Hawkes' habit to circle away from the leaders, trot back, and position his horse to walk alongside the men—his men—encouraging them to keep moving, promising them a good mug of tea and a measure of rum when they stopped, or asking them about their night on the town. He would talk to a few here, one man there, or call out to another—he was becoming known as a soldier's soldier, though he knew that in the eyes of Knowles, his manner was too familiar by half. Hawkes had the measure of Knowles, and understood that his sergeant would have liked to inspire a bit more awe in him. Awe was power in the hands of a sergeant— and to be fair, Hawkes understood his reasoning. With so many new recruits above and below Knowles in the pecking order, it must have seemed like the deaf leading the blind, as far as the sergeant was concerned.

Tom and Cecil marched together, heads bent against sleet peppered with snowflakes the size of mushrooms. At the front of the line someone began to sing, and soon the verse caught on down the column.

> It's a long way to Tipperary,
> It's a long way to go.
> It's a long way to Tipperary
> To the sweetest girl I know!
> Goodbye, Piccadilly,
> Farewell, Leicester Square!
> It's a long long way to Tipperary,
> But my heart's right there.

"If I have to go through this war singing that song every ten minutes, I swear I will ask the Hun to take me prisoner. I will run into the next trench and hold up a white flag," said Cecil. "I might even tell them to shoot me on the spot."

Tom nodded, his mouth set against the cold. His feet were unfeeling in his boots, despite the marching, the heavy thud that should have kept blood circulating with each step. He had never been a smoker, not until he joined the army, and now he couldn't wait for the column to be brought to a halt so he could have a ciggie. He could almost feel the scratchy burning at the back of his throat when he drew on a Woodbine, and now he craved the taste of tobacco in his mouth more than anything. More than anything except, perhaps, a dinner set before him by Kezia.

"Saw you got a letter from your lady wife before we left camp. Everything all right at home?"

Tom nodded again. He liked Cecil, he was a good enough fellow, but he could talk, and for the most part Tom was a listener more than a talker. It surprised him how much he and Kezia talked, long conversations, often into the night. His parents didn't converse, apart from basic greetings. Did they ever talk alone, in their bedroom? He remembered once or twice hearing the low mumble of nighttime voices back and forth, a question asked and an answer given. Tom could talk to his old mate Edward, though not about anything of note, over and above the land, the crops, the harvest, and the price they were getting for cattle. He thought about Edward a fair bit lately. He'd been one of the first to join up, and Tom had wondered where he was. It wasn't as if men sent letters to each other, not like women, not letters like Kezia and Thea would write. His thoughts turned to Thea as they marched along, *One-two, one-two, It's a long way to Tipperary, it's a long way to go, it's a long way* . . . He loved his sister, held her in high esteem—she was his elder, after all, so he had always looked up to her. He'd thought his marriage to Kezia would bring them all together, and imagined Thea, one day, marrying a nice fellow, and them having children, and all the cousins would play on the farm, and there would be Sunday dinners together, and it would be family. He'd imagined himself talking to the man, whoever he was, walking him around the farm while the women cooked a leg of mutton with all the trimmings. Tom felt his eyes half closing even as he walked, even as the sleet stung his cheeks and his ears ached from the sharp wind. It was as if the memory warmed him, made him feel sleepy, as he would if the meal were inside him. Kezia would roast the mutton with rosemary, spearing the flesh with tips of the herb, so it looked almost as if she were creating a garden on top of the meat. And there would be roast potatoes, some greens and parsnips, all doused with rich gravy.

Tom felt the food in his belly, stretched his imagination far into his body so that every cell, every drop of blood, was engaged in digesting a meal that was so real, he could taste it. He could see Kezia taking the plates from the warming oven, bringing them to the table, telling the children to mind their manners if they wanted their Sunday dinner. There would be a girl and a boy, and Thea would have two boys—he knew she would have boys. His girl would have a bow in her hair and her best Sunday dress, and Kezia would tut-tut that there was mud on it already, because his girl would be a tomboy, climbing trees with her brother and cousins. Tom could see it all, could hear the clatter of plates in the kitchen, could see the blurry figure of this man of Thea's and the women, working together, dishing up their Sunday meal, and there would be laughter, and joking, and they would sit, and . . .

The officer riding alongside held up his hand in response to another officer leading the march, and the company stopped, brought to attention. The order was given to fall out, so they staggered to the side of the road and were given leave to sit.

"You all right, Brissenden? You were miles away." Cecil offered Tom a Woodbine.

Tom nodded and took the cigarette. "Obliged, thank you." He paused to light up. "Just thinking of home, that's all."

"Your wife still making up fancy dinners to give you when you get back to Blighty?"

Tom nodded, and laughed. "I'm looking forward to it. New recipe with every letter."

Cecil looked up at the sky, then back at Tom. "It'll be a while, that."

"I know."

"Oh, God, look who's coming down the line."

It was Knowles. The men clambered to attention, the rain dripping from their helmets onto their mackintoshes, then down onto their boots.

"Attennnn-shun!" Knowles stopped in front of Cecil and Tom. "Well, what are you two nancy boys jawing about now?"

"Nothing, sir," Tom and Cecil replied in accord.

He came close to Tom. "Just as well, Private Gravy. Because I am watching you." He waited a moment and then marched down the line, barking orders.

"He's well and truly got it in for you, mate," said Cecil.

"Every bully needs a whipping boy, I suppose," replied Tom.

"I'd watch out if I were you, that's all."

The order came along the line to form a column. Once more they began marching, and once more Edmund Hawkes rode up and down, as if to pull his soldiers along, though there was not a man who felt rested, warmer, or drier, or whose feet ached less for the brief sojourn. The sound of big guns came ever closer, and as the column of British and Canadian troops moved forward, so they began to pass another column, a slow stagger of men moving in the opposite direction, many bandaged, held up by comrades.

"Bloody hell," muttered Cecil.

Tom said nothing, only watched as activity increased, as ambulances groaned along the rutted road or were pulled by blood-spattered horses. He saw Edmund Hawkes cantering back and forth now. It was a slow, measured canter. Tom knew he had already been up to the front line several times, and was—if you looked at the men returning—an old hand. He watched him each time he passed, and saw the pinched look on his face, and though his cap was pulled down and his collar pulled up, he tried to imagine the Edmund Hawkes of old, the young man who'd seemed so very confident in his world. This time it was like watching the ghost of someone who had not died. He cast his eyes sideways at the passing column, saw a few raise their hands in acknowledgement, though the men, who were from an Indian regiment, did not call or sing. They kept their haunted eyes focused in front of them. The strange thing, to Tom, was that though they were alive they seemed dead, their faces whitened by the chalky mud, and whatever it was that awaited him and Cecil and Edmund Hawkes, and every man marching towards the war.

Kezia had not been up to London since before Tom's enlistment. In the early days of her marriage she had taken the gig into the village several times each week, or perhaps more, and now she only found time to visit the grocery shop and post office once a week, on a Friday afternoon, and often persuaded the postman to take her letters, to save her time. The farm sucked up every ounce of her energy. She barely had the power to wash herself at the end of the day, and it seemed the only clothes she ever wore now were Tom's. The men had become used to seeing her wearing trousers and a workmanlike shirt, a weskit, and then, later, her old woolen jacket buttoned up to her neck and a scarf tied to keep her warm. A knitted tam-o'-shanter was pulled down to just above her eyes, and covered her ears. She wore heavy leather gloves, and set about her day's work with the same vigor as any young man who had ever worked on the farm.

It was the Tuesday before Christmas. Kezia had not wanted to go to London on a Monday, for that was the day she, Bert, and Danny discussed the week ahead over breakfast. The linen tablecloth was still put out each day, and Kezia never wavered in her commitment to set the men off on their work with a good meal inside them, which in winter meant a bowl of porridge to line the stomach, before eggs and bacon and strong tea. The price of sugar had gone up, and supplies were limited, so they'd all cut back on the number of teaspoonfuls they'd heaped into the morning brew. The only difference in the morning round was that Ada was left to the house, and Kezia went out onto the farm. But not today.

She'd bathed the night before, delaying her weekly soak from Friday night until the Monday, ready for excursion. She dressed in a matching wool barathea skirt and jacket, with a wrap to keep her warm, and her best winter hat, which was of a nutty brown with a wide grosgrain band and a feather at the side. She had taken a few pounds from the tin in her dressing table drawer, for it was her intention to purchase gifts for each of her workers to go along with the Christmas "box"—not a box at all, but a small envelope with money, an extra week's wages for Danny and Bert, and for the boys who came there would be a few coins. Ada, too, would have a week's wage. Kezia had checked the ledgers before making her decision, which was to give the workers an amount more generous than Brissendens had parted with in the past. She felt she must, for Tom was not there, and she needed their direction as much as they needed her optimism, though she was not aware of the latter.

Danny drove her to the station, and was instructed as to when she would return. But instead of thinking about London and the shops and the approaching festive season—which amounted to her traveling to her parents' home on Christmas Eve, and not returning until the morning after Boxing Day— she was thinking about the extra help she would need for dung spreading in the new year. She asked Danny to stop at the shop as they drove through the village, giving a note to him for the shopkeeper to post in the window. It was to the effect that if any village women needed extra work while their men were away, they should see Mrs. Brissenden at Marshals Farm.

There were times each day that Kezia felt the cloud of doubt envelop her, though for the most part she was so intent upon her work and what had to be done next that she kept it at bay, remaining positive about tasks that needed to be completed on the farm, trusting Bert that they were not getting behind, and hoping Tom would come home soon. She kept up standards in the home, but she wanted him to return to a semblance of order, not the mire of chaos. When she felt the cloud approaching, she would check herself, would push the thought to the back of her mind—perhaps that the apples would fail, or the hops, or they would not get the new pastures ready and the crops planted. She was now adept at handling Ted, a kindly horse, willing and affectionate, but remained wary of Mabel. She had been lead- ing the giant mare up the lane from Pickwick when the cloud of doubt leached into her soul, and it was as if the mare sensed it and took aim with a sharp nip to shake Kezia out of herself. She might be wary of Mabel, but she respected her all the same.

Now, on the train, she had time for worry to bloom again, time for wondering if all would be well in the end. She tried to imagine Tom soldiering, and realized that she could not strike an image in her mind's eye. She could see him in his uniform, in the photograph he'd sent to her before leaving for France, but she could not imagine what his days were like as an army man.

Kezia was taken aback by London. It was not just that she had become accustomed to the quiet of the countryside, where an internal combustion engine was a rarity, but London was more immediate, had more bustle than usual, even for Christmas. Khaki-clad men from across the Empire were on the streets, shopping with everyone else. She had expected some sort of gravity to have seeped into the city, but still people were about the business of the festive season, and there appeared to be little in the way of shortages in the shops. It surprised her that there seemed to be a jollity, especially among the soldiers. She'd noticed more women wearing black in the village, and men with black armbands. The list of boys who would never come home was growing longer, and now, when Mr. Barham came, or the new telegram boy was seen in the village, people asked, "Who've we lost?" Kezia noticed the "we." It had become a collective loss, with mourners attending the mother and father, the siblings and cousins. Here in London there were women in mourning, sharing the pavements with soldiers on the grand adventure.

Kezia, who had in the past looked forward to afternoon tea with Thea or a luncheon with her mother, felt almost as if she had ventured abroad, for posters everywhere encouraged young men to enlist, and young women to plant corms of guilt in a best boy who had not yet stepped forward to serve his country, to protect his family. She was at once proud of and awed by the activity around her.

She bought Ada a set of three delicate lace handkerchiefs in Marshall & Snelgrove. She bought a woolen scarf for Bert, and a pair of gloves for Danny, then wondered if she might swap the two, giving the gloves to Bert, but in deference to his age, and what he called "a bit of a chest," she went back to her original plan. But what would she buy for Thea, who had been invited to join the Reverend and Mrs. Marchant at the parsonage for the holiday? She walked on to Liberty's, where she chose a square scarf of the finest silk and had it wrapped in deep pink tissue before it was placed in a gift box. By the time she had passed Dickins & Jones, guilt was descending upon her. She had sent Tom a knitted scarf—her own creation—and baked him a cake, which she sealed into a tin with candle wax, then wrapped with brown paper before dispatching it to France via the post office. Had it reached its destination? Would the wax fail, and the rich fruitcake arrive moldy and damp? And would the scarf be enough? Kezia felt tears form at the corners of her eyes, and she reached for her handkerchief.

" 'Ere, you all right, love?" called a flower seller outside the Palladium.

"Yes. Thank you. I think some dust flew up into my eye. So sorry . . ." Kezia made to hurry on, back towards Oxford Street.

"Don't worry, love—let's hope your boy'll be home soon." The flower seller stamped her feet and pulled up her scarf against the cold. "Let's hope they'll all be home soon."

"Blimey, Tom, this is good cake," said Cecil.

The military post had been brought to the trench just ten minutes earlier, a surprise because they thought they'd have to wait for letters and parcels until they went down the line again.

"Goes down a treat with a cuppa, eh?" answered Tom, who seemed to stand straighter, despite the snow, the cold, and the promise of more shelling to come.

" 'Ere, Brissenden, heard you got a cake from your missus," said another soldier, Alfred Apps.

"I knew it wouldn't be long before they all came out of their holes for this," said Cecil. "Everybody wants to be your best mate now."

"I heard you got a nice bit of cake, Brissy," said Sidney Harris.

"All right, all right," said Tom. "Come here, and I'll give you some—hold out your hand."

The four men were joined by Arthur Petty and Bill Saunders.

"When's your missus gonna be sending another one, Brissy?" said Harris.

"I'll write and ask for more," said Tom, feeling warmer for the banter, and an affection from the other men, who he thought had been keeping a distance, given the attention from Knowles. No one wanted the sergeant's shadow to fall their way.

"What d'you reckon she put in this? I've never had fruitcake like it," said Harris.

"I think your missus is a bit of an artist," said Cecil, winking at Tom. "You know what I can taste, as well as the sultanas, the orange peel, and the candied cherries? I can taste a little bit of something else in there, and I reckon it's lavender."

"Lavender?" said Petty. "Bloomin' 'ell, ain't that for putting on the sheets?"

"It keeps moths away," said Cecil. "Which means that Mrs. Brissenden has created the perfect cake for the British army—it remains moth free, is moist, has been sweetened by honey, and is just mouthwatering."

Tom blushed and nodded, biting into another piece of cake.

"Yeah, and she turned the spoon with love, eh Tommy!" Petty nudged Tom, making him blush more. The other men grinned, joining the tease.

"Well, I should save the rest for tomorrow, eh, lads?"

"Just for us, then? You won't be spreading all that around, unless there's another one coming a bit sharpish!" Petty emptied his mug, throwing the dregs down into the water-filled trench.

Edmund Hawkes heard the conversation. Every word. And as the men spoke of Kezia's cake, his mouth watered. The sensation, though, was not a salivary gland reacting to the promise of fruitcake with Kentish honey and lavender, but sickness erupting from his stomach with the message, delivered not ten minutes earlier, that on the morrow, in the fog-enshrouded first light, a cannonade would begin at oh seven hundred hours. When it ended, he would wait one and a half minutes for the cordite-laced smoke to rise, and then his men would go over the top and meet the enemy, most of them for the first time.

Chapter 12

*The woman who can write exactly as she
speaks, who can talk on paper to the recipient
of her letter just as easily as if she were
actually conversing . . . is mistress of the art
of letter-writing.*
—THE WOMAN'S BOOK

Dear Tom,

I have not heard from you about the cake yet, so I
expect the post has been caught up somewhere because
of Christmas. Did you like it? I had never before made
a rich fruitcake, and the recipe said to be absolutely
spot-on with the weighing. It was a little hard to get the
flour, but I went directly to Dallings Mill and bought
some. It looked a little brown, but that doesn't matter in
a cake, and I thought it added to the flavor (I made one
for the farm too, and gave Bert and Danny a slice each
to have with their tea, and they said it was very good).

Well, we still have Mabel and Ted, even though the
army have been back three times now, but I don't think
they will come again, after what happened with Mabel.
They decided they would take her and leave us with
Ted, which the officer said was being very generous. I
think they didn't like the look of Ted—you know how
his face can bear that strange look at times, like a dog
who hasn't had any food for months. Bert says it's on

account of Mabel hen-pecking him. He says those two
are like an old married couple. Anyway, they took
Mabel, and Ada cried and I had to hold back my tears.
Danny walked away, as if he was going to start with
the weeping too, and Bert stood at the farm gate, just
watching them walking down the road with her. It was
as if he wanted her to know he was watching her go.
Then she turned her big head—fair pulled the soldier's
arm out of its socket—and looked back. As soon as
she saw Bert watching, that was it. I have never seen
her do such a thing, and I didn't think she could, even
though she's a big strong mare. She reared up all of her
eighteen hands, and she came down so hard you felt
the ground shake. The soldiers and the officer skittered
to get out of the way. Then she gave a buck to reach the
moon, turned tail, and she galloped all the way back
to Bert, who looked down the road at the soldiers and
led her to her stall. The officer came and took back
the money he'd given me for her. I was happy to hand
it over. He said a horse like that wouldn't last two
minutes in France, that they would end up shooting
her anyway because she would cause more trouble than
she's worth. He said omnibus horses and hunters were
the best, because they knew what they were about and
didn't mind the noise so much, then he walked away
saying that it was no wonder the other nag was soft,
he'd never known spoiled horses like it. Well, Tom,
those spoiled horses were back in front of the plough
again as soon as Bert had let them have their talk to
each other and a bag of oats. Bert says that Mabel has
been quite the lady ever since, almost as if it shook her
up enough to make her grateful. He says it was Ted she

came back for, that they've never been parted. I think
she came back for Bert. He's the only one who can
really get the best out of her. She'll work for Danny, and
I sometimes think she only tolerates me. Ted, though,
is different, isn't he? I think I could ride Ted if I had a
mind to. He's a gentleman, and I am glad they thought
he was not good enough, though by all accounts they've
taken lesser horses, and there's some talk in the village
about it, as if we haven't done enough for our boys at
the front, keeping our horses. Then they see how we've
had to plough in the—

Kezia took another sheet of paper and began the page again.
It would be a mistake to tell Tom about ploughing in Micawber
Wood, and the orchards. She closed her eyes and considered her
next paragraph. Tom and Thea both loved Micawber Wood, as
did the village children who played there, all swearing they'd
seen fairies while chasing one another through the trees. The
younger Brissendens had taken Kezia to Micawber Wood on
her first visit to the farm. There was something magical about
it, the way the sun dappled through the canopy overhead, and
the lilting echo of the stream running across rocks and fallen
wood, swishing through narrows and filling out pools where
the water had worn away the banks across the years. The wood
was filled with primroses and bluebells in summer, and when
she'd walked along the forest path in autumn, dried leaves
crunched under her feet, making her feel as if she were connected to the earth in a way that she had not, until then, truly
experienced.

Kezia wondered what she would write next, what meal
would be prepared in her imagination. She smiled at the image
that came to her.

*Do you want to know what I cooked for your dinner
tonight? Knowing you would be full of cake, I have
not cooked a big pudding to follow. I can imagine you
sitting in the tent with your friend, Cecil, and the two of
you with cups of tea and the cake on the table, cut into
big slices—probably bigger than I would have cut them.*

    *Anyway, here's your dinner. I've never cooked duck
before, and once I'd plucked it, I thought it didn't leave
much meat on the bone for anyone to get their teeth into.
I was wondering what to make the stuffing with, and
remembered I'd bottled some plums. So I brought a jar
from the larder, and tipped the fruit into a bowl, keeping
the juice to one side in a jug. I picked out the stones from
the plums—you should see my stained fingers—then I
went out to my kitchen garden to have a look. Being as
it's been snowing, there isn't much to find at this time of
year, but I snipped a sprig of rosemary—you can always
depend upon rosemary, it's hardier than some. I've grown
a few other herbs from seed in pots on the windowsill in
the kitchen, so I cut off a little oregano—it's from Italy. I
chopped up the herbs and added them to the plums, then
I ran some old bread through the meat grinder to make
crumbs, and added a handful to give a bit of body to the
stuffing. Finally, I thought almonds would go well with
it. I bought a couple of ounces when I was in London, so
I chopped them, not too small, then put them in too, and
added half an onion, sliced really small, and stuffed the
bird. I put it in the roasting pan, the one with the lid, and
poured on the last of the sherry—I'll treat us to another
bottle soon. I'd already rubbed the bird with butter, so
the juices and sherry and the butter all together made
the kitchen smell wonderful. The dogs even pawed the*

*door to get in, and you know they respect their place and
would never do that as a rule . . .*

Kezia thought of the collies settled on a blanket in front of
the stove in the kitchen. She would have to get them used to
sleeping outdoors again before Tom came home. Composing the
meal she would have cooked for Tom made her stomach growl.
Soon she would go to the kitchen, but not yet.

*Roast potatoes and parsnips were the best vegetables to
go with the duck, and I thought you'd also like some of
those peas I'd dried in summer. I'm glad I laid out all
those roots—the potatoes, the parsnips, carrots, beets,
and swedes set apart on newspaper—because there is
not a scrap of mold anywhere, and the same with the
apples and pears, although I bottled some and dried
some too, so we have plenty to keep us going.*

*The dinner came out better than I'd even hoped, and
the gravy, which was made from the juices of the meat
and the syrup from the bottle of plums, with a little
browning and some flour to thicken; well, the gravy was
just like you always say you want it, not too thin, not
too thick, but enough to make the bird go down easy.*

*Now, then, knowing you'd be full from the cake, I
made you applesauce with fresh cream and a bit of
cinnamon for your pudding. I know you always said you
didn't care for cinnamon, but it keeps a cold at bay, and
just a little brings a good flavor to an apple. Try it, Tom,
close your eyes and try it all.*

Kezia set down her pen and pressed her hands to her eyes,
feeling the tears run through her fingers. She turned aside so

that they would not fall on the still-drying ink. She thought of the vegetables she'd tried to preserve, but had instead fed to the pigs because they were mold-ridden and ruined, and her poor attempts at drying the peas, which at least she'd been able to put in a broth, and tried not to taste the mustiness. But Tom would not know. She wouldn't want to spoil Tom's picture of home.

She picked up her pen, shook it onto the blotting paper to get the ink running again, and continued.

Keep that cake in the tin, my dear Tom, so it will last you a few days, and try to wrap something around it, so the damp doesn't get in now the wax seal is broken. I believe the sweetness will give you something extra down in your feet when they get you marching up and down the parade ground! I've been thinking about the tents and I hope they're not too drafty. Mind you, Mrs. Pontin told me that her boy wrote that he'd been billeted in a farmhouse with big fireplaces, so perhaps you have too. I'll think of you sitting by a nice blazing fire.

Edmund Hawkes was deep in the dugout, in what passed for officers' quarters in the trench. A series of joists and load-bearing piles held the ceiling and the walls in place, though the ugly headache-inducing smell of mold and fungus, death and rats—so many rats—was inescapable, remaining there even when he went out into the trench, even when it was almost overpowered by cordite, but never quite—always lingering in his eyes, his nasal passages, his throat, so the smell became the taste and the look became the taste, and the taste, always, seemed to be of decaying corpses.

He sat at his desk, upon which a map had been rolled out earlier. A runner had brought orders and a new, freshly printed map of the battlefield. Here it was, all planned by a man in a warm room with not a grumble in his belly—another run over the top, another try for the opposite trench. How long had they been here, in this trench—moving back and forth? Was it days? Or weeks? There had been no respite in between, no comfort at the house, and no solace from the fact that he had brought back some three out of every five men. It was like poker, like roulette, like a gamble at the races; a game of who would run, who would jump, and who would fall. Then begin the wager again— replenish the field, add to the pack, put the chips on the table, and start the wheel spinning. Cannonade ends at oh seven thirty, one and a half minutes for the smoke to clear, then blow the whistle and off they go. And let's see who I can bring back alive, thought Hawkes, amazed at his own survival, at the fact that he still had arms, legs, a brain, that his guts remained inside him.

He lifted the letter and began reading a second time, or was it a third? Letters to the soldiers were not sealed, nor were those from soldiers home to Blighty. But this was the letter he'd waited for, the handwriting he recognized when the post was delivered. He would check enveloped post first, then hand the sack to Knowles to distribute the mail; the letters, the cards, the packages of Wright's Coal Tar Soap, tins of Ovaltine, of Huntley & Palmer's digestive biscuits and Oxo cubes, brown-paper-wrapped parcels of socks and of chocolate; the food, he knew, might be filled with weevil by now.

I've been trying something different with the gravy lately. I put some bottled damsons and pears through the meat grinder (I had to be careful in case the juice went everywhere), and when they were all nicely

*mashed, I fried onions, which I added to the mix. Then
I stirred up a gravy and poured it all into the saucepan
together. At first it looked a bit lumpy and not something
you'd want, but then I added some hot water to thin it
out, with herbs and just a tiny bit of spice, and brought
the lot to the boil while whisking at the same time. It
was hard work, but it turned out perfectly—in fact,
I was thinking of sending the recipe up to one of the
women's monthlies, because this gravy goes very well
with liver, which as you know, I don't even like to touch
as a rule, but I know you like it and this new gravy does
wonders for the meat—makes it good enough for a rich
man's supper, especially with roast potatoes, parsnips,
and peas.*

Hawkes imagined the meal, imagined himself sitting in the
farmhouse kitchen, saw himself smiling as Kezia served the
sweet gravy-drenched liver, and the parsnips and peas, and then
pouring more gravy over the roast potatoes, and he felt himself
watching her, leaning forward with his table napkin and dabbing some of that rich fruit gravy from the side of her mouth,
and he wondered how it would be to kiss that mouth, and how
he might taste the fruit on her tongue, and how she might kiss
him back and lean forward, and how the dinner might be abandoned, how he might take her into his arms and into his bed,
and how they would come to that meal later, still hungry for the
love of each other.

"Sir!"

Hawkes turned with a start. "Oh, Knowles, yes, here's the
mail. Just wanted to check one or two, just in case. As you say,
you never know. Anyway, it's all satisfactory, you can take it to
the men now."

"Yes, sir. And the orders?"

"Of course. Could you find Lieutenant Markham for me? Bring him back here, and we'll look at the maps. Watches at dawn tomorrow morning, artillery at seven, and we're off at oh seven thirty. Right?"

"Right, sir." Knowles lingered.

"Is there something else, Sergeant Knowles?"

"Private Brissenden's letters—find anything, sir?"

"They can be collected and delivered, as with all the men. I will continue to monitor them, but I see no issue with the content—we cannot judge what a man faced with death almost every day might say to his wife, and her to him, knowing his predicament."

"I don't reckon she knows anything about the predicament, sir."

"Not my place to judge, but I would say that not many of our loved ones at home know anything much about our predicament, Knowles, which is probably just as well. Now then, Lieutenant Markham, in ten minutes, here, both of you."

"Sir!" Knowles saluted Hawkes.

The salute was acknowledged in kind, but once the sergeant had left, Hawkes turned his thoughts to Kezia, to the woman sleeping under his tree, resting her head against the roots. And he remembered how he could have lingered there, watching her, for a long time. He yearned to have Tom's place at the table, not the lonely dining room each night, with servants to clatter plates, china dishes, and silver chargers, to be at his beck and call. He wanted to eat food cooked not from duty, but from the heart.

"What've we got here, then? A letter for Private Gravy from his little wife at home. Here you are, Gravy. No nice cake this time." Knowles turned to the other lads. "Amazing, ain't it, that Gravy's wife manages to bake him a cake, and I bet your old mum or your wife can't get hold of a pound of flour, or the eggs, or butter." He passed the letter to Tom and went on along the line, keeping up his line of dialogue. "Makes me wonder, it does, what Mrs. Gravy might be up to, to get things special."

Tom felt the anger rise in his chest, and made to step forward. Cecil put up a hand to block him, even before he moved.

"Steady, Tom. Steady up," said Cecil, his voice low. "He's goading you, so let him go on his merry way. Remember what I said, toe the line and keep your nose clean. He's got it in for you—and if it hadn't been you, it would've been me, or one of the other lads. Hold on, don't bite, and just read that letter from your missus and tell us what she's cooked for you this time."

Once the sergeant turned the corner, the men clustered around Tom.

"Come on, what's on the table, mate?" said a voice from the back, and in the front of the gathering, a younger soldier, a boy some years from manhood, watched Tom as he removed the letter from its envelope.

"You hungry, lad?" asked Cecil.

The boy nodded, and pushed back his helmet. "Not 'alf. Go on, read us the dinner."

Tom cleared his throat and began halfway down the page, changing some of the words as he went on.

> "Seeing as I'd used fruit in the gravy—which as
> I've said, really brought out the flavor of the liver, and
> did away with that bitterness the meat can sometimes
> hold—I thought I should give you something quite
> different for your pudding. Well, I'd never made a
> soufflé before—it always seemed so much trouble—but I

*thought it was time I made my peace with the recipe. It's
just as well you weren't in the kitchen, because I know
your fingers would have been in the bowl for a taster
before I'd poured the mix into a tin for cooking. In fact,
cooking with chocolate gave me another idea for gravy,
so—"*

"What do you think this is—effing storytime?" Knowles had
returned to shout his orders. "Atten-shun!"

The men came to attention. Tom felt his heart leap in his
chest, and with a swift movement crumpled the letter into his
pocket.

"You can all get back to your posts toot sweet, or haven't
you noticed there's a war on? The bleedin' Hun are having a
party over there while you're all listening to Private Gravy go
on about the liver or duck or whatever it is he's having for his
bleedin' dinner. Quick march! And I'll be along the line to check
those shining rifles, so make sure every barrel is fit to blind me."

The men scurried back to their positions. Knowles came
close to Tom, as close as he had ever been.

"You know what I'm going to say, don't you, Private Gravy?"

"Yes, sir."

"Yes, sir is right. And what am I going to say, Private Gravy?"

"You're watching me, sir."

"Too bleedin' right I'm watching you. Now then, I want a
volunteer to go out on sentry duty tonight. Not just standing-on-
the-fire-step sentry duty, but a bit of time-out-there sentry duty.
Lovely starry night it is for it. And who do you think should be
my volunteer?"

"I'm sure I don't know, sir."

Knowles mimicked a schoolboy voice. "I'm sure I don't know,
sir."

Tom remained still, his eyes looking past Sergeant Knowles.

"Well, let me give you a little clue, Gravy, being as you're so nice and warm and filled up with a good dinner inside you, and you know what duck means. You, lad, are on sentry duty. I'll be along after the stand-to, to tell you when to go over, all right, Gravy?"

"Yes, sir!"

Knowles nodded. "You'll have a bit of string on your leg. I'll give it a yank when it's time to find your way back—that's if that sniper over there don't find you first. Thank your lucky stars I'm not sending anyone out on a raiding party tonight. Bit too clear. Now, then, you'll want to get that there rifle shining like the moon, because I'll be back in a minute to inspect it. Thought I'd give you a minute or two to get going with a bit of cloth. Back to your post, Gravy, on the double!"

Tom saluted and marched two steps to his position, where he began to clean his rifle, an almost impossible task in the front-line trench, part of which had collapsed earlier and had been hastily rebuilt with sandbags and an old brass bedstead brought up from a supply trench. But when he was sure Knowles was well away, Tom took out another letter, this one from Thea. He would not have known that Edmund Hawkes read his letter from Kezia, or that the officer had, in his hurry to find a letter to Tom from his wife, missed an envelope bearing Thea's return address. There was only one page, half filled with writing, and in that moment, looking at her distinctive strong hand with large letters looped together, Tom felt a chasm open in his heart. The weight of love in Kezia's pages seemed to shine a light on the shallowness of Thea's message, as if she had nothing to say to him, and he wondered how they had come to this division, though at the same time he suspected he knew—Thea felt left out. In fact, Tom knew she had always felt as if she were something of an outsider, and though he had tried, in his way, to make her feel less so—even in boyhood—it was easier to pretend that everything was all right with Thea. And she would never have spoken the truth of her feelings anyway. Instead she allowed her frustration to emerge in a bitter comment or in something she did—or, more likely, didn't do. She can't even bother to write a decent letter, and she was a teacher! thought Tom.

Dear Tom,

I thought I would let you know that I am leaving for France tomorrow, so you won't be the only Brissenden over there. Father would still say you were the brave one though, wouldn't he? My training has more or less finished, but we will be doing more once we're at the hospital. I was going to say that perhaps I'll see you, but I hope I don't because I'll be driving an ambulance, so you won't want to think about seeing me.

I'll tell you all about Christmas with Kezia's parents when our paths cross again. Kezia and her father are so tight, I've never known two people discuss so many subjects in such a short time. Not only that, but when I look at them together, I can see Kezia in her father. But Kezia's people have always been good to me, and to you as well, so I think a lot of them. Reverend Marchant is a military chaplain now, though I don't think he'll be in France. He wears a uniform, and keeps on at the church while he's back and forth to the camp on the town recreation ground.

In any case, I'll write when I can.

Your sister,
Thea

Night drew in, and as Knowles predicted, it was a clear midnight-blue sky above. Cecil mentioned something about it being like a Vincent van Gogh. Tom had no answer for him. He had no idea who this Vincent was, with his—what did Cecil say? *Starry Night*? Soon Knowles came along the trench, which was quieter now that most of the men were bedded down, though few would sleep more than a snatched few minutes here and there. No one wanted to die in their sleep, set upon by an enemy raiding party, or with a shell landing on them. You had to stay awake, listening, ready to move. Knowles poked Tom in the ribs with the business end of his gun and marched him to the fire step. Though there were only a few men in the trench, Tom felt as if they were watching and waiting. Only a fool or a young too-curious soldier new on the front line was stupid enough to put his head above the parapet, but here he was, sent out into the night on sentry duty. He wondered if Edmund Hawkes knew about this—or was he tucked up in the officers' dugout, toasting tea cakes and drinking tea that tasted like tea? At that moment, Tom longed for the burn of his rum ration bathing the back of his throat.

"Up you go, Gravy, and mind your noddle. That Hun ammo can go straight through your helmet—it makes you wonder why they bother to give 'em to us." Knowles grinned, then looked around him. "Unless any of you lads not kipping want to go too, I reckon you should pay attention. Them of you whose time it is for forty winks had better take it, and them of you who's on watch, well, you'd better watch!"

Tom set one sodden boot on the next rung on the ladder, then the next and the next, keeping his head down as much as he could, his chin almost on his chest. Scraping against the soil, he crawled out of the trench. A few shots came from the German trenches, but they were without target, a discharge of ammunition meant to bring terror into the hearts of the enemy. The evening hate, the lads called it. Dawn would bring the morning hate. Behind him, Tom knew his muckers would be doing some shooting hate of their own. He just hoped they aimed high.

"Don't you worry, Gravy, I'll keep an eye on you. We'll tug you back in time for you to get some shut-eye before the show tomorrow." Knowles seemed almost cheery.

Tom had no reply. He crawled along the ground to the sentry position, the low stump of a shelled tree. He moved to one side, then lay down on his stomach, his Lee Enfield pointed towards his foe. His eyes, now accustomed to the dark and focused on the German trenches, were searching for shadows across no-man's-land, the telltale sign of an enemy raiding party on the move under cover of night.

Was it minutes passing, or hours? Did he see something move? Yes—rats. He'd never tell Kezia about the rats, the size of them, like cats, and the way they feasted on the dead. They said— the boys who'd been up the line a few more times than him— that the rats didn't wait until the cease-fire, until the stretcher bearers from both sides came out to collect the dying. No, they said the rats, especially those big black bastard rats, would be eating a man even before he met his maker, that you could hear them gobbling up intestines while men with just seconds of life left in them called out for their mothers. *Keep still, it's only the rats moving.* Tom knew he would be here again, running past this very spot, the next morning, God willing he made it through the night. And God willing he was able to run that far. Was Knowles trying to kill him, or make an example of him? And why him? He'd never been one to be singled out—mind you, he'd never been anywhere much to be noticed in his entire life, just the college, then back to the farm, and the farm was his. His mind seemed to jump like electricity, a spark bounding from thought to thought. Yes, the farm was his. *We're not serfs with a lease any more, thanks to old man Hawkes.* Tom smiled, then widened his eyes. What was that? He fingered the trigger. *No, better not. Don't make a sound—the minute they know where you are, they'll fill you full of holes.*

Tom felt like two people, one on watch, and one telling him what to do. One looking back and one forward. And looking back, he saw Kezia, in the kitchen, preparing his dinner. He could smell the lavender in the linen cloth as she shook it across the table, and felt the soft fabric as he took up the napkin, pulling it across his lap—embarrassed for himself and the womanness of it all. *Table napkins!* Yet he felt more of a man for having Kezia by his side, a wife who loved him enough to cook a meal even when he wasn't there. He thought of the duck, of the succulent meat falling dark from the bone. He saw it on his fork, pushing into the sweet plum stuffing, and then into the gravy, filling it with a mouthful of flavors. In his mind's eye Tom ate that meal, felt his stomach stretch to satiety and his eyes grow heavy. *She goes a bit silly with that sherry, my Kezia*, thought Tom. Was that a noise? *No, it's only Kezia clearing the plates.* He didn't have enough room for the apple and cinnamon, and the fresh cream, but perhaps, perhaps just a bite . . .

The string tugged at his leg.

"Still watching, Gravy?"

"Sir?" Tom tried to shout a whisper, keeping his voice low.

"Just checking. You can come back to the fire step."

Tom crawled backwards, his eyes still searching.

"Right then. Young Mott here is on watch now. You can go to quarters, Gravy."

"Sir!"

"And remember, Private Gravy. I'm watching you."

"Sir." Tom saluted, and quick-marched to the dugout.

Fresh orders arrived by runner before dawn, informing Hawkes that the attack had been canceled, pending further intelligence. They were to continue their pressure on the Hun but wait for further instructions, which could come as soon as this afternoon.

Hawkes looked at the runner, his grey eyes outlined by rolls of skin. He was a lad who had to depend only upon the speed with which his legs could carry him to avoid death. Killing a runner was a prize shot for a sniper. The young soldier waited for a reply. Hawkes nodded, and wrote a quick note to the effect that the message had been received, and that he awaited orders. He also awaited the engineers, who were supposed to be laying telephone wire. He hoped they'd turn up before this boy was shot for his trouble.

The runner took the envelope, ran back through the zig-zagging front-line trench, to the turning marked "Maidstone Market," and from there to the second line, and then the reserve trench, past the advance dressing station, and out onto the land. Hawkes listened to him splash-splash away, until he could no longer hear his boots meeting the mud with speed in his heels. Then he turned back to his desk and lit a cigarette. He had been in the midst of writing a letter when the message arrived. "I regret to inform you . . . ," it began. Hawkes sighed and picked up his pen, but instead of continuing the letter, he spoke aloud the words in his mind, another message that would not be laid down on paper.

"I regret to inform you, Mr. and Mrs. Mott, that your son could not keep his head away from the parapet, no matter how many times he was told, so he was picked off like a ripe fruit.

Fortunately, Private Brissenden was close by, and managed to catch most of his brains before they hit the ground; however, he was unable to put them back in again. Sergeant Knowles of course says it was all the boy's stupid effing fault—well, not to me he didn't say it, but I heard him. I wonder why it is that the younger men who have just marched up to the front line for the first time feel the need to try to look over at the enemy. Is it part of the adventure they signed up for, this looking out at men their own age with guns? Perhaps you might know, Mrs. Mott, being the mother of boys. How many do you have out here now? Four, wasn't it? Well, let's hope the others listen to the men who manage to march back to camp after a few weeks in the trenches—find out the key to staying alive—"

"Sir!"

Edmund Hawkes turned around. He did not move with speed, but rather his limbs seemed to unfold as he turned his head.

"Sergeant Knowles. Very good. I will inspect the men at oh seven hundred hours. Usual run-of-the-mill orders today, Knowles—weapons, kit, and so on. There's to be sandbagging along the trench, and also a feet inspection, the CO is due here at eight thirty. I want to rotate tonight—we're expecting some cloud, so we'll also have to keep an eye out for the enemy. Here's a list of men who'll be moving back into the reserve trench, and I want you to bring forward Markham's company into the ser-vice trench. Give everyone a taste of something a bit different. Of course, tomorrow morning they could all be moving up here to the front line anyway, if the balloon ever goes up on this show we're all waiting for."

"Right you are, sir!"

"That's all, Knowles."

Hawkes was alone again, and this time he picked up his pen

and wrote to Mr. and Mrs. Mott, telling them how Private Benjamin Mott had died instantly in the service of his country, that he was well liked among his fellow soldiers, who ensured he was buried with full honors. They missed his quick wit and above all his spirit of adventure.

He folded the letter and placed it in an envelope—it would likely arrive the day after the Motts received official notification of their son's death in action. Then Hawkes picked up his notebook. Several lines of verse had been crossed out. He turned the page and began again.

> *Glory*
>
> *Why should I lay dying here*
> *In this strange and foreign land?*
> *Where is the glory?*
> *I cannot understand*
> *Why such as I*
> *Should have to die*

He drew his pen through each line and threw the notebook aside. *Stupid, foolish, childish.* He closed his eyes and wished he could envision Kezia again, sleeping by the lake, snug in the roots of the old tree. But now all he could see was Private Mott sinking into the mud, and Tom Brissenden kneeling over him, the boy's brains in his hands, as if he could push them back into his skull.

CHAPTER 13

*Women in Horticulture and Agriculture . . . Many women
who have lived a great part of their lives in town, and
who think with delight of beautiful summer days spent in
the country, imagine that they would enjoy life on a farm
without really grasping what it means.*

—*THE WOMAN'S BOOK*

K ezia left the milking shed at nine. It was later than
usual, but there were new workers starting, and she
and Danny had to get them used to handling the heif-
ers. Four women from the village had heard that Kezia would
employ them at Marshals Farm and come to the house in search
of work. All had husbands in France, and one, Milly Bamber,
had lost her brother just before Christmas. She'd told Kezia that
his commanding officer wrote that he'd not suffered, and had
been killed "just like that." She'd snapped her fingers to punctu-
ate her words. Kezia said it was a blessing for them all that he'd
known no pain. Then she demonstrated milking the cows, starting with Susie and going on to Sunshine, Bertha, and Molly.
The two women assigned to milking went about the task with
ease, once they'd got the hang of it. There were twenty milkers
in all, and they ambled in at six in the morning, and again at
four in the afternoon, as if they couldn't wait for the easing of
their heavy udders.

Kezia strode out towards the hop gardens, where Bert had
started another two local women workers on the dung spreading—
the two in the milking shed would join them once their first job

was done. One woman was newly widowed, with a baby born after her husband left for France; she'd begged for work, saying she could do with the money. The baby was snug in his carriage at the side of the hop garden, and from the gate Kezia watched Bert and the women for a while. Her foreman was demonstrating how manure had to be spread around the small mounds, known as hills, set about six feet apart in a row and from which each cluster of new hop shoots was emerging. Soon it would be time for stringing the rows, giving the hop bines something to adhere to as they grew. In a few months the young hops would be ready for the women to come again, to weave the shoots along the string, starting them off on their way—and before they knew it, those bines would have reached over ten feet high, some a half an inch thick and as prickly as rope, bearing robust hearty hops ready to be pulled and picked. No doubt it would be almost all women coming from London to do the picking again this year, with per-haps a few elderly men, or some wounded young men. But Tom would be back by then anyway.

Kezia stopped to speak to Bert and the women, then said she was off to get Ted and Mabel to finish ploughing the ground where the woodland used to be. Another few turns, some manure, and it would be ready for seeding. She strode off again up the hill, and as she went she could feel Bert watching her, so she looked back. Three faces were staring in her direction. She waved, and they waved in return, so she continued on her way to the pasture to halter the horses and lead them back to the barn, where she would set them in the traces and get to work.

Had she intuited Bert's thoughts, Kezia might have been sur-prised, for she often felt wanting in his company, as if she were an imposter—a young woman born to a more sedate way of life, yet taking up the reins—quite literally now—and getting on with a job that had to be done. Despite himself, Bert admired her. The farm was running—if not smoothly, it was clear to him that the bumps were fewer than they might have been. He knew she sat with the ledgers twice a week to make sure the books were balanced, and she came to market with him, where she was becoming known as a quick study and no shrinking violet when it came to pegging a price. She allowed him to advise her, but he'd noticed her questions were more, well— more educated—than they had been before Christmas. He was glad for Tom, that his wife turned out to have something about her, but he was worried too. How would they ever rub along together when he came home from the war? She wasn't afraid of Mabel any more, for a start. In fact, it was a funny thing, thought Bert, the way that she and the mare seemed to hold each other in some account now. Kezia commended the mare for her loyalty, and the mare seemed to be more pliable than she had been at first. Mind you, Bert always said that Mabel knew what she was about, and if anything, her temper was due to the fact that she couldn't abide a fool.

It was true, thought Edmund Hawkes. It was exactly as he'd guessed. You couldn't fight statistics, and thus far the statistics— numbers not made freely available to the press—indicated that for every five men marched to the front line, only two would come back down the line. Once again the numbers seemed to rise up and throttle him every time he tried to outflank the statistics and return having lost fewer men. He had a new lieutenant now to replace the one he'd lost. What was his name? He'd forgotten already. He never used to forget names, but now he allowed it to happen, almost encouraging a mental fog to shroud his recollection of names. He never failed to remember their faces, though—especially the faces of men in the throes of death. And with each of those deaths, there it was, another letter, another mother who could be proud of her son, who did not suffer but fought bravely for his country, according to Captain Hawkes.

The new junior officer seemed to have a shine on him, like a freshly minted penny. He was all of twenty and still wet behind the ears. And under the eyes, thought Hawkes. The lad looked as if he'd been weeping, and he wondered if Knowles had tried to wake him up with too harsh a hand before he went up the line for the first time—perhaps in a vain attempt to ensure it wasn't the last. Hawkes didn't always care for the methods employed by Sergeant Knowles, but he could see this bomb-cratered world from his perspective. If Knowles was to give the men the best possible chance, they had to be hardened, they had to be quick-thinking, and they had to be more scared of him than they were of the Hun. They had to fight their way into Knowles' good books, or else rue the day they clapped eyes on him.

Now Hawkes and Knowles had brought back their men— those who remained—and they were in camp for, what? A week? Ten days? Two weeks? During that time Knowles would not cease his nagging for a minute, would not miss a parade or an inspection. It was his discipline that was the true master of this fighting force, this legion of men that Hawkes would march into the eye of the storm once more, taking over the third-line trench, then the second line, and then, finally, the front line— until there was another big show, then those trenches and supply lines would be overwhelmed with stretcher bearers pushing their way through to bring back the wounded before they died, while men alive and adrenaline-riddled would be shoving past to get to the front, their sergeants shouting them onto the fire step and over the parapet into no-man's-land. No-man's-land because no man should ever set foot in such a place, and no man could cross it unscathed. As far as Hawkes was concerned, it killed your soul even if your body was intact. He turned to the notebook on the desk in front of him, and began to write.

To The Armaments Maker

Then he made a series of dots under the title of his new poem. He wasn't sure what he had to say to this mythical armaments maker. The words began to roll around in his mind, informed by the only snatches of recollection he would allow himself— Hawkes knew that memory could take you down faster than a German bullet—from the time he'd overheard a couple of men talking as he walked along the trench. Was it a week ago, now? It began with Carter, the bank clerk, a man more dexterous with a row of figures than the inner workings of his Lee Enfield.

"What I'd like to know," said Carter, "is who makes money out of this business."

"What business?" said the other man.

Hawkes didn't know his name. He was new, one of a cluster of new recruits just come up from the second line to replace men lost the night before, when a German raiding party had thrown a grenade into the trench.

"This business? This war business. What did you think I meant? Being a butcher?"

Ah, yes, the new lad had been a butcher's apprentice from Tonbridge. Private Timothy Letts. Hawkes remembered now, remembered hearing the other men joshing. *Come on, let's go to the front! Let's go over the top. And let's let Letts go to the estaminet when we're let out of this mess. Yes, let's—how about that, Letts?*

Letts had taken it all in his stride—his very long stride,

because Letts was a tall boy, which worried Hawkes. It didn't do to be tall in the trench. His mind came back to the conversation between Carter and Letts.

"So, what've you been talking about then?" said Letts. "Who makes what money?"

"Well, the way I see it," said Carter, "this here war's a business, and people make money in a business. There's your suppliers and your sellers, and the money comes and goes. I reckon we go one way and the money goes the other—look at it, there's the grub, the uniforms, the guns, and just think of the money going into shells and bullets and what not. Your webbing costs money, your boots cost money. Someone's paying—and it's probably us, the ordinary people—and someone's making the money. So, who is it? That's what I want to know. It's what we should all know, eh, before we fling ourselves up that ladder and out there where them Germans can pick us off."

"I'm doing this for my country. I don't want them Germans going over there and killing my mum and having their way with my sister."

"I'm doing it for my country too, Letts. But I want to know where the money goes. Who gets rich from you saving your old mum?" Carter had paused. "What's your sister like, anyway?"

There was some respectful talk about the sister, with Carter trying to wheedle an introduction when he came up for leave, "If I ever get a bloody leave, what with all this." Then Carter continued his opinion-filled monologue.

"Now, I reckon it's not just over here, but what if the whole world was in on it, you know, them as knows? I've been on the foreign desk, you know, at the bank, sending all sorts of money here and there across the world, and I've worked with your French, and your Germans, because they were all over in London. And I've got to speak as I find, I never had a bad word to say about the German on the desk next to me—and he was right sour when he had to leave, because he said he had a good job, and he wouldn't get the same position in Germany. Now you imagine it, all that money I've just told you about, going into the war on our side—well, it's all doing the same over there too. There's them Germans—probably that fellow I worked with—and they've all got to have uniforms, and guns and webbing, and boots and pay, and grub and horses. Where does it all come from and go to? Who gets the hat with the money, that's what I want to know."

Hawkes smiled when he heard Letts reply, "Oh, do leave off. You'll talk your own arse off if you're not careful."

Both Letts and Carter were gone now, buried in no-man's-land during a cease-fire, their names and the location of their remains recorded in the battalion diary so that they might be recommitted to the earth in a ceremony when the war ended. But they lived on in his mind and in the words he struggled to form. Hawkes was still dotting the paper with his pen when Knowles came into the tent and stood to attention. He closed the notebook and pushed it to one side, pulling a map towards him.

"Sergeant Knowles, very good inspection this morning. Good show."

"Sir!"

"At ease, Knowles." Hawkes paused and looked up at the man before him. "I've received a report regarding suspected limited enemy movements to the west, and I want to know more about what's going on."

"I can send a couple of men on a recce, sir."

"No, I will go myself, and I'll take Brissenden with me."

"Brissenden, sir?"

"Yes. He's a farmer, used to looking at the land. I don't want to take an office boy."

"Right you are, sir. Shall we get a horse ready, sir?"

"No. We'll both go on foot."

Knowles left, and Hawkes turned back to his notebook and opened it.

Forty-five minutes after leaving camp, Edmund Hawkes and Tom Brissenden reached several acres of woodland. They had spoken little on their way to a location pinpointed on the map Hawkes now held in his hand. They were on one side of a narrow ribbon of trees and wild shrubbery when they heard voices in the distance. They dropped to their haunches, then onto their stomachs, their guns pointed in the direction of the sounds. The language was German.

"How many do you see?" asked Hawkes.

"Four—not mounted. Christ, they're taking chances, coming out this far."

It was a random thought that came to Hawkes, a conceit that entered his mind and left in a fraction of a second. If Knowles were there, he would have given Tom Brissenden a dressing-down. *They're taking chances coming out this far—what?* he would have said between gritted teeth, as close to Tom's ear as he could. Hawkes knew Tom Brissenden would have then repeated the comment again, adding the "sir" he'd omitted. And Hawkes was well aware that the Tom Brissenden of old didn't care to address anyone as "sir"—and especially not the likes of Knowles.

"They're taking chances all right, but what are they up to?" asked Hawkes.

"They're just doing what we do—probably seeing how far they can come towards the camp without being picked off," said Tom.

"They could be a mapping crew."

Tom nodded. "Getting a read on how much ammo they need to destroy the camp, I reckon." He paused. "See, they're unpacking equipment. Yet they're sitting ducks—Christ, they're brave."

"So are we," said Hawkes.

"What do we do? As soon as we move, I reckon they'll know we're here—and there's more of them." Tom didn't wait for an answer. "If I take the two on the right, you could get the other two."

"We'd be lucky to hit a couple of bloody cows at this distance. If only they were a bit closer. Discretion might be the better part of valor," said Hawkes, his voice even lower.

Tom looked sideways at Hawkes. "You don't want to kill them any more than I do, eh?"

Hawkes shook his head. "I've lost count of the number of my men I've seen killed, but I've also seen enemy soldiers dead in their trenches or sprawled across barbed wire. I've seen photographs of a wife and children spilling out of a German's pocket into his insides, which were outside him at the time. No, I don't want to kill them. But I don't want them to kill us either—if they targeted the camp, it would be a catastrophe."

Tom looked at Hawkes, then back at the German soldiers going about the business of war. "Right then, Captain Hawkes. According to Sergeant Knowles, the Germans reckon we're using machine guns, when it's only the standard-issue Lee Enfield. Because it's so bloody quick." Tom positioned his rifle, stock tight into his shoulder, and pulled back the bolt. His hand appeared not to change position, so swift was his movement as he pulled back the bolt time and again, firing four shots in quick succession. Each bullet hit its target. The German soldiers fell one after the other, dead almost before they'd heard the shot that killed the first man. Hawkes felt heavy and rooted, as if he were being buried, the earth thick upon his chest. At once he was aware of Tom pulling him up by the arm. "Come on. Move, Captain Hawkes. We don't know how many more might be behind them."

Edmund Hawkes and Tom Brissenden made their way back to the camp, keeping close to the tree line, crouching at every sound and both feeling easier as they neared the camp boundary. As soon as they returned, Edmund Hawkes summoned Knowles and made his report. He commended Tom for his quick thinking and courage at a crucial moment, and ensured his name would be mentioned in dispatches to superior officers. His report confirmed earlier intelligence and made recommendations for increasing security. What Hawkes did not know, as he completed his report, was that by mentioning Tom Brissenden's bravery and quick thinking, to say nothing of a dexterity with a rifle that should have singled him out as a marksman, he had made the farmer even more of a target for Knowles. Instead he felt pleased at his generosity towards Tom, and tried not to think of the farm that would have been his, had it not been for a dilettante grandfather. Nor did he think of the wife he coveted. Today had confirmed something he had suspected, that Tom Brissenden was the better man. He sat back in his chair and took out his notebook again. He began again. *To The Armaments Maker.*

Dear Kezia,

We're now back in camp for two weeks. What they don't tell you when you first enlist, and what you can't imagine, is how boring this soldiering business is, and it's even more tedious when we go up the line. It

can get busy now and again, but not always for long—
sometimes I feel like a rabbit, doing not much in my hole
until I have to go out, and then all I do is run in case
that fox gets me. I don't often feel as if I'm going to get
the fox.

So, we're bored and we're hungry. It's not too bad
here, but in the trenches you can get a bit peckish,
especially because we're cooking for ourselves in mess
tins. Did I tell you, they even give us these recipes in
our soldiering manual? You have to be a genius to work
out this one—it's what they call Plain Stew.

"One man prepares two rations of meat—his own
and that of his rear-rank man. The rear-rank man
prepares the onions and vegetables, and passes it to the
front-rank man, who adds them to the meat, together
with a little flour, salt and pepper. The rear-rank man
then prepares potatoes for himself and his front-rank
man, and places them in the mess-tin, with sufficient
water and a pinch of salt. Thus in a kitchen of eight
mess-tins there would be four mess-tins containing meat
and four containing potatoes."

I copied that for you to have a bit of a laugh. As Cecil
says, we're all a bit rank here, so no one knows who
should be doing the cooking.

Tom reread his news so far and wondered if it would be wise
to let Kezia know he'd been a bit hungry—what with her being
able to cook nice dinners, it might make her feel bad about
it. He didn't want to waste paper—ink and paper were at a
premium—so he crossed out "we're hungry" and wrote above
the line "fed up with the same food." Just another little white
lie. He thought it wouldn't hurt to keep in the bit about being

peckish, because everyone gets peckish now and again. And it would make her laugh, telling her about the mess-tins. He continued the letter.

What we really miss is good white bread. I reckon the army only thinks of calories in and calories out, so we don't always get anything you would recognize as food you'd get on a plate at home. It makes us miss home comforts all the more. There's a lot of the lads who are quite put out by not getting proper bread. We're given this stuff called biscuit, which I reckon is more like that hard tack they give sailors. And when I say there are lads who are put out, I mean they are getting very angry, with some wondering why they enlisted in the first place, to not have decent bread. At least I have your cake.

Talking about biscuits, Cecil, my mate, he was sent a tin of Huntley and Palmers biscuits by his wife, which was very nice indeed, but no one gets cakes like you send to me, Kezzie. The cake I received yesterday was spicier than the last one, so I reckon you put a fair bit of something in there—was it nutmeg? Or cinnamon? You probably sneaked in more of whatever it was than usual, but I didn't mind. I had to fight the other lads off— they've become used to getting a slice of your cake or tea bread. You said you weren't much of a cook when we were first wed, but if the cake's anything to go by, well, you're a diamond. I miss you, Kezzie.

Tom finished the letter with questions about the farm, and put the letter in the envelope while imagining his wife in the kitchen, or her garden. He thought of the sweet smell of her hair when just washed, and the fragrance of lavender that seemed to linger on her skin. He imagined her drawing an iron across the linens, and setting the table, and his mouth watered as he envisioned the breakfast laid out, with freshly baked bread and butter churned on the farm. He kissed the envelope and placed it in the military post.

As had become his custom, Edmund Hawkes was the first reader of Tom's letters home. He skipped through other mail from his men to home—letters that asked after Spot the dog, or if Dad was still busy with his racing pigeons, or whether Granddad had won any money on the horses lately—and then lingered over a letter from Tom to Kezia. On some occasions he felt as if he had found love by proxy, though he was a little disconcerted by the almost-eloquence of Tom Brissenden's declarations of affection for his wife. He had thought Tom a much more simple man. At other times Edmund Hawkes felt like a voyeur, one of those men who paid to look through a small round glass in nighttime Soho, men who kept their heads down to avoid recognition, who wore their jacket collars pulled up, and who would give up a few coins to press an eye to a hole as if looking into a kaleidoscope—yet there was no cavalcade of color, just a few moments' worth of excitement to be had while watching a woman reveal herself layer by layer by layer. Silk and lace and bare skin. But he felt a little less guilty when he read this letter, for it contained important information. It seemed his men were restless, though not mutinous. And with good reason, he thought. As an officer, when in camp Hawkes enjoyed a hearty breakfast, a satisfactory luncheon, and a commendable supper, with wine. There was never a shortage of port or brandy. He could rest easy—well, easier than the men—on most nights. Even the officers' more personal comforts were of a better quality—a little more time with a cleaner girl at a different kind of *estaminet*.

His men wanted bread. Good bread that smelled of a bakery at home, and not rough brown biscuit. He had seen men cluster around Brissenden just to hear a description of Kezia's cooking, or taste a morsel of her precious cake. Now he read the letter again, and knew what he must do. He would provide that most basic of staples for his men. He would go into the town and place an order with the baker, and he would bring to his men enough pure white crusty bread, bread thick with the fragrance of yeast and sugar, so that each man would remember that lovely bread from Captain Hawkes dripping in gravy or with a layer of cheese mounted upon it, and the flavor and fullness of this gift of bread would linger long after the men had marched up the line again. Up the line and over the top.

CHAPTER 14

No one can be more trying than the person
who continually gives way to low spirits,
going about with a martyr-like expression.
—THE WOMAN'S BOOK

Thea wrenched the Rover into gear and pressed down hard on the accelerator. Her arms felt filled with cold lead in her heavy coat, while the engine groaned and shuddered as she maneuvered the ambulance along a rutted road towards the casualty clearing station. Though all but ignored by the British powers-that-be, the Rathbone Brigade had been welcomed with open arms by men and women working in the blood-soaked aid posts and casualty clearing stations. Thea ground the gears home again, doubling the clutch and using every ounce of her strength to pull the vehicle over to pass a line of soldiers marching up to the forward lines, their throaty songs lingering on the sleet-drenched terrain.

"I should have stayed at school. I should be in front of a class of nice little well-fed children, keeping my head low and out of sight. I should have stood my ground to support the pacifists. I should not have run away." Thea spoke aloud, as if to hear her own voice imbued her with strength. Men called out to her as she passed.

"Give us a lift, love?"

"Need a mate beside you?"

"How about getting in the back with me, darlin'?"

"You'll be lucky," she yelled back, her voice barely audible, so the soldiers saw only the movement of her mouth, and laughed all the more. At least she'd made them laugh.

The ambulance rumbled past, and soon she was out on the open road, but with another column ahead. This time it was a Gurkha regiment, returning from the front. The noise of the engine dulled the sound in the distance, but she leaned sideways, her head half out of the door so that she might hear. The men did not sing a marching song. There was no resounding "Tipperary" but instead a refrain that seemed to adhere to the very air around her. It was a lament voiced in their native tongue, a song that perhaps echoed a longing deep in the heart, and it pulled at her as surely as if she understood each word in every fiber of her being. These men yearned for home, craved something familiar—she could feel it. Tears began to fall down her cheeks, which she wiped away with the back of her hand, already blood-smeared from an earlier run. She was exhausted, and in the depths of her fatigue, she felt her acute sense of injustice rise up, a renewal of the anger that had led her to risk her freedom fighting for suffrage, and then for peace. *What is happening?* Why wasn't this terrible war being brought to an end? Why weren't the politicians, the leaders of these countries, sitting at a table right now, locked in a room and not allowed to come out until they had brought to a halt this boulder of death rolling down a hill unchecked, crushing everyone caught in its path? Was this how all wars went on?

Thea turned the steering wheel hard to the left and circled at the rear of the casualty clearing station. Using two hands to pull the gear lever into reverse, she then backed the ambulance close to the tent, where wounded would be loaded onto tiered wooden trestles for her to take to the hospital. The shelling was so close, she felt her insides shake with every thud, with every explosion.

"Oh, good, Miss Brissenden," said the senior nurse who

greeted her. "You made fair time since the last journey. I've eight men, two acute with internal wounds, three amputees and some heads, one facial. We have to get them all in somehow. I can't spare a nurse, otherwise I would send one with you."

"I've never had a nurse back there yet, Sister. I'll just plough on through and do my best to keep everyone as comfortable as possible. Let's strap them in to the extent that we can—the holes and ruts in the road are worse than ever this morning. The horse artillery went through with more ammunition for the front, and they've churned everything up."

"I've seen them—even the gun carriages are moving at full gallop," said the nurse. "Both horses and men seem fearless, though we've got a surgeon back there who calls them the arse hortillery. All in good heart though—they're heroes, all." She gave a half laugh, an embarrassed response to her use of soldiers' language. "Brissenden, I should tell you—there's a German boy in this load."

Thea nodded. "That's perfectly all right, Sister. He probably didn't really want to be here either."

The sister looked at Thea. "Be careful, Brissenden. Keep those thoughts to yourself, or you will find yourself back in England—and on a charge of sedition. I don't know that conditions in Holloway Prison would be any better than this for you."

Thea met the sister's eyes, feeling the old fear rise again. She swallowed. "I apologize, Sister. I've just seen a bit too much today, I suppose."

"No more than anyone else here has seen, and a lot less than most of my nurses in the past twenty-four hours. Now then, let's have these poor blighters loaded up and get you on the road. I expect to see you back in about two hours then, perhaps three. Is your colleague on her way?"

"I expect so—I passed her, so she'll have a quick cuppa and

slice of bread and jam, then turn around. I daresay I'll go by her again. Do you have some hot water to top up my flask?"

The sister nodded and reached to take the flask from Thea's hands. "Oh, my girl, your fingers are frozen. Your charges will be on the ambulance and ready to leave in ten minutes, once they're all in. Come on, let me warm your hands—it's not the best remedy, but it's the quickest. Steep them in water with Epsom salts, then make sure you dry them properly and put on some Vaseline jelly—you don't want chilblains."

Thea followed the sister, who she suspected might not have been much older than herself, yet some of the strands of hair that had come free from her cap were grey, and there were lines around her eyes. The tent flap was pulled back, leading into an area where nurses poured hot water from large pitchers into enamel bowls, then ran back into the main operating tent. An orderly came through with two more steaming pitchers. The nursing sister poured a shallow measure of hot water into a bowl, and added a handful of Epsom salts. She nodded to Thea, who dipped her hands into the water, and at once felt an exquisite pain as her fingers began to thaw, accepting the heat. She lifted her hands from the water, then lowered them again. She wondered if the sister intuited that she had not been able to feel her fingers for most of the journey, and she hadn't realized herself that she was frozen.

Thea was soon on her way once more, her hands tucked inside thick leather gloves. She would have to write to Kezia, to ask her to send a pair of silk gloves to wear underneath the leather outer pair—anything to help keep her warm. For now she would have to press on, weighing the requirement for a swift return against the need to maintain the comfort—such as it was—of the wounded men. If she went too fast, she would hit the ruts hard, and hear a cacophony of screams from the back of the wagon. If she went too slow, she would deliver more dead than alive. It was a balancing act, a high wire to be negotiated. And every evening she would do her best, with pails of water, disinfectant, and a scrubbing brush, to sluice the inside of her ambulance, watching the blood run out into the mud—gulleys streaming red with the essence of men, some already committed to the earth before nightfall.

Thea forced the ambulance back and forth to the casualty clearing station, often passing Hilary on the way. Once they almost slid into each other.

"Let's not give the boys any reason to talk about women and motor vehicles, Thea—the last thing we want to do is to lose Mildred and Gertie."

Mildred and Gertie, thought Thea. She'd never considered giving the ambulance a name until Hilary asked what hers was called, and she gave the first name that came to her mind. Now it proved useful. *Come on, Gertie. Just one more mile, Gertie. Let's not get caught in that mud over there. Listen to those boys, Gertie—come on, we'll sing too.* It was as if she had a friend on the long journey to the battlefield, someone to talk to when she was afraid, or angry, or tired in every bone in her body. With Gertie, she was never alone.

"I know one thing," said Jimmy Watson—Private Jimmy Watson. The men in the dugout looked up from the latest delivery of letters.

"What is it now, old son? Who's got on your nerves this time? Ain't Fritz over there enough for you, you've got to go looking for trouble?"

It was Cecil who had replied to Watson's announcement—or rather pronouncement, like a glove thrown down to see who might pick up the challenge of an argument.

"It's all very well you sitting there with your tin of biscuits, Cecil, my old cock, but it turns out"—Watson waved the letter in his hand—"it turns out my old woman's got herself a job and is doing very nicely, thank you. She's making the bullets and I'm firing 'em, so we've got a right little family business going. Trouble is, it seems she don't have much time to write a proper letter, but she's all happy about going off to the music hall with her friends with the bit extra in her pocket. Friends! Makes me wonder what I'm doing here, in all this mud, my feet dropping off, if all she can do is go down to the pub with her mates."

"I'm sure it's not as bad as that, Watsy. Really. She's working hard and it's her night off. She's entitled," replied Cecil.

Tom glanced across at his friend and shook his head. He wondered why Cecil had taken the bait. You didn't want to get Jimmy Watson going—he'd never let up.

"And it's not as if I get a tin of biscuits, like you, or a cake, like old Brissy over there—and didn't you get a new pair of socks as well, and a wrapper of homemade toffee?"

Tom nodded.

"I tell you, I've been over here since last September—so what's that? Almost six months? And what are the two things I'm really interested in?" Watson held the sheet of paper between finger and thumb, as if it were soiled clothing. "Letters from home, and when I'm going to get a decent plate of food in front of me. Now I know two more things."

"Oh, put an effing lid on it, Jim," another voice shouted out. "I've got nits crawling up and down me legs, I can hardly see the writing on the page, and all I can hear is you and your two effing things this, and your two effing things that. Put an effing sock in it, will you?"

Watson returned the volley. "If my feet weren't stuck to the mud, I'd clock you one—rearrange your dial for you."

"Come on now, that's enough of that—we've got plenty on our plates with the chaps in the opposite trench gunning for us, without going for each other's throats." Cecil nodded to Tom. "Read us one of your missus' recipes, Tom. Or has she let us down this time?"

Tom smiled despite himself. He hadn't wanted to read the letter aloud. He wanted to keep Kezia for himself, squirrel away these moments and savor them, cherishing her as if she were here with him, stroking his head until he slept.

"Go on, Brissy, let's have it." Another disembodied voice came from within the rat-stench darkness. "It's going to be that bleedin' bully beef and biscuit again tonight for us, so give us something to make our taste buds perk up, and maybe it'll all go down a bit better.

Tom sighed, and turned back a page. Someone leaned closer with the lantern, and he began to read.

"Bert went out and came back with four nice wood pigeons for us. When we were first married, I knew nothing about preparing a bird, but now you should see me—I'm much quicker about it. Bert said the best flesh is on the breast, but as far as I could see, it was the only flesh. So I took as much meat as I could, then put the carcass on the stove with water and onions and some herbs from the kitchen garden. I thought the boiling would get some more meat off the bones, and make a nice stock for the gravy. As you know, Tom, I don't really care for a plain sauce, and I thought with pigeon

especially, you need something extra to bring the flavor out. I'd put up a good half-dozen jars of blackcurrants in the summer, and I thought the color of them and their sweetish tart taste would do well with the bird, so here's what I did. I simmered the pigeon flesh with some best butter, just to get it going and brown it, then I added blackcurrants, and—"

"I don't know where your missus gets her ideas from. Mine would never think up something like that."

"Ssshhh! Let 'im get on with the story."

Tom didn't know who had spoken, but he felt as if he were a teacher in school, reading a story before the children went home. He remembered Mrs. Willis reading the story at the village school, remembered the sleep-inducing dreaminess of her soft voice. *Once upon a time . . .*

"Are you going to tell us what happened next, or what?" Jimmy Watson winked at Tom. "Get on with it, mate, don't leave us hanging."

Tom cleared his throat. *"I added the blackcurrants and—what do you think I did?"* He paused, looking round at his audience.

"Well, what did she do?"

"I remembered seeing a bottle of brandy in the back of the desk drawer, and I suspected it would really bring out the gamey taste of the pigeon and do very well with the blackcurrants. It's very French, you know, fruit with brandy. They have a liqueur over there called cassis, which is really blackcurrant brandy. Have you tasted any, since you've arrived in France?"

"Chance would be a fine thing."

"Shhhh!"

Tom ignored the interruption.

> "So, I added a few tablespoons of brandy to the pigeon
> and blackcurrant, and then, just for taste, I chopped a
> tiny bit of onion into it, then I let it cool down."

"Then what did she do?"

"Wait a minute, wait a minute," said Tom.

"This is making my stomach rumble," said Cecil. "And I could swear my tongue is swelling up."

"Your tongue will swell up all right, if you don't let him talk. You carry on, Brissy."

> "When it was all cool, I spooned it into a pie dish,
> and made a light pastry. Not flat ordinary water pastry,
> but a light puff pastry. I cut the pastry into a lid, and
> then nicked a little cross in the middle to let it breathe. I
> brushed an egg over the top and put it in the oven. I laid
> the table for us, and put out some roast potatoes and
> parsnips, which went down a treat with the pie. Did you
> like it, Tom? What do you think? Should I have added
> more salt? Or did I overdo the pepper? It might have
> been a bit too peppery."

"I would've gone easy with the blackcurrants, myself," said Jimmy.

"No, not me," said Cecil. "I reckon by the time the gravy is on the pie, the blackcurrants would have really given that bird some body."

"What's for pudd'n?" asked another soldier.

"Let me see," said Tom. "Oh, yes, she stewed some apples and put a little mountain—that's what she said, 'a little mountain'—of whisked cream on the top."

"Nice, you don't want a lot after that pigeon with brandy, do you? I mean, she put that pastry on, which wasn't your ordinary flat pastry, so a bit of apple pie would have fair popped you, wouldn't it?"

The men nodded, then one of the youngest said, "I wouldn't have said no to a slice of apple pie."

Cecil put his hand to his ear. "That sounds like Knowles—better look lively."

The men put away their letters and stood to attention at the very moment the sergeant entered the dugout.

"What's this, a party? Another mothers' meeting? Time you lot started moving again, so look lively about it. No bleeding long sticks of fancy French bread here, you know. No captain bringing the loaves and hoping the fishes would turn up of their own accord. Now then—" He looked at Tom. "Our brave knight in shining armor, Private Gravy, mentioned in dispatches for his skill and fortitude—you'll be on sentry duty again tonight, just after Private Watson here, if he can tear himself away from his wife's mumblings."

As the men filed out, Tom heard Jimmy Watson muttering, "Him and his effing 'look lively,' I'd like to make him look effing lively."

Tom looked up at the stars. It was a clear night, though not moonlit, thanks be to whoever was up there watching them. He'd read only part of the letter to the lads, only the bits they really wanted to hear. He'd begun to wonder how much of Kezia's letter was truth. Was she really eating well? Was the farm really kept up? He wished he knew how things stood. He wished either Bert or Danny had been the writing sort. Perhaps they'd be telling him what he wanted to know. After Knowles had left the dugout, he took the letter from his tunic pocket, and read it again, a candle held down close to the paper.

There's been talk in the village about us being able to keep Mabel and Ted. All the horses are gone now, except our two, and the mare, which the army never wanted anyway, because they said she'd be more useful in the pot than hauling a gun carriage. So I've put the horses to work in the village. It was a blow to everyone, you see—we need horses for everything, don't we? Mrs. Joe does the village milk round now, and Ted is sent down to take churns from the farms to the station first thing in the morning, and when she's done her round, Mrs. Joe collects all the mail from the early train and we take it to the post office for sorting. Bert, Danny, and I, we do what we can before we get down to work on the farm. There's been a lot of post going backwards and forwards to France from the village. You would have thought one thousand men had come from this one small place, not a hundred or so, counting those from just outside. Mabel can get fussy sometimes; you know she hates to leave the farm, but it's as if she knows she's got to work away from home, so Bert has taken her over to Bennetts Farm and Rushley Farm to help them out. The blacksmith says it will put him out of business, now that there's no horses. At least ours won't want for hay. And the saddler in Brooksmarsh reckons he's getting extra work now from a boot maker in Ashford, what with the army having a lot of new feet marching for them! I don't know what the

*village will do, if we don't have a blacksmith. I worry
that the men from the army might come back again and
take Mabel and Ted—the last thing I want is them to
see Mabel looking as if she's turned over a new leaf, or
the mare doing more than just taking me around the
farm and into the village. Mind you, I think everyone's
on the lookout, because Mabel, Ted, and Mrs. Joe are
saving the day here. No one wants to see them go.*

Tom kept the last few paragraphs for the half hour before he
put his foot on the ladder for sentry duty; he wanted to savor
each word as if it were a bite from Kezia's rich pigeon pie.

*But something else happened this week, and I don't
know what you might think about it. A man in uniform
came to the farm. For a minute I was scared he had
come for Mabel and Ted, or to tell us to plant even more
turnips, but he was from the military police—he came
with Constable Ashling from the village. Anyway, he
said he was going round the farms because they've got
prisoners of war, German boys, and they want them
put to work, being as all our men are at the front. I
told him I had village women working, and he said
he could give me one German—he knew we had lost
most of our workers, aside from Bert, who's getting on
now, and Danny, who's lame. I called Bert over to see
the man, and he said he'd be happy to make a German
work on the land, and work him hard, so we had the
German come for the first time on Monday. His name is
Frederick. Bert and Danny call him Fritz. I know this
will be a shock to you, seeing as you're over there, but
even Bert says he seems to be a polite boy. He speaks*

*English very well, and it turns out he was a student in
Heidelberg, but was sent to join the army even before
we went to war. He told Bert that his grandfather is a
farmer, and he has spent all his summers on the farm,
so he knows a lot about what to do when asked. Bert
says he reckons the boy is glad to be here. He told Bert
he hated the fighting, and it was terrible in the army.
He said he was always hungry, and he's grateful for
anything he gets to eat. Constable Ashling comes for him
every evening after work, and takes him off and locks
him in for the night, then he brings him back for work in
the morning.*

*Frederick is a gentleman to the women who come
up from the village and always bows when he sees them
and says good morning, and though they were very
suspicious at first, they say good morning back and then
nothing more. Everybody needs the work, and I have
to say, even Bert said we need the lifting power the
German can give us. They've said we might get a land
girl too. They're training women to work on the farms,
but as Bert said, our village women don't need so much
training, and he'd rather not have a town lass here, even
if she does try her best. I think he was a bit embarrassed
when he remembered that I'm a town lass. Bert reckons
the German is a good ploughboy, leading the horses
from the front while Bert is behind with the plough,
and says he does the turns just right. Danny always had
some trouble leading into the turns, on account of his
lameness. Frederick doesn't look like he wants to escape,
which is what I thought he would do. But where would
he go? I think he likes it here, and he seems very glad to
be away from France.*

Tom felt sick. What was the point of him being here, in France, shooting at Germans, when one of those same Germans was on his farm, saying good morning to his workers, and making a polite little German bow to his wife every time he saw her? And was he eating his food? Was he eating his pigeon pie with blackcurrants and brandy? What was it all about, this war, with him staring up at the stars and waiting for the enemy—the same enemy leading his plough into a perfect turn—to come for him? A wave of fatigue fell heavy across his eyes, as if they'd been covered with a warm towel. He wanted to feel his wife in his arms. He wanted her food in his belly, and her body close to his at night. He wanted to run his fingers across her skin, to feel the sweat of them together.

"Get up there, Private Gravy. Go on, lad, don't be shy. And you'd better keep your eyes peeled for them boys over there in the other trench—we don't want any of their silly-looking grenades coming over that parapet and planting us all minus our crown jewels."

Tom put his foot on the step and assumed sentry position.

"I didn't hear you, Private Gravy. I didn't hear you at all. P'raps it's my ears gone, on account of the shelling."

Tom stepped down and saluted. He did not make eye contact, but looked ahead. "Yes, sir!"

"You've gone and done it again, Gravy. Another smudge on your very stained copybook. Now you get up there, and you scramble where I know you're looking hard at that wire. And you stay there until I tell you otherwise."

"Yes, sir!" Tom marched once in place, turned, and placed one foot on the fire step, again in sentry position.

"Another step, Private Gravy."

Tom took one more step.

"Don't be shy—the Germans won't. Just you be careful you don't get a hole in your brain box."

Another step. Knowles came closer.

"I am watching you, Gravy. I am watching you very hard."

Tom could smell his breath. He was sick of smelling the sergeant's putrid bully-beef-and-Camp-coffee breath. Knowles lingered and then turned away, walking off in the direction of another dugout.

"You're always effing watching me, you bastard," muttered Tom.

He listened into the darkness, his hands firm on his rifle, his bayonet fixed. Sounds of the night descended, and he listened for the rats and the noises that meant feasting for the beasts, and those that meant the enemy was on the move. The enemy that might end up living a peaceful life on his farm if they were caught. He thought about his land, and allowed his mind to walk along the road to the fields, to Twist, to Pickwick, through Micawber Wood, and out to the perimeter line overlooking the Hawkes estate. And where was Edmund Hawkes anyway? Tucked up in his bunk in his officer's dugout—more like a palatial room when compared to the men's, with its soaking wet mud walls. He brought himself back to the farmhouse and imagined walking towards the back door, holding up his hand so the collies would stop at the threshold. He pulled off his boots—his father would have clomped mud across the ancient red tiles, but Tom thought more of Kezia, of the neat, clean, and tidy house she kept for him. He'd married a gentlewoman, so a gentleman he would be when he was in their home. *An Englishman's home is his castle.*

Oh, the smell of her cooking. The waft of pigeon and blackcurrants and that spoonful of chopped onion, and her herbs, dried in the pantry and smelling for all the world like the arid, heady shank of summertime. Ah, now the peppery waft of hops enveloping the farm, a breeze bringing the fragrance through the open window. No more could Tom feel the sharp needle of cold in his boots, or his numb freezing fingertips. He could instead sense his wife's lips on his cheek. And the dinner she set before him, on best china plates. Tom felt the cloud of fatigue spread out and envelop him like a soft blanket as he slipped deeper into the dream. *Oh, Kezia, my Kezzie. Hold me close and never let me go.*

In the bed in his dugout, where a small paraffin stove exhaled pungent fumes and little heat, Edmund Hawkes wrapped the blanket tighter around his body and lifted a flask of whisky to his lips. He wondered what Tom Brissenden felt when he began to read his wife's letters, and he hoped every word she wrote was cherished. He too could almost taste the food she cooked, and he imagined again that it was he who walked through the door to be greeted by Kezia. Sometimes he imagined them in a grand house, but of course, if that were so, then Kezia would not prepare a meal. No, it would be a farmhouse, with low beams and the stove always lit, come summer or winter. He wanted to see the look in her eyes when she brought the dish to the table, when she said, "I made this for you." Oddly, he felt no passionate envy of Tom Brissenden, and found that he admired the man for his fortitude—God knows, he needed it with that Knowles on his back. Hawkes closed his eyes. Soon it would be time for him to rouse himself. He never wanted to be an officer who waited to be woken in the morning; he wanted to be one who would walk the trench at night, would talk to his men on sentry duty, perhaps offer a smoke and a light and ask about home. *Is everyone well? And how are your children? Your daughter's first letter? She has a good hand, doesn't she? Well, thank you—and your mother made the toffees, you say? By jove, they're good. Not long now, Private Hopkins—you'll be able to stand down soon, but keep your eyes peeled and a good ear out for Fritz, won't you?*

Yes, just another five minutes, another sip of the whisky, and Captain Edmund Hawkes would go out and join his men.

CHAPTER 15

*It is a woman's duty to make the life of the
home as happy and gay as possible, and
however depressed she may sometimes feel,
she ought to struggle against the feeling and
not damp the spirits of those around her.*

—*THE WOMAN'S BOOK*

K ezia scraped her chair back from the table and took her
empty bowl and teacup to the sink. Plain broth with
vegetables. No salt. No pepper. No anything extra. She
couldn't taste and she was not hungry, yet she was sure that if
someone else had put a supper in front of her, she would have
shown gratitude by finishing every scrap on her plate. The day
had been long, her back ached, and she had barely the strength to
rise and take herself upstairs. When had she last felt inspired to
open a book before bedtime? When had she memorized a sonnet,
for the pleasure of hearing the rhythm in the verse? When had she
taken a few moments to brush her hair one hundred times before
wrapping the bristles with a silk scarf? She was still wearing the
corduroy trousers she'd put on at five this morning. When was the
last time those trousers had seen suds and the washboard? It was
all she could do to think about bathing.

She leaned against the sink, feeling hot salty tears run down
her dirty, scratched cheeks. How had she managed to graze herself like that? Perhaps clearing winter-dead bramble from the side
of the field. She didn't know. She didn't pay attention any more.
There was a job to be done, and she simply got on with it. And

this was an important job, keeping the farm up for when Tom came home. Oh, she wished Thea were here, helping her, taking some of the load. Thea would not wonder all the time whether she had been doing the right thing. Thea would just know, because this was her history, her beginning. It was Thea who had brought her here. Thea was so strong—and it occurred to Kezia that she might miss her even more than Tom, a thought that set off a fresh bout of weeping. *This will never do. I cannot be weak. I cannot fail.* She'd been all right until this morning, when Mr. Barham arrived with two letters. One from Tom, and one from her father. Perhaps it was her father's voice on the page that unsettled her.

Dearest beloved Kezia,

It seems to have been so long since we saw you last. When was it? January? Your letters fill your mother and me with pride, yet at the same time astound us both, and we find we are concerned for you. We never thought you would be left in charge of the farm, and it seems so much rests on your shoulders, which we are sure are becoming broader by the day. Your mother was rather taken aback when you explained that you were wearing Tom's trousers for work, but when she went up to town last week, she came back shocked and at the same time very proud. It seems that many young women are in trousers, working in all manner of jobs so that men can be released to fight for these British Isles. She said the skirts have become shorter too, and although the observation was voiced in the mildly disapproving manner with which we are most familiar, she said she would be one of the working girls if she had her time again. She may yet surprise us.

Now I must come to the purpose of this letter, to the nub of it, lest I dance around my news and do not get to the point. I leave for France tomorrow, attached to men of the Queen's Own Regiment. I offered myself as chaplain, and even though I was at first deemed too old, it seems I have been called to service in France, where I pray I make a good account in the eyes of the Lord at this terrible juncture. I join the men with the full armor of God around me and with the shield of faith in my grasp, and I pray that I may bring peace to the regiment in this time of war.

I am sure it will not be long before I am home again in the parsonage, with your mother quietly nudging me to have just another cup of tea with Mrs. Johnson, so that we can get the flower roster sorted out for harvest festival. I pray for these quiet staples of life to take us through our days, and I pray for your husband to come home again. I pray, too, for dear Thea, who I believe is a warrior of the heart. Last Christmastide, she left us in no doubt that the passions she carries within her run deep indeed. May God bless you all, and keep you safe until our precious Tom, Thea, and I return.

Your loving father.

Kezia filled two large cast-iron cauldrons with water and put them on the stove, then banked up the fire. She must not lose pride in herself. It was all very well, working on the farm, but she must keep herself clean, wash her hair, and be presentable on the farm and in the village. She was a farmer's wife, granted, but she was also a vicar's daughter, and she had to keep up appearances. The thought of her father brought with it an acute pain to her chest, a discomfort both sweet and sharp. But why so? Was it because he had been her foundation stone—now rarely seen, but there at the beginning of her life's architecture? Or was it because she missed Tom so much, and was worried about the farm? She would be going to market on Friday, and she hated market day. The feeling that she was a fish out of water came upon her whenever she was away from the farm's daily round, and could look back upon what circumstance demanded of her. At the market it was as if she were in a ring where she had no muscle for the fight. Yet, thankfully, Bert would be at her side, telling her, "Now then, I wouldn't take a penny less, you know. You stick to your guns, they'll come up to your price." And for the most part he was right, always congratulating her on a good market day, even if it was in his grudging tone—and if nothing else, she bolstered herself for his sake, and for Tom's. When proceedings didn't go their way, when the tweedy farmers, dealers from London, and rough trading overwhelmed her, he would lean towards her and whisper, "Never mind, Mrs. Brissenden, it was close, so we're not too badly off. The master would've been satisfied enough." And when she came home and worked on the books, as Bert predicted, they were usually not badly off, though the figures told her she often flirted with the red ink, and she had already been to the bank on several occasions to withdraw money from her aunt's bequest to make up the wages.

She stood by the stove and waited for the water to boil, picking up Tom's letter once more.

My Love,

The sun paid us a visit today, much to the surprise of us all. It didn't last long before those dark grey clouds

congregated like gossipy cross old women, and sleet
came down again, but at least it showed its face so we
know it's still there above the weather. The boys in their
flying machines would've been glad of it, I shouldn't
wonder. I've heard they don't like the clouds, because
you never know what might come out of them.

Your last dinner took me by surprise. Lamb's liver
with what? I said to myself. Wild garlic? Now, I thought
it would all be under frost, then you said you dried
some over the hop picking. You are a strange woman at
times, Mrs. Kezia Brissenden. My mother used to give
us a piece of her mind and a clip around the ear if we
so much as got a whiff of wild garlic around our ankles.
She said it was a terrible stink and it would never be
shifted from the house for months, if we brought it in.
And there you go and dry the stuff to put with lamb's
liver. She's probably turning in her grave. Well, I have
to say, it was tasty. Sort of oniony, though I think
adding peppercorns and a dash of cream was a mark of
genius, for a woman who says she doesn't know about
cooking. I suppose I could say that I know I'm a loved
and lucky man because my wife gives me wild garlic. It
makes me think of home, Kezzie, of the streams running
through the woodland. I can't wait to walk through
Micawber Wood, with your hand in mine. I thought
about it when I got your letter, and of course it won't be
long before there's that lovely carpet of bluebells, spread
right through the wood, and the clumps of primroses
and the wood anemones. They generally bloom just
before Mothering Sunday in Micawber Wood. Go down
there for me when they're blooming, and pick some and
press them, then send them to me so I can think of the

wood and you. Don't send any of that dried wild garlic though—the lads here will kick me out.

We had a nice surprise here, a couple of days before we marched up the line again. Captain Hawkes (you know him, from the big house across the lake), went out and bought loaves of bread, like long sticks they were, but very tasty—I reckon a crust of that bread would have gone down a treat with your lamb's liver . . .

Kezia looked up to see the water boiling, so lifted the first cauldron off the hot plate to make room for the second, which she pulled along from the simmer plate so it too could come to the boil. She went into the scullery, took the tin bath from the hook, and carried it into the kitchen, where she set it close to the hearth. One after the other, she took up the cauldrons and poured scalding water into the bath, adding cold to bring it to stepping-in temperature. She shed her clothes and allowed them to drop to the floor. A towel was already hanging over the rail above the stove, keeping warm to envelop her body once it was fresh and scrubbed clean. She opened the fire door so as not to chill. Easing herself into the bath, Kezia reached for another towel she'd placed on the table, folded it into a roll, then set it behind her head. She brought up her knees a little more to get as comfortable as she could, and closed her eyes.

How will I ever tell Tom about Micawber Wood?

She thought about the many letters, about the breakfasts and dinners and suppers she'd concocted, her recipes of love, not cooked on the stove or stirred at the table, not whisked with a bowl encircled by one arm while looking out of the window, but written out on paper. And her darling Tom had loved every bite, had responded to the peppering and the spicing and the cream and the herbs and all the things they imagined together.

But what would she do about the lie that was Micawber Wood? Yes, she would have to wait until he came home. There was nothing else to do. Why worry him now, when he was fighting for his country? For their safety and their future? She sighed. Before she'd left for France, Thea had said that was a lie too, perpetrated by the government to get everyone behind the war. Oh, Thea. Always so suspicious.

On Saturday morning Kezia planned to leave on the early train for Tunbridge Wells. Thea had written asking for silk gloves. Fine silk gloves with good stitching, two pairs. She had said that everything was going well, and that she was working hard. Kezia thought Thea must not be working too hard, to need silk gloves.

"Attention! Private Gravy!"

Tom awoke to the sharp end of a bayonet poking him in the back. He shook his head, pulled up his rifle, and presented arms. A sticky nighttime sweat gathered at the back of his collar.

Sergeant Knowles leaned in towards Tom, and once again Tom wondered what he'd done to inspire such hatred, though at this point he could not say he felt any different towards the sergeant.

"You are in trouble now, Gravy. I've caught you, and you are as good as dead—do you hear me, Private?" Knowles motioned with his weapon, bringing the bayonet up under Tom's chin. "*As. Good. As. Dead.* Sleeping while on sentry duty, putting the whole battalion at risk of being killed in their sleep. Fritz over there could have come running across, and believe me, he wouldn't have been bringing a nice cup of tea. I could shoot you now and be within my rights—and I'd probably be saving us all if I did. But I won't deprive you of your court-martial, Gravy, or a firing squad. And I won't deprive myself of the pleasure of making sure you get your due, either. Over my dead body will you get away with this." He pushed the bayonet harder. *"Over. My. Dead. Body."*

E dmund Hawkes wanted to be a fair man, a man who earned respect. He wanted to be known as a good officer, for there was little time to make deposits into his moral account. And now Tom Brissenden stood before him, with Sergeant Knowles' bayonet pressing into his ribs. *Five minutes.* If only he had left the dugout five minutes earlier for his nighttime walk along the trench.

"I've sent a runner for the MPs, and they'll be here soon, sir." Knowles bore an expression of self-satisfied pleasure, his mouth appearing distorted by the lantern's flickering light.

Hawkes shook his head. *Bloody stupid vermin of a man. He's had it in for Brissenden almost from his first day in the battalion. If only I'd come out earlier. If only I'd found Tom Brissenden, I'd have woken him up and told him to keep his wits about him.* Hawkes closed his eyes for but a second and wished he could put a stop to what he was now duty-bound to do. Tom caught his eye and gave a strange half smile. It wasn't a wry smile, or one filled with the kind of humor that a man indulged in when he was enveloped by fear. It was a smile that spoke to Hawkes. *Never mind*, it said. *Never mind, I know you don't want to do this.*

"Right you are, Sergeant Knowles. Please escort the prisoner into my quarters, where I will question him. I would also like to speak to the MPs when they get here. As we both know, we have time for nothing more than a Field General Court Martial and we certainly cannot summon a judicial adjutant general, given plans for an attack on Wednesday morning. Send runners for

Major Wells and Captain Barclay, so we will have the required three commissioned officers." Hawkes wanted Knowles to know he understood the correct procedures under battle conditions. "I want them here as soon as possible, given what dawn might bring. I know they'll curse at having been dragged along the trenches, but time is of the essence and they are the most senior officers I can get my hands on. I don't want Brissenden moved far, so find somewhere for his imprisonment—shunt some men along if you have to. I suspect the regimental aid post will be the most suitable venue for the hearing—God knows we don't have time to move back to the encampment."

"Sir—"

"Thank you, Sergeant Knowles. Good work. Now then, if you could escort Private Brissenden into my quarters, Knowles, and then wait at the entrance here for the MPs."

A few whizz-bangs jettisoned from the German trenches peppered the sky, and men began emerging into the trench from their infested dugouts. When he looked back, Hawkes could see only the shadowy shapes of soldiers burdened by layers of damp cloth and the weight of their weaponry. And though he could not discern their faces, Hawkes knew they were all looking in his direction. He could feel their animosity begin to expand, and their collective emotion, thick with the understanding that Brissenden's life could be taken by his fellow men, touched him like a blade run through his clothing and into his skin.

"Thank you, Knowles. That will be all," said Hawkes.

"But sir, according to regulations—"

"I am aware of regulations, Sergeant, but we are in circumstances where we have to interpret the regulations to meet the demands of our situation. I would like you to brief the MPs, who I believe will be here shortly. They will guard Private Brissenden until we can convene the Field General Court Martial."

Hawkes waited until Knowles had stepped outside the dugout, and kept his voice low. He did not want to know why Brissenden had allowed fatigue to claim him—God knows, he knew well enough the speed with which sleep could come, even amid shelling so loud it could shatter an eardrum. He had seen a stretcher bearer come off duty, then fall on the ground, fast asleep before his head met the earth. But now Hawkes knew he had to act quickly.

"Brissenden—Tom—I am going to speak up in your defense. And I will tell you that, although men have been found guilty of the same military crime in a Field General Court Martial, I personally know of none. Hard labor or penal servitude might be the worst you have to face, and believe me, both of those punishments can crush a man. We face battle within thirty hours, and I need every man going over the top if we are to take that German trench. Is there anything you can say to help me? Tom, there must be something you can give me, so that I can aid you in this hearing."

Tom shook his head. "No, sir, Captain Hawkes."

Hawkes sighed. "Look, I'm not stupid. I know Knowles has had it in for you. He's old-school—a man of the regiment long before the war—and he thinks all enlisted men are nothing more than town-and-country scruffs who've joined up for a bit of adventure. He doesn't think much of me, either—and I am speaking to you as my neighbor and an honorable soldier of the British army." He shook his head and rubbed his right temple. "And I'm going to admit, I can see his point—he has a job to do and he wants to get it done, and serve the army; he's been wearing the uniform of his country since he was thirteen years of age, and his loyalty is without question—he has seen action in places I don't even want to go. But I've seen his tactics, too—he'll choose one man and make him the scapegoat, the whipping boy. It serves to remind the men of the humiliation everyone can expect if they step out of line."

Tom moved, and in the flickering candlelight, he looked Hawkes in the eye. "I was dreaming of my wife, sir, but I don't believe I was asleep. Simple as that. But if I have to die, I don't want her to think me a coward."

Hawkes turned away, folding his arms. "I am sure Mrs. Brissenden knows only of your bravery, Tom—she married a man of integrity." He paused, then stepped forward to face the accused man again. "You were one of the first from the village to enlist—and you, a married man with a farm to run. Everyone would have understood if you'd remained at home and taken care of your land and your wife. When the time comes, I will speak of your love of your country, and I will point to the swift actions that led to your mention in dispatches—I won't see you taken blindfold before the firing squad, not like this."

Tom frowned and gave a humorless half smile, as if he were having to repeat himself to a fool. "I didn't do any of it for my country, sir—that's not why I went to enlist. I did it for the village, because men from my farm had gone already. We've always looked after our own, at Marshals Farm, and the people of Turndene and Brooksmarsh stick together. It's how it's done, isn't it? But the lads who came before me are all gone now—dead over here and buried in foreign soil." He spoke as if he had indeed been woken from a dream, and shrugged as he continued. "But farm boys buried on farmland seems just about right. I reckon it'll go back to being fields and grazing as soon as all this is over, this fighting." He paused for a few moments, seeming to stare into the darkness. "So if I die with them, then I won't die a poor man, and I'll be buried deep in a farmer's ground, which is not a bad way to leave this world, for a man who made his living on the land. And I have the love of a good wife to remember, don't I? But the way it's going, to my mind there won't be anyone marching back to Kent, will there? Or anywhere in the world, I shouldn't wonder. We'll all be here, dying in bloody France, and most of us wondering why."

Hawkes nodded and looked towards the canvas flap, the opening into the trench. "They're here—the MPs."

Tom stood to attention. Hawkes picked up his cap and checked his uniform. He sighed and shook his head. "How long were you out there, Tom—on sentry duty?"

"Five hours."

"Five hours? You're only meant to do two hours. That's why there's a limit, because men get bloody tired. For God's sake— why did he leave you so long?"

Tom looked Hawkes in the eye without flinching. He said nothing.

"I'll be bringing that up, make no mistake," said Hawkes.

Sergeant Knowles entered the dugout.

"Sir!" He stood to attention. "The MPs are here, sir."

Hawkes nodded. "Very good. And the officers?"

"On their way."

"Right you are. Yes. All right." Hawkes nodded and clasped his hands behind his back so his trembling fingers would not be seen. "I have one more question for Private Brissenden, then he may go."

"Sir, with respect—"

"Thank you, Sergeant Knowles. I don't think Brissenden is about to run anywhere, not with two hefty redcaps waiting with shackles."

"Sir." Knowles tendered his salute and left the dugout.

Tom looked at Hawkes, his stare steady, calm. There was no sign of fear, no twitching lip or eye revealing terror or nerves. "Yes, sir?"

"Tom . . ." Hawkes paused as if to frame his question, again barely realizing he had addressed this man he had known almost from childhood by his Christian name. "Damn this, I've taken enough bloody liberties here already. They'll be court-martialling me next." Another pause. "Look, Tom, what went through your mind on that day? When you took aim and killed each member of the German reconnaissance party?"

"I never wanted to kill a man," said Tom. "It never even occurred to me that I would, in my whole life. And it's funny— even though I enlisted to go to war, I never really thought about raising my gun and aiming at another human being. I'm a farmer—I've only known the land, really. I never took the life of more than a rabbit, a pheasant, or a chicken. And to be honest, I don't even like to see my livestock being slaughtered either, but it's what the farm's for, raising animal and vegetable, and harvesting both so people can eat. But when I caught sight of those soldiers, I knew they would see us or hear us as soon as we moved, and I knew they would take aim and fire, and I reckoned them to be good shots. I always said to myself, ever since I came over here, that I had to consider the enemy a good shot. But all the same, I reckoned I'd have to be better if I was to go home to my farm in one piece." He shook his head. "Funny that, having two ideas about war at once, that you won't have to kill, but you have to shoot to stay alive. And I am a good shot, Captain Hawkes. I'm very good. Always have been. So I knew it was either them or us, and if we let them go on with setting their sights on us, it could be the end for all the lads in that camp, and I wasn't going to let it happen, was I?"

Edmund Hawkes nodded.

"But I want to know something," added Tom. "If this here court-martial goes against me, I want you to swear you'll get men who are even better than me to do the shooting."

Diary, March 8, 1915

Hilary and I have been moved to another location this morning. As volunteers without official military approval (though we're subject to their orders as to where we can best serve), we seem to be shunted from place to place, according to where most wounded are expected to fall and need transport to the hospital. I've been told we are close to a place called Neuve Chappelle today, though half the time I don't know if I've been told the truth, because some of these towns aren't standing any more. I haven't heard from Tom, but I wonder if he is near here, as so many columns of men seem to be marching towards the front.

Thea shook her fountain pen onto the square of blotting paper next to her diary.

"Bloody ink!"

"Now what is it?" Hilary looked up from her book, illuminated by a lantern hanging from a tentpole.

"I think they're watering down the ink—probably to make supplies last. One minute I have watery blue handwriting, and the next, it's gummed up."

"Try a pencil."

Thea sighed. "I know—it would be the obvious thing, wouldn't it?"

She adjusted her lantern and continued writing.

I wouldn't say our previous quarters were palatial, but

the farmhouse was warmer, and we could boil up wa-
ter for a wash—not that there was much time to wash.
Sometimes I have a pang of nostalgia for the dreadful
bathroom at my lodging chambers. At least the WC was
inside, though—a far cry from the farm. I must say, I
was surprised that Kezia has managed to get on so well,
but on the other hand, I've known her for so long now,
and I should have remembered she's like one of those
toffee éclairs; you can sink your teeth in and then you
hit something hard that doesn't give. If I care to admit
it, I think Tom saw that more than me. I wish I hadn't
given her the book. It wasn't given in kindness. It was a
spiteful gesture, and she knew it. And it was a far from
loving welcome into the family—well, family such as we
are, now.

She paused, chewing the end of the pencil she had taken up
at Hilary's suggestion.

"You'll get splinters in your stomach if you do that," said
Hilary, turning a page.

"Old wives' tale," replied Thea.

"Where do you think the splinters go, then?"

Thea stopped chewing and, after a moment's thought, began
writing again.

I admit, I was jealous. It seemed I had not really be-
come used to the idea that Tom had chosen Kezia, and
that they were walking out, then suddenly, before I
knew it, he had asked Reverend Marchant for her hand.
We Brissendens were never churchgoers. The farm
was hard enough, without leaving Sunday's jobs until
Monday morning. But I should be grateful, because if it

hadn't been for Reverend Marchant, I might never have gone on from Camden to the college. I don't know what he said to Father, but he changed his mind. Jack Brissenden could barely see the point of Camden, let alone me becoming a teacher-woman. That's what he called me—a teacher-woman. In any case, I will have to make amends to Kezia. I owe so much to her and her family, and I have realized I love them as if they were my own, if I can admit such a thing.

"Better get some shut-eye, Thea," said Hilary. "There's a lot to do tomorrow. I've heard that Wednesday will be the start of a long few days. We've a couple of tin ladies to oil and check, and we've got the best record for having no breakdowns, you and I, so we've got to keep it."

"You've had a bet with someone." Thea closed her journal, stowed it in her small wooden trunk, and stepped towards her cot. She reached down to unlace and remove her boots, then slipped off her trousers and her thick green cardigan, followed by her woolen blouse. She would sleep in her liberty bodice with the cardigan wrapped around her, and she would keep on the men's long underpants that kept her warm in the ambulance. Her socks remained too, though she wondered if she would ever feel her toes again.

"I stand to make a few francs. That American Red Cross driver, the one with the fair hair and the blue eyes, he said Mildred was an old jalopy and would grind to a halt this week. I tell you, over my dead body will Mildred be allowed to falter."

Thea laughed. "Gertie is as solid as a railway train."

"Well said. Now then, lights out."

CHAPTER 16

*Discipline is a moral force. It is not a natural quality,
and can only be acquired by careful training. It is not
too much to say that its value in warfare is even greater
than courage, for discipline will enable men to conquer
fear and do their duty in spite of it, while courage alone
without discipline may avail little in battle. Discipline
is absolutely essential for the existence of an army in
peace and war.*

—*INFANTRY TRAINING,*
1914

Edmund Hawkes sat in his dugout with his head resting
in his hands. Sporadic gunfire peppered the night, ex-
pletives from the men in the trench salting their artillery response. One man called out, asking whether Fritz wanted
to get any bleedin' sleep that night or not. A call came back, a
taunt in perfect English from the German trench. "You need
your beauty sleep, Britisher?"

From the time Tom Brissenden was brought to him, Hawkes
had felt every sense in his being come to attention. He could
discern each component of the stench around him—men who
had not bathed in two weeks, overflowing latrines, decom-
posing flesh and blood leeching into the mud, seeping into the
swamplike trench. And rats. Christ, those rats stunk to high
heaven. He could smell his own body, thick with dried sweat he
imagined to be green, as if he were coated with mold; crawling
with lice he could barely feel any longer, lice that ran along the
dark seams of his clothing and into his hair, the folds of his skin,

places he would scrub until raw when he saw a bath again. *If.* If he saw a bath again.

It amazed him that at no point following his arrest was Tom Brissenden anything other than respectful and calm. He could have called Hawkes by his Christian name, Edmund, or Mr. Hawkes, as if they had passed on the road to Turndene, yet though they had known each other years—not as friends, admittedly, but that was only due to station and, as they both well knew, family history—Tom let nothing slip. There was pride in his demeanor, though no sign of insolence. That must have taunted Knowles, thought Hawkes. To Private Tom Brissenden, here, in France, even in private conversation, his commanding officer was Captain Hawkes. *Sir.* And the ingrained self-respect and the straight line he walked seemed to elevate the farmer more than it had either a sergeant from the regulars to whom he'd offered his salute, or the village squire, in whose hands his life was now held.

Hawkes began making notes for the court-martial. If there was to be a capital punishment following the hearing—and he hoped to God it would not go that far—then it would take place at dawn. The firing squad always went about their work at dawn. The hearing would be held as soon as a minimum of three commissioned officers were present. Were there witnesses? Who would speak in Tom Brissenden's defense? How could he help Tom make his statement of character, or a statement of mitigation, without demonstrating his lack of impartiality? Of more import, how would Brissenden plead? Hawkes thumped the table with the flat of his hand. And above all, was he telling the truth? Had the man been awake or asleep?

One thing in the accused man's favor was that at this point there were no commissioned officers more senior than a major within a reasonable radius. And the officers Hawkes had summoned were close to their men, not colonels or generals who might be spending their days cushioned in comfort peering at maps amid a self-congratulatory remembrance of fighting Boers on the Veldt, or dealing with native uprisings in India, where a wound might be from a sword, or a knife, or if it were from a bullet, there was a round hole, the blood easily staunched. These men had not seen, could not comprehend, the way a man could be cut in two by rapid machine-gun fire, or how a shell could mutilate a soldier beyond all human recognition. *He would have felt nothing. Death came in an instant.* And the noise, the incessant noise, thumping into the skull, shaking the teeth, and making the heart lose its rhythm; no, they never came close enough to those feverish sounds, so couldn't comprehend how very beyond tired a man might be to fall down and sleep, perhaps even more so in the hours before dead of night, a time when the armies on both sides felt their spirit wane, like a candle flickering before the flame vanishes. It was a wonder they had not all descended into lunacy. Hawkes sat up and shook his head. Perhaps they had.

He took another sheet of paper, and began to write. He would not wait to send this letter; it must go by the soonest mailbag. He would send a runner if necessary. He gave thanks for the speed and efficiency of the army postal service—a letter could reach its destination in England within two days, even from the front, and could be received from home with equal speed. The words he penned came with ease. They had been formed over the weeks since Tom Brissenden joined his battalion, and during the interludes when he read the letters to and from the farmer and his wife, peering over the fence into their union. He wanted this letter to arrive before any other letter he might be required to compose, or any telegram issued by the authorities. He knew of no other way to return

Kezia's husband to her side. And he understood that he could no longer assuage his loneliness by imagining her as his own beloved wife.

Dear Mrs. Brissenden,

I beg your forbearance in reading this letter, which I am taking the liberty of writing and sending to you. I wish to tell you that your husband, Private Thomas Brissenden, is a very brave man. He is a man who has already been mentioned in dispatches, and he is a man of valor.

Since I enlisted and came to France, I have seen men kill each other for perhaps three or four feet of land, and I confess it has altered me. My men are valiant warriors, and I am proud to stand among their number, and honored to lead them. In my opinion, every man who has fought for his country is owed his country. He is owed the very earth of our Kingdom under his feet.

God willing, Tom will return to Marshals Farm, and before long he and I will walk together across our Wealden pastures in the warmth of a Kentish summer, while jawing about the harvest and the price of cattle.

Yours, with my utmost sincerity,
Captain Edmund Hawkes

Hawkes called for Pullings, who was never far from his commanding officer.

"Yes, sir!" Pullings saluted and stamped his feet to attention.

"Pullings, I want to speak to Private Croft. And Pullings, I want you to do some detective work. Find anyone who was within earshot of what went on while Private Brissenden was on sentry duty. I want to know what time he commenced his duty, what was said to him—and I want to know any other tales of discord between Sergeant Knowles and Brissenden."

"Yes, sir!"

"One last thing—try to do it on the QT, Pullings. It's not a simple task, but Brissenden doesn't have much time."

Edmund had confidence in his batman. He might be a young lad, but he was from Brooksmarsh, and he knew the Brissendens and he knew the village. He would not want to see a Kentish farmer sent before his own country's guns.

Kezia could not sleep. Wind was howling across the roof and under the eaves. As the windows creaked in the darkness, she nestled down farther under the covers, burrowing into her loneliness. How would she ever keep the farm running? What if Bert were ill? Danny had been talking about enlisting—not for the army; his lameness meant he was considered unfit for service—but as an orderly at the hospital in Maidstone. He wanted to do something, he said, for his country. Bert had told him his country needed to be fed, so it was just as well he was on a farm. She turned again, stretching out her legs to unlock the cramp, her feet lingering on the cold part of the sheet for just a few seconds before she brought up her knees, huddling to make herself warmer. She wondered what time it was. Two o'clock? Three o'clock in the morning? Why lie awake at three o'clock, when there was never enough time to sleep anyway?

Kezia's mind turned, her thoughts picking up speed. Perhaps when this was all over, when Tom was home and the fighting was done, perhaps she would look back and see her life as being divided into three. There would be Before The War, During

The War, and After The War. She could imagine women in the shop, still wearing fresh mourning, talking about things that happened before the war, or how they did this or that during the war. And then they would say, *After the war, when everything went back to normal* . . . But would anything ever go back to normal? Perhaps normal would be like a town visited on holiday; once seen and vaguely remembered in a haze of sunshine. Normal was when we did this or that. Normal was when we were married. Normal is Tom, sitting at the table to eat his dinner. Normal is going into London to linger in Hatchards, or to have a cup of tea with Thea. Normal is turning the pages of a book, or making a cup of her precious coffee; tending the kitchen garden or driving the gig into the village.

Soon Kezia had exhausted herself and slept the deep, cavernous sleep that could claim the mind one hour before rising, so that, when she wakened, she felt as if it were the dead of night and she had not known rest at all. She could hear Ada downstairs, the grate being shaken and coal added to the stove for morning breakfast. Kezia wondered if she were about to sicken, for the thought of cooking bacon made her heave.

As Thea sat up, her cot creaked.

"Can't sleep?" said Hilary.

"No."

"It's the cold. We should ask for more blankets."

"Shall I light the stove?" asked Thea.

"Then we'll have to open the flap to get rid of the fumes, won't we? No, leave it, Thea. We'll have to get up soon enough anyway."

"I'm usually so tired, I go out like a light. It's probably all this fretting about tomorrow, keeping me awake."

"I don't want to even give tomorrow house-room in my brain," said Hilary. "We're going to be hard at it—they want all patients removed from the casualty clearing stations and field hospitals before the big show they reckon is coming on Wednesday. I've heard they're bringing more bearers in—imagine it, more bearers, and they're digging bloody burial holes already."

"It's the screams I can't shift from my mind, Hil. The terrible sounds coming from the back of the ambulance, when I'm driving. And if we're bringing men who shouldn't really be moved, I dread to think how they'll howl." Thea made fists against her eyelids. "I try so hard not to bump against the ruts, but when Gertie slides in the mud, I can't prevent the shuddering."

"Thea, the vehicle that will get those men from A to B without pain has not been made, and to my mind will never be made. It's impossible. But at least you're not driving an ambulance powered by a team of horses. Think of those drivers."

"I might be better at it," said Thea.

"You very well might," said Hilary. "Now then, I want to try to get at least a little shut-eye tonight. And we've got to get the girls oiled and watered in the dark, if we're going to make a good account of ourselves tomorrow, Thea. Rest your eyes, count glasses of cheap French wine, and try to get some sleep."

Thea lay down in her creaking cot and closed her eyes. It was not long before sleep came at last. She dreamed she was walking with Kezia to the church on her wedding day, the bride's long silken veil caught on the breeze, rising up and brushing against her maid-of-honor's face.

"You look like an angel, Thea, with my veil wrapped around you."

"And we both know I'm no angel!" said Thea, pulling the gauzy fabric away from her eyes.

And they had both laughed.

In her sleep, Thea felt soothed by this laughter, even though their togetherness was happening in the ether of her dream-world. It was a comfort that would remain with her for the rest of her life.

The two officers were escorted into Edmund Hawkes' dugout.

"For crying out loud, Hawkes, I can't believe I'm being dragged along a couple of miles of bloody trench for this—and I do mean bloody. A trench running red bloody water. You would have been well within military law to just have the bugger shot for his trouble." Major Wells slumped into a chair, his greatcoat hanging heavy with red-stained mud.

"I don't think it's as cut-and-dried as that, Major Wells," said Hawkes. He opened a drawer in his desk and lifted out a bottle of Calvados. "Fortitude, anyone?"

"Put that strange Gallic witches' brew away, Hawkes. I've brought something better than that," said Wells, reaching into the inside pocket of his greatcoat. "There you are—an eighteen-year-old single malt. That'll wet your whistle."

Hawkes took three tot glasses from the same drawer and set them on the table. Wells poured. They clinked glasses, then each man tipped back his drink and coughed.

"I have a drop of this every night. Glad it makes me choke a bit," said Wells. "If I get used to it, I might never stop, though I think slightly drunk is probably the best way to get over the top."

Hawkes caught Barclay's eye in acknowledgement of a shared sense of wretchedness.

"Right," said Hawkes. "Sergeant Knowles has made arrangements for the hearing to be set up at the aid post, so there's more trudging back through the trenches, I'm afraid."

"Witnesses?" asked Wells, as he fastened his greatcoat and replaced his helmet.

"Several," said Hawkes. "And I also have information to add, as the man's commanding officer."

"I understand this Brissenden has been mentioned in dispatches. Good soldier, was he? Before this, of course."

"First class, actually," said Hawkes. "But you'll have to come to your own conclusions."

"My conclusion is that I want to go home to my wife and children, Hawkes," said Wells. "And the sooner we can all get back to Blighty, the better. Men like your Brissenden don't make our lives any easier. This sort of thing gets on my nerves, and I'd shoot a man for that."

A tent had been requisitioned for the duration of the hearing, which was expected to last no more than an hour. The three officers were seated at a trestle table positioned along one side, and the place where the accused and the witnesses would stand was marked with a painted white cross on the ground. As the most senior officer, Wells read out the guidelines of the Field General Court-Martial, and the rules of trial procedure according to Military Law, Table Number 7. The charge of sleeping while on sentry duty was read with care, and the particulars of the Brissenden case were seen to correspond with the offence as stated. The three officers agreed that, to secure a conviction, and then to ascertain punishment, there had to be a quorum of opinion so that guilt would be beyond question.

"I'm no bloody lawyer," said Wells, his *Field Service Pocket Book* open at the instructions for a Field General Court-Martial. "But I think I've got this right."

To Hawkes, it seemed that Wells waved the book as if it were a household ledger. He was concerned by the speed with which the major wanted the hearing to be over, and his willingness to dispatch Private Brissenden to the firing squad. Barclay appeared less trigger-happy. Hawkes hoped he could persuade both officers that Tom Brissenden deserved an acquittal—if only on the grounds that he needed every man he could get his hands on for tomorrow's assault on the German trenches.

"All right, let's call Sergeant Knowles to bring in the accused and the witnesses, and get on with this, shall we?" said Hawkes.

A redcap on guard outside pulled back the tent flap as Sergeant Knowles led two more military policemen, who brought Private Tom Brissenden into the tent. His hands and feet were shackled, rendering him unable to move at more than a demeaning shuffle. Knowles seemed less than pleased by the line of four men who followed, and who took up their places alongside the flap, waiting for the call to give evidence.

Wells cleared his throat, announced that the court was duly constituted, and informed those present that the accused would be given the right of challenge, and that after the hearing the accused would remain with the escort and a permitted "friend of the accused." He asked Tom to state his name, rank, and army number. Tom responded, his gaze directly on Wells. The fixed look seemed to shake Wells from his slouch, and he stood taller to ask Tom how he would plead. Tom met the eyes of each officer in turn, as if to ensure they heard every word. Hawkes watched, leaning forward on his elbows.

There was a pause. Tom stood tall.

"Not guilty."

Hawkes sighed with relief and closed his eyes.

"Right," said Wells. "That's a start. No one will be getting out of here in a hurry. Sergeant Knowles, would you take your place.

Identify yourself and give us your account of the accused's guilt in this matter."

Knowles stepped forward and snapped to attention, saluting the officers. He recited his name, rank, and army number, and for good measure gave his number of years in service. He took a short breath before beginning his evidence, telling a clear story of instructing Private Brissenden as to his duty as sentry, and informing him of the hour he would take up that duty. He described finding Tom on the trench fire step with his eyes closed.

"Captain Barclay, do you have a question for Sergeant Knowles?"

"Yes, sir." Barclay turned from Wells to the witness. "Sergeant Knowles, how long had Private Brissenden been on duty at the time of the offence?"

"Five hours, sir."

"Five hours? Please correct me if I'm wrong, but is not sentry duty limited to two hours to avoid the fatigue associated with nighttime duty in one spot, and in the dark, and following a day's work in the trench?"

"Yes, sir."

"Then perhaps you would tell us why Private Brissenden was on the fire step for five hours."

"Two hours is recommended, sir, but if needed, the sentry must remain in place until relieved. We're short of men until reinforcements come up the line ready for the push."

Wells looked at Hawkes, who confirmed in a whisper that new recruits were due to join the battalion within hours, as described by Sergeant Knowles. Wells nodded.

"Do you have another question, Captain Barclay?"

"No, sir."

"Captain Hawkes?"

Hawkes stood up and faced Knowles. "I know this might

appear an obvious question, but as Private Brissenden has pleaded not guilty, it must be asked. Was it dark at the time you discovered the offence?"

"Yes, sir."

"Right. . . . And illumination?"

"We don't want the enemy to see where we are, sir."

"Yes, of course. As I thought. And this was at what time?"

"One o'clock, sir."

"And Brissenden had been on duty for five hours?"

"Yes, sir." Knowles paused. "As I have stated already, under oath."

"Quite." Hawkes took a breath. "So it was dark when you approached Private Brissenden."

"Yes, sir."

"I would like to know how you knew he was asleep."

Sergeant Knowles looked at Wells, and cleared his throat. Hawkes could see his jaw tighten and his eyes turn cold. He knew Knowles hated him. It didn't matter. At that moment he wasn't striving for Knowles' friendship.

"There was no movement coming from him, sir."

"No movement. I see. It occurs to me, you see, that a soldier used to the trench—and this was not Private Brissenden's first sentry duty, nor his first visit to the front line—would be adept at being still. Watching and being still are part of the job of sentry duty. Forgive me for playing devil's advocate, but a man's life could be lost to a firing squad within the next hour and a half, and I think we should look at this with care. How did you know Private Brissenden was asleep?"

Hawkes was aware of Barclay leaning forward in his chair. He looked sideways. Wells was studying the pages on courts-martial. *He's like the rest of us, learning on the job.*

"He jumped when I touched him with my bayonet, sir."

Knowles reddened. Hawkes had set a trap, and he had fallen into it. He was humiliated.

"Sergeant, would it be true to say that being touched with the end of a bayonet would make any man jump? It tends to lead to death. Perhaps you would explain." Hawkes felt confident now. He glanced at the witnesses. They were smiling.

"I have been a soldier in His Majesty's army since our monarch was Her Majesty, and I know when I see a soldier sleeping on the job. It's my job to know and to make sure there is punishment. The lives of all my men depend upon me doing my job." Knowles seemed to grit his teeth again. "Sir."

"Of course. Thank you, Sergeant Knowles. That will be all."

Wells called the witnesses, one by one. Each man was required to swear an oath with one hand placed on the Holy Bible, then recite his name, rank, and army number. Wells sighed again and again as Barclay and Hawkes questioned the men in turn. Finally he held up his right hand, and once again Barclay and Hawkes looked at each other, and at the senior officer's other hand, still clutching the manual open to the page that should have been guiding his every word and action.

"We have heard witnesses for defense, and for character. Personally, I would like to hear what the accused has to say before we adjourn the court for our consideration of findings."

Throughout the trial, Hawkes had felt his animosity towards Major Wells building. They were all tainted by this war, but Wells had a flippancy about him, as if one more dead soldier were just one more dead soldier. He wondered if this was Wells' way of retaining a distance from all that had come to pass, and all that would come to pass before the week was over. For Hawkes it would be one more day of preparation, one more day to make sure every man was ready, that—quietly, with compassion—every man had penned a letter to his family, and if he couldn't write, because God love them, there were those who couldn't, then men like Croft and Brissenden would write their letters and cards for them.

"Now then, Private Brissenden, you will give a full and truthful account of what had been happening up until and including the time you were charged with sleeping while on sentry duty." Wells twisted a pencil in his fingers as he spoke. "Full and truthful."

Tom Brissenden began. He told of taking up his duty at eight o'clock, and of the conditions at the time. He described hearing various sounds coming from no-man's-land, and summoning another soldier at ten o'clock to listen, and they decided it was the rats. There had been some sporadic gunfire, which led him to believe a German sniper was taking aim at any noise he heard.

"Then you fell asleep?" asked Wells.

"No, sir."

"Go on."

"On sentry duty, sir, you have a job to do, and that is to protect the trench, to look out for any enemy movement, anything suspicious. That doesn't mean to say you don't think about other things, does it? Not when you're out there for five hours."

Hawkes looked at Knowles, and looked away again.

Tom continued. "I was awake. I had my eyes closed, but I was listening."

"You had your eyes closed, Private?"

"Yes, sir."

"Then you couldn't see, isn't that so?"

"I couldn't see anyway, sir. It was pitch-black. You only need your ears when it's like that, and your ears work best when your eyes are not trying to do the job as well."

The three officers looked at each other.

"What were you thinking about, Brissenden?" said Wells.

"My wife. My farm. I was thinking how better my stomach would feel for a good meal in it. I was thinking what my wife would do if she had bully beef to cook with, and I was thinking of the dinner she'd just cooked for me."

Edmund Hawkes looked down at the notes he'd scribbled. He felt the heat rush to his face.

"That she had just cooked for you?" said Wells.

"Yes, she cooks for me, sir. Even though I'm not there, she cooks the dinner and the tea and she tells me about what she's put on the table. I close my eyes and I think of that food, sir. But I don't eat with my ears, so I can still do my duty."

Wells turned to Hawkes, and spoke, his voice low but intemperate. "This is turning into a bloody farce. I've a good mind to send this joker out there now with a dozen guns facing him."

"He's an honest man, sir. I will vouch for him."

"Impartiality's not your strong point, is it, Hawkes?" He looked at Barclay. "You'd better continue with this before I take out my pistol and put a bullet in his head and in that sergeant's head along with him."

Barclay stood up, clearing his throat as he looked at the sheet of paper in front of him, then at Tom.

"Private Brissenden, you were one of the first from your village to enlist, is that correct?"

"All the lads from my farm, bar two, went before me, sir. I couldn't see them go unless I enlisted."

"Good man." Barclay blushed, rustling the papers. "Now, Brissenden, my fellow officers and I are rather intrigued by your ability to hear more than anyone else."

Hawkes looked up at Barclay. *Christ, now he's trying to get clever, like Wells.* He looked away, towards the witnesses, each of whom had described the night when Knowles had made Brissenden crawl out of the trench beyond the parapet for his hours of sentry duty.

"Could you explain, Private Brissenden?" Barclay looked at Tom.

"Just as well this lad wasn't planning on being a solicitor, don't you think, Hawkes?" Wells leaned towards Hawkes, whispering with whisky breath.

"I've been a farmer all my life," said Tom. "You get used to listening. I can be fast asleep at home, in my bed, and I'll know if one of my cows is in trouble, or if a fox is about. Part of me's always awake, you see, even when I'm asleep." He looked at the officers before him and added, "Like a mother with her baby."

There was silence in the room, and Hawkes imagined that each man felt a warmth rise within him, and a memory, perhaps not quite forgotten, of his mother's embrace.

Wells coughed, then stood up. "Stand down, Private Brissenden. I think we have enough evidence with which to embark upon a consideration of findings with regard to this Field General Court-Martial." He nodded to the redcaps, who had been standing by the tent flap. "Please escort the prisoner to safe quarter, and Sergeant Knowles, you may march the men outside, where they must remain at attention."

"Yes, sir!" Knowles led the soldiers out, following the military police.

Wells leaned back in his chair. "Gentlemen, now we must decide upon Brissenden's fate. Guilty. Acquittal. Or if we can't get that far, we refer the case to a General Court-Martial under special circumstances. Personally, I don't want a bloody colonel breathing down my neck because he's got better things to do than listen to a farmer who can hear a pin drop in his sleep and thinks his wife is cooking for him. Remind me to ask him if she's got a recipe to make bully beef less likely to turn my stomach to water. No wonder the latrines are overflowing." He paused. "Right, then. Let's get on with it—the Hun's not likely to wait for us, so we'd better cast our votes. It's almost dawn, so we don't have much time. Five minutes, I would say."

Hawkes leafed through his *Field Service Pocket Book*, the guide to how to be a soldier in a time of war. He was tired, worn down by the trenches and by trying to do the right thing when death exhaled its fetid breath at them every single day. He thought how ridiculous it was, how incongruous, that this one book—no bigger than the Book of Common Prayer his mother took to church on Sundays—should have directions on sanitation, on first aid, and on cooking, on marching orders and on the care of horses, along with instructions for sending a man to his death. He flicked through the damp and yellowing leaves of small, almost unreadable print, and came upon a simple diagram. It illustrated the correct way to secure horses by means of linking. The horses stood side by side, touching nose to tail, the bridle of one looped around the saddle of the other. They could not move forward or backwards. They were stuck in one place. And at that moment, studying the diagram, Edmund Hawkes felt as if he were one of those horses, trapped by the circumstance of war. He was stuck in the middle, tied in a godforsaken place.

Chapter 17

*CHARGES. Sec. 6 (1K) When a soldier acting
as sentinel on active service sleeping on his
post. Maximum punishment—Death.*

—*FIELD SERVICE POCKET BOOK,*
1914

Reverend Marchant had woken early and was now in his uniform, seated at a wooden desk in his tent, his arms folded and his chin down, as if he had lapsed back into sleep. Yet exhaustion had not claimed him again. He was deep in thought, considering his role as an army chaplain. He shifted his weight in the chair, raising his head and looking at the center of the canvas in the predawn lamplight, casting his eyes up to a series of triangles joined at the top of the tentpole. He lifted his hands to his face and rubbed his eyes, then sighed, stood up, and began to pace. Marchant had wanted to prove something to his parishioners and to himself by volunteering for service. At the declaration of war, he had received word from the diocese that there should be support for the government, and that it would be policy to encourage enlistment among young men in the parish. And at that moment, in the shadow of war's engagement, it seemed to Reverend Marchant that it was the right thing to do, if in his own way. *Onward Christian Soldiers. God is on your side, boys.* He had considered it best to walk the path of balance, so in truth he had not encouraged enlistment, as such, though he had supported local boys who stood up to be counted.

It wasn't long before a trickle of the buff-colored envelopes began to arrive in town. *We regret to inform* . . . They seemed to come in on a tide—there would be a week with one or two, and then a flood, which diminished to a trickle again before the next run. And his daily round became more urgent, more troubling. He was turned away from as many bereaved homes as he was ushered into, and at once his sermons felt flimsy, as if they were made of gauze that flapped in the wind rather than the fabric of truth, strong, impermeable. A conversation about planning for the Christmas services and the school Nativity play seemed lacking, and his sense that there was something wanting within him came to a head during a discussion with Mrs. Fordham, who complained about rice strewn across the churchyard following a wedding—another hurried wedding before a young man left for France. He realized that he cared little for the rice, and even less for discussion about the positioning of flowers for evensong. After much meditation and a good deal of prayer, he decided to offer himself to the army. He had given war his blessing, and now he would take that blessing to war. But what had he expected?

Being referred to as "padre" was at first unsettling, and seemed to define how his role had changed. *Padre?* Though it smacked of Rome to an Anglican, he felt comfort in the word. *Father.* And had he expected a more enthusiastic greeting for a man of the cloth from the soldiers? His Sunday services at home drew a scattered congregation—perhaps only fifteen, twenty, at best—but he thought the fire and power of battle might bring a man to prayer. He soon discovered he had made an error in his assumption, though the soldiers were always cordial, and would welcome him when he went up the line to the trenches—and increasingly he went up the line with the men, and found that God worked through him just as well when he was helping a man write a letter, or listening to him talk about his young lady at home, or his work, or family. Kezia—bless her—had sent him a cake, which he cut into as many pieces as he could without it crumbling and took to soldiers in the front-line trenches. To a man they commented that they had never tasted rosemary in a cake, and it wasn't half bad. He discovered why those telegrams came in fits and starts—that all the men from a single town could be lost in a "big show" when they went forward into the cannonade as one. In between the battles, there were the boys who were picked off by snipers or raiding parties. It all became so clear once he was in France.

Reverend Marchant had earned respect, for he had shown his bravery in the heat of battle, when he crawled onto no-man's-land to offer succor to the dying, to give the last rites to one soldier after another. He accompanied men to the casualty clearing stations, and if a doctor shouted an instruction, then Reverend Marchant did as he was told, and on more than one occasion discovered himself to be at the center of a battle to save a life, rather than bear witness to its ending. Now, on this day, in the grainy darkness, he felt himself doubting not only his calling but his place in the midst of war. Who should he be? What would God expect of him?

Marchant drew back the tent flap and walked towards another tent where he knew he'd be able to get a cup of tea, and perhaps even a bacon sandwich—though the bacon was crisp enough to break a tooth, and the bread would crack any that the bacon hadn't damaged. The men called it the "refreshment tent."

"Reverend Marchant! Reverend Marchant!"

Kezia's father turned and squinted in the half-light. "Dorr—I mean, Thea—is that you?"

"Yes, it's me. How lovely to see you!" And forgetting all propriety, Thea held out her arms to the man she had clearly always respected, but knew best through the love and regard of her friend. She looked as if she had never felt so happy to see someone. "I heard you'd come out to France, Reverend Marchant, but I never expected our paths to cross."

"I'm not surprised to see you, Thea—you're a brave young woman. But what are you doing here at this time in the morning?"

"Oh, we had to bring supplies in for the big push tomorrow. And there are some patients to take back to the field hospital who couldn't be moved yesterday. We need to make room for a big influx of wounded, so there's a lot to do today."

"Have you had word from our dear Tom?"

Thea shrugged. "I'm his sister—so not only am I probably the last person to whom he would write, but I've moved on from my last billet, so my post hasn't caught up with me yet, and I've not heard from him in a couple of weeks. I've had a letter from Kezia though, and she says she's had communications from Tom—he writes regularly."

"Good. I'm glad to hear it—and I hope he's well." Marchant looked down and stamped his feet to ward off the sudden chill that seemed to envelop his body.

Thea shivered. "It's colder today, isn't it? At least I've got a cake from Kezia back at the billet."

"She's become a very good cook, I must say," said Marchant.

Thea nodded. "Better than anyone expected."

"Yes, and finding out what it means to be a farmer's wife—and probably more farmer than wife, now Tom's away. I'm just realizing what it takes to run a farm, from her letters."

Thea blew out her cheeks. "Well, I'd better get on, Reverend Marchant." She held out her hand. "I do hope we see each other again—I'm sure we will."

Marchant watched Thea walk away, back to the motor

ambulance parked outside the main operating tent, then turned back in the direction of the refreshment tent.

By the time Kezia heard the clatter of hobnail boots on the path, she had been up and about for some time. She had just taken fresh bread from the oven, along with a batch of currant scones. A spoonful of dripping was sizzling in the frying pan, ready for the bacon. Ada had taken a dozen fresh eggs from the chicken house, so breakfast would be on the table almost as soon as the men had washed their hands and dried them on the cloth already placed on the draining board. She might be tired, but Kezia had let nothing slip. The only difference between this day and a time before the war was that the farmer's wife was not wearing one of her day dresses, but was once more clad in a pair of Tom's corduroy work trousers, topped with a flannel shirt and a brown pullover. A tweed jacket had been hung over the back of her chair, along with a plain felt hat.

"That fair makes my nose ache and my stomach rumble— it's beautiful, that smell of bacon and egg. Nice to start the day with a full belly," said Bert.

Danny stepped into the kitchen and removed his cap, nodding at Kezia. She wondered if he would ever get over his shyness with her. It seemed to her that when he came to the house, Danny tried his best to become smaller, as if he were a shadow who could hide behind Bert. Perhaps she could tempt him out of his shell.

"I know you like your eggs poached instead of fried, Dan, so I've put a saucepan of water on to simmer."

"Oh, no, Mrs. Brissenden, you don't have to do that." Danny turned around as he rolled his sleeves and stepped alongside the sink. "I like eggs any way they go on my plate."

"Well, come and sit down then, won't you? The bread's still warm from the oven—Mr. Brissenden loves it like that, spread with butter and jam."

There was a bustle as the two men took their seats, and Kezia went from stove to table, then to the sink, where she left the pans soaking in water. She was about to turn and pull back her chair when she looked out of the window and saw Constable Ashling escorting the young German prisoner of war along the road to the farm.

"Oh, it looks like Frederick is here a bit early today. I wonder if—"

"I'll tell them he can wait outside until we've finished in here," said Bert, standing up.

Kezia watched the two men come closer, and it seemed to her as if they were like father and son on a walk, the older man listening, the younger telling a story, perhaps, and then the older one waving a hand to press a point. For a moment she thought she might invite the policeman and his charge to come in for a cup of tea on this, a cold, cold morning, but Bert's interruption made her think better of it. Even though something had softened in Bert and Danny towards the prisoner, she would not want to embarrass them. It was cold outside, though.

"Bert—it's chilly out there. Do you think the prisoner would want a cup of tea?"

Bert shrugged. "Well, I suppose it wouldn't hurt. He minds his p's and q's, and he puts his back into the job—and he's respectful, I'll say that for him. If you wouldn't mind, I'll get him settled on cleaning the leathers ready for the horses. Old Mr. Brissenden—not Mr. Jack, but Mr. Benjamin before him—well, he always said that even if the work is dirty, once you let the tools go and don't bother to clean off the muck, then you might as well see the whole farm slip through your fingers."

"I'm sure that's good advice. I'm taking Mrs. Joe into the village for the milk round, and Danny's taking Ted so he can do his duty with the coal deliveries this morning. Make sure Frederick knows that everything must shine. If we keep up appearances, it makes people feel better. I'll put some tea in a flask for him, and a knob of bread and jam."

Kezia busied herself making the flask of tea and wrapping a bread and jam sandwich in a square cloth, which she handed to Bert. "There'll be a fresh pot of tea here when you get back," said Kezia.

Bert left the kitchen, and Kezia watched as he lifted his cap to greet the policeman, while the German prisoner bowed to Bert and smiled. She turned back to see Danny standing, craning his neck to see out of the window. He sat down as Kezia joined him at the table.

"Is everything all right, Dan? Would you like more tea?"

The young man lifted his mug and set it down again, his manner troubled.

"I know I should hate him, the German. But I don't. And I heard some of the women saying the same thing the other day, that they were ready to make his life a misery at first, but there he was, polite and nice, and opening a gate for them. And he sings while he's working, songs that no one understands, but you reckon you know all the same. I don't get it, because part of me thinks I'm being a traitor for not hating him. But it's plain from what he's said to Bert that he didn't want to go to war. I reckon the lads from the village were up for a fight more than him. He's glad he got caught, and all he wants is for all this to be over so he can go back and get on with what he was doing before it started."

Kezia sighed. "I suppose he's more like us, then, isn't he?"

"And he told Bert and me something else the other day."

Kezia looked at Danny, setting her cup down in the saucer. "What was that?"

"He's been getting letters, you know, from home—they come in through the Red Cross, according to Constable Ashling. Turns out his older brother was killed in France. And he was a doctor, the brother—well, training to be one, when he had to go into the army. So he's lost his brother, and Bert reckons they must have been very tight, because Frederick was full up, you know, as if he would start weeping any minute. Bert said he looked as if he could do with his mother to put her arm around him. I never thought of them as crying, the Germans. I don't know what to think, really."

"No, neither do I, Dan. Perhaps I should tell Bert to ask the constable if Frederick can come in for breakfast in the morning."

"Oh, I wouldn't go that far, Mrs. Brissenden. Not with Mr. Tom over there fighting them." He shook his head. "But none of it makes any sense to me now, none of it at all."

When everyone had left the tent, only Edmund Hawkes, Major Wells, and Captain Barclay remained. Hawkes was concerned. Wells should take the lead. He should call them to order, even though they knew each other, and even though this was a tent and not a proper courtroom. The court was the process of executing military law, and Hawkes wanted to do all he could to make sure the law was on Tom Brissenden's side.

"Major Wells? I think we should consider the arguments and come to a decision."

Wells was slouched in his chair. He pulled his greatcoat around him. "It's bloody cold in here. You can never get away from the bloody cold, can you? I can hardly believe that just before war was declared, I was in the bloody south of France on my first bloody holiday in years."

Hawkes caught Barclay's eye, and the other man shook his head as if he too was flummoxed by the more senior officer. He decided to take another tack.

"What were you doing, before the war—what was your profession?" asked Hawkes.

Wells looked up. "I worked for my father-in-law—stocks and shares, that sort of thing. And in case you want to know, I enlisted because my wife's family were all for it, what with my bloody interfering mother-in-law saying it was the job of men to go to fight. And my wife agreed, and everyone thought it was a jolly good thing, so the next thing you know, here I am, in a uniform and promoted every time another commanding officer is killed. Terribly proud of me, they are."

"I see," said Hawkes. "Well—Barclay, what about you?"

"I was in pupillage, actually, with a firm of barristers. Lincoln's Inn."

Wells looked up. "So we've a bloody barrister in our midst, and here we are making a donkey's arse of the law. For God's sake, man—why didn't you say, instead of keeping quiet about it and watching us make ruddy fools of ourselves?"

"I'm not a barrister yet, sir."

"And I'm not a judge advocate general, but I'm doing the same bloody work. Right then, you can start."

Barclay fumbled with the papers in front of him, and Hawkes closed his eyes. For a minute he wanted to throttle both of them. They were all three of them neophytes, tripping over themselves in the dark while a man's life hung in the balance.

Barclay cleared his throat. "Sir, I think we should look at the evidence, and I think we should consider what the witnesses had to say, and I would put it to you that we should also look at the military record of the accused."

"I'm impressed," said Wells. "You've hidden your light under a bushel, haven't you, Captain Barclay? Don't get too good at this, or they'll have you at every Field General Court-Martial, doling out the advice." He sighed. "All right, let's make this snappy. For God's sake, the man will probably be dead tomorrow anyway—we could save him the trouble of being sliced in two by the Hun and his machine guns."

"It would be better for an Englishman to die honorably in battle than be cut down in a barrage of British bullets, sir," said Hawkes.

"And there is a plethora of evidence to point to reasonable doubt regarding his guilt, sir," added Barclay.

Wells smiled. "Reasonable doubt, eh? I don't think military law plays by that particular rule, Barclay, but well done. Get through this, and you might make something of yourself in London's cushy Inns of Court."

A silence descended and, as if hanging on Wells' sarcasm, remained for a moment, but to each man it felt like an hour. Hawkes sighed, then spoke up.

"Let's vote now. Let's vote on innocent or guilty."

Wells took out a hip flask from an inside pocket and passed it to Hawkes and Barclay, who each took a pull of the malt whisky. Barclay tore a sheet of paper into three, and handed one piece to each man. Hawkes allowed himself to feel confident. He was sure Barclay shared his feelings, but Wells was the wild card. Wells was mad.

Just a few yards away in another, smaller tent, Tom was seated, though he remained shackled. Cecil—who had been allowed to stay with him as his "friend of the accused"—drew his chair closer so their conversation would not be heard by the military police standing guard outside. Tom tried to rub one wrist with the fingers of the opposite hand, but only caused the rusty metal to cut deeper into his skin.

"Watch that, mate—you don't want lockjaw, do you?" said Cecil.

Tom shook his head. "Makes no difference, does it?"

"Come on, Tom. It's going in your favor, I know it is."

Tom looked at his friend. "But what if it doesn't?"

They were silent again.

"Do you reckon they'll give me time to write to Kezia? Or will they just march me off and shoot me?"

"Tom, don't—"

"But what if I don't get time?"

Cecil reached into his tunic and drew out a small notebook, a diary.

"Christ, never mind me, but you could get shot for that—keeping a diary—you'd better put that away," said Tom.

Cecil opened the leather-bound book and flipped to the back, where the pages where plain, not printed with dates. He tore out several sheets and reached into the tunic again for a pencil.

"Here. I'll keep quiet, and you write to your missus. Be quick about it, because I reckon we've only got about another five minutes. Can you manage?"

Tom nodded. Crossing his wrists to get more movement in his right hand, he placed the paper on his knee and held the pencil above the paper.

"I don't know what to write," said Tom. "I mean, I can't tell her, can I, that I'm about to be shot for cowardice."

"She knows you're not a coward—no one here's a coward. You signed up for this—you didn't look the other way." Cecil paused, pressing his lips together as his eyes reddened. "Tell her what's important—whatever comes to mind. But for God's sake get on with it."

Tom looked down at the torn sheets on his knee and began to write.

Dearest love, my Kezzie,

If you receive this letter, you will know that I'm in a bit of a tight spot. Cecil will tell you all about it, if things don't go my way, but I don't have much time to write this. What's important . . .

He stopped writing, closing his eyes, trying to bring order to his thoughts.

"Keep going, mate," whispered Cecil.

Tom nodded, and pressed the pencil to the paper.

. . . is that you know how much I love you, and have loved you since I was a boy. I always knew you were meant for me, even though I worried that a farmer might not be good enough for you. But you've done me proud, my Kezzie. I've asked a lot of you—I didn't realize it until I left, I suppose. The farm has been all I've known all my life, and what with having Bert and Danny, I thought you'd be able to manage until I came home, but I reckon it's been hard, and you've been a trouper and kept it all going. And you've been cooking me all the wonderful dinners and I've even dreamt about them at night, and—to tell you the truth—when I shouldn't have been dreaming at all. Kezzie, if I don't

*come home, you mustn't let yourself be tied to the farm.
I can't see Thea wanting to come back, so you must do
what you think is best, and you look out for yourself,
even if it means selling up.*

"Hurry up, mate. I can hear people coming," said Cecil.

*I love you, my Kezzie. I will never forget our wedding
day. You looked beautiful, but you've always looked
beautiful to me. It was the best day of my life.*

Tom folded the sheets of paper and gave them to Cecil, who
placed them inside the back cover of his diary, which he returned to his pocket, along with the pencil.

"I'll make sure she gets it, don't you worry, Tom—whatever
happens."

"Not time to say much," whispered Tom.

"Enough to say what matters."

Sergeant Knowles walked into the improvised courtroom first,
followed by Tom Brissenden, who hobbled in the shackles that
hampered every movement. The witnesses also attended, as did
Cecil Croft. Wells, Barclay, and Hawkes were standing.

Wells, unsteady on his feet, took the sheet of paper upon
which the fate of Tom Brissenden was penned in ink from
the fountain pen of Captain Barclay. He asked Tom to state
his name, rank, and army number. He recited the charge once
more. Then he paused. It was a long pause—a theatrical pause,
thought Hawkes.

Wells coughed. It was the throaty clearing of a man well used to the burning nip of alcohol throughout the day, an adjunct to breakfast, dinner, tea, and supper. He looked down at the sheet of paper, then back at those assembled.

"The court has come to a conclusion that the accused, Private Tom Brissenden, is not guilty of sleeping on sentry duty. He is hereby acquitted on all charges and is free to join the battalion once more."

A cheer went up from the men who had spoken in Tom's defense, though Tom did not smile.

Edmund Hawkes nodded at the redcaps, who removed the irons and chains from Tom's wrists and ankles. Sergeant Knowles showed no emotion, but called the men to attention, and ordered a salute and quick march from the tent. Hawkes wanted to talk to Knowles before more time elapsed.

"Right, I suppose we'd all better get back to work, eh, chaps? Got a party to prepare for." Wells pushed back his cap and scratched his forehead. "Bloody lice get everywhere."

The men left the tent, and as they stood outside, Hawkes, Wells, and Barclay swapped their caps for tin helmets, and put on their greatcoats once more. It was lighter now. Dawn had passed, and Tom Brissenden was alive. Hawkes watched Barclay and Wells leave, though he kept his attention on Wells as he wove between tents, and then back towards the trenches that led to his men. And at once he was again aware of his aloneness, another black cloud in the storm.

CHAPTER 18

*Upon Applying For A Job. If we shut ourselves
up from our friends and live entirely within
our own small circle we very soon become
narrow-minded and end in being forgotten.*

—THE WOMAN'S BOOK

K ezia had just returned from taking the gig into the
village for the milk round when Mr. Barham delivered a letter addressed to her. The embossed return
address on the front of the envelope informed both the postman and Kezia that it came from the Camden School for Girls
in Tunbridge Wells. Kezia thanked Mr. Barham, and inquired
after his sister, whose son had joined the navy before the war.
The young man had been killed at Dogger Bank, and his
mother left grief-stricken. The postman replied that she was
as well as could be expected, and that the navy, in a letter
from an officer at Dartmouth, spoke highly of Gregory and his
bravery. Kezia wished she had not asked, for it seemed that
such a question was akin to splashing through a woodland
stream—the inquiry only kicked up silt and made any effort
to understand opaque once again. She thought it might be best
if she stopped asking about the local men and boys altogether.
Then she would not have to feel anything. And if she admitted
it, the feeling she had was a bitter blend of grief for those lost
and guilt for the gratitude when she thought, "Thank God, I
still have Tom."

Ada was blacking the stove when Kezia walked into the

kitchen. Kezia picked up a knife, slit the envelope, and took out the letter.

March 8th, 1915

Dear Mrs. Brissenden.

As one of our most beloved mistresses and a Camden old girl, I am turning to you in an hour of need. In the past two months, four of our staff have volunteered for war work. Miss Ruperts, Miss Oliver, Miss Boulton, and Miss Harrington will be leaving at the end of this term, which leaves us understaffed as we approach the summer term and matriculation examinations for the older girls. I am not in a position to fill all posts before Easter—and anyone settled upon would take time to become familiar with the curriculum and expectations at Camden. I realize you are now a married woman, but the current circumstances have inspired me to cast rules aside and approach you with an offer. Would you kindly consider returning to Camden next term for one or two days each week? If this is of interest to you, perhaps you would be so good as to write by this Friday, March 12th, so that I will receive your reply by the following Monday, and if you are agreeable, the school will then make a more formal offer. I confess, I have already consulted the timetable at Tunbridge Wells station, and have ascertained that in order to meet the demands of the school day, you could catch the London train from Brookmarsh station, which arrives in Tunbridge Wells at twenty to nine, allowing you ten minutes to walk to the school, and another ten minutes before your first class begins at nine o'clock. You

could return home on the five o'clock from Tunbridge
Wells, though there is a half-past four, but that particular
journey requires a change of train at Tonbridge Station.

Kezia put the letter down on the table in front of her. She felt a ripple of excitement cross her stomach. Could she leave the farm for one day each week? She rubbed her forehead. What would it look like if she went off to a job in Tunbridge Wells? No one seemed to bat an eyelid when she arrived at the village store wearing Tom's clothes, so it seemed unlikely that anyone would gossip about her going back to her job. Apart from anything else, even though it wouldn't amount to a lot, she could do with the money. Kezia took up the letter and read again. She would think about it. She would talk to Bert, but not today. And she would have to consider Tom, what he might say when he came home to find his wife ensconced in her former profession, even if it were only one day a week. Yes, she would give the matter time to brew in her mind, and in the meantime, she had work to do.

"Right, Ada, this sitting about won't get anything done, will it? I'll see you when I get back, all right?"

"Yes, Mrs. Brissenden."

They exchanged a few more words about Ada's tasks to be completed, and about the weather, and if it might clear up enough to get a line of washing out. Then Kezia left the kitchen, put her gum boots on by the back door, and marched off towards the stable while putting on her old felt hat. The collies ran at her heels, following their mistress.

Edmund Hawkes asked Sergeant Knowles to pull the makeshift sacking curtain across the entryway so that they might have some semblance of privacy.

"At ease, Knowles." Hawkes pulled out a chair and pointed to another opposite the desk. "Take the weight off, Sergeant Knowles. The day isn't going to get any shorter—there's a lot to accomplish."

"If it's all the same to you, sir, I'll stand," said Knowles.

"Well, I'm not getting up, Knowles," said Hawkes.

Knowles felt himself tense, and became even more ill at ease. Everything he knew seemed to be coming into question. If he was standing, wasn't he supposed to feel as if he had the upper hand? But no, he didn't. As far as he was concerned, Hawkes was just another enlisted man making a mockery of the army, and they were all a disgrace, these new men. Brissenden had made a fool of Knowles, yet . . . yet . . . when he'd glanced at him in the courtroom—and yes, for want of a better word, *court-room* would have to do—there was no emotion registered on the soldier's face. If circumstances had been different, he might consider Private Tom Brissenden to be a very good stamp of a man. But Brissenden had made him look a fool. And though the court had concluded he was not guilty, and had passed down no punishment, Knowles knew there was more than one way to skin a cat, and that being so, he would have his pound of flesh. All in good time. They were a rabble, these enlisted men. You knew where you stood with a regular, and you knew how to control him. This lot were something altogether different.

"I've got the men sandbagging, sir, and making good the trenches where there was that attack the other night."

"Good, yes, very good." Hawkes looked up at his sergeant. "Look, Knowles, I wanted to talk to you about Brissenden and about the trial. The man has been acquitted of the crime, and though I know you wanted to press the ultimate charge, so that others would learn from a perceived error of judgment, we must forge on together here. The men are getting anxious about tomorrow, with some looking forward to the push, but—"

"Gets it over and done with, sir. Waiting to go over the top is hard on the men—it's easier when you get them running."

"Yes, of course. Well, I wanted to ensure that there's no ill-feeling towards Brissenden, or the men who came forward to give evidence."

"Not at all, sir. He's been acquitted, as you say."

"Good. A grudge harbored multiplies, Knowles. It's like a sickness in a man."

"Yes, sir."

"Right. I'll be inspecting at twelve hundred hours. I want every piece of equipment checked and double-checked. I want the trenches cleared to the extent that the mud allows, and I want the men reminded of their job. The artillery begin their show at oh seven hundred hours tomorrow morning. It will last for thirty minutes precisely, and we wait for the smoke to clear, then it's over the top at seven thirty-two on the dot."

"Yes, sir."

"Runners will be bringing synchronized watches before the artillery commence their work. I want you to ensure the bearers are ready for their turn. And finally, tonight the men must rest. No sentry duty is to last more than two hours. Is that clear?"

"Yes, sir."

Knowles was aware of a certain darkness in Hawkes' eyes. As the officer looked at him, he felt it as contempt. If Hawkes loathed him, then the feeling was mutual.

"Just one more thing, Knowles," said Hawkes. "Lay off Brissenden. He's had his scare, and so have the men. They're going into hell tomorrow, and we've got to do our best to get the job done and then bring back as many as we can."

"Yes, sir."

"That will be all, Knowles."

Sergeant Knowles pulled back the sacking and left the dugout. He swore under his breath, and if Hawkes could have met his eyes then, he would have known that as far as Brissenden was concerned, the sergeant was not finished. No, not by a long chalk.

Again Kezia could not sleep, so instead of struggling with the covers, she wrapped herself in Tom's woolen dressing gown and made her way into the kitchen. The dampers were all but closed, and the fire, banked up for the night, provided a gentle warmth. The collies, ears unfolded at Kezia's footfall, wagged tails as she pulled out a chair to sit at the kitchen table and set her writing paper and pen in front of her. She turned up the wick on the lamp she'd carried from the bedroom, and wondered what dish she might conjure to tempt Tom. She flicked through her cookery books, though nothing Mrs. Beeton or anyone had to say took her fancy. She opened the book Thea had bought her, the wedding present given with no knowledge of what lay ahead. Kezia closed her eyes and pictured Tom on their wedding day, his face as he turned to her, and remembered how she felt as she walked towards him, her hand resting on her father's arm. The congregation on either side of the aisle had seemed a blur, molded into one smile, one sea of goodwill. She felt her father lay his hand upon hers as they reached the altar. And dear Thea, dear beloved Dorrit, stood behind her. She opened the book and read the inscription.

To dearest Kezzie,

Thinking of the day you will be my sister in name as well as the sister of my heart.

With all my love to you, my most cherished friend,
                                                        Thea

Kezia felt tears prick the corners of her eyes. She realized that she had never given due thought to the inscription, never lingered over the words, but instead had closed the book after flicking through the pages, so hurt was she by Thea's apparent dismissiveness of her future role. They had made up—that was true. But she missed Thea, grieved for those days of school and college and easy friendship—a time before Thea became at odds with herself, before anger set her apart from those she loved and who loved her in return.

Turning the pages, now, Kezia found almost nothing to mirror her life. There was no tribe of servants to concern herself with—and Ada couldn't be considered a tweenie maid or a housekeeper, not by any stretch of the imagination. There was no butler's pantry, and no footman. She would never have to worry about seating the King and Queen at table if the Prime Minister were present—this was a guide for a different, more ordered existence. Now her life began and ended with the farm. She picked up the pen and, closing her eyes, composed a letter to Tom—her words creating an alchemy to bring them together, if only in their imagination.

Dear Tom,

I wonder if the weather there is any better than here. It's early morning now, and soon I will have to get the breakfast ready, and I think it's about time we all had something a bit different, don't you? So here's what you can look forward to today, you and the men. This will set you up! I've read a recipe for pancakes, using two sorts of flour—corn as well as wheat—and it occurred to me that it would be very nice with some ground almonds mixed in. Now, ground almonds are not the easiest thing to get—usually you only see them around Christmastime, to make marzipan for the cake. So, I went into the pantry and found some marzipan left over from Christmas—do you remember the cake I sent to you? Well, I didn't use all the marzipan, so I sealed it in another tin, just like I've been sealing the cakes when I send them out to France, with a bit of candle wax. Your mother had quite a few old tins stacked in the larder, and now, what with sending cakes to Thea and to my father, and to you, we're down to four. I shall have to get some more if I carry on like this. Bert says I should open my own bakery in the village. Marshals Farm Bakery, he said I should call it.

So, to make the pancakes, I chopped the marzipan in tiny pieces and warmed it a little, then I mixed in an egg and more flour, and made it into a batter—I never even knew you could do that; it wasn't easy, but it worked! The pancakes are light and fluffy, and I didn't cook them thin, not like on Shrove Tuesday, but left them a bit thick, more like a flat Yorkshire pudding. I heated up some jam with a little hot water and made a sauce. It's not the thing I would usually do, but I bet your mouth is watering, isn't it?

Where are you, Tom? Where are you, in France? Are you in a tent? Or a farmhouse? Kezia closed her eyes and tried to imagine where her husband might be, how he would be sleeping. Was he warm enough? Did he miss her? She wiped the tears again and said aloud, "Oh, Tom, please come back to me. Wherever you are, come back to me."

It was Ada who woke Kezia at seven o'clock.

"Oh, my goodness. Where are the men? I didn't cook the breakfast. Where are they?"

"Don't you worry, Mrs. Brissenden. They saw you through the window, sleeping, so they went off to the oast house, and they had their dinner for breakfast. They made a pot of tea on an old paraffin stove they keep up there—they bring it out and boil a kettle outside. Bert said there's nothing like a cup of tea brewed in the elements."

"Oh, dear. Oh, dear. I've got to get ready, there's work to do."

"It's all right, Mrs. Brissenden. The women are in the milking shed now, and Danny took the mare into the village for the usual round."

Kezia rested her head in her hands.

"Ada, would you be a dear and make me a cup of tea?"

"Of course I would, Mrs. Brissenden. You just rest now. You've had a lot on your plate since Mr. Brissenden left the farm." Ada went to the stove and put the kettle on the hot plate. "Oh, do you want me to take that letter down to the postbox when I leave? It'll be no trouble."

"Thank you, Ada—the sooner it gets over to France, the sooner I'll get a letter back, eh?"

Tom did his best to keep out of Knowles' way for the remainder of the day, and was grateful to be in his dugout once darkness fell. He was not assigned sentry duty, which was just as well, as far as he was concerned.

"Oi, Brissenden, read us one of them dinners what your missus cooked." A voice broke the silence. The men had been writing letters and cards home. For the most part, they did not mention the battle to come, but instead asked questions of their loved ones, and petitioned the recipient to "Give my love to Gran" or "Tell Uncle Charlie I said hello." Another asked his mother to give Trixie, his dog, a rub around the ears, and tell her that her master had a leave coming up soon. Yet another asked his wife if the baby was ever going to come—the whole battalion was waiting for news so they could go out and have a drink to wet the baby's head once they'd marched back to camp.

Someone held a candle closer, enabling Tom to see as he leafed through the clutch of envelopes, each one thick with news from home.

"How about this one—her roast chicken?" said Tom.

"Go on—she's written about three of them roast chicken letters, all of 'em different, and each one's tickled my taste buds."

"Shhhh," warned Cecil, "everyone quiet now."

Tom began to read:

> *"I thought I'd try something else with the roast chicken. First of all, you would be proud of me, because I cleaned the chicken myself. It was about time, and I know I made a good job of it, though you should have seen the kitchen floor, there were feathers everywhere."*

Tom paused, leaning closer to the light.

> *"I bought a lamb's heart from the butcher—which I am sorry to say came from New Zealand, which I know is a thorn in your side, what with all that wheat coming in from America and cutting prices at the market. They say*

*they've ploughed up half the country to plant wheat over
there. But the U-boats have slowed some of that coming
in, and Bert reckons we'll get good prices come harvest
time—mind you, there might be price pegging going on."*

"Never mind about that bit, Brissenden. I don't want to know
about the effing prices, just the food."

"All right, all right," said Tom.

*"I cut the heart into pieces and sautéed—that's a
French word, you pronounce it 'so-tayed,' and—"*

"French words—I've had all I can swallow of the bleedin'
French words."

"Shhhh!"

Tom smiled at the voices, though Kezia's was loud and clear
in his mind.

*"And so-tayed them in some best butter with rosemary.
I know you don't like too much rosemary, but it brings
out the flavor of the meat. I put in some more herbs, such
as I could scratch from the kitchen garden in winter, and
I added onion and a little celery seed. Then came the
bread crumbs, and some chopped dried apple. I mixed it
up well and packed the whole lot into the cavity."*

Tom felt a lump grow in his throat, imagining Kezia working
in the kitchen, her hair tied in a loose bun on her crown and
her sleeves rolled. She always seemed to be wearing a different
day dress and clean pinafore from the housewifery part of her
trousseau.

"Keep going, mate—dinner's not cooked yet."

"I sealed the cavity with a spear of rosemary, then I rubbed best butter into the skin with salt and pepper and a little curcumin. It gives something extra to the taste, though it isn't spicy. Then I put the bird in the oven to roast. Oh, you must have loved that dinner. Instead of just roasting potatoes on their own, I added some turnip and some parsnip and carrot, and I rolled the whole lot in olive oil—I treated us to a small bottle from the shop; they ordered some in because I kept asking for it. I chopped some thyme into the vegetables, and roasted them at the same time. It all came out perfectly, and there are even leftovers. There was so much food, I reckon we could have fed your whole battalion."

"I'll drink to that, mate," another voice came from behind Tom.

"Do you think she overdoes that rosemary a bit? It sounds all very nice, but I wonder about that stuff."

" 'Ave you ever tasted it?" asked another man.

"No, but all the same."

"The thought of that lamb's heart in the middle—well, your missus does you proud, Brissy, I will say that for you."

"Reckon we could do that with a tin of bully beef?"

"I don't know. But I reckon all you can really do is make stew."

"I tell you, Tom, mate, if I cop a Blighty tomorrow, I'm going to tell them to just send me back to your missus. I won't take liberties, mind. All I want is grub like you get."

Tom laughed, and the men joshed for a while longer, talking

of food, of their favorite dishes, cooked by a mother, wife, or sweetheart. And soon something akin to sleep claimed each man, though his hand remained on his rifle, and his ear was tuned to the outside of the dugout. Who knew what tomorrow would bring? For now it wasn't worth thinking about, but home was. Yes, home was always worth thinking about.

Thea had not slept. She was up long before dawn, by lamplight checking and rechecking Gertie. She drank tea with Hilary, and each woman managed to eat a couple of slices of bread with plum jam. Soon they would be on their way, soon they would be driving towards the fighting, towards the casualty clearing station to bring back wounded from battle. Sometimes she thought it was like a conveyor belt in a factory, with fresh human raw material moving up the line to the front, which she brought back to the hospital after that material had gone through the regimental aid post, the advance dressing station, the casualty clearing station, then her ambulance, and on to the hospital. But both she and Hilary prided themselves on their speed, despite the fact that they felt so very slow most of the time.

Thea packed her own first-aid pack into her coat pocket, filled a flask with hot tea, and wound a scarf around her neck. Before leaving the billet, she put on two pairs of silk gloves—dear Kezia had embroidered her initials on the inside of each glove—before pulling on the thick leather gloves, solid with dubbin to keep the water out. The flask was pushed underneath her seat, and she looked out towards Hilary.

"I hope this doesn't take too many turns to get going today—my back is calling for me to return to my bed," shouted Hilary, her voice thinned by the rain and wind.

"Me too. Take care, Hil—this is going to be a long one."

They waved, then Thea moved to the front of the engine, slotted in the starting handle, and began to turn. Once, twice, three times . . . *This time, please go this time, Gertie, love.* The engine rumbled and shuddered into life. Thea ran to the driver's seat, placed the starting handle on the floor beside her, and turned the steering wheel. In the near distance shells crumped and boomed, while overhead aeroplanes dived and swooped, avoiding enemy fire and ready to drop messages. They were the eyes of the army, keen eagles watching khaki-clad specks of life running in the mud below.

Captain Edmund Hawkes had received his watch, synchronized so that along the extent of the front line, a phalanx of men from the battalions would move over into no-man's-land and towards the enemy trenches. He inspected his men one last time and, walking along the trench, he stopped to talk to them, individually and in clusters. He spoke of their bravery, of loved ones at home waiting, proud, behind them all the way. He reminded them to run, then go down, then rise again, go down, fool the enemy, don't let him get his eye on you. He spoke of taking the opposite trenches, of honoring the regiment, and the whole of Kent, the Garden of England.

And still the barrage raged. *Don't worry, lads, the artillery boys will have knocked Fritz for six.* And then it stopped, and Hawkes began counting. He was on the fire step now, men were at the ladders, and Knowles was to the side of him. He began counting down the seconds. *Hold on, lads. Ready.* Tick-tock, tick-tock.

"Bearers up," shouted Hawkes, and the stretcher bearers stood ready behind the men.

He lifted the whistle. *Five—four—three—two* . . . everyone

counting in his mind, now, then the whistle reverberated through his ears and into his brain.

"Charge! Charge!" Hawkes could hear himself screaming, could feel his legs clambering over the parapet, men around him, all screaming in the charge, bayonets fixed, struggling to run with sixty-pound packs. Once again he felt himself slowing, yet he was running as fast as he could. His legs felt heavy, as if coated with treacle, though he knew he had not lost speed. Hawkes could feel every sense in his being come alive, while his soldiers were falling around him, hitting the ground amid those still on their feet. The waft of smoke and the acrid smell of cordite filled his lungs, and it seemed the only color he could discern was red. Red across the chest of a man whose heart had been blown clear through, red across thighs, red wounds in the stomachs of boys. And still Hawkes ran, onward, towards the enemy's trench. For some reason he would never be able to understand, as hard as he might try, later, to recollect these seconds, Edmund Hawkes turned to look back. And as he squinted into the smoke, he saw Knowles lifting his weapon and taking aim. Once again Hawkes felt as if time were waiting for him to catch up, as he perceived the trajectory of the as-yet-unshot ammunition from Sergeant Knowles' gun, and he realized that the person who would fall was not the Hun, not the enemy, for he was still too far away. Knowles was intent upon blasting a hole through Tom Brissenden.

Hawkes' scream was long and loud as he lifted his revolver, yet his entreaty to stop was not to be heard across the landscape, across fields that had once grown sugar beet and barley, and into which the blood of hundreds of men was now seeping. "No! Stop!" he shouted again, and at that moment Tom Brissenden looked to his side—not that he could have heard, but Hawkes wondered, later, if he might have sensed the bullet that Knowles would never live to fire. Edmund Hawkes felt his hand on the pistol stock, felt his finger hook the trigger and then pull back. And he saw Knowles rise up and fall in a shower of blood. Then he remembered nothing else of that day, except sometimes, afterwards, in the weeks before wounds claimed his life, he thought he could recall a smile on Tom Brissenden's face just a mere particle of a second before the enemy's shell exploded between them.

Reverend Marchant was walking from the casualty clearing station operating tent when Thea pulled up in Gertie, turning the steering wheel sharp to the left and reversing as close as she could to the opening where eight wounded men would be transferred from a recovery tent to the slatted wooden bunks in the back of her ambulance. It was her fourth journey of the day. Though he was close enough, she was in a hurry, so had not noticed him as he watched her, taking account of red-stained leather gloves as she leapt from the driver's seat and ran to the back of the ambulance. She pulled open the doors, and did not flinch as blood ran from the ambulance floor back out onto the dirt.

"Thea! Thea! Over here." Marchant walked towards her, and waved when she turned.

"Oh, Reverend Marchant—so sorry, I didn't see you. I must hurry, as men are coming in so fast, they need to make room here." The noise of an engine roar caused her to look over her shoulder. "Oh, here's Hilary—I wondered where she'd got to." She turned back to Kezia's father. "Look, I have to get on. So sorry. Perhaps a cup of tea later?"

"Yes, of course, Thea—can I help you?"

"Not really—unless you're a dab hand with a spanner. We've got to sort out Hilary's engine. Shouldn't take too long—it can't."

Then she was gone, running towards Hilary's ambulance,

whereupon she unlatched the bonnet and, taking an oily cloth from her pocket, began unscrewing something Marchant could not see. In any case, Reverend Marchant had no knowledge of engines, any more than of the working of the human body. His faith in the spirit was strong though, and never more so than today. He returned to the line of men lying on stretchers outside the operating tent. Nurses were moving back and forth, stopping here and there to mark a man's forehead, or to call orderlies to remove a man to the operating tent, or perhaps to the line of stretchers bearing those who had died, with blankets drawn across their shattered bodies. Marchant went back to work, turning his attention towards the living—the dead he could deal with later.

It was some twenty minutes later that he saw Thea bringing the ambulance to the other side of the casualty clearing station. All around, it seemed people were shouting—there was no other means of making oneself heard. The cannonade was becoming louder and louder, the sound of gunfire ricocheting into his mind and distorting his thoughts. *Where is she going?* Then Thea saw him, and waved from behind the steering wheel. He ran over to her.

"Where are you off to? Shouldn't you be driving away from the battle, not towards it?"

Thea raised her voice to be heard. "The advance dressing station is full to overflowing, so they need more ambulances to bring wounded up here. I said I'd go."

"For God's sake, Thea, you're going right into the shelling. Let one of the men go."

"Don't worry, I've a red cross on my roof and on the side, I'll be all right—Gertie and me, well, we can get through anything."

"I'll come with you," said Marchant.

"No, they'll need you here—and believe me, I have enough to do worrying about the boys in my wagon. I don't want to be worrying about you too—no offense meant, Reverend Marchant, but I don't know how I would explain it to Kezia if it was down to me that you got so much as a shrapnel splinter in your finger." Thea waved and pushed the ambulance into gear, while Marchant stood back so she could proceed. It was then that Thea stopped the vehicle and smiled at him again, and did something he would remember always, for though somewhat unseemly—he was a man of the cloth, after all—it was as if she knew. Thea reached out from the ambulance and, having removed the thick leather glove, held her silk-covered hand to his cheek. "You know, there are times you do so remind me of our beloved Kezia." She smiled and shook her head. "She worries too, doesn't she? But I am quite safe. Tell her I'm safe, when you write. And give her my love, won't you? My heart misses her so much."

For but a second Marchant covered her hand with his own, then she raised her eyebrows, signaling that she must be on her way, and pulled back her hand. She replaced the leather glove, waved, and pressed down on the accelerator.

The man of God watched the ambulance rock from side to side as Thea negotiated the rutted mud-filled road, manoeuvring around stretcher bearers moving the wounded. Then he turned away, and began to walk back to the cluster of tents, pausing to look up at the flying machines overhead.

It was as he took his third step—and he remembered that it was his third step, one for the Father, one for the Son, and one for the Holy Ghost—that he felt his whole body lifted by an explosion that seemed to pull the ground from under him, causing a riptide of terror and falling bodies. And he would remember landing upright, his feet on the ground, and that his legs began to move before he could even think, before he could even see in the direction of the explosion, before he heard his own voice screaming through his mind. *Thea! Thea!*

CHAPTER 19

*Self-sacrifice in the cause of duty may become
almost a fetich [sic] with many women. No
woman, however, is justified in making
herself a domestic drudge.*

—*THE WOMAN'S BOOK*

Kezia decided to travel into Tunbridge Wells on Friday. She was familiar with the home of Camden's headmistress, a flat in a Georgian house only a few steps away from The Pantiles. When she was a new teacher at Camden, she had been invited to tea with Miss Hartley, and had thought how lovely it would be to have the flat as her own, with such a perfect view of the bandstand. Miss Hartley said it could be noisy at times, but Kezia had only imagined sitting on the window seat and watching the world go by. She remembered these things while on the train, the gentle side-to-side rocking taking her back to another time. *Before the war.*

In the headmistress' modest sitting room, Miss Hartley greeted her guest with an unaccustomed gusto, revealing the level of her concern regarding the lack of teaching staff. Miss Hartley was even happier to know that Kezia had considered the proposition and was agreeable to teaching one day a week, and perhaps more if she discovered that, in time, her responsibility to the farm allowed a greater absence from its demands. A doughty housekeeper full of bustle brought the women tea, although as she reached for the cup, Kezia was embarrassed to realize that her soil-stained fingernails were in full view of her hostess. She took the cup with care to hide the offending nails, and did not sign the letter of agreement until she had put on her gloves once more. She would begin work as soon as school resumed after the Easter holiday, and at term's end would be free by the time the farm became busy with summer harvesting. Tom was bound to be home by then anyway. It was unlikely, she explained, that she would be in a position to sign an agreement for the autumn term. At this point, anyway.

"Some things have changed at Camden, Mrs. Brissenden," said Miss Hartley, setting down her cup, a signal that their time together was coming to an end. "The girls now have a knitting circle at school, where they are making scarves and gloves for our soldiers, and first-aid and nursing classes have been added to the curriculum. However, I am intent upon maintaining high academic standards and do not want Camden girls to become khaki followers, especially in this town where so many men are in uniform. Our young women must matriculate with first-class results—I predict that for many of them there will be no young men to wed if this war continues as it has started, so they must be well able to stand on their own two feet!"

Kezia wanted to counter the headmistress's opinion, but felt it best to nod her head and agree that the school's academic record must be held before all else.

Once the informal interview had concluded, Kezia decided to walk around the town, and made her way towards Mount Pleasant, where she went into Wickhams for a new raincoat, something to wear for work on the farm that fit her. Tom's old coat hung on her shoulders when it was wet, and there was enough heavy lifting to do without the extra weight of sodden fabric. Having made her purchase, she lingered in the ladies' wear department, and wondered if she should buy two new dresses for school, though it was not yet a year since she had last stood in front of a class. No, even though she was in possession of funds from her precious savings, profligacy was unattractive in a married woman.

As Kezia walked along familiar streets, it was not more recent memories that came to mind, but recollections of her years as a Camden girl. She missed Thea as much as she yearned for the return of her husband, so it was as if with each step she slipped a little further into an abyss of nostalgia. Even though the streets were familiar, and it was business as usual in the shops, it seemed to Kezia that more women than she might have imagined were wearing black, while most of the men she saw were in uniform. Here and there a Belgian accent pushed into her consciousness, and she remembered reading in a local newspaper about the many refugees who had sought shelter and work in the town. At first blush the daily comings and goings had not altered, but a closer look revealed so much that was new.

Walking back towards the station, Kezia was glad she had the farm to welcome her, glad to be going home to a purpose, and satisfied with the plan to return to her teaching post. She felt a certain confidence rising within her, as if she could keep the wheels of their married life turning so that, when Tom marched home, it would be as if he had never left the farm.

Monday brought a lightness to the sky, and showers promised to recede for a while at least. Indeed, Kezia thought the sun might break through, and went about her work with a sense of renewed energy. On Saturday she had received a letter from Edmund Hawkes, who had spoken so well of her Tom that she felt a welter of kindness towards him. She wondered what might have inspired so comforting a letter; she had always known she'd married a man of good conduct, and the letter proved it. Indeed, she felt as if Tom were with her now, watching her, proud of her mettle. *My Kezzie*, he would say. *My girl, my lovely Kezzie*. And it was as if the words had been whispered in her ear, ever to be remembered.

She had taken Ada home in the gig before midday, for the girl felt headachy. Kezia put a cold damp cloth to the back of her neck, and felt her forehead. It was obvious she was too ill to go on. Kezia instructed her not to return until she felt like her old self.

Mr. Barham had just made deliveries of the buff-colored envelopes to half a dozen houses in the village, and now made his way along the road to Marshals Farm. The recipients of these envelopes—containing messages he had come to detest delivering—were to a person polite. They thanked him for the delivery as he placed the envelope in their shaking hands, before touching his cap and turning away. These were the letters sent to the next-of-kin of enlisted men. Officers' families received such news via telegram. Often, by the time he had reached the gate, Mr. Barham had heard a wail, or a shout, or some terrible sound by which he measured the contents of the message. *Wounded—Army Form B.104—80. Missing Presumed Dead. B.104.83.* Or *Killed In Action. B.104.82.*

Now he walked slowly, his shoulders rounded under the weight of his burden, though his bag was not heavy. At last he arrived at the farm door, and lingered for a half moment, looking down at the two envelopes, one from Reverend Marchant. He lifted his hand to knock, but the door opened, and before him stood Kezia Brissenden, wearing her husband's trousers, her husband's shirt and pullover. She was in the process of pulling on a mackintosh quite obvious in its newness—there was not a scrap of dry mud to be seen—and she smiled when she saw him.

"Oh, hello, Mr. Barham. Not bad weather today, eh? Those clouds have become rather grey, though, so I thought I'd put my mackintosh on before I go out. Ah, you've letters for me?"

The postman felt the color drain from his face, and his voice lost its timbre even before he opened his mouth.

"I'm very sorry, Mrs. Brissenden. I've got a letter for you—well, two letters. One's official."

Kezia stood with her left arm in the sleeve, and the right to her chest.

"Mrs. Brissenden?"

"Yes. Yes, of course. Yes. Yes. Well, thank you, Mr. Barham." She pulled her arms from the sleeves and dropped the new mackintosh on the doorstep. She took the two envelopes, turned, and closed the door.

Barham lingered for a second or two, trying to decide whether he should find Bert or Danny. He wondered whether Ada was in the house. Yes, of course she was, so Tom Brissenden's wife wouldn't be alone. Nothing worse than being on your own when bad news comes calling.

Kezia read the words "OHMS—On His Majesty's Service" at the top of the envelope, and for a moment she could not allow her eyes to read any further. Then, like a fearful child creeping along a landing in the dark, she allowed herself to read the date. She held her breath as she hooked her finger into the flap of the envelope, tore it across, and took out the letter.

We regret to inform you that Private T. J. Brissenden was killed in action March 14th, 1915. Lord Kitchener sends his sympathy. Secretary, War Office.

There was more, but Kezia had felt her stomach loosen, and bent double across the table. No sound issued from her open mouth. No tears came, though they would, in time. Instead she remained holding on to the table, for without it she would fall. It was her father's handwriting on the second envelope that pushed her into a chair. Yes, it would be her father's comfort, reaching out to her from France. Each breath came deep and rasping as she took the pages out and unfolded the news. Her hands were shaking. She could not hold the paper still, and squinted as perspiration stung her eyes.

My dear beloved Kezia,

It is with a heavy heart that I write to you today, though I suspect with the battle now in progress my letter might take a few days to arrive at your door. I am afraid I have tragic news, for which you must fortify yourself.

Kezia's eyes skimmed across the words, seeking the solace her father's letter must contain, for surely someone had told him about Tom.

I have also written to your mother, so I am sure she will be on her way by the time you read this letter. I have instructed her to travel to the farm without delay. My dear daughter, I know there is no simple way to impart bad news, but I wanted this to come from me, your father, so that if a messenger is to be the subject of your hatred, it is I, who has had so much of your love.

It was then that Kezia saw the word she had intuited was on the page, even though she had hoped it to be different,

even though she had persuaded herself it was about her husband.

Thea.

"No-no-no-no-no," Kezia could hear herself saying, over and
over and over again. "No-no-no-no . . ."

*Dear Thea volunteered to drive closer to the battlefield
to bring out wounded men. I had barely turned my back
when I heard the explosion. I ran to her side, and I can
only tell you that the Lord took her in an instant and
without pain.*

There were many more words of consolation from Reverend
Marchant to his daughter. But Kezia could read no further.
Thea. Thea. My dearest Dorrit. She was numb in every part of
her body, so she stamped her feet on the hard kitchen floor and
banged her fists on the table. *Thea . . . Thea . . .* Still she could
not feel. She turned to the range, reaching with splayed fingers
towards the hot plates—but pulled back just before touching
the searing metal. She brought her hands together and dropped
to her knees.

"Help me," she said. "Please help me . . ."

Kezia knew, then, that she had to move. She could think
of no other way to wrench control over time, to slow it down,
to give herself time to think, and to restore her life's rhythm.
But what? What could she do? What could she do to set her
body to work, to ground the lightning bolt that two simple envelopes contained? She wanted Tom in her kitchen. She wanted
to touch Thea again, to have something of her to hold. And as
she pressed her knuckles to her eyes and felt each breath, each
heartbeat as it sustained her life, she remembered something
she had read in the book Thea had given her. She had not been

looking for anything in particular at the time, but it was while leafing through, wondering how much of the book might be useful, that she had seen the passage.

> *The gloom cast over a family by the death of a dear one leaves the bereaved relatives without much heart for forms and ceremonies.*

Hadn't she always brought ceremony to her days with Tom? Hadn't she brought rhythm and song to the loves of her life, when she set the table with linen and silver, and a towel on the draining board, and lavender soap? And hadn't she and Thea enjoyed their ceremonies? The cake on the table, the picking out of walnuts and cups of tea in Thea's lodging, or Kezia's room?

Had she been observed, some might have noted that Kezia Brissenden was in the midst of experiencing a profound shock. But there again, another would have said that, no, this woman is not at all perturbed. *See how she puts on her mackintosh. Look how she pulls on her boots and strides along the path to the chicken house.* With little hesitation Kezia selected an older hen, one she knew to be a poor layer. She took up the bird and with a deft movement snapped its neck. On her way back to the house, she stopped only long enough in the kitchen garden to pick whatever herbs she could find. March in England was never a good month for herbs.

Kezia walked back to the kitchen and placed the bird in the sink. She removed her boots and set them together by the back door, and then she put on an apron. She plucked the chicken in the sink, as she had been taught by Ada, and pulled the innards out with her bare hands. She stopped for a few seconds to look at the new eggs forming inside the chicken, a row of soft yellow eggs-to-be, each at a different stage of growth, from tiny rounds to one white larger oblong that the hen might have laid, come evening. Having prepared the bird, Kezia set herself to chopping herbs. She brought an onion from the larder, as well as plums she'd bottled the summer before. She made up the fire, drawing the blaze high as if to fuel a locomotive. She felt the roar of logs and coal, and began pulling pans and dishes this way and that, simmering, sautéing, stirring, and checking for tenderness.

She looked up at the clock on the mantelpiece above the stove, and knew the men would be leaving the farm soon, that it would not be long before she heard the rhythmic soft thud of boots marching along the lane from the oast house. Bert and Danny would look through the kitchen window and wave to her—*please don't let them knock at the door*—and be on their way. She could not speak to them now. *I will tell them on the morrow.* Yes, she would tell them after she had screamed up into the rafters, after she had cried her tears and wailed into the night. She would tell the men, and then she would tell Mabel and Ted and Mrs. Joe. Mabel would nip at her, would be inconsolable, turning her head into the corner of her stable until Bert came. Ted would nuzzle her and move away from Mabel, and Mrs. Joe would hang her head and want to be held. Kezia knew she would walk to the cattle shed, then to the hives, where worker bees clustered around their queen, vibrating to keep her warm. She would walk through orchards and hop gardens, from Pickwick Field to Barnaby and Twist, and across to Dickens' two cities; she would step out across the freshly turned field that was once Micawber Wood, and she would tell the farm that the master was dead, and brave, dear Dorrit had perished.

She listened for the footfall of her men to diminish in the distance, then looked out of the window once more, waiting for Frederick to take up his place by the gate. She was doing this, preparing the meal and setting the table, because Tom and

Thea—and especially the sister of her heart, her brave, beloved Thea—would say it was the right thing to do. This was her ritual to honor a time before the war.

Kezia turned her attention to the table, remembering—but not quite—something else she had seen in the book Thea gave her. She went to the shelf next to the fireplace and took down *The Woman's Book* from its place next to her mother-in-law's recipe books, and began turning the pages until she found the paragraph she was seeking. And she so wanted to laugh when she imagined Thea reading the instructions aloud—mimicking Camden's Miss Hartley perhaps, while rolling her eyes as if she was above such housewifery:

No matter how simple a meal may be, it should be put neatly on the table and made attractive to the eye. There are certain table requirements which are within the reach of the very humblest; they may not be essentials, but they are beyond doubt among the ameliorating influences of life, which help to cultivate the mind and improve the manners.

Kezia returned the book to its place and, still smiling as if Thea were with her, brought out her fine linen cloth, her wedding silver and white wedding napkins. She carried a vase of flowers from the parlor and set it on the table, then put plates in the warming oven and opened the kitchen door. Frederick was waiting by the gate, his hair slicked back by a fine late-afternoon drizzle.

"Frederick! Frederick, come here, please," she called.

The German looked around, as if there were another of the same name behind him. He glanced along the road—he would not want to miss Constable Ashling, though there were times when he'd had to wait long enough for the policeman—then walked to the farmhouse door and bowed.

Kezia smiled. "Come in, Frederick. Sit down."

"I beg your pardon, Mrs. Brissenden?"

"Come into the kitchen, Frederick, and sit down, please. At the table—sit there." Kezia pointed to the chair that was usually hers. "I know you don't get enough to eat, do you?"

The fragrant aromas of rosemary and plum, of onion and roast chicken, filled the kitchen. Kezia watched as Frederick breathed in deeply, then turned to her with tears in his eyes.

"Are you sure, Mrs. Brissenden?"

"Of course. You've time. I will talk to the constable when he comes. There will be no argument. And you can take some more when you go. I'll fill a bowl for you. Now then, wash your hands first. There's soap and a clean towel for you on the draining board."

Kezia watched as Frederick took up the soap and scrubbed his hands, using his thumbnails to scrape deep into his skin before rinsing. She watched as he picked up the white linen towel, bringing it to his nose as if to savor the moment.

The German boy took his seat, and Kezia returned to the stove, where she spooned chicken with plum and herb stuffing, three vegetables, and sherry-laced gravy onto her best china. She came back to the table and set one plate in front of Frederick and one in front of Tom's seat at the head of the table. Then she pulled out Tom's chair and sat down, though she did not touch the knife and fork. Instead, she folded her arms on the table to watch.

"Eat, Frederick," said Kezia Brissenden. "Please. I want you to eat."

AUTHOR'S NOTE

The Woman's Book (subtitled "Contains Everything a Woman Ought to Know"), edited by Florence B. Jack, was first published in London in 1911. It not only covered household management but also had comprehensive sections on cookery, children, home doctor, business, dress, society, careers, and citizenship.

ACKNOWLEDGMENTS

The collection of early twentieth-century women's journals and magazines (or "books" as they were called by women of the era) held by the Women's Library—now located at the London School of Economics—proved to be an invaluable resource, along with the archive of documents pertaining to the suffrage movement in early twentieth-century Britain. Thanks must go to the very professional and always helpful staff at the library.

I am so very fortunate to have a wonderful editor in Jennifer Barth at HarperCollins—thank you, Jennifer, for your enthusiasm from the moment you saw my brief description of *The Care and Management of Lies*, and for your wise counsel, always. Thanks must also go to the amazing Katherine Beitner, to Stephanie Cooper, and to Josh Marwell and his first-class team of publishing pros at HarperCollins. To the enormously accomplished Andrew Davidson, and creative wizard Archie Ferguson—thank you for the brilliant (in my humble opinion) covers for my novels.

To be blessed with an agent who believes in your work, who is honest and supportive beyond measure, must be the dream of every author—if that is so, then I am filled with gratitude to have literary agent Amy Rennert at my right hand. Thank you, Amy, for really believing in *The Care and Management of Lies*, and for helping make my dream come true.

And last, but never least, to John Morell—thank you for reminding me to celebrate each milestone on the road to publication day.

ABOUT THE AUTHOR

Jacqueline Winspear is the author of the *New York Times* best sellers *Leaving Everything Most Loved*, *Elegy for Eddie*, *A Lesson in Secrets*, *The Mapping of Love and Death*, *Among the Mad*, and *An Incomplete Revenge*, as well as four other national best-selling Maisie Dobbs novels. She has received numerous honors for her work, including the Agatha, Alex, and Macavity Awards for the first book in the series, *Maisie Dobbs*, which was also nominated for the Edgar Award for Best Novel and was a *New York Times* Notable Book. Originally from the United Kingdom, she now lives in California.

About the author

About the book

Insights,
Interviews
& More...

Read on

Meet
Jacqueline Winspear

I HAVE LONG BEEN DRAWN to the period— the Great War—WW1—and its aftermath, inspired by a curiosity that began in early childhood, when I was deeply aware of the lingering pain of "war wounds" suffered by my grandfather, who had seen action during several of the war's most notorious battles. I was aware of the effect those wounds and his lingering shell-shock had on my family, and though it was at first a childish curiosity, it grew into a deep adult interest by the time I reached my teens, when I was also studying the war poets in school and becoming very emotionally affected by the work. My interest brought me back to the same question—what does war do to ordinary people swept up in its chaos? The history of any war is drawn on a massive landscape, but I'm interested in zooming the camera in, then asking what might have happened to a person in this or that situation. My grandfather was still removing shrapnel from his legs when he died some fifty years after the Battle of the Somme (1916), and my grandmother was partially blinded during an explosion at a munitions factory where she was working with volatile explosives in 1915—those examples underscore a comment from one of the characters in my novel *Birds of a Feather*: "That's the trouble with war, it lives on inside the living."

Writing *The Care and Management of Lies*
A Conversation with Jacqueline Winspear

*The Care and Management of Lies
tells the story of girlhood friends Kezia
Marchant and Thea Brissenden as they
navigate the tumultuous time in which
they are living. Thea has become a
passionate suffragette and Kezia,
engaged to marry Thea's brother Tom,
is bound for a traditional married life
of domesticity—until war breaks out.
The novel paints a moving picture of
a friendship strained by a world in
turmoil and the shifting notions of the
roles of women. Are there ways in which
the questions the novel raises echo in our
own time?*

There are several aspects of the book
that mirror our times. The passage of
time can test any friendship—change of
job, moving house, choice of life-partner,
and then children come along, and life
separates people who have once been
inseparable. The transition from
girlhood into womanhood, and the
opportunities and changes that come
as part and parcel of that move—leaving
school, going out to work, moving house,
or choosing to live another life—have
made this crucial time in the lives of
women throughout the past century.
This test of change is what has happened
to Kezia and Thea. Although quite
different, they have been friends since ▶

Writing *The Care and Management of Lies*
(continued)

girlhood and have truly admired each other's strengths—then the choices that each has made separate them, and they move apart. Passionate Thea becomes involved in the fight for women's suffrage, which was far more heated and violent in the UK than in the US. Her beliefs put her at odds with Kezia at the onset of war—and Kezia, as one who is about to be married and wants nothing to stand in the way of her envisioned happiness, would like to think that the threat of war will go away. But it doesn't, and life is again changed for both of them—yet in that unexpected transition, it seems they gain a new sense of mutual respect, and each draws upon strengths the other holds dear. Kezia surprises Thea with her backbone when she effectively steps into her husband's shoes after he goes away to war, while Kezia admires Thea's choices despite the fact that she fears for her friend's well-being. I think many women can identify with the fact that cherished friendships can be threatened by the life choices each woman might make—and this was a time when opportunities never before available to women became part of the equation.

You have said that **The Care and Management of Lies** *first began to form in your mind twenty years before you wrote your first novel. What inspired this story and why did you wait to tell it?*

When I was in my mid-twenties, I had great fun working weekends with a friend at her stall in London's Portobello Road Market. We dealt mainly in art deco pottery, jewelry, and other odds and ends. But you have to keep a stall stocked, so I often went to jumble sales (rummage sales here in America) to find pieces I could resell. It was while sorting through a pile of other people's unwanted "stuff" that I found a very battered copy of *The Woman's Book* (edited by Florence B. Jack, published 1911). The spine was cracked, the pages were foxed, and the cover was completely battered and falling off. But it was the inscription that captured my attention and imagination, for the book had been given to a young woman on the occasion of her marriage in the summer of 1914. It took my breath away. I wondered if her young husband had gone to war, whether her fledgling marriage had been ended by the conflict—had she been widowed? Did he come home? Was he wounded? How did they keep their love alive in wartime, and what did life look like for this bride after the war? The book cost me five pence. Over the years a story seeded itself in my mind, though sadly the book left my hands (I gave it to a friend who thought she could have it re-bound, but of course as these things happen, she married and had children, then moved, and I emigrated). It was after I became a published author that I knew I wanted to write my story one ▶

Writing *The Care and Management of Lies*
(*continued*)

day, and I managed to acquire another copy of *The Woman's Book*—in fact, I have acquired a few! In *The Care and Management of Lies*, the book is given as a gift to Kezia Brissenden on the occasion of her marriage, by her best friend and sister-in-law to be, Thea—but it is given as a bit of a dig, a comment on the bride's life to come.

I took so long to tell the story because it was more than a few years before I became a published author, and then I was deep into writing about another strong woman character, Maisie Dobbs. But the time came when I just knew I had to write the book that had been with me for so long, and fortunately, my publisher was incredibly supportive of my dream—because to write this story has been something of a dream come true. I've found it quite hard to leave the work behind, because I became so engaged with these characters.

Most chapters of the novel begin with a quote from The Woman's Book. *At a time when women were fighting for the right to vote, this book seems to have all the hallmarks of a tome meant for the housewife to be and yet you describe it as being so much more, as demonstrating the very best of womanhood in all domains of endeavor. Do you see its relevance today? Or . . . does anything compare to it today?*

The Woman's Book was a very popular book in its day, so quite a few were published. The amazing thing about the book is that, although at first blush it looks like yet another tome on household management—and certainly Kezia has assumed that, because she hardly uses it—deeper reading reveals it to be very much for the modern woman. Though you can read sections advising you on topics such as where to seat the Prime Minister if the King is present for supper, there are other sections on women in the workplace, women in politics, how to be a political canvasser. Another section covers women in agriculture, and though you can learn how to black a stove, or get stains out of your whites, you will also find out how to make money from freelance writing. I liked that section!

Frankly, I have never seen anything similar today—probably the last book that mirrored *The Woman's Book* was *Superwoman* by Shirley Conran, published in 1976.

It bears adding that in *The Care and Management of Lies* there are also quotes from military handbooks issued in 1914 to officers and men sent to fight for Britain and the Empire—what these books have in common with *The Woman's Book* is a deep sense of order, as if everything has its place, and must be in that place, or chaos will reign. And that mirrors one of the key elements of the time I find so very interesting— ▶

Writing *The Care and Management of Lies*
(**continued**)

that at the outset of war in 1914 there was a cherished Edwardian veneer of order, yet with the war came such disorder. From the rise of the middle class to the development of opportunities for women (the vote was a result of women's involvement in the war), right up to enormous developments in world geopolitics and alliances—1914 really was the true start of a bold new century.

Food plays out deliciously as a core theme throughout your novel. In her letters to Tom, Kezia describes the mouthwatering meals she might cook for him, and even Tom's fellow comrades in the trenches find comfort in the meals Kezia imagines on the page. You write: "Tom Brissenden was eating the same food as any other man in the encampment. But with these letters, he was tasting love. . . ." It is said that soldiers at the front—then and today—often write about the food they miss from home. What is the relationship between food and nostalgia in The Care and Management of Lies?

When people are away from home for an extended period of time, away from the comforts of home and those they love, food becomes something of a lightning rod. I know just from being on a book tour, for example, that towards the end of my travels I am aching to come home so I can sit down in my kitchen and have a cup of tea with my homemade oatmeal for breakfast!

A war zone is invariably a desolate, unforgiving place, and food—thoughts of home-cooked food especially, or a favorite dish—takes on a new level of significance. With food comes a sense of being cared for, a sense of being nourished and, above all, loved. Army rations have changed dramatically over the years, but the same equation still holds true—the military is primarily interested in calories in and calories out. Men and women in combat situations use an extraordinary amount of energy, and military cooks have the task of meeting the calorific needs of a fighting force. Today's army cooks have more ways of producing and transporting large quantities of food, but there is probably not a deployed serviceman or woman who does not dream of that first meal back at home. The son of my oldest, dearest friend returned last year from his third tour of duty in Helmand Province, Afghanistan. On one occasion during his deployment I was visiting their home, and he phoned to speak to his parents at dinner time. The phone was put on the table, on speaker, so we could all talk to him, and he wanted us to tell him all about what we were eating—one of his favorite dishes, as it happened, cooked by his mum. I talked about it later to my friend, and she said that for both her husband—an army officer—and son, food became the most important ▶

thing for them when deployed, and receiving a special food item from home—perhaps a cake or some cookies—was tantamount to being given something very precious. When my friend's son called it was always at dinner-time, and he always wanted to know exactly what was on the table, in great detail.

Nostalgia is fed by the emotions that come with separation—and in wartime that separation becomes more acute, encompassing a sense of loss of home, family, loved ones, warmth, comfort, freedom from fear, along with so many other emotions. How the men were fed in WW1 became a crucial component in the issue of morale.

As Tom enlists to fight for his country and heads off to battle, he and Kezia are forced to learn to love in a time of war. We have watched the moving images of soldiers these last many years in this country and elsewhere separate routinely from their loved ones to serve a tour of duty. What differentiates love in a time of war from love in a time of peace? How does war affect marriage, and how do we see this played out in Tom and Kezia's marriage?

I think love becomes more urgent in a time of war. One only has to read stories about the number of couples who were wed when war was declared in 1914, then later in the Second World War

and subsequent conflicts. Men and
women are changed by war—and
a military spouse is as affected as
the serviceman/woman. Keeping
relationships immediate and remaining
connected is much easier with today's
technology, whereas in the past the
spouse at home had to depend upon
letters and cards, and of course for the
soldier, those packages from home held
enormous importance, for they often
contained food items. The British army
had a very efficient postal service in
WW1—probably more efficient than
the post today—with letters often taking
only two days to arrive from the front to
a house in England. In Tom and Kezia's
marriage, we see how they keep their
relationship immediate with letters—
but those letters are written as if they
were together, rather than apart. This
keeps their love very much alive, in the
present. ⁓

"You've Got Mail"— in the Trenches

ONE OF THE KEY THEMES in *The Care and Management of Lies* is that of food in a time of war, and particularly how important food was to the soldiers sent to fight overseas. In those days all the army cared about was "calories in and calories out"—how to keep energy reserves replenished. Nowadays military planning encompasses food in a different way—yes, calories matter because fighting is a high-energy job, but there is more of an understanding of how important it is to provide foods that give a sense of home, and the contribution of those foods to morale.

In WWI soldiers yearned for the taste of food they recognized, so loved ones at home would send special packages with foods such as homemade cakes, packets of biscuits, jars of Bovril and any jam other than plum (the army provided plum jam, which as you can imagine, was not a favorite), as well as chocolates, boiled sweets, and breads. And the fact that much of this bounty arrived in fairly good order was down to an extraordinarily efficient postal service which conveyed mail to and from the front lines and camps overseas.

Letters between Tom Brissenden and his wife Kezia are at the heart of *The Care and Management of Lies*, and not only does Kezia write to her husband regularly, but she sends him cakes wrapped in paper, then placed in a tin which she seals with candle wax, before wrapping again and taking to the post office. The cake is still fresh when Tom opens the tin—surrounded by his trench-mates, all hoping for a slice.

Over the years I have spent many hours using the archive at the Imperial War Museum, foraging through the massive collection of letters sent to and from soldiers during the years 1914–18. I have garnered a sense of what people wrote about—ordinary things, for the most part. And I know that soldiers would read out their letters from home—probably not the personal details—because in the sharing of stories, home became a bit closer, and the warmth of affection in a letter could be contagious. And of course it was entertainment—trench life could be a boring round of monotony interspersed by the horror of the charge across no man's land and the terrors of witnessing death of a most terrible kind.

But what of the men and women who worked around the clock to make sure those letters and packages reached their destination?

All mail directed overseas to men in the trenches was sent first to a huge wooden building erected in London's Regent's Park almost immediately after war was declared. When mail left London, it was sent to a forward Post Office in Le Havre that had been set up as a matter of urgency within days of war being declared in August 1914. Apparently, by the end of 1914, the sheer volume of mail—letters, packages of food, and clothing—had overwhelmed resources. The General Post Office (GPO) then built a depot covering five acres, thought to be the largest wooden structure in the world. At its peak in 1918, some twelve million items of mail were being processed weekly.

And who do you think was processing all this mail? Yes, you've guessed it—approximately 100,000 women were brought in to work for the Royal Mail. Before the war, the Royal Mail was the world's largest employer, with some 250,000 on staff—but over 75,000 men left to join the war effort. Many enlisted in the Post Office Rifles, a 12,000 man regiment. At the Home Depot in France, 2,500 workers on the site were women, and from that depot during the war an estimated two billion letters and 114 million packages were dispatched out to men. Most reached the western front within two days, processed in post rooms closer to the front lines. ▸

"You've Got Mail"—in the Trenches
(continued)

. . .

In addition, the GPO delivered mail to ships at sea, and to British POW's incarcerated in Germany.

And here's something to consider in these times when we think we are all so very connected—in 1913 the average rural town in Britain could expect some twelve deliveries of mail per day, thanks to the Penny Post, which had heralded in an age of mass communication. At the outset of war, the deliveries were cut to two per day, and in 1918 the Penny Post—that cheaper means of sending a letter—was ended.

Few records remain of the GPO during the Great War, as the large depots were dismantled within months of the end of hostilities.

So, when you read the letters between Kezia and her beloved Tom, give a thought to the mounds of mail sent via Britain to the trenches, to the battleships and to the hospitals and POW camps—letters from around the world in a time of war. Whatever they wrote about—between the lines, if not in words—I would imagine both soldiers and those at home could not help but wonder what might come to pass by the time the letter reached its destination. ∿

Discover great authors, exclusive offers, and more at hc.com.